Praise for #1 *New York Times* bestselling author Sherryl Woods

"Sherryl Woods writes emotionally satisfying novels about family, friendship and home. Truly feel-great reads!"
—#1 *New York Times* bestselling author Debbie Macomber

"Launching the Chesapeake Shores series, Woods creates an engrossing...family drama."
—*Publishers Weekly* on *The Inn at Eagle Point*

"Sparks fly in a lively tale that is overflowing with family conflict and warmth and the possibility of rekindled love."
—*Library Journal* on *Flowers on Main*

"Warm, complex, and satisfying."
—*Library Journal* on *Harbor Lights*

"Sure to satisfy."
—*Publishers Weekly* on *A Chesapeake Shores Christmas*

"Woods's amazing grasp of human nature and the emotions that lie deep within us make this story universal...this latest novel in the Chesapeake Shores series does not disappoint."
—*RT Book Reviews* on *Driftwood Cottage*

"Once again, Woods, with such authenticity, weaves a tale of true love and the challenges that can knock up against that love."
—*RT Book Reviews* on *Beach Lane*

"Engaging and satisfying... A sweet, affecting holiday-themed read."
—*Kirkus Reviews* on *A Seaside Christmas*

SHERRYL WOODS

THE CHRISTMAS BOUQUET

MIRA

ISBN-13: 978-0-7783-1760-9

The Christmas Bouquet

Copyright © 2014 by Sherryl Woods

Bayside Retreat

Copyright © 2015 by Sherryl Woods

Recycling programs
for this product may
not exist in your area.

www.MIRABooks.com

Printed in U.S.A.

CONTENTS

Dear friends,

This holiday season, there's a special gift for all of you who've been following the O'Briens from the very beginning. *Bayside Retreat* is an original novella in the Chesapeake Shores series, included here as a bonus.

Emma Hastings is a relative newcomer to town. She's working part-time for her mother, the town librarian. What not everyone knows, though, is that Emma wrote a bestselling novel based in large measure on her crumbling marriage. Now, with that marriage in the past, her creative well seems to have run dry—until she meets Jaime Alvarez, a man who could definitely inspire a few intriguing fantasies.

Jaime, Mick O'Brien's longtime assistant and second-in-command, is recovering from a leg injury suffered in a construction site accident. Of course, as always, Mick's determined that Jaime will leave town not only healed, but with a wife! Typical of Mick, right?

I hope you enjoy *Bayside Retreat*, as well as Caitlyn's story in *The Christmas Bouquet*. She's living proof that, even for determined O'Briens, life doesn't always go according to plan!

Above all, I wish you the happiest of holiday seasons, touched by just a little of that special Chesapeake Shores magic!

All best,

Sherryl Woods

THE CHRISTMAS BOUQUET

1

It was all because of that blasted bridal bouquet, Caitlyn Winters thought as she stared in dismay at the positive pregnancy test in her hand. From the moment she'd caught the bouquet at Jenny Collins's Christmas wedding in New York a little over a year ago, she'd been doomed. That instinctive grab of an object flying straight at her had changed her life.

Her twin sister, Carrie, who'd all but shoved her aside to try to snatch the bouquet from the air, was going to laugh herself silly at what had transpired since that night. So were the rest of the O'Briens, for that matter. They loved irony.

Noah McIlroy, the family medicine resident whom she'd met soon after the wedding and with whom she'd been having a serious relationship since last September, tapped on the bathroom door.

"Caitlyn, are you okay?"

A hysterical laugh bubbled up, but she fought to contain it. This was no laughing matter. "Fine," she managed to squeak out just as the door opened. Noah's gaze shifted from her face to land on the test strip she was holding. Concern immediately evolved into astonishment.

"You're pregnant?" he asked, his eyes filled with surprise, but a smile already tugging at his lips.

His wonderful, sensual lips, which had gotten them into this mess, she thought wryly. Of course, she was well aware those lips hadn't caused her pregnancy. Heck, she'd known about the birds and bees long before that, thanks to all the romances in Chesapeake Shores and among her amorous O'Brien relatives.

But it was her inability to resist Noah's heated kisses that had led to all the rest. That and an apparently defective condom. Given her cautious nature, she probably should have insisted on at least three methods of birth control, but no, she'd trusted Noah when he'd assured her that the condoms would be sufficient.

The man had cast a spell over her from the minute they'd met, literally one week after she'd caught that blasted romantic bouquet with all its superstition attached like streamers of satin ribbon. The deft catch had earned hoots of laughter from her family and a stunned, disappointed scowl from her twin, who'd been angling for the bouquet all evening.

And now, here she was, barely more than a year later, and pregnant. She hadn't even accepted Noah's repeated pleas that they live together, even though he was in her apartment more often than he was in his own. She'd drawn a line at that, knowing that she'd never be able to keep his presence in her life a secret from her nosy family if they were actually living under the same roof.

And she'd wanted to keep this relationship a secret. After all, she was supposed to be the grounded, goal-oriented sister. Carrie was the one everyone had expected to

fall madly in love and marry before her college graduation. Instead, Carrie was jetting around the world, leading a completely carefree life, building a career in public
relations for a big fashion designer and tossing away men
like used tissues while she pined for one unobtainable
man. And Caitlyn, thanks to that bouquet, was standing
here with a positive pregnancy test in her hand!

She recalled the forget-me-nots that her aunt Bree had
tucked into Jenny's simple bridal bouquet and fought
back another hysterical laugh. She was hardly likely to
forget this moment, that's for sure.

She drew in a deep breath and finally dared to meet
Noah's gaze. For a man supposedly as dedicated to
his medical career as she was to hers, he looked awfully pleased about this unexpected bump in the road.
Of course, he was just a couple of months away from
launching his career, while she still had the long years
of an internship and residency to complete.

"Wipe that smile off your face," she instructed him
firmly. "This is not good news."

His smile only spread, revealing that appealing dim-
ple that had also sucked her right in. "It's the best possible news," he contradicted.

"Noah, you may see the light at the end of the tun-
nel, but be real. You'll finish your residency at the end
of June and you still have to decide where you want
to go into practice and get established. I haven't even
started my internship. We might not even be living in
the same city a few months from now. A baby doesn't
fit into the plan."

"You know what they say," he began.

"Don't you dare remind me that God laughs while
we're making plans."

She frowned for emphasis as she passed him on her way into the bedroom, where she sank down on the side of the bed. Maybe if she sat for a minute, she could think. Thinking clearly had always been her best trait.

She'd known what she wanted for her life by her teens. After spending a summer volunteering in a doctor's office in a medically underserved community in Appalachia and seeing reports about villages in third-world countries that were even worse off, she'd found her calling. Her reward had been the healthy children who'd clustered around her at the end of the summer to say goodbye, the moms who'd hugged her with tears in their eyes.

Just like her ambitious mother, Abby O'Brien Winters Riley, Caitlyn had thought her future through very carefully. There would be college, medical school, an internship and residency. Then she'd use all that knowledge to help children in parts of the world where medical help was severely lacking. She'd make a difference, just like everyone else in her family had in their own way. This was her way to shine, to live up to all those family expectations and at the same time do the kind of meaningful work she'd been born to do.

She'd been so focused that she'd managed to complete college in three years, then set out to whip through medical school and all of her rotations as fast as they'd allowed her to. Every summer she'd either crammed in more courses or served in another needy community, most recently in Africa with the Red Cross. While Carrie was the social butterfly, Caitlyn had been driven, not allowing a single distraction. Not until Noah, anyway.

She glanced up at him as he studied her with a worried expression. He was so incredibly gorgeous, it was little wonder that her heart seemed to stop whenever she looked at him. But it wasn't his looks that had made her fall in love. He'd seemed as driven as she was, determined to be the kind of old-fashioned doctor who was more concerned with treating his patients with compassion and dignity than racking up huge bucks on office visits and unnecessary testing.

They'd met on her rotation through the family medicine service right after that fateful wedding. She'd been immediately smitten by his dedication, the thoughtful kindness he displayed to everyone from patients to the most inept medical students still struggling to adapt book learning to practical experience. He'd turned her into a better doctor by example, no question about it. He'd suggested she waver from her original intention to focus on pediatrics and steered her into choosing family medicine. He'd helped her see that she could serve even more people with that well-rounded specialty.

Until she'd worked with him, she'd understood everything in her textbooks, but she hadn't mastered the instinctive diagnostic skills that made the difference between being competent and excelling. He'd taught her to listen to more than a list of symptoms, to hear what her patients weren't saying, as much as to what they said.

By fall, when she'd started her final year of medical school, they were in an exclusive relationship, stealing time to be together whenever they could. With their competing, demanding schedules, those stolen moments had been few and far between. Given the test strip she was holding, they'd been more than sufficient to alter her life, apparently.

Noah dropped down beside her now and took her

hand in his. "We're going to be okay," he said softly, his warm brown eyes filled with tenderness.

When she didn't answer, he touched her chin. "Look at me, Cait." Only after she'd turned her head, fighting tears, did he repeat, "We're going to be okay."

"How?" she asked him, unable to imagine it, unable to accept his confidently spoken reassurance.

"We'll get married," he said without hesitation. "I know we haven't talked about that yet, but you know I love you. I want a future with you. This just bumps up the timetable. I'm all but finished with my residency. I'll go into practice in July. You'll finish your internship and residency. Then you can join me in the practice."

She listened to the logical simplicity of his plan and regarded him incredulously, panicked by the certainty in his voice.

"That's *your* dream, Noah. Not mine. You know what I want, what I've worked so hard for. There's a big world out there in desperate need of medical help. I want to save the lives of babies in third-world countries who might not make it without a doctor in their village. The two weeks I spent in Africa last year..." Her voice trailed off and hitched as she thought about the desperation she'd seen everywhere she'd turned. "That time confirmed everything for me. I was meant to do that kind of work. I promised I'd be back."

To his credit he didn't dismiss her dream or the promise she'd made. They'd talked about it often enough. He knew how much it meant to her to go where she was needed. It was what she'd stayed up nights studying for. She'd known it from the first time she'd seen those malnourished children with their wide desperate eyes on the news. Every volunteer assignment she'd taken after that had only solidified her resolve.

"Then how do you see this going?" he asked quietly.

She wanted to blurt out that she'd have to end the pregnancy, but how could she? While she might believe in every woman's right to choose, she knew she'd never be able to live with herself if she chose abortion. She was a healer. And this was Noah's baby, an unexpected blessing under any other circumstances.

"I don't know," she whispered, hot tears falling.

Noah pulled her into his arms and held her against his chest, surrounding her with his strength and heat and that scary, unwavering certainty. "We'll figure it out," he promised. "Together, we'll figure out what's best."

For just an instant, Caitlyn allowed herself to believe that. She desperately wanted to hold on to the possibility that there was an answer that worked for both of them. But in every scenario she envisioned, she lost.

Noah knew a baby wasn't in Cait's plans, not right now, anyway. It killed him to see her so utterly miserable when he wanted to shout his joy from the rooftop. The timing might be lousy in so many ways, but the news filled him with hope that this child would bind the two of them together forever.

She'd been right about one thing: marriage and sharing a medical practice *was* his dream. He'd wanted that from the minute she'd started on his service at the hospital with her exhaustive textbook knowledge of medicine, her instinctive diagnostic skills that even now she didn't recognize that she possessed and her unquenchable thirst to learn everything he had to teach her. Her silky skin and untamed red curls had captivated him, too, no question about it. Every male at the hospital stared after her as she bounced through her days with boundless energy and optimism, spreading smiles in her wake.

Over the next few weeks they'd shared enough late nights and coffee it was a wonder either of them had ever slept a wink with all that caffeine racing through their systems. He'd never been much of a talker, but with Caitlyn, he hadn't been able to keep quiet. There'd been so much he'd wanted to share, so many things about her he'd wanted to learn.

She'd made him laugh with her endless stream of stories about her large Irish-American family and teased him unmercifully because his own background was Scottish. She'd claimed she could never take him home because of it.

He'd thought at the time she was joking, but now he couldn't help wondering. They'd been inseparable for most of the past year, but he still hadn't been invited to Chesapeake Shores, which wasn't that far away. Was he wrong about how much he meant to her? Was he only someone with whom she could spend time until the day she finished her residency and went off to begin her "real" life? Did she view him as safe, someone she could leave behind without regrets?

No, he thought heatedly. He wasn't wrong about their feelings. He couldn't be. He wasn't the only one in love. Cait loved him, too. He might not have a lot of experience with serious relationships—how many doctors had enough time to properly date during all those years of school and training, after all?—but he could recognize that what he'd found with Cait was special.

Sitting across the room on the edge of the bed where she'd left him, he watched her now as she pulled her strawberry-red hair into a severe knot intended to tame the curls. He smiled as a few escaped to brush her cheeks. It reminded him of the way she lived her life, desperately trying to control everything, but a wild streak coming out when she least expected it. He could recall with total clarity the last time she'd cut loose with total abandon. He liked imagining that was the night this baby had been conceived, with neither of them thinking of anything but each other.

"Cait," he said softly. "I think it's time I meet this crazy family of yours."

In her mirrored reflection, he saw her eyes go wide with alarm.

"Now?"

"Can you think of a better time? They have to be told about what's going on."

She shook her head. "Not a chance, Noah. Not until we know what we're going to do. Maybe not even then. My mom, she's great. She'll handle this okay. My great-grandmother—"

"Nell O'Brien, right?"

She nodded. "She'll be worried, but she'll support whatever I decide to do." As she spotted his frown reflected in the mirror, she quickly corrected herself. "Whatever *we* decide to do."

Noah let it go, shoving aside his sense that she really did intend for this to be her decision and hers alone.

"With the two of them in your corner, what's the problem?" he asked. "Maybe that's just what you need right now, two women you respect giving you some advice." He held her gaze. "And the advice will be more meaningful if they've met me and know how committed I am to you."

"I can't deny that talking to them might be helpful," she acknowledged, her expression turning wistful. "And Nell is incredible. She's wise and compassionate. She won't judge me."

"Well, there you go," he said, as if that settled the matter. "It's time to head to Chesapeake Shores."

She shook her head. "For me, maybe. Not you."

"But I'm in this with you," he protested, digging in. "They need to know that. I don't want them to think for a single minute that I've left you to deal with this alone."

"You're forgetting one thing," she said, looking visibly worried. "Two, actually. My grandpa Mick is likely to beat you to a pulp first and ask questions later and my stepdad will help him. Trace has managed to convince himself that I have never, not even once, gone on a date, much less slept with anyone."

"You have to be joking!" Noah said. "What does he think is going on with you and me?"

She flinched. "I haven't mentioned you."

He froze as the implication sank in. "Your stepdad doesn't know you're in a committed relationship?" he asked slowly, not able to believe she'd kept something like that secret given how close she was to her family.

"It hasn't come up," she said defensively. "Actually, no one back home knows."

Shock nearly rendered him speechless. "But your mother works less than an hour away," he said at last. "She's been here. Surely she's wondered about finding my clothes scattered about."

"The past few months I've managed to steer her away from here," she admitted. "The couple of times she has stopped by, I've had enough notice that I've had time to tidy up."

"Meaning exactly what?" he asked, trying to remain calm. "You've hidden away all traces of me?"

"Pretty much," she said, then gave him a defiant look. "It was better that way, Noah. You have to trust me on that. If anyone in my family knew about you and me, they'd be pestering us every minute about our plans for the future. Neither of us needed that kind of aggravation or distraction."

He resisted the urge to confess that he'd be interested in hearing her response to that question about their future himself, especially now. If he went down that path, they'd only wind up arguing and there was a more pressing issue on the table right now: the baby.

"How have you managed to keep your mother and everyone else so conveniently out of your personal business? I thought they were constitutionally incapable of not meddling."

"Which is exactly why I haven't mentioned you," she reminded him. "It keeps their attention on my work. They think I'm a bit of a boring drone."

"You've deliberately steered all of them away from visiting, too, haven't you?" he said, realizing how deliberate her actions had been. "How did you pull that off so well? You told me yourself that their drop-in visits were constantly disrupting your study time, yet you couldn't seem to prevent them from showing up."

Cait flushed guiltily, then shrugged. "I guess I finally got through to them that my schedule is even more demanding now that I'm doing all these rotations at the hospital. Half the time I'm there, so they'd miss me if they did drop by the apartment. After a few wasted trips up here, they gave up. Instead, I've gone home when I can. That seems to satisfy them, that and about a million phone calls a week."

"But your mom is close by most of the week," he persisted. "How do you get away with keeping her at arm's length when it's no big deal to pop over from her office?"

"Her schedule is just as crazy as mine and this is actually out of her way. She's always rushing through her day to get home to Trace and my brother. We grab a bite to eat when we can, usually at her desk. If I take the initiative and call frequently, there's no reason for her to come by."

"And if she does announce an intention to visit, you 'tidy up,'" he said, unable to keep an edge of irritation from his voice. He was offended and saw no reason to hide it. "What about your sister, then? You and Carrie talk at least once a week. How have you kept her away? From the way you've described her, it seems doubtful to me that she'd take a hint."

"No, Carrie definitely wouldn't respond to subtlety," she agreed. "She's been out of town a lot, thank goodness. And she's mostly so self-involved with her own chaotic personal life that she doesn't ask a lot of questions."

Noah could see that Cait had been much more circumspect with her family than he'd realized. He understood that she was a private person. He certainly understood her not wanting their colleagues at the hospital to know they were involved, though most did, of course. But keeping her own family in the dark? It defied everything he knew about how important they were to her.

Right now, though, there was no time to delve into her reasoning. This pregnancy news changed everything. It was hardly something she could keep from them, not for long, anyway.

"Cait, how far along are you? Do you have any idea when the baby might be due?"

"I won't know for sure until I see the doctor," she said.

"But you must have some idea," Noah pressed.

"I missed a couple of periods," she finally admitted, her expression chagrined. "I was stressed out. I didn't think too much about it. Then I had a couple of bouts of morning sickness this past week and it dawned on me I might be pregnant. I guess I'm not such a great diagnostician, after all, huh?"

He allowed himself a small smile. "More like a woman in denial, I imagine."

She sighed. "Denial was lovely," she admitted.

Noah could understand why she might think that, but with reality setting in, there was no more time to waste. "So, you're about two months along?"

"Something like that. I think the baby's probably due in December."

"Sweetheart, I know you're not exactly overjoyed about this. You need to open up with someone."

"I just told *you*," she said.

"But right now, I suspect you're thinking of me as the enemy," he told her. He scrambled for an alternative. If she didn't want to talk to her mother or Nell O'Brien, then perhaps her sister. Weren't twins supposed to have an extraordinarily strong bond?

"Couldn't you talk our situation over with Carrie? Get some family backup before you spill the news to everyone else? Would that help?"

She looked horrified by the thought. "Good heavens, no! If Carrie knew about us or about the baby we're expecting, every O'Brien in Chesapeake Shores would know by the end of the day. The situation would spin out of control."

"Are you absolutely sure they don't already know that something's up?" he asked. "With us, anyway."

"Did you not hear what I just said about my stepfather and my grandfather?" she asked impatiently. "If either of them had a clue, you'd be a dead man."

Noah couldn't believe she was right about their likely reaction. "Come on, Cait. You're in your twenties. You've been away at school for years now. Surely they can't believe there's never been a man in your life."

She finally smiled, the tension in her shoulders visibly easing. "Well, they knew about Ronnie Jessup in fourth grade," she told him. "That was after we moved from New York to Chesapeake Shores. He sent me a dozen valentines that year. Grandpa Mick immediately wanted to have a talk with his parents, but Nell stopped him. And my mom managed to keep Trace from following me to my high school prom. I'm pretty sure Grandpa Mick was lurking around somewhere in the shadows, though."

Noah laughed, then realized she was serious. "They're that protective?"

"Carrie and I were the first grandchildren. Grandpa Mick might have gone a little overboard. While I can't imagine building my entire life around dating the way Carrie has, she might have had the right idea. She's trained them to deal with it. I was the responsible, serious one. I was in love with my books. I probably lulled them into a false sense of complacency thinking I'd never do anything outrageous. This is going to come as a huge shock to them."

"Oh, boy," Noah whispered, then regarded her with

a renewed sense of determination. "Sweetie, we need to get this over with. Neither of us is on duty this weekend. It's the perfect time to go to Chesapeake Shores."

"But I have to study," she protested.

He met her gaze. "With all of this on your mind, do you actually think you're going to be able to concentrate?"

"I can *always* concentrate," she insisted.

Noah thought that actually might be true, but he shook his head. "Cait, I won't have your parents or anyone else thinking I'm reckless and irresponsible or that I've treated you carelessly. That would be a terrible way to be introduced to any family, but especially to one as protective as yours. I want them to like me or at least to accept me."

"Noah—" she began.

Since a protest was undoubtedly coming, he cut her off. "I know how much you love and respect your family. If you're determined to stay here and avoid this, go right ahead, but I'm going to speak to them. They need to know my intentions are honorable, even if we ultimately decide not to get married."

She looked stricken by his vehemence. "You wouldn't."

"I would," he told her solemnly. "I love you, Cait. More than that, I respect you. I'd like to prove I'm worthy of your family's respect, too. They need to know that I'll do whatever it takes to protect and support you and our child." He lightened his tone. "And if you're right about your grandfather and stepdad beating me to a pulp, at least I'll have time to heal before our child gets his or her first look at me."

She scowled. "That's not even remotely amusing." She sat down beside him and wove her fingers through his. "Look, I love you for wanting to stand beside me and face my family, but maybe that's not the best idea." She drew in a deep breath, then conceded, "You are right about one thing, though. I should probably go down there this weekend and fill them in on what's going on, even get some of Nell's sage advice. The whole family relies on her to put things into perspective."

Noah frowned, not entirely pleased about her plan. "And then you'll do what? Come back here and announce your decision to me?"

She winced at his caustic tone. "No, of course not. We'll decide this together. I promise. Going home will help me to think everything through, though. I'm reeling right now. I need this space, Noah. You know how I am. I ponder things, especially important decisions, and I won't be able to do that with you watching me every second. Please don't push to go with me."

He nodded finally, reluctantly accepting her decision. "As long as you swear you'll come back and talk it over with me before you do anything crazy."

She obviously knew what he meant by *crazy,* because she rested her hand against his cheek, tears in her eyes again.

"There won't be an abortion, Noah. That much I do know. I swear it."

A wave of relief washed over him at the sincerity he heard in her voice, at the commitment shining in her eyes. He knew he could trust her to keep her word. Now he just had to pray that whatever went on with her family would work in his favor.

2

With every mile that brought her closer to Chesapeake Shores, the knot of dread in Caitlyn's stomach seemed to tighten. It was the first time ever she hadn't been eager to get back to see her large rambunctious family. They could be overwhelming at times, but she'd grown up never doubting how much she was loved. In fact, that had given her the strength and confidence to choose the path she'd chosen for her future. She'd known there were too many children in the world who didn't have that powerful support system, who didn't even have the basic necessities.

She'd spent most of the drive trying not only to summon the courage to reveal her secret, but trying to decide the first person she should tell. There was little question that her mother would empathize. She'd had to make her share of difficult decisions to balance love and career and family. She'd even given up her dream job as a successful stockbroker in New York to take over the Baltimore office of her brokerage company so she could be closer to Chesapeake Shores and her new family with Trace.

Caitlyn pulled to the side of the road. She drew in a deep breath, then hit speed dial on her cell phone. When her mom's delighted voice filled the car, she immediately felt her anxiety ease.

"Hey, sweetheart, how are you?" her mother asked. "I've been thinking about you a lot this week. We miss you."

"I miss you, too," Caitlyn said. "As a matter of fact, I'm on my way home. Are you in Chesapeake Shores or at the Baltimore office?"

"Lucky for you, I've been working from home today," Abby said. "Why didn't you let us know you were coming? I'd have cooked."

Caitlyn laughed. "No, you wouldn't. You would have called Aunt Jess and asked her to send over some food from the Inn at Eagle Point," she teased. "There's still time to do that. I'm about thirty minutes away. I could pick it up."

"What a great idea! Why don't you do that. I'll call Jess as soon as I get off the phone." She hesitated. "Caitlyn, are you sure everything's okay? You never pop in unexpectedly like this. You always let us know when you're coming. Has something happened at the hospital? Is your work going okay? Medical school's not getting to be too much for you, is it?"

"Everything's fine," Caitlyn assured her automatically. She forced herself to amend that. "But maybe you and I could find a little time to talk after dinner. I'd like your advice about something."

"Now I'm really worried," Abby said, only half in jest. "I'll tell Jess we're going to need one of those chocolate decadence cakes to go along with some serious conversation."

Caitlyn laughed despite her somber mood. "You *always* want one of those cakes. I've just given you the perfect excuse to order it without guilt. You can blame all those calories on me."

"Too true," her mom said. "My hips won't thank you, but I do. See you soon."

Caitlyn disconnected the call and sighed. There, she thought. She'd laid the groundwork. She doubted, though, that in her wildest dreams her mother could possibly imagine the news that she was coming home to share.

Noah didn't have a lot of buddies, at least not the kind he could call and join for a beer and a serious discussion about what was going on in his life. He had a few basketball pals, but their conversations were superficial and mostly limited to medicine and sports. On top of that, they were rarely available on a Friday night. If they weren't on duty at the hospital, they'd be home with their families or out on dates.

Since he knew he'd probably lose his mind sitting around his apartment and waiting for word from Caitlyn, he switched rotations with one of the other residents and went to the hospital for the Friday-night shift.

Thankfully, it was a quiet start to the weekend, because his concentration was shot. He knew he was in bad shape when the head nurse on duty pulled him aside after rounds.

"What's with you, Noah?" Jill Marshall asked. "I've known you since the first day you set foot in this hospital, and it's the first time I've ever seen you be abrupt with a patient." She gave him a long look, then added, "Ray Simpson."

He regarded her with dismay and went over his conversation with Ray in his head. He winced when he realized she was right. He'd practically cut the man off in midsentence.

"I'll go back in there and apologize," he said at once. "I have a lot on my mind, but I shouldn't be taking it out on a patient."

"It must be pretty serious," she said, regarding him worriedly. "How about a cup of coffee instead? I'm a good listener. Maybe you should get this off your chest before you tick off another patient. You can go back to see Mr. Simpson afterward. He's in traction. He isn't going anywhere."

Since Jill was in her fifties and had been a head nurse long before he'd turned up at the hospital as a green intern, Noah knew the offer was well-meant. She might treat the physicians with the utmost respect, but she mothered the med students, interns and even the residents. If anything other than Caitlyn's pregnancy were on his mind, he'd accept her offer eagerly. She'd proven herself to be a good sounding board on many occasions.

"I could probably use the coffee," he admitted. "But can we skip the heart-to-heart?"

She frowned at that. "How am I supposed to help if you won't tell me what's worrying you?"

"Just knowing you care helps a lot," he said.

She rolled her eyes at that, but led the way to the empty nurses' lounge and poured them both cups of coffee strong enough to keep the most exhausted person on staff wide-awake and alert.

"I thought you took this weekend off so you and Caitlyn could have some time together," she commented as she handed him his coffee.

Noah chuckled at her attempt at an innocent interrogation. "Something came up. She had to drive down to Chesapeake Shores to see her family."

"And you didn't want to go along? You had the time off, after all."

"It wasn't the right time," he said.

She gave him a direct look. "Okay, I know I'm butting in here, but are the two of you serious or not?"

"We are," he said a little too emphatically.

"Then I really don't get it. Have you even met her family? They live practically up the street."

"It's a little farther away than that," he responded, then sighed. "But I know what you mean. It's complicated."

"Complicated how?"

"I can't explain it," he admitted.

"Because she won't explain it to you," Jill guessed. "Noah, you know we all love Caitlyn to pieces. She's going to be an incredible physician, every bit as talented as you. Personally, I think the two of you are perfect for each other. But if she's holding you at arm's length, whatever her reasons for it, maybe you need to think about moving on. It's not normal for a woman supposedly in love to be deliberately keeping you away from her family."

She allowed that to sink in, then added, "You're an incredible man. I know a half-dozen women on staff who'd give their right arms to have you glance at them twice. Believe me, any one of them would be thrilled to drag you home to meet Mom and Dad."

Noah appreciated what she was saying, but he wasn't interested. "That's very flattering, but Caitlyn's the one for me."

She held his gaze and asked gently, "But are you the one for her?"

"I am," he said readily.

He had to be, he told himself. Especially now.

Caitlyn managed to get through dinner with her mother and Trace without giving anything away. She even played with her little half brother, Patrick Donovan Riley, for a few minutes before he went down for the night. Her last words as she tucked him in were, "Don't you dare let Grandpa Mick insist on calling you Paddy, okay? It should be enough for Grandpa that your cousin Luke has an Irish pub called O'Brien's right here in town. We don't need to be obsessive about the whole Irish thing."

"'Kay," he mumbled sleepily as his eyes drifted shut.

She lingered in his room, trying to imagine herself with a child his age in a few years. How crazy would that be? And how on earth would it work if she were in some isolated part of the world? Would Noah insist that their child remain with him wherever he located and opened his practice? Was that one of the possibilities? Could she accept being separated from her child, even temporarily? And what about Noah? Could she live with being separated from him? Until now it had seemed a distant problem, one it would be years before she had to resolve. Now it was all too depressingly complicated with no obvious solutions, at least none she'd managed to come up with on her own.

When she got downstairs, she found her mother in the kitchen, putting the last of the dishes into the dishwasher.

"Where's Trace?" Caitlyn asked.

"I told him we wanted some mother-daughter time,"

Abby replied. "How about going for a walk? It's a mild night for this time of year. After the endless winter we've had that dragged on through April, I can almost believe that spring is finally right around the corner."

"It's a little too dark for a walk on the beach," Caitlyn responded, regretting that. She'd done some of her best thinking and planning on the shores of the Chesapeake Bay.

"We could walk along the road into town, burn off a few calories from that cake," her mother suggested. "We could even grab a cup of coffee or shop. I imagine one or two of the stores are still open, even though most of them won't start extending their hours for the summer season until Memorial Day weekend."

Caitlyn smiled. Her mom had always loved shopping, a trait she shared with Grandma Megan. She'd been in heaven living in New York. There was no comparison in Chesapeake Shores certainly, even though the small downtown area was thriving.

"We can certainly window-shop at least," Caitlyn agreed. "No more food, that's for sure. That cake is so rich I may not eat for the rest of the weekend."

"You'll eat at Grandpa Mick's on Sunday," her mother said. "Otherwise, you'll never hear the end of it. He'll lecture you on insulting Nell."

"Don't I know it," Caitlyn said. "Besides, sometimes I actually crave Gram's pot roast and her chicken and dumplings and her Irish stew."

"Any preference for Sunday? I'm sure she'll make whatever you ask her for."

"Irish stew," Caitlyn said at once. "I tried making it myself a couple of weeks ago. It was awful, and I know I followed the recipe you gave me."

Her mom winced. "Maybe you should have gotten it directly from Gram. You know how I am about things like that. I could have left off half the ingredients. To her everlasting dismay, your uncle Kevin is the only one in the family who inherited Gram's skill in the kitchen."

Caitlyn shook her head. "That would explain the disaster, all right. My stew was all but inedible."

"I've already called to tell her you're here. I'll let her know first thing in the morning about Sunday dinner," her mom promised. "Shall I tell her you'll be stopping by for a cooking lesson in the meantime?"

"That would be great," Caitlyn said at once. It would give her time alone with Nell to get some much-needed perspective to go right along with the recipe.

Abby grabbed a jacket off a peg by the kitchen door. "You ready for that walk?"

Caitlyn plucked her own jacket off a peg and left the house with her mother. The night air was brisk, even for May, but there was a full moon that cast a stream of silvery light across the Chesapeake Bay just below the road.

They walked the first half mile or so in silence until Caitlyn couldn't stand it any longer.

"How's work?" she asked.

"Challenging," Abby replied. "Handling the job full-time now with Patrick seems a lot harder than it did when you and Carrie were his age. It doesn't make sense since there were two of you."

"That's because we were little angels," Caitlyn said wryly, knowing perfectly well that she and her sister had been anything but angelic.

Her mom laughed. "As if, but it's true that Patrick's a real handful. Trace is a trouper, but he's more in demand for graphic design work than ever, especially for these new start-up web companies. Even though he works at home, it's hard for him to juggle work and child care. Thank goodness for kindergarten. He manages a few uninterrupted hours of work before Patrick gets home."

"You could afford help," Caitlyn suggested.

"And have your grandfather complain that strangers are raising his grandson?"

"It's not as if he has a lot of room to talk," Caitlyn reminded her. "Didn't he leave Nell to raise you and the rest of his kids when he and Grandma Megan were apart?"

"But Nell is his mother. He'd say it's not the same."

"Then tell him he can step in and babysit Patrick."

"Oh, no," her mom protested at once. "That child is stubborn enough without letting my father influence him on a daily basis."

Caitlyn laughed, well aware of her grandfather's personality. *Stubborn* was just the tip of the iceberg. Controlling and meddling also came to mind. "I can see how that would be worrisome," she said.

Silence fell again until they reached downtown Chesapeake Shores. The shops were all closed, but one or two of the restaurants along Shore Road appeared to be open.

"Panini Bistro?" Caitlyn asked.

"That works for me," her mother said, leading the way inside and heading for a table in the back.

There were a few other tables occupied, but they were far enough away that their conversation wouldn't be overheard. As soon as they had cups of decaf coffee in front of them and Caitlyn had taken her time adding sugar and cream, her mother reached over and covered her hand.

"Talk," she said gently. "Whatever's going on, you know you can tell me. Is medical school not going well? Are you having second thoughts about medicine?"

It was interesting that her mother had focused on her career first. Clearly she understood it was the most important thing in Caitlyn's life.

Caitlyn shook her head. "Work at the hospital is good. And I'll never change my mind about medicine and what I want for my future. That's part of the problem."

"How so?"

Tears welled up in Caitlyn's eyes. Unable to bear the thought of the disappointment she might see on her mom's face, she looked down at the table and whispered, "I'm going to have a baby."

There wasn't even an instant of shock or hesitation from her mom. "Oh, sweetheart," she said, squeezing Caitlyn's hand tightly. "That's wonderful news!"

Caitlyn looked up and spotted the tears in her mother's eyes and realized her words were totally sincere. Among the O'Briens, babies were a blessing, no matter what.

"Seriously? You're not disappointed in me?"

"I could never be disappointed in you," Abby replied fiercely. "You're brilliant and loving and the best daughter imaginable."

"But this is something Carrie would do, not me."

Her mother actually chuckled at that. "It's true that it might be less of a shock coming from your sister, but that doesn't mean it's not wonderful. Tell me about the father. Why haven't you mentioned that you're with someone special?"

"How do you know it's someone special?" Caitlyn asked, amazed by her mother's perceptiveness.

"Because you're you," Abby said, a smile on her lips.

"If I know nothing else about you, I know you don't have casual flings. Given how focused you've been about school and your career, I can't imagine you'd get involved with anyone if he weren't really important."

"That's true," Caitlyn said, grateful for the vote of confidence.

"Any particular reason you haven't mentioned him before?"

Caitlyn flushed. "You know how Grandpa Mick and Trace would get. The whole family, for that matter. Add in what happened at Jenny's wedding and Grandpa Mick would never leave us in peace. Catching that bouquet all but signaled that there'd be a wedding in my future. If he knew about Noah, he'd have a date scheduled on the church calendar. I didn't want to subject Noah or myself to the pressure."

Her mother smiled. "No question Dad would pile on the pressure," she agreed. "But you've always been able to handle that. Did you think your young man wouldn't be able to?"

"Not at all. Noah is incredible," Caitlyn confided to her. "He's smart and funny and gorgeous. He's finishing his residency in family medicine next month."

"He sounds perfect for you." She studied Caitlyn with a penetrating look. "Am I wrong about that?"

She shook her head. "No, he is perfect. It's the timing of all this. He wants to get married."

"Let me guess. You don't."

"Not because I don't love Noah," she said quickly. "I do. More than anything. And I want this baby."

"But marriage and a baby weren't part of the plan," her mother said, holding her gaze. "The one you thought through so carefully and wrote down before you even finished high school."

Caitlyn nodded. "That was the plan, all right. This was supposed to happen years from now. *After* I'd accomplished everything I wanted to accomplish," she stressed.

Her mother regarded her with sympathy. "Oh, my poor girl, I can totally relate to how you're feeling. I know all about plans and how disconcerting it is when they go awry. I was just getting started as a stockbroker in New York when I met your father. I had this fast-paced timetable for success, and believe me, there was no room in that for a man, much less marriage and a family."

Caitlyn chuckled. It sounded so familiar and oddly reassuring. Her mother had figured out a solution. Perhaps she could, too.

"But bad timing or not, there was your father," her mom continued. "He was very determined and persuasive. Eventually he overrode all of my objections and convinced me to get married. I figured I could juggle marriage and work okay, no problem. I am, after all, an incredible multitasker."

Caitlyn laughed. "So you've always claimed."

"I am," her mother repeated with a hint of indignation. "My point is that I adjusted my plan and it was working very smoothly." She sighed. "At least until I discovered I was pregnant with twins."

After a moment, she continued. "You know the rest. Your father wanted me to quit work and be a full-time mother. When I refused, we fought. Endlessly, as a matter of fact, until there was no other choice but to get a divorce. Then I had two babies and a full-time career. I panicked, but I did it. You'll be able to do it, too. You'll make whatever adjustments are necessary. You have my genes, after all."

"I've been to med school," Caitlyn reminded her. "I know genetics will only get me so far."

"Well, you have the O'Brien grit and determination going for you, too," she added. "What does Noah have to say about all this? Beyond wanting to get married, that is."

"He says we can figure the rest out, but I don't see how. The only way I see it working is if I give up on my dream and settle for practicing medicine in some traditional way, rather than going overseas."

"Did Noah insist you abandon everything you've worked for? If he did, perhaps he doesn't know you as well as he should. The right man would be incredibly proud of your dedication."

"Noah would never insist on something like that, even if it's what he really wants. Sure, he'd be thrilled if I finished up in a few years and went into practice with him, but he does get where I'm coming from. He's always been incredibly supportive. If there's a way for me to do what I've always hoped to do, he'll back me. I'm the one who's not seeing any alternative but sacrificing the one thing that's been driving me for years now. I feel as if I'm caught up in one of those either-or moments."

"Maybe you just need to start thinking outside the box. You won't know what's possible until the two of you really sit down and talk about all your options. Have you done that yet?"

Caitlyn shook her head. "We just found out this week. He encouraged me to come home to talk to you and Nell."

"He didn't want to come along?"

"He practically insisted on it," she admitted. "I talked him out of it. I told him I needed to think this through in peace and break the news myself." She regarded her mother worriedly. "Do you think there's any chance at all that Grandpa Mick and Trace will take this as well as you have?"

Her mother laughed. "Not a chance," she said. "But we'll deal with them. Given what a handful you and Carrie were as teenagers—well, Carrie, anyway—I've had a lot of experience at keeping them from freaking out."

"I know that, but I'm not sure your skills have been put to a test like this before. Besides, I'm the one who needs to tell them."

"How about we do it together?" her mother suggested.

Caitlyn wanted to seize the offer, but she shook her head. "Thanks for offering, but no. I'm an adult. It's up to me." She sighed, then added, "Noah really did want to be with me when I tell them, but I told him I wouldn't risk his life like that."

"Probably a wise decision," her mother concurred. "But I suggest you get him down here very soon. Otherwise, I can't promise they won't go looking for him. The entire O'Brien posse is likely to take off for Baltimore before you can get all your words out."

Unfortunately, Caitlyn knew her mother was absolutely right about that. "I'll talk to Trace and Grandpa Mick in the morning. After I'm convinced they've recovered from the shock, I'll see if Noah wants to drive down for Sunday dinner. At least if there's a crowd, someone will pull Trace and Grandpa Mick away if they attack him."

Her mom nodded. "Good plan." She hesitated, then asked, "What about your father?"

Oddly enough, Caitlyn hadn't even considered how her biological father might react. While Wes Winters had remained in their lives after the divorce, he'd married again, had two more children and taken less and less of an interest in what was going on with Caitlyn and Carrie.

"I'll call him next week. It's not as if he'll accidentally find out in the meantime," she said. "I doubt the news will be much more than a passing blip on his radar these days."

Her mother gave her hand another reassuring squeeze. "It's all going to work out," she promised. "And I can't wait to meet this young man of yours."

"You're going to love him," Caitlyn predicted.

"What matters is that you love him," her mother responded.

"I do," she said, and for the first time since she'd seen that positive pregnancy test, she was able to focus on the fact that she loved Noah more than she'd ever imagined possible. She needed to concentrate on that. Maybe then everything else really would fall into place.

3

It was nearly midnight and Cait had rarely been far from Noah's thoughts for more than a few minutes at a time all evening. He'd checked his cell phone a half-dozen times to see if she'd tried to reach him. When it finally vibrated and he saw her name on the caller ID, he breathed a sigh of relief as he answered.

"Hey, you," he said, his voice low even though he was alone in the on-call room at the hospital. "I was hoping I'd hear from you tonight. Is everything going okay in Chesapeake Shores? Have you broken the news yet?"

"It's actually going better than I expected, so far," she told him. "I told my mom earlier."

"And?"

"She can't wait to meet you."

The tension he'd been feeling all day eased. "That's a good sign, isn't it?" he said. If Cait's mother could keep an open mind about him after learning about the pregnancy, perhaps she'd get through to others in the family.

"One down and a long list to go," Cait warned him.

"But that one is crucial. I imagine you had to talk fast

and create quite an impressive list of my sterling attri-
butes to counteract the baby news."

"To be honest, my mom's pretty excited about the
baby, too. She believes we can figure out a solution."

"Word is that we're both pretty smart," Noah replied
with a smile. "I think she's right. What about the rest of
the family? When will you tell them?"

"I'm going to talk to Trace and Grandpa Mick in the
morning." She sighed heavily. "I'm really not looking
forward to that."

"I'm still willing to hop in the car and drive down there
to be with you when you tell them. I can take the heat."

"And I appreciate that," she said. "But I need to be
the one to break the news. Once I see how that goes, I
thought maybe you could come down on Sunday. We
have this big family dinner at Grandpa Mick's every
week. Remember, I've told you about that."

Noah, whose own family was small and apparently
very sedate by comparison, had envied the chaotic meals
she'd described. "I remember."

"It's a bit of a mob scene, but you know what they
say about there being safety in numbers. I doubt even
my grandfather would do anything crazy with that many
witnesses."

"Gee, you make it sound like a fun time," he said. "But
if you want me there, I'm game." He was, in fact, surprisingly eager to take this next step. He sensed that despite
Cait's fears, he'd have allies there.

"I'll call you once I've seen them tomorrow and we can
decide what's best," she promised. "Now tell me about
what's going on at the hospital. Did you work tonight?"

"I did, though my mind kept wandering. Jill called
me on it. I was abrupt with poor Mr. Simpson," he con-

fessed. "He was just looking for more reassurance that he'd be okay and able to go back to work once the worst of his injuries from the accident heal, but I snapped at him."

"I can't believe you were short with anyone," Cait said, sounding shocked. "You never lose your temper with the patients, no matter how many times they ask the same questions."

"I apologized." He recalled that uncomfortable conversation. It was one he hoped never to have to repeat. "Do you know what he told me?"

"What?"

"That for the first time it made him realize I was only human, too."

Cait laughed. "Could be a lesson in there for all of us," she said. "Not that I recommend losing your cool on a regular basis, but we need to remember we're not gods and the patients need to know that, too. Aren't you the one who's always preached that we need to connect with them as real people?"

"And I do believe that," Noah confirmed. "Tell me about Chesapeake Shores. What's it like this time of year?"

"I was pretty distracted as I drove into town, but the weather's nice. Mom and I took a walk along the bay after dinner, then went for coffee. Decaf," she added quickly.

"Good for you. I know how you love your caffeine."

"Way too much," she conceded. "Maybe this is one sacrifice that will stick with me and I'll stop craving it to get through those long days at work."

"Describe the town for me again," he said. He'd never tired of hearing about it. He'd grown up in the middle of a blighted urban area that had made him long for a more peaceful and serene setting.

"The daffodils are fading on the town green," she reported. "But the tulips will be in full bloom soon. And the little patch of lily of the valley at the house smells wonderful. That was Grandma Megan's favorite flower, so Mom and all of her siblings have planted it by their front walks. They say back then it reminded them of her when she was away for so long and they never want to forget how much they missed her and how grateful they've come to be that she's back in their lives."

Noah was familiar with the story of how her grandmother had walked out on her workaholic grandfather, a famed architect and urban planner. She'd left behind five children, convinced by Mick O'Brien they'd be better off growing up right in Chesapeake Shores, a town he and his brothers had built along the shores of the Chesapeake Bay. While she'd left with the best of intentions for her family, it had caused a serious rift with her children that had only recently healed. Now Mick and Megan had patched up their differences, as well, and were far more happily remarried. It was proof, he thought, that with true love there was always reason to hope.

"I can't wait to see this town that's so special to you," he told Cait. "And to meet your family."

"You're going to love it here," she said. "It's an idyllic setting and a great community." She yawned sleepily. "I'm beat. You must be, too. I'll give you a call tomorrow and we'll decide on a plan for Sunday, okay?" She hesitated, then added, "Or I'll warn you if it would be wise to leave the country."

Noah laughed, though he could tell she wasn't entirely kidding. "I'll wait to hear from you," he said. "I love you, Cait."

"Love you, too. Good night, Noah."

Even after she'd disconnected the call, he held tightly to the phone, reluctant to sever the connection himself. Cait had definitely sounded more upbeat than she had before heading home. He counted on that being a promising start for this new journey.

Maybe by Sunday they'd have a real strategy for the future that would work for both of them. He'd certainly been putting the pieces of his own plan together in his head ever since he'd discovered that Cait was pregnant. And once she'd calmed down, he knew she was more than likely to have her own very specific ideas. Somewhere in there, he hoped, was exactly the right compromise.

Caitlyn lingered at the kitchen table, pushing French toast around on her plate.

"You need to eat that," her mother scolded.

"I know, but I can't seem to swallow." She met her mother's worried gaze. "Thanks for making it, though."

"Even I can dip bread into eggs and manage not to burn it," Abby said. "Enough butter and maple syrup and nobody ever notices that's all it is—bread, eggs and a little milk. Trace acts as if I've taken breakfast to a whole new level of culinary achievement."

Caitlyn chuckled. "In his view, maybe you have. This is an improvement over cold cereal, frozen waffles or even scrambled eggs."

"You and Carrie survived on that, didn't you?" her mom retorted.

"Doesn't mean I can't appreciate the extra effort that went into this."

"If you appreciate it so much, finish it," Abby prodded.

Caitlyn shook her head and pushed away the plate.

"Okay, then, you might as well get your big announcement over with. Trace is already in his office working. I can call Dad and get him over here, so you can speak to both of them at the same time."

"It would be easier to break the news just one time," Caitlyn agreed. "Maybe they can prop each other up as the shock settles in."

"Or I can stand just outside the door with smelling salts," her mom suggested.

Caitlyn laughed despite herself. "Probably an even better idea, especially for Grandpa Mick. Maybe you should ask Grandma Megan to come over here, too. She can usually calm him down."

Abby gave her a wry look. "But it's Nell who's able to peel him off the ceiling when he's about to lose it."

Caitlyn thought of Nell's soothing influence on all of them and nodded. "Fine. Call her, too. Though I hate to imagine what they're going to think when you summon them over here first thing on a Saturday morning and they see me."

"They're going to be delighted to get a glimpse of you," Abby assured her.

"That won't last," Caitlyn predicted. "I'd better go and pull myself together. Let me know when the cast has been assembled for the big reveal."

Her mom gave her an amused look. "Your aunt Bree, the playwright, will be thrilled you've inherited her sense of drama."

"Don't even mention her to me. It's that bouquet she made for Jenny's wedding that I blame for all of this," she said as she left the kitchen and headed to her room.

Far too quickly she heard a tap on her door and her mother announced that her grandparents and Nell were in Trace's office. Abby walked downstairs with Caitlyn.

"Are you sure you don't want me with you for moral support?" she asked.

Caitlyn shook her head. "Too bad I can't drink. I could use a stiff shot of something about now."

"It's going to be okay," Abby reassured her. "Just remember that they all love you. And once they're past the shock, they'll agree with me that this is great news. I'm counting on them to help me convince you that it doesn't have to derail your life."

Caitlyn opened the door to Trace's spacious home office with its tall windows letting in lots of morning sunshine. When they'd all moved in years ago, she and Carrie had spent hours in this room playing as Trace worked. Taking a huge breath, she stepped inside.

"Well, look who's here," her grandfather boomed, enveloping her in an exuberant hug. "My favorite granddaughter." Mick leaned close to whisper, "Don't tell the others."

It was a familiar refrain, one repeated with every single grandchild at one point or another. They were all Mick's favorites to hear him tell it, and they grew up believing it and counting on that exuberant and unconditional love, even as they chafed at his well-meant interference in their lives.

Caitlyn crossed the room to kiss her grandmother, then sat down next to Nell and reached for her hand. That garden-roughened hand had soothed away many hurts over the years. It was a shock to realize how frail it felt in Caitlyn's grasp.

"You okay?" Nell asked, regarding her with worry. "I know perfectly well we're not here just so you can say hello."

"If only that were the reason," Caitlyn told her with a heartfelt sigh. She looked across the room at her stepfather. Trace had been such a powerful force in her life. He'd been present in ways her biological father never had been, not just physically present, but emotionally supportive, too. She could recall the candy he'd brought to her and Carrie from Ethel's Emporium, the trips into town for ice cream and pizza as he'd wooed them as determinedly as he'd tried to win back her mother's affections. Theirs was just one more story that proved true love really could have a second chance.

"What's up, kiddo?" Trace asked quietly, his gaze steady and expectant. It was evident he knew something was up.

Holding tight to Nell's hand, she began, "I thought you all should know that I've been seeing someone."

Her grandfather frowned. "You'll need to define just what that means. I thought you didn't have time for dating?"

Caitlyn smiled at the claim she'd made so many times over the years. "To be honest, it's a little more than dating," she confessed.

Now Trace's shoulders visibly stiffened. "Meaning?"

"It's serious," she told him, looking directly into his eyes. She sucked in a deep breath, then blurted, "We're going to have a baby."

The commotion that ensued wasn't entirely unexpected. Grandpa Mick immediately started blustering about going after the man responsible. Trace seconded him, even as Nell and Grandma Megan were circling the wagons around her, beaming. Her mom, who'd clearly been listening at the door, came into the room and poked Grandpa Mick in the chest.

"Sit down," she commanded, then went to sit on the edge of Trace's desk, her gaze all but daring him to make a fuss.

To Caitlyn's shock, her grandfather fell silent and Trace sat back and closed his eyes, clearly gathering his composure. They looked shaken, but no more so than she'd expected.

"Tell them about Noah," her mom suggested, then added meaningfully, "He sounds like a wonderful man to me."

"You knew about this?" Trace asked, regarding her with a hint of hurt in his voice.

"Only since last night," Abby told him. "I would have said something then, but Caitlyn wanted to tell you all herself. I had to respect her decision."

"Well, personally, I couldn't be happier to hear that we'll have another baby to celebrate," Nell said, giving her son and Trace a defiant look.

"Of course we'll be celebrating this gift, Ma," Mick responded impatiently. His scowl deepened. "But I want to know what this young man intends to do to make things right. Have you set a wedding date?"

Caitlyn shook her head. "We've barely had time to absorb the news. We haven't made any plans yet. There's a lot to consider."

"There's only one thing I can think of," her grandfather contradicted. "Whether the church is available."

"Mick, let the girl talk," Grandma Megan said quietly, then faced Caitlyn. "Sweetheart, have you discussed marriage?"

"It's on the table," Caitlyn acknowledged, reluctant to make the admission because of the pressure that was bound to follow for her to say yes.

"Well, of course it is," Trace said, proving her point. "It's the right thing to do."

Her mom frowned at him.

"I'm just saying," he said defensively.

"Caitlyn's decision," Abby reminded him.

"And Noah's," Caitlyn added. "I've thought of inviting him to join us for dinner tomorrow, but I won't do it unless you all promise to treat him decently." She looked directly at her grandfather and then at Trace as she said it. "I want all of you to get to know him, but I don't want any pressure about wedding dates."

"They'll be on their best behavior," Nell assured her before glancing sharply at both men. "Won't you?"

Silence fell.

"Won't you?" Nell repeated.

Trace sighed. "Of course."

Mick's scowl settled in. "I reserve the right to say whatever I please in my own home."

Megan lifted a brow. "Do you want to meet this young man of Caitlyn's or not? You'll guarantee politeness or the rest of us will be having dinner at Brady's without you."

Caitlyn choked back a laugh at Grandpa Mick's stunned expression. "Maybe that would be best," she said innocently.

"Over my dead body!" Grandpa Mick blustered. "Okay, okay, I'll promise to keep a civil tongue in my head, but if I don't like what I'm hearing, none of you can hold me to that."

That wasn't quite the assurance that Caitlyn would have preferred, but it was more than she'd anticipated. She crossed the room to give him a fierce hug. "Thank you."

When she looked into his eyes, she saw they were damp with tears.

"You love this man?" he asked, his tone quieter and far more reasonable.

"I do."

"Then we'll start from there," he said. "Everything else can be worked out."

Caitlyn wished she were as confident of that, but knowing that her family was on her side was a huge relief. It already felt as if a tremendous weight had been lifted from her shoulders.

"I think we've had enough surprises for one morning," Nell said. "Sweetheart, why don't you come back to my cottage with me? You can help me make a big pot of Irish stew for tomorrow's lunch."

"I'd love that," Caitlyn said eagerly.

And it wasn't just because it meant she could escape from this room before either her grandfather or Trace could go back on their word and start asking questions she was nowhere near ready to answer. It had just as much to do with the soothing effect of being around Nell, and maybe finally learning to cook a favorite Irish meal that would be edible.

"Okay, now that they're gone, what are we going to do about this?" Mick asked his son-in-law.

Trace gave him a startled look. "I was under the impression that we've been given clear marching orders. We're to be nice and keep our mouths shut."

"Oh, balderdash!" Mick retorted. "Have you ever known me to sit back and wait to see what happens?"

Trace smiled. "And how has that worked out for you?"

"Perfectly fine," Mick replied at once, then sighed. "Mostly."

Trace gave him a rueful look. "It's those exceptions that worry me."

"But you agree with me that Caitlyn and this man need to get married as soon as possible?" he pressed.

"Not necessarily," Trace said.

Mick was startled by Trace's apparent indecision. "You don't agree? What kind of father doesn't want to see his daughter married to the man who got her pregnant?"

"Stepfather," Trace corrected.

Mick rolled his eyes. "We both know you've been more of a father to that girl than Wes Winters ever was. Why are you hesitating about doing what we both know is right?"

"Because this is Caitlyn's decision. If she has second thoughts about marrying this man, maybe there's a reason for that. I think we need to meet him and then decide on the best course of action."

Mick took his son-in-law's suggestion under advisement. "You could be right," he admitted eventually. "We'll know more tomorrow, then first thing Monday we can get busy making plans. Maybe I'll call the priest this afternoon just to get the ball rolling."

Trace laughed. "So much for waiting until we know more."

Mick waved off his sarcasm. "Oh, we both know that Caitlyn's smart as a whip. If she's involved with this man, then we're going to approve of him, too."

"Probably so," Trace conceded.

Mick nodded, satisfied. "Then we have a plan."

"Well, at least you do," Trace said. "I just hope it doesn't blow up in your face."

"Now, why would it do that?" Mick asked, bewildered.

"Because you seem to be forgetting one thing. Caitlyn is your granddaughter. She has a mind of her own."

Now it was Mick's turn to sigh. That was, indeed, a little worrisome.

In the kitchen of Nell's cozy cottage overlooking the bay, a fire had been lit to take off the morning chill. Dillon O'Malley was waiting for them, the water already hot for tea.

"How did you read my mind?" Caitlyn asked him, giving a hug to this man who'd come back into her great-grandmother's life only a few brief years ago.

"How are you, you darling girl?" he asked, studying her closely with his perceptive gaze. "Do I detect a certain glow about you?"

Nell regarded him with amazement. "What makes you ask a thing like that? The girl just told us not a half hour ago that she's pregnant."

Dillon winked at Caitlyn. "I'd love to have you believing that I've a touch of second sight, but the truth is Abby called to fill me in. She said it had turned awfully damp and cool to be walking outside and thought you might want a bracing cup of tea when you got here. I've herbal for you, Caitlyn."

A pleased smile spread across Nell's face. "Is there any question about why I fell for you so many years ago and all over again when we went to Ireland for Christmas a few years back?" She turned to Caitlyn. "If your young man is half as thoughtful, you'll have a good life."

"Noah is patient, kind and considerate," Caitlyn assured her. She smiled at Dillon. "But it probably wouldn't hurt if you want to give him a few lessons in catering to a woman's needs."

"I'd be happy to," Dillon said. "Will we be seeing him soon?"

"Tomorrow more than likely," she said. "I called him before we left to walk over here. He's coming for Sunday dinner, unless I've scared him off with all the warnings about the interrogation he'll likely face."

"Why don't I stick close and see that he's not overwhelmed," Dillon offered. "I know all too well what Mick can be like when he's feeling protective. I imagine he's a little crazy right now."

Caitlyn laughed. She recalled her grandfather's reaction when he'd discovered that his mother was being courted by an old flame in Dublin. He'd been all but impossible to reason with.

"We'll both be keeping a sharp eye on Mick," Nell promised. "Now, let's get to that stew. I've all the ingredients ready to go. Do you have paper and a pen?"

Caitlyn took them out of her pocket. "Right here."

Apparently satisfied that she and Nell were warmed up from their walk back to the cottage, Dillon left them to their cooking.

"You really did luck out with that man," Caitlyn told Nell.

"I was twice blessed," she replied. "You didn't know your great-grandfather, but he was a fine man, too. I think that was one reason it took Mick so long to warm up to the idea of Dillon being back in my life. He loved his father. I think he thought I'd always mourn him."

"But he finally realized that we have an unlimited capacity for love, didn't he?" Caitlyn said. "Do you think the O'Briens mate for life like a few of the creatures in nature? You're with the first man you ever loved, even after having a whole family with another man. Grandpa Mick and Grandma Megan got back together after years of being divorced. Even Mom eventually came back to Trace, her own first love."

"Are you really wondering if this Noah of yours is your soul mate?" Nell asked gently. "Or if you're going to be acting too hastily by marrying him just because of the baby?"

Caitlyn was relieved to have Nell recognize her real worry. "Exactly," she said.

"Only you know the answer to that," Nell said as she diced vegetables and put them into a pot of water on the stove along with various spices. As they began to simmer, filling the air with a wonderfully rich aroma, she sat across from Caitlyn. She took a sip of her tea and waited, then smiled. "Since you haven't had a word to say to that, I assume you don't know the answer."

Caitlyn shook her head, yet another batch of tears forming in her eyes. At this rate, she'd be dehydrated throughout her pregnancy.

"I don't," she whispered. "I really don't. It's disconcerting. It seems as if I've always understood what I wanted to do professionally, what I was meant to do, but when it comes to love, I never had a plan at all. I certainly didn't have any idea how to combine the two."

"Then you won't make a decision until you do. And we'll all of us wait for that moment, even your grandfather."

"Grandpa Mick's never been very patient," Caitlyn said with a sniff. "He's going to push to book the church. You know he is."

Nell squeezed her hand. "This time he'll find a way

to wait for your decision, and that's a promise from me to you."

"Thank you."

"No thanks necessary," Nell said. "This is your life to lead as you think best. If you want our guidance, you'll ask for it. As for our support, that's a given."

Caitlyn looked into her great-grandmother's blue eyes, faded now with age, and felt better than she had at any time since she'd first read that positive pregnancy test.

"I love you," she said, hoping she'd have years and years left to say those words to Nell, praying that her child would have time to get to know this wise and wonderful woman.

"Now don't be getting all sentimental on me," Nell said briskly, though she wiped away a tear of her own. She tapped a finger on the blank page in front of Caitlyn. "Start writing or your second attempt at making traditional Irish stew won't be any better than the first."

Caitlyn pushed aside all other thoughts and started writing down the recipe, just the first of many that would connect her to her Irish roots.

Despite all of his brave declarations about facing the O'Briens at Cait's side, Noah was decidedly nervous as he drove into Chesapeake Shores and followed her directions to her grandfather's house on a cliff overlooking the Chesapeake Bay.

Before he made the turn onto the shoreline road, he caught a glimpse of the town green, which was still bright with the few remaining yellow daffodils in the May sunshine. It was just as Cait had described. There were shouts of childish laughter coming from the colorful playground at one end of the green. He couldn't help thinking what a wonderful place it would be to raise a child. He doubted, though, that Cait was ready to hear his thoughts on that or on the research he'd done that revealed that the nearest local doctor's office was miles away.

As he approached Mick O'Brien's impressive home a few minutes later, he sucked in a deep breath. Even though Cait had assured him she'd paved the way by speaking to both her grandfather and her stepdad, Noah couldn't help feeling he was about to walk into the lion's den, albeit a cozy-looking one with a sprawling front porch crammed with rocking chairs and old-fashioned wicker furniture. Fortunately, it was a little too cool for those chairs to be occupied by shotgun-bearing O'Briens.

As he pulled to a stop, Cait must have spotted him from inside the house because she emerged and ran across the grass to meet him. He studied her face, trying to guess how things might be going inside.

"You okay?" he asked, taking the time to kiss her thoroughly despite whatever prying eyes might be watching.

"Getting there," she said, a little breathless from their kiss.

"Does everyone inside know what's going on?"

"I've only told Mom, Gram, Trace, Grandpa Mick and Grandma Megan, but I think we can assume the word has spread. I was getting an awful lot of speculative looks just now."

"What about Carrie? Is she around?"

"Nope, she's at some fashion thing in Milan or Paris." She shrugged. "Someplace in Europe. I'll tell her next time she calls."

He grinned. "Are you sure you two are identical twins?" he asked, checking out her loose-fitting linen slacks and oversize sweater in a shade of purple never intended to be worn with her coloring. He thought she looked amazing, but he imagined her fashion-conscious sister would have been appalled.

"I know what you mean," she said, glancing down with a rueful expression. "I'm a mess."

"Not even close," he objected. "Just oblivious to the designer racks, thank goodness. I think you look perfect."

"And that's why I love you," she said, linking her arm through his. "Are you ready to do this?"

"Are you?"

"I think so," she said. As they neared the house, she leaned close and whispered, "Don't worry. Whatever happens, I'll protect you."

Noah smiled at that, then stopped her when she would have opened the door. "Cait, have you made any decisions?"

She shook her head. "I told you I wouldn't, not until we'd talked. Did you think I'd go back on my word?"

"No, it's just that you seem more at peace than you did the other day."

She paused, her expression thoughtful. "I think I am," she admitted, sounding surprised. "It must be the Chesapeake-Shores effect."

Whatever it was, if it had put a sparkle back into her eyes, Noah counted that as a blessing.

4

Caitlyn watched carefully as her family chatted with Noah. He seemed to be holding his own with all of them, even Grandpa Mick and Trace. The tension in Trace's jaw had finally eased. He'd even nodded approvingly when her mom appeared at his side. Abby had looked ready to intervene if things got out of hand, but Trace's glance evidently reassured her.

Still, Caitlyn held her breath as her grandfather pulled Noah aside. When she stepped in their direction, Noah gave a subtle shake of his head and Grandpa Mick regarded her with a forbidding expression.

"Let them talk," Nell advised. "You come and give me a hand in the kitchen. I'll give you a few more tips on the finishing touches for the Irish stew. And I've made Irish soda bread to go along with it. You can take notes on that."

"I doubt I'm up to baking bread," Caitlyn protested.

"It's a great stress reducer," Nell promised. "It'll come in handy whenever you've worries on your mind."

"In that case, bring it on," she said. "I've plenty of challenges ahead, it seems."

As she turned to go into the kitchen with Nell, she

cast a last worried glance in Noah's direction, then dutifully followed her great-grandmother. She still couldn't seem to concentrate on Nell's words, though.

"Child, my first impression of Noah is that he's a fine young man with a quick wit and a good head on his shoulders. I think he's capable of putting Mick's fears to rest," Nell said at last. "All your grandfather wants is to know that you're loved."

"Love doesn't always solve all the problems, though," Caitlyn said, thinking of how many things needed to be resolved to make this situation right. Some of the obstacles seemed insurmountable.

"Of course it does, at least if it's the real thing," Nell said impatiently.

"Then why do people say that love isn't always enough?"

"Because they don't understand that the problems don't just vanish when you love someone. Love takes work and compromise and understanding and respect. Do you and Noah have those things?"

"I'm willing to work at the relationship and I respect Noah more than anyone I know outside of this family," Caitlyn said. "I think I understand his hopes and dreams."

"And he understands yours?"

"He says he does."

Nell smiled. "Then it's the compromising that's the sticking point?"

"For me," Caitlyn admitted. "I'm half-O'Brien, after all. We're stubborn and sure of ourselves and we want what we want."

"I can't deny any of that," Nell agreed. "But look around at this family, Caitlyn. Is there a single one of us who hasn't compromised on the important things at one time or another? Your own mother is here, rather than in New York where she'd envisioned her future. Even your grandfather—and we both know how stubborn he can be—has given up control of his company and stopped most of his traveling, so he can spend more time with your grandmother the way she always hoped he would. Dillon gave up his life in Ireland to live here with me, when I told him I couldn't be separated from my family." She met Caitlyn's gaze. "I could go on and on. Do I need to?"

"No," Caitlyn said. "But Mom and Grandpa Mick both got to live their dreams at least for a little while before they compromised. And you and Dillon visit Ireland every year."

"And you feel as if your dream will be lost forever if you don't grab on to it right now?" Nell asked, smiling.

"Something like that," Caitlyn conceded, realizing that was part of her O'Brien need for immediate gratification.

"And those places you've dreamed of going, will they disappear?" Nell asked.

"Of course not. But I made a promise to be back soon," Caitlyn said, clinging to her plan. "I don't like the idea of breaking that promise. Promises are meant to be kept, especially one as important as this. You taught me that."

Nell smiled. "Don't throw my old lessons back in my face," she scolded. "A delay doesn't mean you'll never keep your word."

"I'm not sure that people who are counting on me for so much will be able to see it the same way," she argued.

Once more Nell regarded her with a touch of exasperation. "This need you've seen in these places? Will that be wiped out anytime soon?"

"I'd like to think so, but realistically, no."

"Then you and Noah could start this life together, perhaps, and then follow your dream a few years from now. You could even do it together, am I right? You'd be twice the help to people who need it."

"But once we have children, we can't just run off to save the world at the drop of a hat," Caitlyn said.

Nell smiled at that argument, clearly dismissing it. "Haven't you noticed the size of this family?" she asked. "I imagine there's someone who could care for your children for a month or two if you wanted to volunteer in another country. Isn't that what we do for one another?"

"It's what you did for Grandpa Mick when Grandma Megan left," Caitlyn replied, beginning to see what she meant. "You stepped in to help raise Mom, Kevin, Bree, Jess and Connor."

"And your Grandma Megan helped out with Little Mick while Connor and Heather were working things out. We all did our part with Davey, too, while Kevin was getting over Georgia's death and before he met Shanna." She gave Caitlyn a penetrating look. "See what I mean?"

"Actually, I do," Caitlyn said.

It just remained to be seen if she and Noah could reach the sort of compromise Nell was talking about, one they could both live with. The first step, she thought, was releasing that tight grip she had on the plan she'd formulated for her future.

Mick O'Brien's office was lined with bookshelves and littered with architectural blueprints. There was a sweeping view of the bay through the French doors. A leather chair sat behind a massive mahogany desk with clean modern lines. The presence of toy trucks and even a few scattered dolls, though, told the real story of the man who ruled the O'Brien clan. He had a soft spot for his grandchildren. Perhaps he would, as well, for this unexpected baby who'd be his first great-grandchild.

"Sit," Mick told Noah, his tone gruff. "And don't look so worried. My instincts are telling me that you and I might be on the same side."

"Really?" Noah said, not convinced of it. He suspected Mick was about two critical answers away from wanting to draw and quarter him.

Mick chuckled. "I'm sure you've heard the stories, that I'm a meddler, that I'm overly protective when it comes to my family."

Noah smiled. "Those are the rumors."

"Definitely true," Mick confirmed. "But I'm also a pragmatist. This baby's coming, whether I approve or disapprove. I just want to ensure that the baby's interests and my granddaughter's are protected."

"That's all I want, too," Noah told him with complete candor. "I love Caitlyn, sir. I've been very clear with her about that and you need to know it, too."

"Are we agreed, then, that marriage is the answer?" Mick asked, though it was less a question than a statement.

"I want to marry her, no question about it," Noah confirmed. "I've been eager to start a family with her for a long time now. The only thing preventing me from asking was knowing how dedicated she is to this dream of hers to go back to Africa to practice medicine."

"And I totally admire her for that dedication," Mick

said. "O'Briens understand all about how blessed we've been and our obligation to give back."

"I understand you've been dedicated to supervising the building of homes for Habitat for Humanity since you retired from your company," Noah said. "I imagine that was part of Cait's inspiration for her own goals."

"I'd like to think so, but she's young. She has years to make her own contribution to society. Right now the important thing is this child she's carrying and what's best for the baby."

"I think Cait is mindful of that," Noah said. "But it's a delicate balancing act for her between knowing what's best for our child and what she needs for her own fulfillment. This pregnancy came as a shock to her. I'm not surprised that she's having a hard time adjusting."

"It came as a shock to you, too, I imagine," Mick said. "But you're not lollygagging about doing what needs to be done. You want to get married."

"Absolutely," Noah confirmed. "But if there's one thing practicing medicine has taught me, it's to keep an open mind, to be flexible when it's necessary. Cait's not learned that lesson yet."

Mick gave a nod of satisfaction. "So, how do we get her to that point?"

Noah gave him a startled look. "I was hoping you'd have the answer to that. You've had a lot more practice dealing with her stubbornness than I have."

Mick laughed, then shrugged sheepishly. "According to my wife and even my son-in-law—Caitlyn's stepfather—my ways tend to backfire, at least at first. I thought maybe you'd have more finesse."

"I think getting Caitlyn down the aisle is going to take more than finesse," Noah replied candidly. "She's worried about giving up on something she's been working toward for a long time now. You probably know a lot about that kind of drive and determination."

"I certainly do," Mick said. "Took me a little too long, though, to figure out there's more to life than a career. I'm a happier man since I discovered that."

"You could tell Caitlyn about your epiphany," Noah suggested.

"I'd be happy to, but it took me years to figure out what's truly important. I lost all that time with my wife because of it. Caitlyn knows that, too. We don't have that kind of time to waste. There's a bit of urgency to this situation."

Noah could hardly argue with that. "But she respects you, sir. She doesn't want to disappoint you."

Mick shook his head. "At the moment, anything I say is considered suspect. She knows what I'm expecting, an engagement and then a wedding. She won't think I'm taking her needs into account."

Noah actually found himself commiserating with this man who'd apparently always thought he possessed all the answers when it came to his family. For a man who'd had his own life planned out for some time, Noah had been feeling a bit at a loss himself now that he had to take Cait's dreams into account. Balancing her goals with his own required some of that finesse Mick was talking about.

"I'll do whatever it takes to make sure Cait's happy," he told Mick. "Even if that doesn't include me."

Mick regarded him with shock. "You'd give up without a fight?"

Noah shook his head. "Not without a fight, no."

Mick nodded happily. "Okay, then, let's talk this

through and come up with a plan," he said eagerly. "I spoke to our priest yesterday and he's ready to cooperate."

Noah smiled. "You don't leave much to chance, do you?"

"Not if I can help it," Mick confirmed.

"She's not going to be happy thinking we're in cahoots," Noah reminded him.

"Play this right and she never has to figure that out," Mick replied confidently.

Noah wanted to believe that was possible, but he knew better. Cait, of all people, had her grandfather's deviousness pegged. As Mick began to toss out ideas, some more outrageous than others, Noah started to realize the depths of it himself.

Caitlyn was trying to focus on Nell's instructions, but she was too distracted by the thought of Noah being interrogated by her grandfather. They'd been alone too long. Just when she was about to burst into her grandfather's office to rescue Noah, Jenny walked into the kitchen, a grin on her face.

"You!" she exclaimed, giving Jenny a mock scowl.

Jenny Collins Green, whose mother was married to Caitlyn's great-uncle Thomas O'Brien, laughed. "My mom called about your news. I understand you're blaming this situation on my bridal bouquet, so naturally I had to fly home from Nashville to defend myself. Caleb's in the recording studio night and day with his new album or he'd be here, too. He's thinking there might be a hit song in this predicament you blame on the two of us."

"Of course he does," Caitlyn said, then asked plaintively, "You couldn't have tossed that bouquet in Carrie's direction?"

"She didn't need my help," Jenny replied, pausing to give Nell a warm hug before turning back to Caitlyn. "Your sister will fall in love all on her own. She's had lots of practice at looking for the right man." She shrugged. "Besides, everybody knows I was never a tomboy. I had very little control over where that bouquet went." She looked around the kitchen. "Where is this man who managed to slip past your defenses?"

"In Grandpa Mick's office being grilled," Caitlyn said with a shudder. "Do I need to be worried for his safety?"

"You don't have a ring on your finger yet, so no," Jenny said. "Mick's not about to kill the groom-to-be before he has the two of you married."

Caitlyn laughed, relaxing at last. "I hadn't thought about that, but you're right. Grandpa Mick has a single goal right now and it trumps any desire he might have to make Noah pay for his role in this."

Jenny regarded Nell fondly. "Mind if I steal your helper? I think a walk in the fresh air before dinner will be good for her. She seems a little tense."

"Go," Nell encouraged. "She's been of no help to me with her mind totally focused on what's going on between Noah and her grandfather."

Outside Jenny headed straight for the pier that jutted out into the bay. There was a bench at the end. At this time of day, it was drenched in sunshine that had finally managed to take the morning's chill out of the air. They sat down on the warm weathered wood. Jenny turned her face up to the sun.

"God, I love it here," she murmured. "I don't think we've had sunshine for a week in Nashville. Spring is usually gorgeous there, but this year, not so much. I actually think I'm waterlogged from all the rain."

Caitlyn drew in a deep breath and felt the last of her tension drain away. "I miss this, too," she confessed. "I was so eager to be gone on my big adventure I hadn't expected to, but I do."

"Ever think about coming back here to live?" Jenny asked.

"Sure, maybe someday."

"Once you've gone off to save the world, I imagine."

Caitlyn smiled. "Something like that. How about you?"

"I already have my house here," Jenny reminded her. "The one I grew up in."

"That's right. After your mom married Uncle Thomas and he built a house for her, they fixed your old house up for you, didn't they?"

Jenny nodded. "Caleb loves it here, too, and of course, he feels this huge debt of gratitude to Bree for giving him a chance by casting him in her play so he could get his career back on track. Oddly enough, though he's new to town and we live most of the time in Nashville, we have real roots here."

"I imagine he's also grateful to Bree for giving him the perfect excuse to stick around, so he could try to win you back," Caitlyn said. "No one was very happy about that, me included." She gave Jenny a penetrating look. "We were all wrong, weren't we? You're happy."

Jenny nodded. "You were and I am. Caleb is my soul mate, no question about it." She glanced over. "Can you keep a secret?"

"I may be one of the few in this family who can," Caitlyn said. Before Jenny could say another word, Caitlyn's jaw dropped. "You're pregnant, too, aren't you?"

A beaming smile spread across Jenny's face. "Two months, so we're not telling anyone just yet. I'm only telling you because I think it's so amazing that no matter where we live, our kids will probably spend time here together on summer vacations or something. Maybe they'll even be best friends, the way my mom was with your mom and your aunts."

"Does anyone else know?"

Jenny shook her head. "Caleb is about to burst trying to keep the news to himself. We both know, though, that once the word leaks, our agents are going to want it plastered all over the tabloids. They're publicity hounds."

"And it makes great news after that whole nasty scandal that tore the two of you apart when they printed photos of him with another woman," Caitlyn said.

"You'd think our secret wedding in New York would have done the trick with that," Jenny said with a touch of bitterness. "But I suppose it never hurts to reinforce the fact that we're very happily married now, thank you very much. If it can keep a few female predators at bay, I'm all for it."

"Living in the limelight must be tough, especially with a sexy country singer for a husband."

"It has its drawbacks," Jenny agreed. "Nobody knows that better than we do, which is one reason I like the privacy that comes with being back here from time to time. Mick would probably personally break the kneecaps of anyone in town who spread gossip about us. He even terrified Ethel into silence after Caleb and I reconciled, and you know how she loves to spread the latest news about everyone in town. Her shop may sell souvenirs and penny candy, but all the locals know it's gossip central."

Caitlyn laughed. "Grandpa Mick's protectiveness and meddling do have their positive benefits, don't they?"

"Try to remember that," Jenny advised. "Now, let's

go back to the house and get Noah out of Mick's clutches before he's brainwashed."

Much calmer after her conversation with Jenny, Caitlyn nodded. "Let's do it."

As she stood up, she gave Jenny an impulsive hug.

"What was that for?"

"Just a reminder that as much as I might grumble about catching your bouquet, I am grateful that it brought Noah into my life."

"The bouquet didn't do that," Jenny told her. "All it might have done was open a tiny crack in your heart so you'd recognize him when he came along."

Mick had given Noah a lot to think about. He'd been surprisingly helpful with suggestions for getting Caitlyn on board with the idea of planning their future together sooner rather than later.

And when Noah had shared a few of his own thoughts, cobbled together after a little computer research on Chesapeake Shores, Mick's expression had brightened with delight. In some ways the gleam in his eyes had been worrisome, but he'd assured Noah he'd trust him to handle things...until he couldn't.

Noah understood the warning implied by his words. Mick had a timetable in mind and he expected Noah to get the ball rolling quickly.

Now he glanced around the living room, then finally drifted toward a window to admire the scenery and, hopefully, avoid another interrogation from any of the other O'Briens milling around.

Eventually he spotted Caitlyn coming up the walkway from the cliff overlooking the bay with another young woman by her side. Since the two of them looked nothing alike, he assumed it was someone other than her twin. He walked outside to meet them.

"This is Jenny Green," Caitlyn told him. "Jenny, this is Noah."

He regarded Jenny appreciatively. "Something tells me I owe you a debt of gratitude for tossing that bridal bouquet in Caitlyn's direction."

Jenny laughed. "You sound much happier about that than she does. Nice to meet you, Noah. I'll leave you to fill Caitlyn in on your grilling by her grandfather."

As she went inside, he felt Cait's steady gaze studying him. Her expression was filled with concern.

"No need to look so panicky," he told her. "I'm still in one piece. And Mick hasn't dragged me over to the dark side and gotten me to agree to any conspiracies where you're concerned." That much was true. He hadn't actually agreed to any of Mick's proposed schemes, not a specific one, anyway. They'd merely agreed to a goal. He doubted, though, that Cait wanted to view them as allies on any level whatsoever.

"I think that may bother me even more," she claimed. "It tells me Grandpa Mick is being even sneakier than usual. What did the two of you talk about?"

"How much we have in common," Noah said, keeping the response truthful, but not exactly enlightening.

Cait frowned. "Such as."

"How much we both love you," he replied simply. "And how much we want you to be happy. Those two things create an unbreakable bond between us. We both agree on that."

Before she could ask a lot more questions he didn't particularly want to answer, he told her, "Now we need to get inside. Nell pulled me aside on my way out here and told me she's about to put that famous Irish stew of hers on the table." He grinned at her. "It's nothing like what you made for me, is it? Do I need to prepare myself to be politely enthusiastic?"

"Trust me, this will be an experience like none you've ever had before. Nell's food is like manna directly from the Irish gods."

"Then I'll look forward to it," Noah told her.

"She's given me the recipe."

"I thought your mom had already done that."

"It seems she left out a few essential ingredients," Caitlyn admitted. "Mom's not exactly an attentive student when it comes to cooking, apparently."

Noah nodded. "That explains a lot."

Cait's laugh rang out. "It does indeed. Hopefully that culinary gene skipped over a couple of generations and landed in me, but don't count on it."

"You have plenty of other things going for you," he told her honestly.

"Ah, flattery," she said. "Is that part of your tactic these days?"

"I didn't know I needed a tactic," he claimed innocently.

"You've been closeted with my grandfather for close to an hour. Only a fool would believe there weren't tactics being discussed, no matter how you'd like me to believe otherwise."

Now it was Noah's turn to laugh. "I guess you'll have to wait and see."

The game, if he wanted to think of it that way, was just beginning.

5

"Well, we got out of town without a shotgun wedding," Caitlyn remarked to Noah when they finally had some time to sit down and talk. Their schedules had been so hectic once they were back at the hospital and on duty that they'd barely crossed paths for the past week. He'd even slept at his own place or in the on-call room at the hospital. That should have been a relief since it had postponed any serious discussions, but her bed had felt awfully lonely without him.

Noah grinned. "I'm not sure I see that as a good thing. I half wonder if it's not going to take something as dramatic as that to get you down the aisle."

Caitlyn frowned at him. "Pressure's not helping," she remarked. Even though Nell's words and the reassurances from her mother had helped, she still wasn't ready to take the plunge into a marriage she wasn't convinced would be best for her and Noah both. And a marriage license under those circumstances would not guarantee the best life for their child, either.

With time on her hands, she'd spent the afternoon trying to master Nell's recipe for Irish stew and thought she'd finally gotten it. She spooned it into bowls and set it on the kitchen table in the small apartment that she'd made cozy with mismatched castoffs from a variety of O'Brien homes. A bouquet of daffodils that reminded her of home sat in the middle of the old oak table.

"Try this," she said, still standing. "I think it might be a huge improvement over last time. Of course, it was probably a mistake to make it so soon after you had Nell's. I doubt there's any comparison."

Noah took a taste, while she watched him nervously.

"It's good," he said slowly, then grinned. "Very good, in fact. You might have a very limited repertoire of recipes, but we won't die of starvation."

Her expression brightened at his teasing. "Seriously, Noah? It's actually good?"

"Would I lie to you?"

"If you thought it would put me in a good mood, you might," she said. "You are anxious to get your own way, after all."

"Sweetheart, if I thought praising your cooking would do the trick, I wouldn't be in the kitchen cooking most of our meals myself when I'm over here."

She frowned at his attempt at humor. "You're losing ground, pal." Then she couldn't help chuckling. "Okay, I now have one edible dish I can safely prepare for company. It's better than last week, when I had none."

She joined him at the table and took her own first bite of the stew, then sat back in astonishment. "Wow! It really is good."

"I told you."

She sipped her water and peered at Noah over the rim of her glass. "We haven't had a chance to talk about the weekend. Or maybe I should say you've been pretty evasive whenever I've asked." She gave him a stern look. "No more, Noah. I want to know what you and my grandfather discussed while I was in the kitchen with Gram. I doubt it was sports. Other than knowing there are football and baseball teams in Baltimore, you don't know enough to hold your own in that conversation."

"Hey, I play basketball."

She rolled her eyes. "With a bunch of medical residents, who are equally clueless about other sports. When I mentioned the Ravens to Mike Hardesty, he thought I'd gone bird-watching."

"He did not," Noah said. "He was just pulling your leg."

"I'm telling you the man didn't have a clue." She waved off the subject. "Not the point. I want to know what you and Grandpa Mick *did* talk about."

He shrugged. "The future, my plans, the state of medicine today, things like that."

Though he'd made a valiant effort to sound casual, as if none of it had amounted to much, Caitlyn knew better. She sat up a little straighter. "What future?"

"Yours and mine," he replied readily.

"That's what I was afraid you meant. Did you tell him we'd be getting married?"

"Of course not. You haven't agreed to that."

She saw the loophole. "But you said you were eager to get married, didn't you?"

He gave her an innocent look she didn't come close to buying.

"I told him it was a possibility, that it was certainly what I wanted," he conceded.

Caitlyn groaned. It was every bit as bad as she'd feared. "So now he knows if there's a holdout, it's me.

No wonder you're still in one piece and I have a half-dozen messages from him on my cell phone."

Noah shrugged, his expression unrepentant. "I gave him the facts about where I stand. He drew his own conclusions."

"So you got out of that room looking heroic in his eyes and left me swinging in the wind," she accused.

To her exasperation, he laughed. "That's one way to look at it, I suppose."

"You are shameless. You tried to turn my own grandfather against me."

"Not against you," he corrected. "I doubt I could do that if I wanted to. He obviously adores you. He also recognizes how stubborn you are."

"Because I take after him," she muttered, suddenly regretting that. Up till now she'd always considered that hardheaded O'Brien determination to be a positive. It had given her the self-confidence and will to go after what she wanted. Her grandfather had respected that. Now he was likely to see it as an impediment to getting his own way and redouble his efforts to get her down the aisle.

"He trusts you to make the right decision," Noah said.

She shook her head. "No, he trusts me to make the decision *he* thinks is right. And if I don't, he'll be knocking on our door to try to change my mind."

She put down her fork, resignation settling over her. "I'd better call him back."

"Now?"

"I've ignored a lot of calls," she said. "He doesn't like being ignored. Trust me, I'd better get to him before he turns up here."

She braced herself for her grandfather's brand of pressure, which could start with subtle coaxing, but could easily lead from there to stern lectures and sneaky manipulation if his family didn't fulfill his expectations. He'd never used any of those tactics on her before. He hadn't had to. Which meant she had no idea if she could bring herself to tell him to butt out or not.

"Maybe you should forget about making that call until we've had a chance to talk about what we want," Noah suggested. "I know you think I've been evasive, but you haven't exactly been forthcoming about what you thought about while you were visiting your family. Let's have that discussion."

She wasn't crazy about his reasonable tone or the suggestion. "Are you thinking you can persuade me to fall into line with your plan in the next half hour?"

"I'd like the chance to try," he replied without hesitation.

She shook her head. "I'm not going to let you bully me into making a hasty decision we'll both come to regret," she told him. "And that's exactly what I intend to tell my grandfather."

A frown settled on Noah's face. "Since when have I ever tried to bully you into doing anything my way?" he demanded.

"Never before," she conceded, to be fair. "But there's never been a situation quite like this one."

"Which is exactly why we need to talk and work things out," Noah said. "We're in uncharted territory. I know this isn't what we planned, Cait, but the baby's going to be a reality in a few months. Pretending otherwise isn't going to change anything."

"Believe me, I'm well aware that the pregnancy is real. I'm the one who had to hightail it out of rounds today because of morning sickness."

He immediately regarded her with worry. "Are you feeling okay now?"

"Perfectly fine," she said, then gestured toward her empty bowl. "I've eaten every bite of stew and may have seconds."

"That's good, then," he said, his voice filled with relief. "Did you tell Dr. Davis you're pregnant so she can cut you some slack while you're on your pediatrics rotation?"

"Absolutely not," she said, horrified by the thought. "I'm having a baby. I'm not an invalid. Things are competitive enough in med school without me suggesting I be treated differently because I'm going to have a baby."

"I'm just saying it might be helpful if she knew," Noah said.

"So everyone at the hospital will know and can voice an opinion about what we ought to do? Do you really want the whole world to gang up on me? Trust me, it's not the way to get me to see things your way."

He sighed. "That is not what I was suggesting and, believe me, I know all about how perverse you can be. If too many people start trying to push you into doing anything, you'll do exactly the opposite."

She gave a nod of satisfaction. "Something you definitely need to keep in mind."

Noah met her gaze and held it. "There's something *you* need to keep in mind," he said evenly. "I love you, Cait. And I won't stop fighting for us to be a family."

She regarded him with puzzlement. "I don't understand how you can be so sure that marriage is the answer. You have dreams on the line, too, Noah. I'm not the only one who had the future mapped out."

"That's true," he said without hesitation. "But for me,

you've been a part of that future practically from the moment we met. This baby?" A smile lit his eyes. "It's just an unanticipated blessing. I'll do whatever it takes to make everything work out for us."

She shuddered a little at the determination in his voice. If she knew little else about Noah, she knew this. He might bide his time, he might use subtle tactics, but he was a man who usually got his way. He'd won her heart against all odds, after all.

After Noah's quiet declaration a few nights before, Caitlyn never did get around to making that call to her grandfather. Therefore she wasn't all that surprised when she looked up from a patient chart at the hospital and saw him standing there, a frown on his face.

"It's a relief to see you're still alive," Mick O'Brien commented dryly.

She winced. "Sorry I haven't gotten back to you. I've been busy." She came out from behind the desk and kissed his cheek. "I hope you didn't make a special trip up to Baltimore. I'm on duty."

"But you can take a break," he said with certainty. "I spoke with that lovely Dr. Davis and she assured me it would be fine."

"You spoke to my boss?" she said incredulously. "What were you thinking?"

"That I need to have a conversation with my grand-daughter, who's about to have my first great-grandchild," he retorted unrepentantly. "You slipped away from the house before we could talk and you've been avoiding my calls."

When she was about to protest, he held up a hand. "Don't bother trying to tell me how busy you've been.

You've never been too busy to talk to me before. I imagine you've been giving that caller ID thing a real workout lately."

Since she could hardly deny it, she opted to go on offense. Scowling at him, she said, "I hope you didn't say anything about your great-grandchild to Dr. Davis," she said. "My pregnancy is not your news to share, especially around here."

"Of course not. I know there are boundaries at work. Though she did seem to think you might have something on your mind."

Alarm flowed through Caitlyn. "She said that?"

He nodded. "She said you're one of the best students she's ever worked with, but you've been off your game for the past couple of weeks."

"Oh, God," Caitlyn murmured. Maybe Noah had been right. Perhaps she did need to fill the doctor in before the head of pediatrics drew her own conclusions about what was going on with Caitlyn. Speculation could be a whole lot worse than the facts.

Grandpa Mick clearly saw her distress, because he put an arm around her shoulders. "Don't look so anxious. I told you, didn't I, that she thinks you're an excellent doctor."

"Who's messing up," Caitlyn reminded him.

"I didn't say a thing about you messing up."

"You told me she thinks I've been 'off my game.' Isn't that the same thing?"

"Absolutely not. She's a doctor, after all. I imagine she knows why someone might turn a little green around the gills from time to time."

"She actually told you that she thinks I'm pregnant?" Now she truly was horrified. How many other people had guessed? Were there whispers all over the hospital? Had Noah been protecting her from that? And why had she thought for a single second that an entire hospital of physicians might not recognize the signs? Apparently there were a whole lot of things about which she wasn't thinking too clearly these days.

"Pregnancy wasn't mentioned," her grandfather said. "Not by me, anyway. And she would hardly speculate to me, even if I am family. Do you really want to debate who said what to whom right here in the middle of the pediatrics wing?"

"Do you think the cafeteria will be any more private?" she asked.

"I guess we'll see," he said, steering her toward the elevator.

They rode to the first floor in silence. In the cafeteria, her grandfather got himself a cup of coffee and put two pastries—one with a blueberry center, the other cheese—on his tray, along with a hefty serving of scrambled eggs. "You want decaf, juice or water?" he asked.

"Water's fine. And I don't need a pastry or eggs."

"Who said anything on this tray was for you?" he replied, a spark of amusement in his eyes. "Your grandmother's had me on a diet of oatmeal and fake eggs. Since she's not here to challenge me, I thought I'd treat myself."

Caitlyn laughed. "So I get to hold this over your head?"

"You can try, but I guarantee she'll have it figured out before you do. That woman knows my every move. I haven't gotten away with a thing since we got back together. I'll enjoy my eggs and pastry now, but believe me, I'll pay later."

When they'd found a table with some privacy, she looked her grandfather in the eye. "You and Grandma Megan are happy now, aren't you?"

"Of course we are. Winning her back was the biggest blessing of my life." He glanced longingly at his second pastry, then shoved it in her direction. "Which is why you probably need to save me from myself. Eat this."

She absentmindedly tore off a piece and popped it into her mouth, then regarded him with suspicion. "This is what you intended all along, isn't it? For me to eat this cheese Danish?"

"You think I'm that sneaky?" he asked with a straight face.

"I *know* you are," she replied, laughing. "And now that I think about it, you've never liked cheese Danish, but you know I do."

He grinned. "Okay, you caught me."

She gave a little nod of satisfaction at having won the admission. "Since we've established that I'm on to you, you might as well just tell me why you're here, instead of trying to be subtle about it. You've never been any good at subtlety."

"Okay, then, I want to know why you haven't said yes to Noah's proposal yet."

"What makes you think he's proposed?"

He waved off the question. "Of course he has. The man's in love with you. You're having his baby. He all but guaranteed me he'd have this matter settled in no time."

"Did he now? Or was the timetable just wishful thinking on your part? It's only been a little over a week since we were in Chesapeake Shores, after all."

"Why are you being so stubborn about this?" he grumbled impatiently.

"I'm an O'Brien. It's in my genes," she retorted glibly, then decided a more serious reply was called for. "I don't want to make a mistake."

"You think it would be a mistake to marry the father of your child?"

"Not because Noah's not an amazing man," she said quickly. She wanted to be very clear about that. If and when she and Noah did marry, she wanted the family to like him, to have faith that she'd made a good choice. She didn't want them to be holding on to any lingering resentment or judging him for not stepping up, when, in fact, he had.

Her grandfather gave her a penetrating look. "Is he the right man for you?"

"I thought so."

He frowned at that. "If he's not, say the word and I'll back off. You can have this baby on your own. You have an entire family who'll be there to support you."

"I'm grateful for that," she said, touched. "But my hesitance isn't about Noah, not exactly, anyway."

"Then it's all about this crazy idea you have that you're more needed over in Africa than you are right here?"

She bristled at his question and his dismissive tone. "That is not some crazy idea," she said heatedly. "You were all in favor of it not that long ago. You said you were proud of me for wanting to do work that could make a difference."

"That's before you got pregnant," he said. "Now you have another priority, unless you're telling me that those other children are more important than your own."

"I'm certainly not saying that," she said defensively. Or was she? Surely it wasn't what she intended to imply.

"Do I need to remind you what a mistake I made by

running all over the world building houses and whole communities, instead of being right here for my family?" Mick asked.

"I know the story." It had been a cautionary tale for every O'Brien, a warning to put family first. With Nell preaching that on a regular basis, Caitlyn had no idea why her grandfather hadn't gotten the message. Most likely, he'd simply chosen to ignore it because it didn't mesh with his ambitions. Was she doing the same thing? Quite possibly.

He held up a hand. "Just hear me out. I lied to myself all those years, Caitlyn. I told myself I was doing it for my wife and children, that it was important work that would be financially rewarding and make our lives easier. That was true as far as it went, but the real truth is I was feeding my own ego. I liked being a big-time, world-renowned architect."

His eyes grew misty. "But you know what?" he said. "When your grandmother had had enough and left me, it wasn't so much fun being the loneliest man on the planet. The accolades and money couldn't make up for that so I worked even harder and lost time with your mother and her sisters and brothers, too. The decisions I made back then nearly cost me everything that truly mattered."

Caitlyn blinked back her own tears at the real pain she heard in his voice. She didn't want that for herself, but she wasn't ready to give up everything she'd worked for. Not yet, anyway. Not if a compromise was possible. Didn't she owe it to herself to find a better solution? Didn't she owe it to Noah, for that matter, so she didn't wind up resenting him or their baby for robbing her of her dream? Was she really so selfish to want it all?

And what about Noah? She'd meant what she'd said

to him. His dream of going into practice in some under-served rural area of the country was in jeopardy, too. Sure, he sounded certain that it was a sacrifice he might be willing to make, but would he be so sure if the right opportunity presented itself? And then what?

She pushed aside all her doubts and said, "I'm not going to lose Noah, Grandpa Mick." She wasn't entirely sure if the reassurance was meant for him or herself.

"I hope not," he said quietly. "But no matter what I think is best, if you do lose him, I'll be around to pick up the pieces, same as always."

More tears stung Caitlyn's eyes, then spilled down her cheeks. She covered his hand and held on tight. "Thank you."

"No need to thank me," he said gruffly. "But just so you know, I'm not giving up on seeing you walk down the aisle before this baby gets here."

She smiled through her tears. "Never thought you would."

Noah looked up when Mick O'Brien stepped into his office. "Well, did you have any better luck getting through to her than I've had?"

Even before Mick settled into the chair opposite his desk and spoke, Noah could read the answer on his face.

"She's not listening, is she?"

Mick shook his head. "I do think I gave her some food for thought, though. I suppose we have to acknowledge this will be a marathon, not a sprint. How's your patience?"

Noah smiled. "Better than yours, I imagine."

"Little question about that," Mick acknowledged ruefully. "I had the church on hold for the first Saturday in June."

"Even I wasn't that optimistic," Noah revealed.

"So, what's your next step?" Mick asked. Before Noah could reply, the older man got a worrisome gleam in his eyes. "There are a lot of pretty nurses around. You could try making her jealous."

"That's a terrible idea," Noah said at once. "If nothing else, Cait needs to know I'm committed to her and to the baby. I don't want her to think I'm the kind of man who'd turn to another woman just because things with her aren't going my way."

Mick nodded, though there was no mistaking his disappointment. "That makes sense," he acknowledged. "You don't want her thinking you're a cheater. That would just be another hurdle for you to overcome."

Noah had to hide a smile as Mick wrestled with the dilemma. He clearly hated not being able to control the situation.

Eventually, though, his expression turned thoughtful as he seemed to be pondering a new strategy. Since Noah was fresh out of ideas himself, he waited to see if Mick reached any conclusions.

"It might take something dramatic to shake her up," Mick said slowly. "You said this residency of yours ends June 30. What does she think you're going to do after that?"

"We haven't discussed the specifics, but I'm sure she knows I want to go into practice for myself at that point."

Mick leveled a look at him. "But you still haven't mentioned that you're thinking about opening an office in Chesapeake Shores? That might get the ball rolling."

Noah shook his head. "To be honest, I'm not sure

she'll consider that a plus right now. She's going to think I'm trying to manipulate her. I have a hunch she's going to see it as me joining forces with her family."

"Could be," Mick agreed. "And she'll probably assume I'm behind it. It's exactly the sort of tactic I might have come up with if I'd had a little more time to think things through." He gave Noah an approving look. "You and I think alike, son."

Noah had a hunch that might not work in his favor with Caitlyn right now. "But you didn't plant the idea in my head," he reminded Mick. "I did my own research. And once I saw the town, I knew it would be perfect for me and for a family. You just confirmed that for me."

"When do you plan to fill her in?" Mick pressed.

"When the time is right," Noah said, wishing he had the first clue about when that might be. Cait would probably be a lot more receptive if he announced that he'd joined a medical team heading to Africa.

Mick sighed heavily. "I suppose I'll have to leave you to be the best judge of that."

Noah smiled at his resignation.

"When's this baby due?" Mick asked.

"December," Noah told him.

"Okay, then. Just try to get a ring on her finger before she goes into the delivery room, okay?"

Noah laughed. "I'll do my absolute best."

He was no happier about the prospect of not being married when his child came into the world than Mick O'Brien was.

"Was that your grandfather I saw heading into Noah's office a little while ago?" Jill Marshall asked Caitlyn when they crossed paths as Caitlyn was on her way to

Noah's office herself. "I thought I recognized him earlier when he was asking Dr. Davis where to find you."

"And he was going into Noah's office?" Caitlyn said, not surprised that he'd apparently gone straight from seeing her to see Noah, but thoroughly exasperated by it just the same. Of course the two of them were in cahoots. She'd expect no less of her grandfather. He'd found himself a natural ally, despite what he'd said about being on her side no matter what decision she made.

"Fifteen, maybe twenty minutes ago," Jill confirmed.

"Thanks," Caitlyn said, picking up her pace.

She tapped on Noah's door, then opened it without waiting for his response. He was behind his desk, his back to the door, staring out the window. He was also alone.

"Company gone?" she inquired with feigned cheer.

He swiveled the chair around to face her, his expression brightening. "Hey, you. What brings you by?"

"Well, I started over here to see if you'd have time to grab lunch later. Then I found out my grandfather was closeted in here with you, so my mission changed."

"Oh?"

"The thought of the two of you conspiring behind my back scares me, Noah."

"We're not conspiring," he insisted.

"Then what are you doing?"

"Commiserating."

"Excuse me?"

"I'm in love with a woman who won't marry me, even though we're having a baby. He's got a granddaughter he'd like to see married to the father of her child."

She shook her head. "So, misery loves company," she concluded.

"Pretty much." His expression brightened. "You have the key to putting us both out of our misery."

"All I have to do is say yes, shop for a white dress and walk down the aisle," she said.

"That would do it," he confirmed.

She sat down on the edge of the chair opposite his desk, then leaned forward earnestly. "What about living happily ever after, Noah? Where does that come in?"

"Same place it always does, after we say our vows."

"But if we're both not a hundred percent on board, there's no guarantee of that."

"Sweetheart, marriage is always a leap of faith. No matter how committed two people are, no matter how right they think the marriage is, vows don't come with guarantees."

"But if I say yes now, if we jump into this without a plan we can both live with, the odds against us will be huge," she predicted. "I need the plan, Noah. I need to know how we're going to make this work, or at least give it a fighting chance. And it can't be with me giving up everything and you giving up nothing."

"I know that," he said softly.

"Then do you have a plan? A workable one? You haven't mentioned one so far."

"I have some ideas. I'm still working out the details."

"And you don't want to share these ideas of yours with me?"

"Not until they're a little more settled."

"How is that any more fair than me making a decision all on my own?" she asked. "Isn't that exactly what you were afraid I might do when I went home?"

"Double standard?" he suggested wryly.

She smiled despite her mood. "At least you can see that much."

"So, how about lunch?" he asked. "Or am I still in the doghouse for hanging out with your grandfather?"

"We can still go to lunch, but can we declare the topic of marriage off-limits? It'll ruin my digestion."

"I can do that."

But even Caitlyn recognized that she was only postponing the inevitable. Marriage was clearly on the table and one of these days they were going to have to deal with it. If only she weren't so terrified that once they talked, the only solution that felt right to her would mean walking away from the man she loved because the timing was all wrong.

6

Caitlyn disconnected the call from her aunt Bree and sighed. She'd also heard from her aunt Jess, both of her uncles—Kevin and Connor—and their wives in the past forty-eight hours. They'd all had opinions and offers of moral support. She wondered exactly how long it had taken her determined grandfather to get them all on board with his strategy. For all his talk of restraint and patience, the pressure for Caitlyn to do the sensible thing—marrying Noah—was mounting.

Drawing in a deep breath, she hit speed dial for her mother.

"Call them off," she pleaded when Abby answered her cell phone.

"Call who off?" she asked, sounding harried.

"The O'Brien troops. Grandpa Mick has obviously called them into action and it's freaking me out. I can't think seriously about any of this if I have to keep defending myself and making excuses for not getting with the program. I swear to you, Mom, if this keeps up, I'm going to toss my phone into the bay, which will deeply offend Uncle Thomas. Then he'll be on my case about pollution and recycling, which frankly would be a lot more fun than the current calls."

Her mother laughed, which was not the response Caitlyn had hoped for. "Mom!"

"I know. Believe me, I've been on the receiving end of all these good intentions a time or two myself, but you're made of tough stuff. Just let them ramble on and then do what you want to do."

"But I don't know what I want to do," Caitlyn said in frustration. "Didn't you hear me? I can't think."

"Where are you?" her mom asked.

"In my apartment. Thank goodness I'm not on duty today. I'm half-afraid to go to the hospital. Grandpa Mick turned up there earlier this week. I almost expected to run into Trace every time I turned a corner after that."

Abby groaned. "I am so sorry."

Caitlyn thought about her stepfather's surprising silence since she'd first made her revelation. It wasn't like him to be so quiet. "Mom, is Trace furious with me? Is that why he hasn't added his voice to everyone else's?" she asked, fearing the answer. She knew without a doubt that her stepfather loved her every bit as much as if she were his own. The thought of disappointing him broke her heart.

"Of course not," Abby said with reassuring conviction. "You can thank me for his restraint. I've told him additional pressure won't help and for once he's listened."

"Then please, please do the same thing with the rest of the family," she pleaded. "I can't take much more of this."

Apparently her desperation got through to her mom,

because Abby said, "Sit tight, sweetie. I'm on my way. We'll figure this out."

"Now *you're* going to tell me what to do?"

"As if I could. No, I'm just going to let you rant and rave till you get this out of your system and then I'm going to listen some more while you talk through your options and make your own decision."

"You're as bad as Noah. You're both so blasted reasonable," she grumbled. "If I had solutions, don't you think I'd have acted on them by now?"

"The solutions are there. You just need to clear away all the distracting clutter."

If only it were that simple, Caitlyn thought. But at least the person heading over to save the day was a whole lot more empathetic than the ones who'd been calling all day. At least her mom hadn't fallen victim to Grandpa Mick's latest machinations.

At least, she hoped not. For all she knew this could be another trap with her mom offering emotional sanctuary only to slip past her defenses. Even as the thought crossed her mind, she shook it off. No, her mom wouldn't do that. She wouldn't conspire with Grandpa Mick.

Unless she believed in the plot, Caitlyn realized with a sigh. In which case, agreeing to this visit was going to be just one more regret in what was turning into a long list of them.

She pressed her hand against the slight bump in her belly. Not this baby, though. For all of the commotion that had ensued since the news broke, she couldn't make herself regret the baby. It would be the best part of her and Noah. It wouldn't hurt, though, if maybe it was just a little less mule-headed and conniving than the rest of the O'Briens.

* * *

Noah walked into Caitlyn's apartment and found her asleep on the sofa. She looked more peaceful than she had in a while. As much as he wanted to sit in a chair and watch her sleep, maybe try some mental telepathy to get inside her head to figure out what she was thinking these days, he opted for going into the kitchen to start dinner.

In the refrigerator, he found a large container of what looked to be homemade spaghetti sauce. He knew Cait hadn't made it and it hadn't been here when he left this morning, which suggested a visit by an O'Brien. Either the visit had worn Cait out or left her more at peace. He wouldn't know till she woke up. Given the unpredictability of her moods these days, there was no telling what to expect.

He put the sauce in a pan and started the water for pasta. He'd just put the finishing touches on a salad when Cait wandered into the kitchen. To his surprise she wrapped her arms around his waist and rested her head against his back.

"Everything okay?" he asked.

"Not too bad, if you consider that I spent the day being badgered from all sides."

He nodded in the direction of the simmering sauce. "At least someone brought food."

She smiled. "Mom, though I'm pretty sure Nell actually made it. And, of course, since she came with spaghetti sauce, my mother couldn't very well deny that she'd been counting on me calling her when the rest of the family pushed me to the brink. It was the one big flaw in their plot. No plausible deniability."

Noah laughed. "Did she even try to deny it?"

"Oh, she hemmed and hawed for a minute, then gave

up. It was actually pretty interesting to watch her squirm. It kept me from tossing her right back out the door once I realized she was in on the whole plot."

"She's just trying to be supportive. So are all the others," he suggested. "Do you know how lucky you are to have that much backup?"

"Of course I do," she said. "But they're not in your face every minute, so it's a lot easier for you to be appreciative."

He chuckled at that. "Who says they're not in my face? Your uncles Kevin and Connor and your stepfather have been by the hospital."

"Trace came to see you?" she repeated, an odd look on her face. "What did he say?"

"Not much, really. He asked a few questions about my plans, nodded and said he'd be in touch. It was actually a little disconcerting. Not two hours later Kevin and Connor invited me to join them for a drink. Call me crazy, but I sensed a connection."

"More than likely," Cait agreed. "Did you go? You never mentioned it."

He nodded. "I know a command performance when one comes along. I think they left reassured. Connor and I even bonded a bit over our inability to understand women."

Cait frowned at him. "You understand women just fine. And, as I recall, Uncle Connor was completely opposed to the whole concept of marriage thanks to my grandparents' divorce. It kept him from marrying Heather when Little Mick was born, even though he was in love with her. If he's bonding with anyone these days, it should be me."

"He did mention that," Noah acknowledged. "But then when he saw the error of his ways, Heather didn't buy it."

"Can you blame her? After months, actually years, of listening to him decry marriage, why would she believe any epiphany he claimed to have had? Would you if I'd awakened from my nap just now, walked in here and, out of the blue, said 'let's get married?'"

"I think I'd just be relieved that you finally changed your mind and wanted to make a commitment," Noah told her.

Cait regarded him with disbelief, then rubbed her temples. "All of this well-meant advice and interference is giving me a headache."

"Then let's go away," he suggested at once. It was something he'd been thinking about all day. With a little encouragement from Trace, he'd almost gone ahead and made reservations, but then he'd thought better of it. Cait didn't need a decision about anything being taken out of her hands right now. Every bit of the control she prized most had been ripped out of her hands the instant she'd seen that positive pregnancy test. But if she did want to go away, he'd make it happen.

He held her gaze. "Come on, Cait. Just you and me. We can sit on a beach down in Florida and maybe start to hear ourselves think."

Caitlyn's expression turned wistful. "Wouldn't that be wonderful?" She sighed. "You know we can't do it, though. We can't get away from the hospital for more than a day at a time and generally it's not even the same day. We're lucky to sit across the table from each other at dinner one night a week."

"I know you're right," he said, resigned to accepting reality. "Maybe after my residency ends in June."

"I'll still be working, more than ever, in fact," she reminded him. She poured herself a glass of milk, wrinkling her nose when she took the first sip. Milk might be great for the baby, but he knew she'd never been a big fan unless, of course, it came with a pile of home-baked cookies. Since her cookie jar was perpetually empty unless Nell sent up a care package, she was stuck with just milk.

"I'm glad you finally brought up the end of your residency," she began. "I've been wondering what you intend to do next. It is a decision that affects both of us under the circumstances. Have you been looking into communities where physicians might be needed?"

"I made a list a few months ago and sent out some feelers," he said. "But things have changed. Any decision I make now depends on you."

He was increasingly enthusiastic about opening a practice in Chesapeake Shores, but would that work if he and Cait didn't agree to marry? He'd want to be wherever his child was, though. Staying here in Baltimore was an option. Or Annapolis. But neither was the fit he'd always envisioned. A place like Chesapeake Shores was, a small community that had been unable to find a full-time family-practice doctor. Many physicians who'd been approached assumed that residents would want to head to the city for their care, according to Mick.

Cait regarded him with a troubled expression. "You're considering sticking close to Baltimore, aren't you?" she said, not with any hint of anxiety that he might be leaving, but more as if the idea horrified her.

"I won't be far from the baby," he declared, prepared for an argument.

"But you've never wanted to practice in a big city," she protested. "Your dream is to set up a practice in an underserved area, a place where you can be a real part of the community. That's been your priority ever since I've known you. I thought you wanted to go to Appalachia or maybe out west someplace."

Now was the time he should mention his thoughts about Chesapeake Shores, but he held back. "Priorities evolve," he told her.

"Meaning mine should, too," she said, bristling at what she had clearly inferred as a criticism.

He held up his hand. "Don't, Cait. Nobody's made any decisions yet. Let's not argue over maybes."

"So what? You want to just drift along?"

"Not indefinitely, no. But I'd rather we take our time and get it right than have either of us dig in our heels and take a position from which we can't back down. That's why I've been pushing to sit down and get all of the possible options on the table, no matter how crazy they might seem. It's the only way I can think of that would be fair to both of us."

Her expression turned incredulous. "You want to make lists? Maybe assign numbers and rank the choices until something emerges as a winner?"

Despite her derisive tone, he nodded. "Can you think of a way that's any easier? If so, put it out there and we can talk about it. You're the one who's always claimed that lists help you to stay organized."

"Sure. I can check off the things I need to do, like picking up the dry cleaning or getting milk at the grocery store. Little stuff."

"Are you telling me you didn't have lists when you were trying to decide which medical school you wanted to attend?" he asked, knowing better. There were Post-it notes all over the apartment with her to-do lists for everything, big and small.

Instead of answering, she rested her head in her hands, then finally looked up. "I hate this, Noah. I hate that we suddenly find ourselves tiptoeing around, trying not to offend each other or pressure each other or declare war on each other."

He allowed himself a smile, even though the situation was far from amusing. "We've hardly declared war. I suggested we make a list. If you don't like that idea, then tell me how you'd like to proceed, because you're right about one thing. Drifting along isn't the answer."

"Maybe we haven't declared war yet, but it's coming," she said direly. "I'm afraid of that, Noah. Just as you said, once either of us digs in our heels, we'll lose everything."

He saw the genuine misery in her eyes and pulled her up and into his arms. "We're not going to lose anything," he said firmly. "Not if we're honest and if we love each other."

"I wish I believed that as strongly as you do."

He brushed another of those wayward curls that he loved from her cheek. "Then it's a good thing I have enough faith for both of us."

After a surprisingly tension-free meal, Cait went into the living room and found a legal pad and a pen, then returned to the kitchen table to sit across from Noah. He was right. Putting their thoughts on paper might help them to find clarity. At the very least they could eliminate anything either of them truly hated. That should narrow down the options.

"Okay, let's do it," she said when she returned. "Let's make a list."

Noah put the last of the clean dishes away and joined

her at the table. "Maybe it should be two lists," he suggested. "You make yours. I'll make mine. Then we can see where there's a workable overlap."

She nodded and handed over a piece of paper. She frowned when he immediately started jotting down notes.

"You've obviously been thinking about this a lot," she said.

He glanced up. "And you haven't?"

"Well, sure. It's all I've thought about, but you've obviously drawn some conclusions. I haven't."

Noah flipped over his piece of paper. "Then let's try this a different way. We'll come up with relevant questions and each of us will write down our answers. Then we'll compare notes."

"What sort of questions?"

"Let's start with where we see ourselves a year from now," he suggested.

Caitlyn nodded. That was easy enough. She'd be right here, working at the hospital and raising her baby. Noah would be...where? How did he fit into the picture? He wanted to be married, but she knew with absolutely certainty he didn't want to be in Baltimore, no matter what he'd said earlier.

She told herself not to get bogged down in trying to figure out his answers. The whole purpose of this was to focus on her own replies.

"Okay, what next?" she asked after writing down her answer.

"Where do we see ourselves in five years?" he suggested.

That was easy, too. She'd be working in that village in Africa where she'd found such fulfillment. She glanced over at the latest photo she'd received of half a dozen smiling faces. Those children were healthier because she'd been there, even for such a short time. No way, though, would returning to that village mesh with anything Noah might write down, she thought wearily. She crumpled up the paper and tossed it in the direction of the trash can.

"This isn't going to work," she said.

"You haven't given it much of a chance."

"We want different things. Unless you've undergone some major transformation, that is." She looked him in the eye. "You haven't, have you?"

He held her gaze. "Have you?"

She shook her head. "No. There's no middle ground here, Noah."

"There isn't if you won't even try to find it," he said, clearly frustrated. "What will work for you, Cait? Me saying I'll come with you to Africa? Me saying I'll care for our child while you go off to save the world? If those are the only solutions you see working, write them down."

She frowned at his tone. "You're starting to sound like my grandfather, as if my goal is horrible and selfish." She gestured toward that snapshot. "Look at them, Noah. Those kids matter."

He sighed at the heartfelt comment. "I didn't mean to make it sound as if they didn't. It's a noble dream, Cait, and if we didn't have a baby to consider, I'd be backing you a thousand percent."

Tears, always a threat these days, filled her eyes. "I know you're right. I have to accept reality, but I hate it, Noah. I really hate it."

She saw the color wash out of his face and knew he'd misinterpreted her meaning. "Not the baby. I could never hate our child. It's the circumstances, the timing. I never expected to be in a situation like this, having to make a seemingly impossible choice."

"Cait, if marrying me and making a home for our family isn't what you want, if you can't imagine ever wanting that, just say so. I'll take custody of the baby and you can follow your dream. I love you enough to let you go."

She found herself actually considering what he was offering. It was yet more proof of the kind of man he was, and she loved him even more because of it, but the thought of walking away from him, from her baby, left her feeling hollow inside. That wasn't an answer she could live with, either.

"I don't want to give up on us," she admitted tearfully. "I just don't know what's right anymore."

Noah reached across the table and enveloped her hand in his. The heat and strength were a surprising comfort.

"Then we'll give it more time," he told her quietly. "The last thing I want is to push you into making a decision you'll regret. There must be some way we can all win—you, me and the baby."

"I hope so," she said fervently. "That's what I want, too." She held his gaze. "You do know that none of this indecision is because I don't love you, right? You're the best man I've ever known outside of the O'Briens. They set the bar high and you've exceeded it. Please don't ever doubt that."

He smiled. "Okay, then. One day at a time, and no pressure from me."

Cait laughed at that. "You're not the one I'm worried about. I've had a few more messages from Grandpa Mick just since he told me the very same thing. Trace's

silence is almost as hard to take, because now I know
he's only biting his tongue because my mom told him
to and it didn't stop him from coming to see you. Just
about the only person in my family who hasn't been in
my face is my sister, and that's only because no one has
filled her in yet."

Noah regarded her with surprise. "Carrie doesn't
know yet?"

"I haven't spoken to her. Mom says she's having problems with a temperamental boss. Personally, I think
Carrie's addicted to drama. Mom thinks I'm imagining
things, but I'm pretty sure Carrie's crazy about the designer, not the job. He is one serious hunk. The fact that
he's difficult would only be more appealing to Carrie.
If I were wrong, she'd have quit by now."

"I'm surprised you haven't called to see what's going
on," Noah said.

"Carrie only wants to talk to me when things are
going her way. She's convinced I think her world is frivolous." Caitlyn shrugged. "And I do, but it's important
to her. I respect her for finding something she's passionate about and sticking with it. That's what all of us
need in our lives."

"I agree," Noah said pointedly. "That's why I will
never dismiss your goal, no matter how much it might
stand in the way of our future."

Caitlyn regarded him seriously. "I want the same for
you, you know. Baltimore or even Annapolis were never
in your game plan, Noah. You shouldn't have to lose your
dream, any more than I should."

"I won't lose anything important, Cait, not unless I
lose you."

The heartfelt simplicity touched her in a way nothing else had. Regret washed over her because no matter how badly she wanted to say the same thing held true for her, she couldn't get those words out. Not yet. Not without fighting hard to hold on to the future she'd envisioned for herself.

The too-thin not-quite-three-year-old boy who'd been admitted to the pediatrics wing the night before was listless and pale. He flinched when Caitlyn put the stethoscope on his chest. Reacting to the fear, she immediately withdrew it and placed it on her own chest.

"Yikes, that's cold!" she said with an exaggerated shiver. She rubbed it dramatically between her hands to warm it. "Let's see if that's any better." She put it against her own chest again. "Definitely better. Want to see for yourself, Mason?"

He held her gaze with his big blue eyes and finally nodded.

This time she approached more slowly before gently placing the stethoscope against his skin. "Better?" she asked.

He didn't answer, but the fear had left his eyes. She made quick work of taking his vitals, then started to leave.

"No!" he protested, tears spilling down his cheeks. "No go."

Caitlyn walked back to the crib, where he was standing now on legs too wobbly for a child his age. She touched his pale cheek. "How about I stay for a couple more minutes and read you a story?"

She didn't really have time for that, but she simply couldn't ignore his plea. It must be terrifying to be all alone in a strange place and not feeling well.

His expression immediately brightened at her offer. "Story," he echoed excitedly, showing more animation than at any time since he'd arrived the day before.

"Okay, then," she said, smiling at him. "You put your head down for a little nap and I'll read."

Hopefully he'd drift off before Dr. Davis wondered why she hadn't completed her rounds. She chose a book from the pile nearby. Instead of lying down, though, he regarded her wistfully as she read. She'd been around enough children his age to recognize that he wanted to be held. When she stood, he immediately held out his arms to her. She picked him up and settled into a nearby rocker.

"This is not part of my job description," she said as he snuggled against her trustingly. The weight against her chest, the little-boy scent, the tiny finger pointing at the pictures in the book, filled her with surprising contentment.

So, she thought, this is what it will be like, more aware now of the simple act of reading to a child than she'd ever been with any of the O'Brien babies. Was it possible for even a couple of months of pregnancy to sharpen her maternal instincts?

"Caitlyn!"

A disapproving voice cut through her reverie and she looked up to find Dr. Davis regarding her with dismay.

"He was scared," she said in her own defense. "He just needed a little attention."

The pediatrician's expression softened. "I know your instincts are good, Caitlyn, but we don't have a diagnosis yet of what's going on with him. Until we've ruled out an infection of some kind, you should be taking precautions, especially under the circumstances."

There was little question about the circumstances to which she was referring: the pregnancy.

"He doesn't have a fever," she protested. "I just checked his vitals." She sighed. "But you're right. I shouldn't be taking chances." She'd just seen a scared little boy and wanted to make it right.

Dr. Davis removed Mason from her lap, gave him a tickle that had him giggling as she set him back in his crib. "Outside, Caitlyn," she instructed, even as she smoothed the hair back from the boy's forehead and gave him a little pat before following.

"I think we need to talk about this," she told Caitlyn. "I haven't asked because your personal life really isn't my business, but you are pregnant, aren't you?"

Caitlyn nodded. "I don't want that to affect my work, though."

"No reason it has to," Dr. Davis agreed. "As long as you're sensible. If we're dealing with a patient who might be contagious, you either take the appropriate precautions or we assign that patient to another student."

"I don't want the pregnancy to turn into a big deal," she said. "I need to pull my weight."

"Don't worry, you will," the doctor assured her. "Now, tell me what you found when you were with Mason just now."

Caitlyn described his listlessness and his fearful reaction when she went to touch him. "He might have something that makes him especially sensitive to touch, but I don't think that's it."

"What, then?" the pediatrician prodded.

"He was afraid of me at first," she said. "He moved away when I first reached out to him. Who brought him in? Why weren't either of his parents with him?"

"They've been ordered to stay away," Dr. Davis told her. "Until we rule out abuse."

Caitlyn frowned. "But there aren't any bruises."

"Not all abuse leaves physical scars," the doctor reminded her.

"Shaken-baby syndrome," Caitlyn said at once.

"That's definitely a possibility. You're new to this service, but this isn't the first time he's turned up in the emergency room with signs of a mild concussion. A CT scan will tell us more."

"Have you done one before?"

"Twice, as a matter of fact. They were inconclusive, which is why Mason is still at home, rather than in foster care. I dread the day, though, that he comes back here and it's too late to help him. My instincts are telling me I'm right about this." Worry darkened her eyes. "I have to find some way to protect that child."

Her heartfelt reaction demonstrated a level of caring that Caitlyn hadn't seen in her before. Dr. Davis was always the consummate professional, kind but a little distant. Caitlyn liked seeing this side of her.

"So you were never really worried about an infection," she concluded.

"I always worry about everything until I've ruled it out," Dr. Davis told her. "Let that be a lesson to you. Being a good diagnostician is a wonderful attribute. Jumping to conclusions isn't."

Caitlyn got the message.

As they walked down the hall, Dr. Davis said casually, "Did you know that I spent five years working in Africa before I came back to the States to practice?"

Caitlyn regarded her with surprise. "I had no idea. Did you love it?"

"It was the most rewarding five years of my career, but the most frustrating, too."

"Why?"

"Because I realized that no matter how idealistic I might be, I simply couldn't save the world. I could barely make a dent in all that needed to be done."

"So you gave up?"

"Hardly. I came back here where I could fight to get research funded and needed supplies to other doctors who were as well-equipped as I was to do the actual healing. I simply redirected my need to help to something that could benefit even more patients in more villages. I still go back for a few weeks every couple of years. It renews my commitment to making sure the doctors there have everything they need to do the job the best they can."

Caitlyn regarded her suspiciously. "Have you been talking to Noah about this?"

"No. Why?"

Since she didn't want to explain how far apart she and Noah were on planning their future, she shrugged off the question. "I just wondered. Could we talk some more sometime about your work over there and what you're doing now? I'm surprised I haven't heard more about it around here."

"I like to keep the two things separate," Dr. Davis explained. "I never want anyone here to think I'm not fully committed to what we're doing. I do the other work because it matters to me, not to win any accolades."

"Then I won't mention it," Caitlyn assured her, respecting her all the more for her attitude. "But I would like to know more."

Dr. Davis nodded. "We'll have lunch one day and I'll

fill you in. Now, let's get busy." She beckoned for Caitlyn to follow as she walked briskly down the hall, reading charts as she went, asking for Caitlyn's perceptions of the patients they had yet to see this morning.

From then on, Caitlyn didn't have time to think about the future. The sick and injured children right in front of her were the only ones who mattered.

7

Noah had been in the pediatrics unit checking on one of the other patients when he'd spotted Cait with little Mason Waycross. The sight of her cuddling the boy in her arms while reading him a story had made his breath catch. She was such a natural with children. An image of her holding their child formed in his head and wouldn't go away.

He had to find some way to ensure that happened, he thought as he left the unit and went back to his own rounds.

The next time he'd caught a glimpse of Cait, it was more than forty-eight hours later and she'd been deep in conversation with Dr. Davis in the cafeteria. Since she'd never given him any indication that she was close to the pediatrician, he couldn't help wondering what that was about, but he didn't interrupt them. He and Cait had an unspoken rule about keeping their distance at work, except for shared meals, coffee or professional conversations. The past couple of days, there hadn't been time in their schedules for any of that. Even their phone calls had been hurried.

All of their discretion was probably wasted. Their relationship wasn't much of a secret, he acknowledged dryly. Two weeks after they'd started seeing each other, his basketball buddies had been taunting him about it. Jill Marshall had put two and two together even more rapidly. Gossip spread as quickly in a hospital as it possibly could in Chesapeake Shores or any other small town.

That was just one of the reasons he'd hoped for a quick resolution to their current situation before word leaked out about the pregnancy. He was finally coming to accept, though, that there wouldn't be one. They were just going to have to deal with the speculation in the meantime.

When his cell phone rang with an unfamiliar number on the screen, he answered to hear Mick O'Brien's booming voice.

"When can you get down to Chesapeake Shores?" he asked.

"My schedule's pretty jammed up," Noah told him.

"Well, *un*jam it," Mick ordered. "There are some people I want you to meet."

"Who?" Noah asked, immediately on high alert.

"The mayor, a few others."

"Mick, what have you been up to?"

"Just laying a little groundwork," he insisted. "I think you'll be pleased."

"I thought you were going to stay out of this."

"I've had a couple of conversations," Mick protested. "No big deal. You don't like what they have to say, you're free to say no."

"And how do I explain to Caitlyn that I'm going to Chesapeake Shores without her?"

"Bring her along," Mick said without hesitation. "She might as well know what's going on. Keeping it a secret doesn't make a lot of sense since it'll affect her life, too."

"Mick, this is a bad idea. It's premature, for one thing."

"You finish your residency at the end of June. It's already the middle of May. What was your timetable, to wait till July 1 and then wing it?"

"I was hoping to let Cait come around to my way of thinking on her own. My taking a step like this is going to back her into a corner."

"If you ask me, the girl needs a push," Mick grumbled.

"She's a woman, not a girl, and you of all people should know how she'll react to being pushed. The same way you would. She'll push back."

Mick heaved a sigh. "More than likely," he conceded. "Okay, I'll tell them you're swamped at work. That kind of dedication will impress them, but don't put this off too long, Noah. We need to get the ball rolling. There's a house on the market that would be just right for your home. With a few modifications, you could set up your practice there, too. I can have a crew ready to go, as soon as you give me the go-ahead."

Noah began to see what Cait meant when she said her grandfather liked to take charge. "Now you really are getting ahead of things, Mick. I appreciate your wanting to help. I really do, but you have to give me a little credit for understanding Cait and you have to let me go at this at the pace that I think best."

"I've known her a lot longer than you have," Mick reminded him. "Sometimes you have to take a firm stand."

Noah laughed at that. He could imagine that working when Cait was in preschool, but certainly not now that she was grown. "I wouldn't even dare," he said. "Not if I expect this to turn out the way I hope it will."

Mick sighed. "I knew my granddaughter was stubborn. I didn't expect you to be, too."

"Can you imagine her with a man who isn't?" Noah asked. "She'd run roughshod over him. And I do have the added benefit of being patient, especially when something's worth waiting for."

"Not familiar with the concept," Mick said. "We'll talk again soon."

"I'm sure of it," Noah responded wryly.

He shook his head as he hung up. No one in his family had ever been a meddler, so this was a whole new experience. It remained to be seen whether the O'Brien gene for it was going to be a blessing or a curse.

Caitlyn listened in amazement as Naomi Davis described what her foundation had accomplished to see that doctors working in villages in third-world countries had the medical supplies they needed.

"We're barely scratching the surface, though," Dr. Davis lamented. "Ask any of the organizations dedicated to helping and they'll tell you that there will never be enough resources."

"That's why I want to go back," Caitlyn said. "Every pair of hands matters."

"So does having adequate medicine and supplies," the pediatrician reminded her. "So does well-funded research."

"I know that," Caitlyn said. "I'm certainly not diminishing the importance of what you're doing. Frankly, I'm amazed at how much you've accomplished."

"Did you know that your grandfather is a major donor?"

Caitlyn regarded her with shock. "He is?"

"He made his first donation after you volunteered. He called me, said he understood I had a foundation doing work in that part of the world, and he wanted to know how he could help."

"I had no idea," Caitlyn said. "He's never said a word about it." She was well aware of his work with Habitat for Humanity and had known how fervently he believed in giving back out of gratitude for all the blessings in his life, but that he'd chosen this particular project astounded her.

"When I asked him how he'd found out about us, he said he'd done some homework after his granddaughter had volunteered on a medical mission," Dr. Davis revealed. "He'd found that our foundation put the bulk of every dollar received into actual help. Very little goes to administrative costs. In fact, we operate on a shoestring, mostly with volunteers and a paid staff of two." She smiled. "I'm not one of those two, by the way."

Caitlyn wasn't really surprised by that. She'd come to realize the level of commitment Dr. Davis had made to this cause. She wouldn't be using it for either recognition or personal gain.

"May I share something with you?" the pediatrician asked. "An idea I've had? Perhaps you can help."

"Of course," Caitlyn said eagerly.

The doctor's eyes sparkled with excitement. "Your grandfather's not the only one who's done his homework," she confided. "I know a little bit about his background as an architect. I know he and his brothers created Chesapeake Shores from his vision, and that he's built other communities around the country from scratch, as well."

"He's retired now, though," Caitlyn told her.

"Except for supervising projects for Habitat for Humanity in this area," Dr. Davis said, proving that her research on Mick O'Brien had, indeed, been extensive.

"True," she replied.

"How do you think he'd feel about tackling a new challenge?"

"What sort of challenge?"

"Building medical facilities in some of these villages," she explained.

Caitlyn's pulse picked up. What an incredible idea! She knew it would appeal to her grandfather on many different levels. She also knew, though, that her grandmother might hate the thought of him being gone for months at a time to oversee construction.

"I don't know," she said, unable to keep a hint of regret from her voice.

"You don't think he'd be willing to consider it?" the pediatrician asked, her disappointment plain.

"Oh, I think he'd love the challenge of it," Caitlyn admitted. "It's just that he made a commitment to my grandmother that he'd limit his travel. How can I ask him to break his word to her? That is what you're suggesting, isn't it? That I be the one to persuade him to do this?"

"It did occur to me that you might be a more effective advocate for the idea than I would, but if you're reluctant, I can speak to him myself. I've put together a proposal for him to consider. I even have some funding set aside. It's far from enough, but I'd hoped he would have some thoughts about where we could go for contributions of building materials. I think we'd have all the labor we could ask for, albeit mostly unskilled. That's why we'd need someone with experience not only at construction, but at working with volunteers to oversee it all."

"He certainly has the contacts and experience to do all of that," Caitlyn agreed. She drew in a deep breath. "Let me talk to him. I'd like very much for him to take this on, but I need to lay the groundwork."

She thought of Grandma Megan's likely reaction and winced. Laying the groundwork wasn't going to be easy. In fact, it could cause a rift between her grandparents just when things between them were better than ever.

Still, if this was something she could do for the cause in which she believed with all her heart, she had to take the chance.

"Give me a little time," she told Dr. Davis. "I'll get back to you as soon as I've had a chance to talk to him."

"Thank you."

"Don't thank me yet," Caitlyn said, then smiled ruefully. "You might actually be the one doing me a favor."

"How so?"

She thought of how this request just might redirect all of the family's attention to a new topic and away from her pregnancy. "Don't ask me to explain," she said. "Just know that I'm grateful on more levels than you can possibly imagine."

"I was thinking I might run down to Chesapeake Shores on Saturday," Caitlyn told Noah over a quick coffee break just a few hours after he'd seen her with Dr. Davis in the cafeteria for the second time in a few days.

"I thought you were intent on staying as far away from your family as possible," he said, surprised by her announcement.

"There's something I need to discuss with my grandmother," she admitted, then added, "With Grandpa Mick, too."

"Want to fill me in?"

"It's an idea that Dr. Davis had," she told him. "Did you know about her foundation?"

He nodded. "I went to a fund-raising event a while back."

Cait frowned. "You never mentioned that."

"It was a few months before we met."

"Still, you know I'm interested in medicine in that part of the world. Why wouldn't you tell me she's actively involved in that cause?"

"To be honest, I forgot about it," he said. "She doesn't make a big deal about the foundation. In fact, I think she was a little embarrassed that one of her donors insisted on throwing this big dinner and invited all the doctors from the hospital. She kept telling the residents they didn't need to feel obligated to attend or to make a donation. Of course, we all went, out of respect for her, but also because it was such a good cause."

Cait's expression was still disgruntled. "Were you afraid I'd jump on the bandwagon or something? Is that why you never mentioned it?"

"Of course not," he said, though he wasn't able to keep a defensive note out of his voice. Had he remained silent because he'd feared that Cait would find an ally in Dr. Davis, someone who would only fuel the dream that could take her away from him? Was he that insecure or selfish? He didn't like thinking he might be.

In an attempt to divert her attention, he asked, "How does your grandfather fit in?"

He listened in amazement as she explained the pediatrician's idea for having Mick design and oversee construction of basic medical facilities. "And you're going to take that suggestion to him?"

She nodded. "First, though, I need to speak to my grandmother. When his work was taking him away all the time, it destroyed their marriage. This would require travel, I'm sure."

"And she might object," Noah guessed.

"I wouldn't be surprised if she hated the idea," Cait admitted.

"Then what?"

"Then I'll have my work cut out for me trying to win her over," she said.

"Maybe you should leave it to him to persuade her," Noah suggested, then added, "If he's actually interested in pursuing the idea in the first place."

"He's going to be interested," she said with certainty.

"But do you really want to be caught in the middle? I thought you were sick of everyone being in your business. Now you want to get involved in a decision that should be between the two of them."

"But somebody needs to present the idea to him," she argued. "Isn't it better if it's me? At least I'll be sensitive to the possible fallout."

"Will you really?" Noah asked skeptically. "Or will you be pushing to get the answer you want because you're personally invested in this cause?"

He could see that Cait knew he was right. She just wasn't quite ready to admit it yet. There was no mistaking that she was warring with herself, so he sat by silently, sipping his now-cold coffee.

Eventually she frowned at him. "You know I hate it when you're right," she grumbled.

He laughed. "I know, and it happens on such a regular basis, it must really be a trial for you."

"Not amusing," she commented. "So, what do you suggest? That I leave it to Dr. Davis?"

Since a trip to Chesapeake Shores fit in nicely with his own plans, he shook his head. "No. I think we can drive down for the day. You can fill your grandfather in, give him whatever proposal Dr. Davis has prepared, then leave it to him from then on."

"You want to go, too?"

"I have the day off. Why not?" he said with an innocent shrug. "It'll be good for everyone to see that I'm still in the game."

"Is that what our situation is to you, a game?"

He backed off at once. "Sorry. A poor choice of words. I meant to say that they'll see that my commitment to you is as solid as ever."

"Better," she said, smiling. "But what will you do while I'm talking to my grandfather?"

"I might wander around town for a bit," he suggested. "Maybe Connor will be available for coffee."

"Boy, you two really must have bonded," she said. "I'm not sure how I feel about that."

"Would you prefer it if the members of your family hated my guts?"

"No, of course not. I just find it worrisome. Conspiracies among O'Briens are the norm."

"I'm not an O'Brien."

"But you might not be above conspiring with them, if you thought it would help your cause," she said.

"You're the only O'Brien I want to conspire with," he said with what he hoped was convincing sincerity.

"Good answer," she told him. "Not that I believe it for a minute."

Noah laughed, understanding her skepticism. "What time shall we leave?"

"I'd like to be there by midmorning. I have a craving for one of Sally's raspberry croissants and they're almost always gone before lunchtime."

Noah nodded. "Then that will be the first stop."

Her expression turned thoughtful. "I wouldn't mind some penny candy from Ethel's, either. Trace used to buy that for Carrie and me. And Grandpa Mick always had some in his pocket, too."

Noah gave an exaggerated sigh of resignation. "I suppose there's no hope that our child won't be spoiled rotten by the two of them, too."

She regarded him with indignation. "I am not spoiled rotten."

"It's okay," he soothed.

"I am *not* spoiled," she repeated.

"Tell me one single person who's ever denied you anything you wanted," he taunted.

The request seemed to stump her, just as he'd anticipated. "Don't fret. I love you, anyway."

"And I love you, despite this annoying tendency you have to gloat whenever you're right."

Noah stood up. "See you at your place tonight?"

She shook her head. "I'm on duty."

"Then I'll see you here in the morning. Make sure you get some sleep." He pressed a kiss to her forehead. "Love you."

"Love you, too."

The second he was out of sight, he flipped open his cell phone and called Connor. "Your father said there's a house that might be perfect for Cait and me and for my medical practice. Do you know the one?"

"I do," Connor said.

"Can you arrange for me to see it late Saturday morning? Cait and I are driving down. She's going to be tied up with Mick for a while, so I thought I'd use the time to take a look."

"Can do," Connor said eagerly. "What time?"

"Eleven-thirty?"

"Perfect. I'll make the arrangements. Does Caitlyn know anything about this?"

Noah sighed. "No. And it might be better if your father didn't know that I was checking the place out."

"Oh, boy," Connor murmured. "Don't you think Caitlyn ought to be in the loop?"

"She will be," Noah promised. "As soon as there's anything to mention."

"A fait accompli?" Connor said. "Man, that's just asking for trouble. I've been there, done that, and paid the price."

Noah had a hunch he might be right. Even so, he wanted to have a plan in mind before he filled Cait in. She needed to know he was serious, that this was something he really wanted and not just a means to an end.

He sighed, suspecting he was delusional. No matter how he dressed up the idea and tried to sell it as his own, he doubted she'd buy it for a minute. Up until now neither one of them had ever included living in Chesapeake Shores as part of a dream for the future. But more and more, Noah believed it was the right answer for both of them.

Cait stood on the porch at her grandparents' house on Saturday morning and watched Noah drive away. Something was up with him, no question about it. She pondered that as she popped the last bite of raspberry croissant into her mouth, then pushed her suspicions aside. She had her own mission for today. She'd worry about what Noah was doing later.

Opening the unlocked front door, she walked inside shouting for her grandparents. To her shock, the only response came from the kitchen from her great-grandmother.

"Caitlyn!" Nell said, stepping into the foyer and regarding her with surprise as she wiped her hands on a dish towel. "Where'd you come from?"

"Noah dropped me off. I came to see Grandpa Mick and Grandma Megan."

"Well, you're too late to catch either one of them. Your grandmother's already gone to her art gallery and your grandfather left at dawn for the Habitat for Humanity site."

"You're kidding me," she said, deflated.

"You didn't think to call ahead and let them know you were coming?" Nell asked. "Those two are never still for a minute. The only reason you caught me here is that I brought up the pies I'd baked for tomorrow's dinner."

"What kind of pies?" Caitlyn asked at once. "Strawberry-rhubarb, by any chance?"

Nell laughed. "Do you mark strawberry season on your calendar?"

"It's etched in my brain," Caitlyn told her. "Did you happen to make an extra one?"

"Won't you be here for dinner?"

"Afraid not. Noah and I have to go back this afternoon. We're both on duty tomorrow."

"Where is Noah?"

"He told me he was going to wander around in town."

Her great-grandmother regarded her skeptically. "He didn't strike me as much of a shopper. Most men I know aren't."

"Now that you mention it, that explanation doesn't make a lot of sense to me, either. He said something about tracking down Connor, too. What do you suppose they're up to?"

"Knowing your uncle, it could be anything," Nell said candidly. "If I were you, I'd want to find out. Want me to drop you off in town? I drove over here since I had the pies to deliver."

"Take me to Uncle Connor's office," she suggested. "I'll start there. I know it's Saturday, but last I heard he kept office hours in the morning to be accommodating to people who work. If he's not around, maybe his secretary will know where he is."

Nell locked up, then dropped her off in town a few minutes later. Even before Caitlyn could walk inside, she spotted her uncle and Noah down the block walking into a house with a for-sale sign on the front lawn. Just as all the houses on this block were, it was one of the original Chesapeake Shores homes designed and built by her grandfather. Seeing Noah heading inside set off alarm bells.

Caitlyn changed directions, marched down the block and walked straight into the house through the open front door just as Noah and her uncle walked back into the living room.

"Caitlyn!" her uncle said with exaggerated enthusiasm. "Where'd you come from? I thought you were with Dad."

"It seems I missed Grandpa Mick. Nell was at the house, though, so she dropped me off at your office," she explained. "Noah mentioned he might stop by to see you." She glanced in Noah's direction, then back at her uncle. "He didn't mention anything about this, though. Whose idea was it to go house-hunting?"

"I'm not house-hunting," Noah claimed. "Not exactly, anyway."

"You're in a house that's for sale," she pointed out. "What would you call it?"

Connor looked from her to Noah and back again, then headed for the door. "I think I'll leave you two to debate this," he said, then murmured to Noah, "Good luck, pal."

Caitlyn put her hands on her hips and tried to stare Noah down. "I'm waiting," she said softly.

"For?"

"An explanation."

"And I'll give you one," he promised. "But first tell me what you think of the house?"

"It's a great house. Every house my grandfather designed for this town is terrific. They all have charm. They're all built to last. I'm sure this one is no exception."

"Do you want to take a look around?" he asked hopefully.

"Not until you tell me what you're doing here," she said, though she very much feared she already knew the answer.

"I thought it might be the perfect place to raise a family," he said, meeting her gaze with an unflinching expression.

"You thought that or Grandpa Mick did? Or was it left to Connor to plant the idea in your head?"

"Your grandfather mentioned this specific house, but only after I told him I was thinking of opening my practice in Chesapeake Shores after I finished my residency."

She stared at him incredulously, stunned by his casual announcement of something that to her was earth-shattering. "You want to start a medical practice in Chesapeake Shores and you never thought to run that by me?"

"I wanted to think it through first, check into the possibilities."

"I don't believe this," she said, feeling as if the walls of the house were closing in on her. She finally saw what he was up to, him and her entire family, and she didn't like it. "I have to get out of here."

She turned and ran from the house. Noah was slowed down when he stopped to lock up, but he still caught her before she reached the corner.

"Caitlyn, it's just an idea. Nothing's been decided."

"Really? Do you honestly expect me to believe that you, Connor and my grandfather all accidentally landed on the same page and that no decisions have been made?"

"I can't tell you what the two of them are thinking, but my mind isn't made up," he insisted. "I'm exploring an option that holds a lot of appeal."

"Not to me, it doesn't," she declared. "I love this town. I love my family." She looked him in the eye. "I do not love this idea. And if you'll be honest with yourself, you can't tell me you love it any more than I do." She was all but trembling. "I can't believe this. I knew my family would do everything in their power to try to manipulate me, but I didn't think they'd do it like this or that you would let them get away with it."

Before he could even try to argue with her about that, she spun around and took off down the street. This time Noah was wise enough to let her go.

8

Caitlyn didn't stop walking until she reached her grandmother's art gallery on Shore Road in a strip of shops facing the Chesapeake Bay. Since she'd passed her aunt Bree's flower shop, her uncle Kevin's wife's bookstore and Connor's wife's quilt shop on the way, she wasn't surprised when the trio of women entered right on her heels.

"What on earth?" Grandma Megan asked when she saw them. She enveloped Caitlyn in a hug, then stood back to take a longer survey. Clearly, she didn't like what she saw. "What's wrong?"

"We don't know," Bree said. "I just saw Caitlyn practically running down the block in this direction and set out after her."

"And I joined in," Shanna said.

"Me, too," Heather said. "She looked upset."

Caitlyn felt her eyes fill with tears. She wasn't sure if that had to do with Noah's blatant attempt to manipulate her by deciding he wanted to practice here in Chesapeake Shores or the show of unconditional solidarity from her aunts.

Her grandmother must have felt the shiver that ran

through her, because she rubbed her arms, then ordered her to sit. "Whatever's happened, we can put our heads together and figure it out. I'll make tea."

Caitlyn managed a watery smile. Thanks to Nell, they all thought a cup of tea could make everything better. "Tea would be good if you have herbal."

"Of course I do," her grandmother said.

"I'll get it," Heather offered, already moving toward the back of the gallery.

"Talk to us," Bree said. "Do we need to call anyone? Your mom might be working at home today. As upset as you are, she should be here."

Caitlyn shook her head. She'd already set off enough alarms. "It's okay. I've taken her away from work too much lately with all my drama. I just need a few minutes to process what's going on."

"We won't call your mother, if that's what you prefer, but who else would you turn to, if not your family?" Grandma Megan said briskly. "Now tell us why you're so distraught and what we can do. I had no idea you were planning to come to town today."

"It was a last-minute thing," Caitlyn told her, thinking of the mission that had brought her to Chesapeake Shores. "And then, just now, I caught Noah..." Tears welled up and spilled down her cheeks.

Bree immediately regarded her with shock. "Caught him what?" she asked indignantly. "Cheating on you? I didn't realize he even knew anyone who lives in town. I swear I'll tar and feather the man myself."

An hysterical sob bubbled up at the image of her aunt going after Noah. Caitlyn didn't doubt for a minute that she'd do it, that any of them would. The image of him being pummeled by O'Brien women held a certain appeal, one she wasn't particularly proud of. She didn't need anyone fighting her battles for her and, as she knew perfectly well, physical violence never solved anything. She'd seen the damaging results a few too many times in the emergency room. Little Mason immediately came to mind, along with the test results that indicated he had been shaken by someone. The authorities were now involved.

"No, no," she protested quickly to reassure everyone on that point. "Noah wasn't cheating. He was looking at a house."

She frowned at Heather, who was coming back with a tray filled with a steaming pot of tea—a soothing chamomile, if she wasn't mistaken—and a perfectly matched set of delicate porcelain cups. The set was in an antique chintz pattern that was so typical of her grandmother's taste it brought a smile to her lips, despite her sour mood.

She faced Heather. "Noah was with Connor. What do you know about whatever's going on between those two?"

"Absolutely nothing," Heather said, looking genuinely mystified. "Connor hasn't said a word to me. Oh, he admitted that he and Kevin had gone to Baltimore to have a word with Noah, that they'd all gone out for a drink, but I thought that was the end of his involvement."

"Kevin hasn't said a word since then, either," Shanna reported. "He just told me he was satisfied that Noah was a good guy and that his intentions were honorable. You know how these men are. They pound their chests for a bit, demand answers, then go back to their own lives as quickly as they can."

"Except for Mick," Megan said with certainty. "He's behind this. I'd bet money on that."

"Well, of course he is," Bree agreed. "I can see him

now, backing Noah into a corner, finding the ideal house for the two of you, then persuading Connor and Kevin to do his dirty work."

Caitlyn sighed. "Noah swears none of them pressured him. He claims he *wants* to live in Chesapeake Shores when his residency ends this summer, that he wants to set up a medical practice here. He told me it was his idea, that he first thought of it before he even met them at Sunday dinner a few weeks ago."

The women scoffed at that.

"That's why Mick's so clever," Megan reminded them. "He convinces people they thought of things themselves, when all along he's the one who planted the seeds, poured on the water and fertilizer, then sat back to await the expected results."

"Agreed," Bree said at once. "He's my father and I love him, but he's sneaky."

Caitlyn thought about what Noah had said, then shook her head. "Not this time," she finally conceded reluctantly. "I don't think Noah's that easily manipulated. I think his idea just fit very neatly with what Grandpa Mick was trying to accomplish, getting the two of us married and settled right here. Noah probably mentioned it when they were closeted together before dinner, then Grandpa Mick seized it and ran with it."

"You have to admit, it's not a totally terrible idea," Heather said hesitantly. "Chesapeake Shores really could use a doctor."

"And you'd be close to family, so we could all help with the baby when it comes," Shanna suggested, glancing quickly from one woman to another as if to assure herself she wasn't adding to the pressure. "You wouldn't have to rely on day care while you're finishing up your internship and residency. That would be a good thing, right?"

Caitlyn frowned at the very rational comments. "You're sounding awfully eager to jump on the bandwagon. Were you all in on this? Did Grandpa Mick supply you with a pro-con list in case the subject came up?"

"Absolutely not," Bree said. "This is the first I've heard about any of this. Jake wasn't part of the mission to see Noah. I doubt the two of them have exchanged more than a handful of words, and that was on the day you brought Noah to the house to meet us all. And I try to steer far away from Dad when he's plotting."

Caitlyn gave her a wry look. "That didn't stop you from making a dutiful call to me with a few suggestions about how to run my life. Are you saying Grandpa Mick wasn't behind that?"

Bree flushed. "Okay, he might have mentioned something."

"Oh, just admit it," Heather scolded. "He stood right over you till you made the call, the same as he did with the rest of us." She gave Caitlyn an apologetic look. "Sorry."

"No problem," she said. "I get it. He's a hard man to say no to."

She glanced up to see her grandmother regarding her speculatively. "If you didn't know anything about Noah's plan to look at a house, what did bring you to Chesapeake Shores today?"

Now it was Caitlyn's turn to flush. "I needed to speak to Grandpa Mick about something. It's nothing to do with me, Noah or the baby," she added quickly.

"Really?" her grandmother said, suspicion written all over her face. "If it's all so innocent, why do you suddenly seem so jumpy and why does that make me nervous?"

Caitlyn sighed. "Because you might not like what I wanted to talk to him about," she confessed.

"Oh, boy," Bree said. "That's it. Since the immediate crisis has been averted, I'm going back to my shop. I have a flower order coming in any minute. If I'm lucky, it might be delivered by my husband."

"And I occasionally have actual paying customers," Shanna said. "I ran out so fast, I didn't even lock the door. They could have walked off with half the books by now."

"I'm not actually open for another hour, but I have things to do," Heather claimed. She leaned down to give Caitlyn a hug. "Good luck."

"What makes you think I'm going to need luck?" Caitlyn asked, but one look into her grandmother's icy gaze told her the answer to that. "Can I come with you guys?"

"You stay right where you are," her grandmother ordered in a do-it-or-die tone she'd rarely used with her grandchildren. In Caitlyn's experience, that tone had been reserved for keeping Grandpa Mick in line.

Caitlyn poured herself another cup of herbal tea, then waited. Grandma Megan didn't seem any more eager to force the issue than she was. It was Caitlyn who finally couldn't stand the silence another minute.

"I guess I should explain," she said reluctantly.

"That's what I'm waiting for," Grandma Megan replied.

"There's a woman I work with at the hospital, a doctor," Caitlyn began. She explained about Naomi Davis's foundation and her work in third-world countries.

"I can see why you'd find that fascinating," Grandma Megan said. "But how exactly does that involve your grandfather?"

"It doesn't. Not yet, anyway." She drew in a deep

breath and blurted out the idea about having her grandfather design medical facilities.

For an instant her grandmother seemed to relax, but then all too quickly, she sat up a little straighter. "This is about more than designing the facilities, isn't it? She wants him to supervise building them."

Caitlyn nodded. "It's an incredible idea," she ventured tentatively, keeping a close eye on her grandmother's expression. The annoyance seemed to have drained away. Now she simply looked resigned.

"And she knew your grandfather would never say no to something that means so much to you," Grandma Megan said softly, a hint of bitterness in her voice. "Very clever of her."

"It wasn't like that," Caitlyn protested. "She was just running the idea by me to see what I thought about it, but she was willing to talk to him herself. I understood right away how much you'd probably hate the idea, so I insisted on filling in Grandpa Mick. I knew he'd want to talk it over with you."

"Since when?" her grandmother asked.

Caitlyn regarded her with alarm. "It's not like that anymore," she said hurriedly. "He doesn't just go off and do what he wants the way he used to."

"I suppose not," her grandmother conceded grudgingly. "But this is going to appeal to his ego. He won't be able to resist."

"I'm sorry," Caitlyn said, regretting the potential fallout from what had seemed like such an incredible use of her grandfather's talents. "Noah was right. He told me I shouldn't get caught in the middle."

"And yet you are," her grandmother said wearily.

"If you're really opposed to this, I won't say a word to Grandpa Mick," Caitlyn offered.

"How can I possibly object when it's such a worthwhile cause?" Grandma Megan asked, her frustration plain. "I can't be that heartless."

Caitlyn felt terrible for putting her grandmother in this position, but she could see that no matter what her personal objections might be, her grandmother wouldn't stand in the way of whatever Mick decided to do.

"There might be a compromise," she suggested hesitantly.

Her grandmother's expression brightened perceptibly. "Really?"

"I've given this a lot of thought since Dr. Davis and I talked," she said. "Grandpa Mick wouldn't have to oversee all the construction. If he made it a project of his company, rather than a personal cause, different people could be assigned to each construction project. He'd hardly have to travel at all himself. He'd just have to authorize the commitment of company resources."

"An interesting idea," her grandmother admitted.

"I know Matthew would want to do it," Caitlyn said, referring to one of her great-uncle Jeffrey's sons who was working with her grandfather. "And maybe some of the other men, too. Jaime is Grandpa Mick's second-in-command. He's in charge of the day-to-day oversight on a lot of the projects. He loves to travel."

Her grandmother smiled. "You really want your grandfather to say yes to this, don't you?"

"Of course," she admitted at once. "But only if it won't upset you. I know how hard the two of you have worked to make your marriage stronger this time. Long separations weren't part of the deal."

"No, but perhaps I could go along with him now, at least occasionally," her grandmother said, her expression thoughtful. "It wouldn't be like it was all those years ago with me being left behind to raise five children practically on my own. Would there be things I could do in these villages?"

"Absolutely," Caitlyn told her, instantly seizing the opening. "They're in desperate need of help of all kinds. You could assist the doctors or teach the kids to read, help them to learn English. Even just cuddling a baby or teaching the moms about nutrition would be a huge help. It's so rewarding, Grandma Megan. It's an experience you'd never forget."

Her grandmother reached for her hand. "You've certainly not forgotten it, have you? You're eager to go back."

"I *need* to go back," Caitlyn told her, then sighed. "But I'm beginning to think I won't be able to."

"Perhaps not right away as you'd planned," her grandmother agreed. "But just look what you've been able to accomplish for the cause by coming here today. I'd say you're making a worthwhile contribution even now."

Caitlyn thought about it and realized she was right. If her grandfather agreed to do this, she'd played a role in helping a lot of doctors and a lot of families in a lot of villages. It might not be the same as a hands-on contribution, but in some ways it was even more important. That was a lesson Dr. Davis had learned and tried to impart just the other day.

"Thank you for reminding me that there's more than one way to make a difference," she said.

She still wasn't quite ready to give up on her dream entirely or to plunge into a marriage that she hadn't anticipated, but she felt more at peace than she had since she'd first discovered she was pregnant. Now, with her state of mind improved, she just needed to find Noah and tell him she was at least a little less angry that he'd been making his own plans for the future behind her back.

Noah took refuge in Sally's Café, sipping coffee and staring out at the kids playing across the street on the town green. He knew that sooner or later Cait would find him here once she was ready to talk.

He'd just about decided to go ahead and order lunch and was studying the menu when he looked up and saw her at the window, regarding him with a serious expression. He gave her a tentative smile, then watched with relief as she headed for the door and came inside. She slipped into the booth opposite him.

"Are you okay?" he asked quietly.

She nodded. "Better than before. You can relax. I've stopped being furious with you."

"Good to know. Mind if I ask what calmed you down? I might need to know the secret for next time."

She smiled at that. "Are you anticipating a lot of fights?"

"We're both strong-willed," he said with a shrug. "Disagreements are going to come along."

"But hopefully I won't be as irrational as I was earlier," she said. "I'd like to blame pregnancy hormones for that."

"So this newfound serenity I sense in you is just another mood swing?" he suggested cautiously.

"No, the truth is that the minute Bree, Shanna and Heather started lumping you in with Grandpa Mick and the rest as part of the big conspiracy, I suddenly knew better. Setting up a practice here really was your idea, wasn't it?"

Noah nodded. "I'll confess that I hadn't considered the idea before we found out about the baby, but once I knew you were pregnant, I started seeing the future a little differently. I knew I'd want our child to grow up surrounded by family. Since yours is a lot more convenient to Baltimore, it seemed to make sense."

"You do have family of your own," she reminded him.

"Chicago's definitely not an option," he said at once. "It's too far away from where you'll be, for one thing. For another, I have zero desire to go back there. It hardly qualifies as a small, intimate community."

She regarded him curiously. "You never say much about growing up there or about your family."

"Let's just say I was anxious to leave it all behind. My parents tried, but it was hardly an idyllic life, not like the one you lived. And the area we lived in was dangerous. It was no place for a child to grow up. I doubt you can imagine what it's like for a kid in those circumstances. I was scared all the time. I had friends who died. They were just kids and they never had a chance to see their dreams come true. Some of them didn't even dare to dream."

"Noah, I'm so sorry. I had no idea."

"Don't be sorry. It's just the way it was. I was one of the lucky ones. My parents might not have had much, but they did keep me focused on my studies. They told me that was the way out, an option neither of them had had."

"Your mom must be so proud of you," she said softly.

"She is. You know that my dad died a couple of years ago. He had a heart attack when someone robbed the store where he was working. He might have made it if the ambulance hadn't taken so long to respond, another fact of life in that neighborhood." He forced a smile to counteract the grim reality of the life he'd left behind. "I'd love to make a home in a place like this, give my mom a better life. The thought of our child growing up here in a community that's safe, surrounded by a huge family..." He met her gaze. "It's even better than I ever imagined."

Caitlyn reached for his hand and clung tightly to it. "Thank you for telling me this. I wish you had sooner."

"I don't like to dwell on the past."

"I can understand that, but it did shape who you are. I think I understand you so much better now."

"Then you can see why Chesapeake Shores seems so amazing to me?"

She nodded.

"Even before I came down to meet you for dinner at Mick's, I was fascinated by all your stories about the town and your family. I started doing a little research online. Then when I drove into town that day, I just knew that this was where we should be raising our family."

He gestured toward the town green. "Look out there, Cait. How often do we see kids playing in the parks where we are, at least without their parents hovering a couple of feet away."

"There are parents out there, too," she said. "Nobody is going to let their kids roam free at that age, not even in Chesapeake Shores."

"I suppose not," he said. "It just seems more serene somehow, more the way I always imagined small-town life would be."

"It is idyllic in many ways," she agreed. "But it's not perfect."

He shrugged, not giving up. "Close enough."

"And you really see this as someplace you could be happy practicing medicine?"

He heard the skepticism in her voice. "It's not in the middle of nowhere, but yes," he said. "The town needs its own doctor, somebody to deal with the everyday sniffles and the flu, somebody to do blood pressure monitoring and preventative medicine. Why should they have to drive to the next town or all the way to Baltimore or Annapolis for basic care?"

"I'm just worried that you're making this compromise because you think it will satisfy me, get me to go along with setting up a practice with you once I've completed my residency. What if I don't see myself in Chesapeake Shores, surrounded by family? They haven't driven you crazy yet, but I've had a lifetime of their meddling."

"And their support," he said quietly. "And their love. Is that really such a bad thing?"

"Not when you put it that way, no," she replied, then sighed. "And maybe this would be the right place for me and a family...someday."

"Just not yet," he concluded. "But the family's coming now, Cait. Or in a few months. Even if you leave me out of the equation, there will be a baby to consider."

"I'm not likely to forget that," she said. "It's all I think about. And just now Shanna pointed out all the built-in child care I'd have available if we lived here. It's hard to argue with that."

Since her family seemed to be making his case for him, Noah nodded and backed off...for now. "Well, we're not going to decide anything right this minute and I'm starved. You must be, too."

She looked momentarily startled by the unexpected reprieve, but then seized on it. "A tuna melt," she said at once. "With fries." She paused, then added, "And apple pie for dessert."

He smiled. "Are you sure that's all?"

She frowned at his amusement. "Ice cream on the pie," she added with a touch of defiance.

"Done," he said, and beckoned for the waitress, an older woman who'd been hovering nearby for a while now. He realized they were the only customers left in the place.

"Sally!" Caitlyn said, looking up with delight. "How are you?"

"I'm good. You're certainly a sight for sore eyes." She winked at Noah. "She and her sister were two of my best customers when they were teenagers. And where they went, the boys trailed along. I think they were single-handedly responsible for paying for my last car."

"Stop it," Caitlyn protested, then confided, "This is my second visit today. I was in earlier for a raspberry croissant."

Sally laughed. "I sure hope you're sticking around. I could use a new wardrobe for summer."

"Afraid not," Caitlyn told her. "But Noah's a good tipper. Maybe that'll help."

"Let me go put your order in before the cook takes off on his break. I heard what you want." She turned to Noah. "How about you?"

"A crab cake sandwich," he said at once. "With slaw and fries."

"Got it." She headed for the kitchen.

"She seems nice," he said when she'd gone.

"She's as much of an institution in this town as Ethel, who owns the gift shop down the block."

"Ah, the one who sells penny candy."

Cait nodded. "Of course, none of it costs a penny anymore, but we always called it that. Carrie and I were her best customers, too." A grin spread across her face. "You know, it occurs to me that given all the candy she sells, Chesapeake Shores probably needs a full-time dentist more than a doctor."

"I can't help with that," Noah said. He clasped her hand again. "I love you."

"Just keep reminding me of that," she told him.

"Do you think if I do you'll eventually stop viewing me as the enemy who got us into this fix?"

Dismay washed over her face. "I've never thought of you that way, not once."

"How could you not?"

"Because I always take responsibility for my own actions. We were in that bed together, Noah. We made this baby together. And we're going to figure out what comes next together, too."

For the first time in recent days, Noah felt reassured that he might not be fighting a losing battle.

9

Caitlyn's cell phone rang just as she and Noah were finishing their late lunch at Sally's. She looked at the caller ID and sighed.

"My grandfather," she told Noah, then connected the call. "Hey, Grandpa Mick."

"I heard from Ma that you were at the house earlier looking for me. You still in town?"

"Noah and I are at Sally's. Are you at the house now?"

"Just got here. I'm about to take a shower. I'll be cleaned up by the time you all get here." He hesitated, then said, "You here because you have news?"

She grinned at the hopeful note in his voice. "Probably not the news you've been waiting for, so don't bother rallying the troops for a celebration. We'll see you soon."

"Stubborn kids," he grumbled, then disconnected the call.

She frowned at Noah. "Anything we say now is going to disappoint him."

"Not everything," Noah said. "I'm ninety-nine percent certain I'm going to buy that house, unless you vehemently object."

"How can I after what you told me?" she said. "And if I'm finishing up my internship and residency in Baltimore, it makes sense for you to be close by. I just wish I weren't so worried that you're choosing this because of the baby, and not because it's the right situation for you."

Noah chuckled. "You almost sounded enthusiastic for a second there. Then you had to go and ruin it."

"Do you want me to pretend I don't see the obvious pitfalls?" She regarded him intently. "Noah, what if one of those opportunities you dreamed about presents itself? Are you going to resent me?"

"Never!" he said so adamantly that she had to believe him.

"Okay, then," she said, accepting his decision. "I suppose we ought to get to Grandpa Mick's."

"Don't you want to let your grandmother know we're heading over there? From what you told me about her reaction earlier, she should be there to voice her concerns."

"I honestly think she was warming to the idea," Caitlyn said.

"Then she can say that. Don't leave her out, Cait. Not when this affects their life together."

She nodded. "You're right. I guess I was just hoping I could make Grandpa Mick see all the positives before she chimed in."

Noah smiled. "Exactly why she needs to be there to play devil's advocate, if she so chooses."

"That's why you have such a reputation for being fairminded," she grumbled. "In my family, we learned to divide and conquer."

"In other words, you and Carrie could wind your stepfather around your little fingers and he'd do your dirty work in convincing your mom to let you have your way."

"Hey, it was very effective," she said, then sighed. "At least till Trace caught on. Sadly, it didn't take him that long."

"How are you going to feel when our child tries the same tactic with us?"

She laughed. "We'll be on to him or her from the beginning," she said. "It's Grandpa Mick we'll need to worry about. He's an easy mark for his grandchildren. I imagine he'll be even worse with his first great-grandchild."

As confused as she was most of the time these days, the thought of seeing her grandfather with her child brought a surprising smile to her lips. Maybe she was finally starting to see the bright side of this pregnancy, after all.

Noah figured he could learn a thing or two about compromising to make a marriage work by keeping a close eye on Mick and Megan O'Brien as Cait presented her grandfather with Naomi Davis's idea for those medical facilities overseas.

Mick's eyes brightened with interest as Caitlyn described the importance of the contribution he could make with his expertise and commitment of company resources. When she'd finished, he turned to his wife.

"Okay, Meggie, tell the truth," he said, regarding her solemnly. "How do you feel about this?"

"It's a worthwhile cause," she told him with surprisingly little hesitation. It seemed she'd had time to warm to the idea. "And it would be wrong for you to turn your back on it," she added, startling all of them.

Mick looked the most surprised. He seemed reluctant, though, to take her words at face value. "You really mean that? When we remarried, we agreed that my travel would be limited. It's been working out okay."

Megan smiled. "You've been tolerating it," she corrected. "And I appreciate that, but Caitlyn and I have talked about this. I'm thinking I could go along, at least some of the time."

Mick finally allowed his own delight to show. "You'd be willing to do that?" he asked eagerly.

"Somebody will need to keep you from overdoing it," Megan said. "And maybe I could make an important contribution myself. This is something that would mean a lot to both you and our granddaughter. How could I not want to be a part of it? You're the one who advised me to hire someone who could run the gallery so we could travel. I might as well start trusting her to do that."

"And after you oversaw the construction of one or two facilities, I thought maybe you could send Matthew, Jaime or one of the others from your company to oversee the rest," Caitlyn suggested.

Mick chuckled. "So, now you're running my company for me, too?"

"Not running it," she said at once. "Just pointing out that a win-win is possible all around. Dedicating some of your company's resources might pave the way for other companies to follow suit. You'd be setting an example. Eventually, if things go well, the whole project would need someone to oversee and expand it. That could be done from right here."

Mick turned to Noah. "Now it's not just my company, but the entire world. Watch out for this one. She knows how to get her way."

"So I'm discovering," Noah said.

"I wonder where she learned that," Megan commented wryly.

"Nothing wrong with going after things you believe

in," Mick responded with a pointed look in Noah's direction. "Okay, enough about this. I'll give it some more thought, Caitlyn, but I think you could safely tell Dr. Davis that I'm interested in talking some more to her. I'll want her to fill me in on the sort of facilities she's envisioning, what sort of work force I might find there, whether building supplies are available, that sort of thing."

Caitlyn rushed across the room to envelop him in a hug. "Thank you."

"Don't thank me just yet," he said, holding her in place and giving her a direct look. "Now tell me what you and Noah have decided."

Cait glanced in Noah's direction.

"I'm going to make an offer on that house," Noah told him.

"And establish your medical practice here?" Mick said, his satisfaction evident.

Noah nodded. "That's what I'm thinking."

Megan gave Cait a worried look. "Are you okay with that? You didn't seem so enthused earlier."

"Of course she is," Mick said. "No reason not to be."

"Mick!" Megan kept her gaze on Cait. "Sweetheart, how do you feel about it?"

"I'm convinced it's what Noah wants, so I'm fine with it," she said. "I just felt completely blindsided when I saw Noah looking at a house. I needed to be sure he wasn't doing it to pacify Grandpa Mick or to back me into a corner. He swears it's the right situation for him."

To Noah's relief, she said it without any hint of reservation.

"All right!" Mick said with enthusiasm. "Now we can start planning that wedding."

"Hold on," Cait said. "Nobody said anything about a wedding. This decision is about what's best for Noah and maybe even for the baby. That's the only thing anybody's committing to right now."

A frown settled on Mick's face. Noah had the sense he was about to launch into a tirade that would only defeat his purpose, so he quickly stepped in. "That's enough for now, Mick."

"Exactly," Megan chimed in. "Leave them be, Mick. They have to reach their own conclusions."

"They're having a baby," Mick protested. "This is no time to be dillydallying."

"And it's no time to be piling on the pressure," Megan told him firmly. "Haven't you always said that Caitlyn is incredibly smart? Now trust her to make a wise decision when it comes to what's best for her life."

"Please," Caitlyn implored, adding her voice to her grandmother's.

Noah almost felt sorry for the older man, who obviously just wanted things to go well for his beloved granddaughter. "It will work out," he assured Mick. "I promise you that."

"Just not on your timetable or in the way you might envision," Cait told him. "Be patient with us, okay?"

"Looks as if I don't have much of a choice," Mick grumbled, then added with frustration, "I can't say I understand why Abby and Trace aren't all over this."

Megan laughed. "Because they're both smart enough to see that pushing usually backfires with O'Briens."

Noah was glad he'd figured that out all on his own.

Caitlyn went back to work at the hospital after the quick trip to Chesapeake Shores, satisfied with the outcome of her visit with her grandfather. She'd also reached a new understanding of Noah's priorities, one that had left her at peace with his decision. Now if only she could be as certain about what needed to come next for her.

She was on a break when she noticed that she'd missed a call from her sister during rounds. She quickly hit speed dial to return the call.

"You're having a baby!" Carrie squealed when she answered. "How on earth did that happen?"

"The usual way," Caitlyn replied.

"Oh, I know that, but for heaven's sake, Caitlyn, you've never expressed even the slightest interest in dating, much less hopping into some man's bed. This man must be something extraordinary."

Caitlyn laughed. "He is pretty special. I can't wait for you to meet him. When will that be? And where are you now?"

"At the airport on my way home," Carrie said, her tone sobering. "I quit my job."

"But you loved that job," Caitlyn said, not even trying to hide her shock. "Or was it Marc Reynolds that you loved?"

"You don't have to sound so smug," Carrie said, bristling. "You told me I was trailing all over the world after him for all the wrong reasons. I thought eventually, if I worked my backside off, he'd notice me."

"If noticing you is a euphemism for sleeping with you, I thought he had noticed you," Caitlyn said.

"Sure. Turns out I was handy and a whole lot easier than dealing with some demanding, temperamental model like Patrina."

"That's who he's hooked up with?" Caitlyn said. The supermodel had been on the cover of at least three magazines in the past few months, to say nothing of quite a few tabloid editions. Her romantic exploits were almost as notorious as her ability to sell the dozens of fashion and cosmetic brands with which she was associated.

"Seems Marc is like most men. He only wants what's unattainable. I finally realized I was just convenient and doubly handy because I worked harder than anyone else on his staff."

"Oh, sweetie, I am so sorry."

"Hey, lesson learned," Carrie said. "At least I got some invaluable experience in the fashion world. I've already put out a few feelers. I'll have another job in no time."

"Maybe you should spend a little time in Chesapeake Shores and get your feet back under you and your priorities straight before you dive right back in," Caitlyn suggested, then added, "It would be nice to have my twin close by for a while, especially now."

"If that's true, why didn't you call me yourself to fill me in? Why did I have to hear your news from Mom?"

"Because you were working," Caitlyn said candidly. "And you were a hundred percent absorbed in that. Last time we spoke, I barely got a word in edgewise."

"You could have told me to shut up and listen," Carrie argued.

Caitlyn laughed. "Last time I tried that, you got offended and hung up on me."

"Okay, I can be a little self-absorbed," Carrie conceded. "But I do love you and I want to hear all about Noah and this baby you're expecting the minute I get home. Maybe I can stay at your place for a couple of days before I brave Chesapeake Shores. Would that be okay or will I be in the way?"

"You could never be in the way," Caitlyn told her. "And if you're asking because of Noah, we both work so much we rarely even cross paths. He still has his own place, in fact."

"Well, you must have found time to do something," Carrie joked. "I have to admit, it makes me very happy that I'm not the twin in the family headlines for the moment. Quitting a job nobody in the family respected can't possibly compete with having a baby. And, just so you know, as soon as you know the sex of the baby, I'm going to call in a lot of favors in the fashion world to ensure your baby is the best-dressed kid ever."

"Just what I need, a tiny fashionista," Caitlyn protested.

"Maybe you'll learn something," Carrie teased. "Your wardrobe is seriously lacking in style." She fell silent for a full half second, then said excitedly, "We can go shopping for maternity clothes when I get there. That will be so much fun."

"That will be torture," Caitlyn told her. "Besides, white coats are very in at the hospital. And just so you know, it was never your job we didn't like. It was the way we all thought Marc was taking advantage of you. Count your blessings that Grandpa Mick didn't fully grasp what was going on or he'd have been in Paris dragging you home himself."

"Mom says he's taking your news surprisingly well," Carrie said.

"That's because he likes Noah and is convinced I'll fall into line and marry the man."

"You don't want to get married?" Carrie asked, sounding stunned. "You're the ultimate traditional woman, at least compared to me."

"I don't want to be *pushed* into getting married," Caitlyn corrected. "Not if it's for all the wrong reasons."

"But you love this man, right?"

"I do."

"And he loves you?"

"Yes."

"Then I really don't get it," Carrie said. "You should be jumping at the chance to marry him. I certainly would be."

"Let me ask you this," Caitlyn said quietly. "If your dream job in Paris was waiting for you, would you be jumping to get married if it would keep you from accepting it?"

"So this is about going back to Africa," Carrie concluded. "Oh, sweetie, I know that's been your goal, but I'm here to tell you that even the best job in the world can't compete with being in a relationship with the right man. Trust me on that. I may have been delusional where Marc was concerned, but I believe I was meant to be married with a bunch of kids underfoot."

"Well, I want it all," Caitlyn told her.

Carrie laughed. "Just like all the O'Briens. We were led to believe that was possible, weren't we? Mom is responsible for that."

"Absolutely. She set the bar pretty high."

"Did you ever stop to consider that maybe it's just not possible for most women?" she asked, real regret in her voice.

"Not for a minute," Caitlyn responded emphatically, then sighed to herself. What if she'd gotten it wrong?

The rest of May and June passed by in a blur. Though Cait and their future were never far from Noah's thoughts, he had a million and one things to do to finish up his residency and get all of his ducks lined up to open his medical practice in Chesapeake Shores.

He found it worrisome that Cait always seemed to have some excuse for not joining him when he drove down for the closing on the property or to check on the progress with the renovations. While it was true that her schedule was every bit as demanding as his and there had always been conflicts, he got the feeling that she'd deliberately found a way to ensure that their time off never coincided.

And with her sister's surprisingly prolonged stay at her apartment, they hadn't spent any time alone together in weeks. That didn't seem to frustrate her half as much as it did him.

"I thought Carrie was only planning to spend a few nights with you," he'd said a week ago when she'd shown no signs of leaving after her visit had already lasted nearly a month. For once he made no attempt to hide his exasperation.

"I can't very well toss her out," Caitlyn had told him, a defensive note in her voice. "She's going through a big transition right now."

"And her presence actually fits into your plan at the moment, too, doesn't it?"

She'd scowled at that. "Meaning?"

"You're using her as a buffer, Cait. As long as she's there, we can't spend a minute alone together. You get to postpone the sort of serious conversation we need to have. With my residency ending and my move to Chesapeake Shores imminent, we need to settle things."

"We're alone right now," she'd countered, though

there was a telltale blush on her cheeks, proving that he'd guessed accurately about her motives.

"Sure, in the middle of the hospital cafeteria," he'd replied, then shook his head in frustration. "Never mind. I need to get back upstairs."

A few weeks ago on their visit to Chesapeake Shores, he'd allowed himself to hope that they were moving forward. Now he wasn't sure of that at all. If anything, they seemed to be drifting further and further apart. He didn't know Carrie all that well yet, but he couldn't help wondering how much she might be influencing Caitlyn. She was, after all, used to flitting all over the world, unattached. Could her lifestyle be more appealing to Caitlyn than she'd ever acknowledged?

He was still pondering that when he arrived at his new Chesapeake Shores home and office. Mick's crew had finished the renovations yesterday. Mick himself was there to meet him.

"What do you think?" Mick asked after they'd toured the house. "Is this what you had in mind?"

"It's amazing," he acknowledged. The waiting room was warm and friendly. The examining rooms were filled with natural light. Upstairs, the family quarters had been renovated with the latest appliances and designer touches. No expense had been spared. Noah recognized that Mick hadn't charged him even half of what another builder would have charged.

"Think my granddaughter will like it?" Mick asked, a gleam in his eye. "If she'd given me any input, we could have modified it along the way. She may be the only woman I know who ever claimed to not care about a home she intends to live in."

Noah sighed. "I wish I thought she was planning to live here."

Mick gave him a startled look. "What's that supposed to mean? I've been trusting you to close the deal. Are you losing ground?"

"I honestly can't tell anymore," Noah said, not even trying to hide his annoyance. "Something changed after Carrie came back home and moved in with her."

"Well, I can take care of that," Mick said at once. "That girl belongs down here, anyway. I'll have a word with Abby and tell her that Carrie's in the way."

Noah laughed at his naïveté. "And as soon as you do that, you'll have two granddaughters furious with you. For whatever reason, this current arrangement seems to suit both of them."

"I can take a little backlash," Mick insisted. "Right now we need everybody to stay focused on the goal. We need to get you and Caitlyn married by Christmas."

"I'm all for that," Noah agreed. "But more and more I'm wondering if we're not deluding ourselves that it will happen."

Mick sighed heavily. "I thought once she got me to agree to helping design and build those medical facilities, she'd realize she could make a difference without being in some godforsaken village herself."

"I thought so, too," Noah admitted. "But in some ways, I think it's made her more determined to get back there herself. I honestly think she's jealous that you're going over there to work in a few months and she can't go herself."

"That's just crazy," Mick said. "Of all people, Dr. Davis ought to be able to get through to her how much she can do from right here. Maybe I need to have another talk with Naomi. I imagine she could dream up a few things Caitlyn could do from right here to make herself useful."

Noah shook his head. "It won't help. Cait knows all about the work Dr. Davis is doing. She's told me herself how much she admires her. She's even been volunteering with the foundation in her spare time. But it's not enough to replace the dream she's had for herself for years now. She made a promise to the people in that village. She wants to keep it." Noah sighed. "I can't help admiring her dedication."

"Well, nobody's telling her she can't keep her word eventually. People don't always get to do what they want to do the minute they want to," Mick responded.

"O'Briens do," Noah reminded him.

The lines of worry on Mick's brow deepened. "Yeah, I should have known that lesson would come back to bite me in the butt eventually. So, what do we do?"

"*We* don't do anything," Noah said. "I just have to let her know I love her, that I respect her dreams, and hope that one of these days she'll realize that the baby and I are as important as the future she had all lined up for herself."

"You're suggesting patience," Mick said.

"I am."

"I'm not much good at being patient."

Noah laughed at that. "Try, Mick. I'm convinced it's the only way to get what we want."

Caitlyn pulled the tattered letter out of her purse and opened it. Written in pencil in awkward lettering, it was from a young man in the village where she'd worked the summer before.

"We miss you," he began. "It is not good here. Three babies died this week. Mothers are too sick to feed them. There is not enough food or milk. The doctors say there is little they can do without more help. Can you help us, Missus Caitlyn?"

Tears spilled down her cheeks at the simple request for basic food and medical supplies, things everyone here took for granted. She knew that she alone couldn't save everyone, but what about this one village? How could she turn her back on them? How could everyone expect her to, especially Noah? Shouldn't the man who claimed to love her understand her need to help?

Ironically, the one person who seemed to get it was Carrie. Her twin had been surprisingly supportive of her commitment.

"I wish I had a goal that was half as important," Carrie had said more than once. She repeated it now when Caitlyn showed her the letter. "All I've ever cared about was catching a man and doing things that were fun."

"You worked hard at your job," Caitlyn corrected.

"Because I thought it would impress Marc," Carrie admitted. "Not because I was passionate about it. It's fashion, for goodness' sake. Even I know that's not exactly a meaningful world."

Caitlyn found herself in the odd position of defending a career she'd often thought to be frivolous. "If it's something you love, that's what matters."

"Tell Grandpa Mick that. He spent an hour on the phone yesterday telling me it's time to get serious about my life. He says I'm wasting time."

"Did he have any suggestions?" Caitlyn asked, knowing perfectly well he usually did.

"Of course. He wants me to go to Africa with him

and Grandma Megan. He said it would be good for me to do something for other people for a change, to realize that not everyone has the charmed life we've led."

Caitlyn felt as if the wind had been knocked out of her. "Are you going?"

"If I don't come up with a suitable alternative, I suppose I'll have to," Carrie said, looking resigned. "As he pointed out, I can't just sit around twiddling my thumbs. O'Briens don't do that. And none of the job offers that have come my way have amounted to much. Quitting my job with Marc with no notice may have burned more bridges than I anticipated. Or maybe he's been trashing me, rather than giving me the references I deserve."

"Have you considered spending some time in New York?" Caitlyn asked, a desperate note in her voice. "That is where the fashion industry jobs are, after all. Or even Los Angeles or Miami."

"I know. My lack of motivation may be telling me that I don't belong in that field, after all. Maybe going to Africa would be good for me. I could be doing something worthwhile, even while I'm thinking."

Instead of being overjoyed that there would be yet another pair of hands to help out in the part of the world where help was so desperately needed, Caitlyn was filled with envy. It should be her going back.

She realized Carrie was studying her with a worried expression. "Caitlyn, what's wrong?"

"Nothing," she said tightly. "Nothing at all."

She shoved the letter back into her pocket and steeled her resolve. She would go back. She just needed to figure out how to make it happen.

And how to explain it to Noah.

10

After their confrontation in the cafeteria over Carrie's presence, Noah decided that the best way to handle things with Caitlyn was to back off. Forcing the issue certainly wasn't working. Every time he had tried to broach the subject of marriage or even the baby after that, Caitlyn had regarded him with a defiant expression and left the room. It hadn't taken long to realize that pushing her to talk was counterproductive. In what he'd come to recognize as true O'Brien fashion, anything she perceived as pressure just made her dig in her heels.

Lesson learned, he concluded. He needed to take his own advice and be patient and let her come to terms with their situation in her own time, no matter how frustrating he found the delay. Even trickier was tuning out Mick's unrelenting pressure. Noah needed to keep the long-range goal in mind.

He was at the nurses' station going over patient charts when Peyton Harris, the chief of obstetrics and gynecology, joined him.

"Do you have a minute?" the obstetrician asked.

"Sure," Noah said. "What's up?"

"Look, this is a little awkward and I'm probably violating who knows how many privacy rules, but you and Caitlyn Winters are close, correct?"

Noah nodded. "For once the hospital grapevine got it right," he confirmed.

"Then you know what's going on with her?" Peyton asked, phrasing the question in the most circumspect way possible.

"I know she's having a baby," Noah confirmed.

Peyton looked relieved that Noah was aware of the situation without him having to violate any confidentiality rules. They could speak frankly, physician to physician. Noah suspected Peyton also knew that the baby was his or he never would have initiated this conversation in the first place.

"She just canceled her latest prenatal visit for the second time," Peyton told him. "Believe me, I know how overworked the medical students are around here, but of all people, she should understand how important prenatal care is."

"I'm sure she does," Noah said tightly, wondering what Cait had been thinking. He was willing to give her space, willing to let her deal with the situation in her own way, up to a point. He would not allow her to risk the pregnancy. He simply couldn't. He could already envision the fight they were about to have when she accused him of trying to run her life.

"If she's found another doctor, I won't be offended," Peyton said. "But that's not what she told the nurse. If you have any influence at all, could you see what's going on and try to get her in to see me, or someone else, for that matter? Just make sure she's getting her prenatal vitamins and proper care. That's all I'm concerned about."

"I'll take care of it," Noah promised. "Do you have any openings tomorrow?"

"Just call my office. I'll see that they work her in," he assured Noah.

"Thanks, Peyton. And I appreciate your coming to me."

Even though he was seething, Noah forced himself to complete the patient charts before he went in search of Cait. He told himself it was probably a good thing that there was time for his temper to cool, especially when Jill Marshall took one look at him and asked why he was so angry. If she could read his mood that readily, he needed even more time before confronting Cait. Their conversation needed to at least begin calmly. If it escalated after that, well, so be it.

"Just a personal matter," he told her. "Have you seen Cait?"

"I have, but judging from your expression I'm not so sure I should point you in the right direction," Jill said. "And, to be honest, she seems to have been responsible for your being in a lousy mood more than once recently. I don't like that."

Though he might have appreciated the protective attitude another time, he simply couldn't deal with it now. "Jill, please. There are just some things we need to work out. If you know where she is, tell me."

"Okay, fine, but it's against my better judgment."

"So noted."

"She went on break about fifteen minutes ago. I'm not sure if she went to the on-call room or the cafeteria. She looked pretty beat, though."

"Thanks."

He was about to leave when she touched his shoulder.

"Noah, I'm seriously worried about you. You don't look happy. Are you sure she's the right woman for you?"

He forced a smile. "Thanks for the concern, but I know she is," he said. "I mean it, Jill. Thanks."

"Anytime."

Noah nodded and, despite his warning to himself to get his temper in check, he headed straight for the on-call room. With any luck, Cait would be there alone. This was not a conversation he wanted to have in public.

To his initial relief, he found her stretched out on one of the uncomfortable beds, eyes closed. Then he noted with dismay that there were dark circles under her eyes. Clearly she wasn't taking proper care of herself. How had he not noticed that sooner? Maybe because she'd gone to such great lengths to keep some distance between them lately.

He sat down beside her. "Cait?"

Her eyes immediately blinked open and she bolted upright. As with all med students, interns and residents who needed to be alert at an instant's notice, she had mastered the art of shaking off even the deepest sleep.

"Oh, it's you," she said, and fell back against the pillow. "Noah, I need a nap. Can whatever's on your mind wait?"

"Not this time," he responded firmly.

Something in his tone must have gotten through to her, because she swung her feet around and sat next to him, their shoulders touching. "What's going on? Is it one of my patients?"

"No, though it's nice to hear that you put them first," he said, shifting so he could look directly into her eyes. He touched her pale cheek, then gently traced the dark circle under one eye with his thumb. "What about you,

Cait? Where do you put yourself on your endless list of duties and obligations?"

She regarded him blankly. "Noah, I'm half asleep. What are you talking about?"

"I just had a conversation with Peyton Harris," he said, then waited for the implication of that to sink in.

Her eyes widened when his meaning registered. For an instant guilt flitted across her face. "Oh," she said softly.

"What's going on, Cait? Why have you canceled two prenatal appointments? And why hadn't you told me about them in the first place? You knew I'd want to go with you."

"You know what it's like around here, especially at this time of the year," she said, clearly scrambling for convincing excuses. "The residents are about to leave, so they're distracted. The interns are expected to pick up the slack until the new residents take over. Medical students fill in wherever we're needed. Things came up. It's not as if I don't know what I need to be doing, Noah."

He leveled a look straight into her eyes. "I know you did an obstetrical rotation, so I'm sure you do know the basics," he agreed. "Above all, I'm sure you understand how important good prenatal care is. It's something we preach about all the time to our pregnant patients."

"I know and, believe me, I get it. In case you didn't notice when we were at Grandpa Mick's, O'Briens have a lot of babies. Why are you making a big deal about a couple of canceled appointments? I'm taking the vitamins. I'm in good shape. There's nothing about this pregnancy that puts me at high risk."

"And you know that how? Have you been examined by some other obstetrician on a regular basis?"

She faltered at the anger he couldn't contain. "No."

"And my finding you just now so exhausted you can barely keep your eyes open, that's your idea of being in good shape?"

"It's just the nature of the job," she reminded him. "You know what it's like around here, Noah. I can handle a little lost sleep. I'll catch up when I'm off duty. That's what medical students do."

"*Pregnant* medical students take better care of themselves," he argued heatedly, running his hand through his hair in frustration. "Cait, you have to know what you're doing isn't good for the baby or for you."

"Noah, I will see Dr. Harris," she said, adopting a tone meant to placate him. "I just couldn't do it today."

"Or the time before that," he reminded her. "Why should I believe you'll show up the next time?"

"Because I'm giving you my word," she said, holding his gaze. "I'm not going to endanger our baby, Noah."

"I wish I could believe that," he said wearily. "But let's say I buy that you just got busy and needed to reschedule, what about not telling me? Why are you shutting me out?"

The question clearly flustered her. She was looking everywhere in the small room except at him. "That's not what I was doing," she claimed.

"Really?" He made no attempt to hide his skepticism. "That's certainly how it feels."

"Come on," she pleaded. "Be reasonable. I know your schedule is even crazier than mine, especially with all these trips down to Chesapeake Shores."

He shook his head. "I'm not buying it."

She frowned. "Then why do you think I did it?"

"Because you didn't want me there. I want to know

why. Have you started to regret your decision to have the baby? It's too late to terminate the pregnancy now."

She looked genuinely shocked that he would even suggest such a thing. "I've told you that was never an option," she said fiercely, her hand dropping protectively to her belly.

"Then what's going on? You know how much I want to stand beside you, Cait. I want to *marry* you, for goodness' sake."

"I know," she said. "I'm sorry. I guess I just thought it would be for the best not to drag you into this in a public way."

"You need to explain that one to me."

She swallowed hard. "Once I see Dr. Harris again, the word will be all over the hospital that I'm pregnant. You know how everyone loves to gossip. This will be hot news."

"So you were trying to protect me from gossip?" he asked incredulously. "Sweetheart, there's no disguising that baby bump. I imagine a few people might be oblivious, but most are simply being discreet. Whether you see an obstetrician once or every other week, it won't matter. We're way past the time when you can keep this pregnancy a secret. Wearing loose shirts isn't disguising a thing."

She uttered a sigh of resignation. "I know. What I don't understand is how you can be so blasé about that. Your reputation is going to be affected, too."

"No doubt about it, there will be talk," he said, understanding it probably even better than she did. He'd witnessed the grapevine in action a whole lot longer than she had.

He held her gaze. "And since we've been together for

quite a while, it won't take great mathematical skills to add two and two and conclude the baby is mine. I'm willing to make a public declaration about that. In fact, I'd like to tell the world. It's only out of respect for you that I haven't. My silence is much more likely to be misconstrued than the pregnancy itself."

She regarded him with a bemused expression. "You really are thrilled, aren't you? You don't even care if people talk."

"No, I don't. I am thrilled about the baby, Cait. I haven't regretted this pregnancy for a single second. And I honestly thought you were starting to come around. What's suddenly changed? Something has. There's been a difference these past few weeks. You've been deliberately avoiding me, for one thing. I know that's not just my imagination."

She regarded him miserably. For a couple of minutes, he thought she might remain stubbornly silent, but she finally drew in a deep breath and faced him.

"It doesn't paint me in a very good light," she whispered, averting her gaze as a tear leaked out.

"Cait, there's nothing you could tell me that would make me think any less of you," he swore. "I love you unconditionally. Don't you know that? I want to be here for you, not on the outside trying to guess what I can do to be supportive."

For a woman who'd been loved and accepted her entire life by such a large family, she had to believe she was lovable. He couldn't understand how she could harbor even the tiniest doubt about being worthy of his love. Nor could he imagine anything so terrible that it would cost her his respect. She was an amazing woman, who'd been dealt an unexpected monkey wrench to her well-considered plan for her life. She might not have reached any conclusions as quickly as he had, but she was dealing with their situation the best way she knew how.

"Talk to me," he pleaded. "I need to understand."

"Okay, here it is," she said. "I know this shouldn't matter to me, but now Carrie's talking about going to Africa with my grandparents." She blurted out the explanation as if she were embarrassed by it, then added, "Carrie, of all people!"

The news came as almost as much of a shock to Noah as it likely had to Cait. It didn't fit with anything he knew of Carrie's personality. No wonder Cait was shaken by it.

"And you think it should be you," he concluded, guessing that to be the real root of her distress.

She nodded. "Yep. I told you it was ugly. I'm jealous that my sister gets to do something I was meant to do."

He almost smiled at the way she was condemning herself for a perfectly human reaction, but he knew she wouldn't appreciate that. Instead, he focused on trying to connect the dots. "But what does that have to do with canceling these appointments?" he asked.

"I know when I finally hear the heartbeat and see the sonogram, this baby is going to be real to me. Up till now, somehow it was like this vague thing that was going to happen months from now. On some level, I just hadn't dealt with the reality of this little person growing inside me."

"And that reality scares you?"

She nodded. "I'm terrified that I'm going to wind up resenting the baby, especially right now when Carrie's going to do what I should be doing."

"And you think you'll take that resentment out on the baby?"

"I won't mean to," she said at once. "But you know how resentments build up and then you do or say things you shouldn't. What if I make our baby feel unwanted?"

"Cait, you're one of the most caring, compassionate people I know. That's why you want to go back to Africa in the first place. You'd never do anything to make the baby feel unwanted. With every fiber of my being, I know that about you."

"I wish I did," she told him. "But you don't understand how I felt when Carrie made her big announcement. It knocked the wind right out of me. It seems so unfair. She's not committed to this cause the way I am. She's just going so she can get Grandpa Mick off her case for not finding another job."

"Maybe so, but isn't the important thing that there will be help for the people who need it?" he asked reasonably, understanding even as he spoke that it wasn't about being reasonable. It was about how she felt deep inside despite everything rational she might tell herself. That sometimes-destructive trait of envy had reared its ugly head, and she wasn't used to feeling that way, so she was condemning herself for it.

She gave him a rueful look. "I'm not quite ready to be that calm and understanding."

Noah smiled at that. "Okay, let's get back to Dr. Harris. If I make an appointment for the two of us for tomorrow, will you promise to show up?"

She gave him a long look. "If you make the appointment, is there any chance at all you won't drag me there yourself?"

Noah laughed, finally releasing the last of his anger now that he had a better grasp of what had been going through her mind lately. "Not really."

"Then make the appointment," she said, sounding resigned.

He tucked a finger under her chin. "Don't look so miserable. We're going to see our baby for the first time!"

And if she wasn't quite as excited about that as he was, that was okay. He believed with everything in him that once she heard the heartbeat and saw the sonogram there was no way she wouldn't be every bit as emotional as he was. All of these other issues would fall by the wayside.

The steady *thump-thump-thump* of the baby's heartbeat seemed to fill the examination room. Tears sprang to Cait's eyes at the sound and she reached for Noah's hand. She'd heard that sound before, of course, but this was her baby, hers and Noah's.

She'd anticipated this reaction, known that it would change everything for her, but she hadn't fully expected the level of joy coursing through her, not under these circumstances. She found herself grinning at Noah.

"We're having a baby," she whispered as if it were breaking news.

He laughed. "So I've heard."

Noah leaned down and kissed her, lingering a little longer than was appropriate with the obstetrician sitting right there. Caitlyn allowed herself the luxury of savoring the kiss in a way that had been all too absent recently.

"Pretty amazing, isn't it?" Noah asked eventually.

"Amazing? Listen to that heartbeat," she said proudly. "It's beyond incredible."

"It's strong and healthy," Dr. Harris confirmed. He gave her a hard look. "And we're going to keep it that way. No more cancellations, understood?"

Caitlyn nodded. "Absolutely."

"I'll see to it," Noah chimed in.

For once she didn't object to his take-charge attitude. She certainly hadn't done anything to reassure him that she was taking good care of herself. Well, no more. It was time to grow up, accept where they were and move forward. She had a brand-new life depending on her. It might not be what she'd envisioned for the immediate future, but it was the reality.

Dr. Harris handed her a printout of the sonogram. "I'll see you in a month. Call me anytime, day or night, if anything comes up before that."

Cait nodded.

Beside her, Noah was studying her intently. "Are you okay?"

"A little shell-shocked," she confessed. She patted her belly. "There really is a little person growing in there." She regarded him with amazement. "I've read the textbooks. I've been around a lot of expectant moms, but until right this second I don't think I ever understood what it would feel like to know that I'm going to be a mom."

"If it's anything like how I feel knowing that I'm going to be a dad, it's pretty mind-blowing," Noah said. "Why don't we go celebrate? Are you ready to do that yet?"

She smiled at him. "I think I am. I think I'd even like a glass of champagne, the nonalcoholic kind, anyway."

Noah looked relieved. "Done," he said readily. "Pick the place and we'll toast our baby."

"It's about time, isn't it?" she said, regretting all the weeks she'd thought only of how this was going to disrupt her life, rather than thinking about the miracle they'd been given.

Eager now to embrace the excitement, she dressed quickly and met Noah in the reception area.

"I want to go to Brady's," she announced.

"You want to celebrate in Chesapeake Shores?" he said, clearly surprised by the choice.

"It's where my family always goes for special occasions, at least the ones we don't spend at Grandpa Mick's. Do you mind making the drive?"

"Of course not, if it's what you want."

"If it gets late, we can spend the night with Mom and Trace and drive back in the morning."

"Do you want anyone in the family to join us for this celebration dinner?" Noah asked.

Caitlyn shook her head. "No, this needs to be just the two of us. We have a lot to talk about."

"Wedding plans, perhaps?" he asked.

She winced at the hopefulness in his expression. "Sorry. Not yet. I was thinking more along the lines of baby names. I understand that the process of elimination can take a very long time."

Noah looked surprised. "You want to choose a name for the baby? That's quite a leap from barely wanting to acknowledge that he or she is on the way."

"I don't want our child to arrive in the world and have to wait around for us to come up with a name," she said simply. "It needs to know we gave the matter some thought. If we hit on the right choices, I'm expecting a couple of good solid kicks in my womb."

Noah laughed. "I think we might be more at the flutter stage right now."

She gave him a defiant look. "The point is that our baby is going to be brilliant and will react when we get it right."

"Okay, then," Noah said, clearly fighting a smile. "Do

we need to buy a book of baby names on the way down there? Your aunt Shanna probably has one at her store."

She shook her head at once. "We'll look up popular baby names on our phones," she said. "If we set foot in her bookstore, the whole family will find out we're in town. If we're careful, we might actually have an entire evening to ourselves with no one in the family the wiser unless we decide to stay over."

"Sounds like a plan," he said readily. He started to the door, then paused and put his hands on her shoulders and gazed into her eyes, his expression softening. "I love seeing you like this, Cait. I've been waiting and waiting for you to be as happy about the baby as I am." He searched her face with a long look. "You really are happy, aren't you?"

"I'm really happy," she assured him, winding her arms around his neck for another of those slow, sensual kisses that reminded her of how good they were together.

Right this second, with her blood humming and her heart full of joy, she could almost believe that the future would sort itself out in a way that was best for all of them.

Brady's really was the perfect spot for a quiet celebration, Noah concluded after they'd been seated at a table with a view of the bay. The attentive staff brought a bottle of chilled, nonalcoholic bubbly to the table at once, then discreetly left them to look over the menu.

"Nice place," he said.

"Wait till you try the food," Cait told him, her expression eager. "Nobody makes better crab cakes or any other crab dish, for that matter. And the rockfish is excellent, too. The desserts here can't compare to those at Aunt Jess's Inn at Eagle Point, but everything else is first-rate."

"I heard that," a man said, feigning a scowl as he looked down at Cait.

"Brady!" she said, jumping up to embrace him.

He wrapped her in a warm embrace, then held her away. "Look at you. I hear you're about to be a doctor and a mother."

Cait flushed. "Word does get around in this town, doesn't it?"

"Especially if it involves an O'Brien," he confirmed.

"This is Noah," Cait told him.

"Ah, the new doc coming to town," Brady said, reaching out to shake his hand. "Welcome to Chesapeake Shores." He glanced toward the open bottle chilling in a bucket of ice. "You two celebrating?"

Cait nodded. "Please, please don't spread the word about that. Noah and I were hoping for a quiet evening to ourselves."

"Take back what you said about my desserts and I'll keep my mouth shut," he countered.

"Your desserts are sublime," she said at once.

"Then my lips are sealed," he promised. "Why don't you let me put something special together for you?" He glanced at Noah. "Any seafood you hate or are allergic to?"

"Not a thing," Noah said. "Surprise us. Is that okay with you, Cait?"

"Perfect," she said at once.

Brady took another long look at her and shook his head. "I remember you in pigtails. How'd you get to be all grown-up when I haven't aged a bit?"

"Chesapeake Shores magic," she told him.

Brady left them to themselves. Within minutes, small appetizer-size plates started arriving with a half-dozen different seafood delicacies from little crab tarts to scallops wrapped in bacon. Each bite was more delicious than the one before.

"He knows what he's doing in the kitchen, doesn't he?" Noah said approvingly. "I don't think I've ever had anything better in Baltimore."

"Brady's is a hidden treasure," Cait confirmed. "He and Aunt Jess have done a great job of keeping their menus unique so that people will always have a reason to go to both places. That doesn't mean they're not competitive. Aunt Jess is an O'Brien, after all, and Brady was here first. The locals benefit from that rivalry."

"How does Jess feel about the family celebrating special events here?"

Cait laughed. "Oh, she gets her share of things. Between weddings, receptions and baby showers, we keep her in business, too."

"Interesting you should mention weddings," Noah said.

She gave him a warning look. "You promised."

He grinned at her. "It just seemed like a natural opening. What sort of wedding would you like, Cait? Big and fancy? Small and intimate?"

"There's no such thing as small in my family," she said. "There are a lot of us. But family only would work for me."

He nodded. "Good to know."

"When the time comes," she added pointedly.

"You said *when,* not if. I'll take that as a good sign."

"And drop the subject?"

"Dropped," he said at once. Victories might come in

small increments, but they were coming. "How about baby names? You ready to talk about those?"

Her eyes lit with surprising eagerness and she took her phone from her purse. "Here we go," she said eventually. "The most recent list of common baby names."

She began to read them off, wrinkling her nose from time to time. Noah saw the precise instant when something appealed to her.

"What?" he asked.

"Megan," she said softly. "After my grandmother. We have a Little Mick, but none of the girls have been named for her. I like Megan McIlroy. How about you?"

He nodded. "Put it at the top of the list for girls," he agreed. "How about a boy's name?"

"Noah's a great name," she said.

"I don't think so. We'd only end up calling him Junior."

"But it needs to capture your Scottish heritage," she said. "Rory?"

"And throw my Scottish roots into the faces of your Irish family? Maybe we'd better avoid that."

She grinned then. "How about Scott? That could be fun."

"Do you really want to taunt them that way? Or make life miserable for our child?"

"Oh, come on. Scott is a great name for a boy. Kids won't notice that we're making a little joke between us."

"Trust me, someone will figure it out and torment him," Noah said. "Let's just find something nice and traditional."

"Robert's a good solid name," she suggested. "We could call him Robby or Bobby. We don't have any of those in the family."

"And it wouldn't have anything to do with him being named for a famous Scottish poet," Noah said wryly.

"Not every Robert in the world was named for Robert Burns," she argued.

"But ours would be," he taunted. "Admit it."

"Okay, yes, it did cross my mind."

Noah gestured toward her phone. "What else is on that list?"

She read off a few more names until Noah stopped her. "That's it," he said. "Jackson."

He wasn't surprised when her eyes lit up.

"From *Grey's* Anatomy," she said with a grin. "You know he's my favorite. Those eyes of his..." She practically swooned as she said it.

"There are worse reasons to choose a name for a baby. We could call him Jack. That's a good old-fashioned nickname."

"I love it," she said at once. She touched a hand to her stomach. "What about it, kiddo? Are you a Megan or a Jackson?"

Noah laughed at the suddenly startled expression on her face.

"The baby kicked," she told him, eyes wide. "I swear it did. We have ourselves a Megan or a Jackson."

"Well, I for one can't wait to find out which it is. What about you?"

She looked hesitant. "I'd kind of like to be surprised."

"You don't have some compulsive need to decorate in either pink or blue?" he asked.

"No," she said. "This baby has been a surprise from the get-go. I say we run with that all the way."

Delighted with her suddenly light mood, Noah nodded. "Okay, then. We'll be surprised."

Thank goodness he'd let Connor and Mick talk him into that pale green nursery with its decor of bunnies and ducks. It seemed the safe choice was going to work out just fine.

11

Over the next couple of weeks as the end of Noah's residency approached and he was more and more absorbed with making plans to open his practice in Chesapeake Shores, Caitlyn looked back on their celebration at Brady's as a turning point. She'd slept better and felt more at ease with him from that moment on. Their easygoing rapport was what she'd missed during those first tense weeks after discovering she was pregnant. They might not have set a wedding date, but she felt as if their relationship was back on solid ground. She'd remembered all the reasons she'd fallen in love with him—his compassion, his strength, his generosity of spirit.

Whatever resentment she'd felt over the pregnancy had faded, too. She'd begun to embrace the blessing that had been given to them.

Oh, she still had her share of moments when she was angry about the choices she was faced with making, but in general she was too busy to spend much time dwelling on that. And, though she'd sworn to Noah that she'd never blamed him for any of this, she recognized that on some level she had. She'd let go of that anger, too, and accepted her own share of responsibility. She'd said that before, but it had been no more than giving lip service to it. Now the knowledge that she and Noah shared responsibility for this child had settled into her heart.

"What happened when you and Noah went to Chesapeake Shores?" Carrie asked over popcorn as they settled in on a Saturday night to watch an old movie musical marathon with Fred Astaire and Ginger Rogers.

"What makes you think anything happened?"

"You seem different. Happier and more at peace." Carrie grinned. "And you've stopped looking at me as if I've stolen your favorite toy."

Caitlyn frowned. "I never looked at you like that," she protested.

"Oh, yes, you did. And I know the look, because I was always stealing your favorite toys when we were kids."

Caitlyn thought back to what seemed like a million years ago when rivalries had sprung up over the most inconsequential things. "Come to think of it, you did, you little brat."

Carrie laughed. "Now there's the twin I know and love. Seriously, though, what happened with you and Noah that night at Brady's?"

"We celebrated the baby. I told you that."

"And I think that's fantastic, but you didn't set a wedding date. Why not? Why are you holding out?" She gave Caitlyn a questioning look. "I have to assume you're the one who's not ready. After all, Noah's moving to Chesapeake Shores to be surrounded by O'Briens. That tells me he's more than ready for marriage and a lifetime of meddling relatives." She gave an exaggerated shudder. "Brave man!"

"I know," Caitlyn agreed, acknowledging her own

sense of shock at his willingness to do that. "At first I thought he was nuts for even considering a move to the middle of the enemy camp, but then I realized that from his perspective all those people are allies. I'm the one they're not so happy with at the moment."

"You could change that with two words," Carrie suggested. "Or even one."

"Oh?"

"*I do* or even a simple *yes* would satisfy them. So, why aren't you saying either one?"

Caitlyn had wondered about that herself. Why was she still holding out against what increasingly seemed to be her inevitable fate? "I don't know," she confessed softly. "I love Noah. And we're having this baby. Getting married shouldn't be this huge obstacle for me. It would solve so much, not the least of which would be getting Grandpa Mick off my case."

Carrie gave her a thoughtful look. "I do have one thought, if you're ready for one more person to butt in."

"Why not?" Caitlyn responded. She certainly wasn't reaching any conclusions on her own. Pretty soon, she was going to have no choice but to accept her family's opinion that she was just being stubborn because none of this had happened on her timetable.

"I think if you say yes, it will mean accepting that your goal is no longer an option, at least for now," Carrie suggested. "I imagine that's why you were so mad at me, too. I'm getting to do what you'd envisioned for yourself."

"I'm definitely still in mourning for that dream," Caitlyn agreed. "And yes, I envy you, no question about it. This is much bigger than stealing a toy, Carrie. Going to Africa will be some sort of lark for you. I was *meant* to help those villages. My whole identity, at least in my mind, was based on that. I made a commitment to those people to come back."

"And we all admire you for that, me most of all," Carrie told her. "But your dream doesn't have to be dead. You need to stop looking at it that way."

"How can I look at it any other way? Once I'm married and there's a baby to consider, I'll be trapped forever in Chesapeake Shores. It's not what I bargained for."

"Oh, stop whining," Carrie said impatiently, shocking her. "You're every bit the O'Brien that I am. We know we can make things turn out the way we want them to, even if it takes a little longer than we planned. If Noah truly loves you—and even I, after a few weeks, can see that he does—he's going to do everything in his power to find a way for you to get whatever you need to be completely and totally fulfilled."

"How? It's not as if Africa is right around the corner. I can't go off and leave my husband and a baby behind."

"Are you still stuck on that?" Carrie asked even more impatiently. "Marriage and five kids didn't stop Grandpa Mick from following his destiny."

"And look how that turned out," Caitlyn argued. "He and Grandma Megan were divorced for years. Nell raised Mom and her siblings. I don't want to marry Noah and then wind up divorced because I was constantly running off to pursue this other passion of mine. Maybe I should just accept that the two things can't be reconciled. That would save us all a lot of misery."

"When did you, the very spirit of optimism, become such a pessimist? Sure, it was hard on all of them back then," Carrie said. "But it's turned out okay in the end. Focus on that."

"Happiness might reign now, but they all paid a terrible price," Caitlyn contradicted. "Even Grandpa Mick."

"It's different," Carrie insisted. "We're talking about one child, not five. Don't you think Noah—a family-practice doctor, for heaven's sake—is more than capable of child care? Or how about the million and one O'Briens who are always happy to pitch in? Hey, for that matter, what's wrong with spinster aunt Carrie looking out for the little one while you save the world?"

Caitlyn rolled her eyes. "You're hardly a spinster aunt. In fact, if you weren't hiding out here with me, you'd have a new man in your life by now," she said, seizing on the change of topic like a lifeline. "We both know you're over the breakup with Marc. He simply isn't worth any more grieving."

"I can certainly agree with that," Carrie said, then breathed a sigh. "Finally. Better late than never to figure that out, huh?"

"Then get back out there. Start dating again."

"I need a breather," Carrie said. "Ever since my first day in college I've been ridiculously single-minded about finding the right man and getting married. How many times did you get on my case about that and, much as it pains me to admit it, you were right. Look where it's gotten me. I've let myself be defined by the men I've been seeing. I don't even know who I really am or what I want aside from marriage and a family."

"There's nothing wrong with that goal," Caitlyn told her. "You just got a little obsessed with it to the exclusion of everything else. And who's to say there's not the perfect guy who'll be totally in favor of your being a stay-at-home mom if that's what you want?"

She took the time to truly study her sister. Carrie, who'd

never lacked for self-confidence, looked surprisingly lost. "Is a family still what you really want, Carrie?"

"I honestly don't know anymore." She sighed deeply. "Do you have any idea how much I envy you? You've always known exactly what you wanted. You set your goals that first summer after you volunteered in Appalachia. You made me feel like such a slacker because not only weren't my goals as noble, I didn't have a single one that I felt passionate about, at least in terms of a career."

"I've been obsessed with my career the same way you were driven to get married," Caitlyn told her. "Maybe we're both finally realizing that life isn't about either/or. Nell would tell us it's about making compromises and choices and maybe taking a completely unexpected path. She'd be reminding us we have to keep our hearts and our minds open if we're going to get the most out of life."

Carrie's expression suddenly brightened. "You know what I need? I need a dose of our great-grandmother's wisdom. I think I'll go to Chesapeake Shores tomorrow."

"You do realize that Nell's wisdom will also come with Grandpa Mick's meddling," Caitlyn warned.

"He has my cell phone number, so I'm getting that here," Carrie said with a shrug. "If our grandfather starts getting on my nerves, I'll tell Trace or Mom to call him off."

"You're delusional if you think either of them have any influence over Grandpa Mick. If you want him to butt out, go to Grandma Megan or Nell," Caitlyn advised. "He occasionally listens to them, and I stress the word *occasionally*."

Carrie regarded her worriedly. "Will you be okay if I go? With Noah leaving, maybe you shouldn't be here alone."

Caitlyn frowned. "Of course. Why would you think

otherwise?" A terrible thought occurred to her. "Have you been here all this time because Mom and the others were worried about me?"

"Mom might have mentioned that my sticking around could help," Carrie said. "She thought you might need a sounding board. Even though we're as different as night and day, nobody knows us as well as we know each other."

Caitlyn laughed. "And Noah thought I'd planted you here as a buffer. To be honest, I wasn't so sure I hadn't."

"Well, if you need me to stick around in any capacity, I will."

"Not necessary. Noah will be on his way to Chesapeake Shores any day now himself. Maybe with both of you gone, I'll be able to hear myself think. I need to figure out why I can't take that final leap of faith into marriage."

Carrie frowned at that. "It's when you overthink things that you get into trouble. If you want my final piece of advice, which I know you don't, just take the plunge and marry the man. You can figure out all the rest later."

Caitlyn shook her head. "You're the impulsive one, not me."

"And right now that's not much of a recommendation," Carrie concluded with a sigh. "Okay, then, think away. I'm going to make more popcorn."

"Double the butter," Caitlyn called after her.

Right this second, buttery popcorn, Fred Astaire and Ginger Rogers were all she wanted to think about. Everything else seemed way too complicated.

Noah had his car loaded up with the last of his belongings. He'd said his farewells to everyone at the hospital. Jill was the last one on his list.

"Don't you bother saying goodbye to me," she said, even as she gave him a fierce hug. "Thanks to Caitlyn's presence, I imagine I'll be seeing you around here for a good long while. If I don't, I know how to find Chesapeake Shores."

"You get lost coming to work," Noah teased.

"Which is why I have an excellent GPS in my car," she retorted.

"Are you absolutely sure you don't want to come down there and whip my office into shape?" he asked. Though he was only half-serious, he knew he'd never find a nurse who'd be even half as dedicated.

"As much as I'd love to move to a small town and boss you around, I'm needed right here," she told him. "The residents and interns need me to keep them in line and the hospital needs me to keep this floor running smoothly. To say nothing of the fact that my husband would probably object to me running away with a younger man. Come to think of it, Caitlyn might have a few reservations of her own if she knew I'd always harbored a secret yearning to run off with you."

"No way," Noah said. "She knows exactly how invaluable you've been to me around here. I doubt she'd begrudge you any fantasies you claim to have envisioned."

Jill actually blushed at the compliment.

Noah held her gaze. "Will you do something for me?"

"Anything," she said at once.

"Keep an eye on Cait for me," he requested. "She's going to push herself to do everything that's asked of her."

"And you're worried that she won't cut herself any slack because of her pregnancy," Jill concluded.

Noah wasn't surprised that she knew. He assumed she'd been among the first to figure it out, long before that telling baby bump had appeared. What was surprising was that she hadn't mentioned it before now. It was yet more proof that she was capable of discretion when it was called for.

"She won't want any special favors," he confirmed.

"And I admire her for that," Jill said. "But I will watch out for her. That baby she's carrying is going to be pretty amazing with your genes and hers." She studied him. "I know I'm heading onto dangerous turf, but why aren't the two of you already married?"

"It's complicated. She'll be here. I'll be in Chesapeake Shores."

She gave him a disbelieving look. "It's about distance? I don't believe that for a second."

Noah bent down and pressed a kiss to her forehead. "I appreciate your protective instincts, but we're going to work this out, Jill. You can stop fretting."

"What would I do with myself if I didn't fret over my residents and interns? You're all like family to me. And moms never stop worrying about their kids. I just want you to be happy, Noah. You're meant to have a family."

"And one of these days I'll have that," he assured her. "With Cait."

She sighed. "I surely hope so, if that's what you want. Now, go find your girl before I get all misty-eyed and dream up some excuse to keep you right here where I can watch over you."

"There's nobody I'd rather have watching my back," he told her. "You really are the best friend any doctor around here could have."

He walked away then, not looking back till he came to the end of the hall. When he cast one last glance over his shoulder, he saw her wiping her eyes. Even so, when she caught him looking at her, she managed a bright smile and a wave.

"You're one in a million," he called back.

"Send a note for my personnel file," she replied, then bustled away, off to meet another group of green interns and a new staff of residents.

Caitlyn hadn't expected it to be so hard to say good-bye to Noah. When he arrived at her apartment, she saw that his car was loaded with his belongings and suddenly had to face the fact that he wouldn't be around anymore. She hadn't realized just how much she'd come to count on his presence. On a professional level, he'd offered advice and the support she'd needed on the most difficult days. On a personal level, he'd come to mean so much more. A quick touch on her cheek, a stolen kiss in the on-call room, always left her smiling. Nights in the same bed had been amazing. That was where she'd discovered just how deep passion could run.

And while there were bound to be difficult days ahead as she continued her internship and residency, she finally understood that what she'd miss the most was simply his unfailing support of her, the love she'd come to count on seeing in his eyes when they passed each other in the hallways at the hospital or before they fell asleep in each other's arms at night.

"Okay, let me warn you ahead of time," she said, settling next to him on the sofa, her head on his shoulder. "I'm going to have another one of those incredibly selfish moments right now."

"Duly warned," he said with a smile.

"I wish you were staying right here," she admitted. "I know I said you needed to follow your dream and had to be convinced that Chesapeake Shores fit into that, but now I want you here, in the big city, where I can see you every day."

He tucked a finger under her chin. "And I wish you were coming with me to Chesapeake Shores," he said. "But we're both doing exactly what we need to do right now."

"Are you sure you want to be in my hometown with my grandfather bugging you every ten minutes about marrying me?"

"I'm tough enough to handle Mick," he said with certainty. "We've reached an understanding."

Caitlyn shuddered. "Why does that strike terror in my heart?"

"Because you know that eventually you'll reach the same conclusion that he and I have reached, that you and I belong together."

She heaved a resigned sigh. "I probably will," she conceded.

Noah chuckled. "You'd be rough on my ego if I weren't so sure that this is going to go my way eventually."

"I'm not just being stubborn," she told him, hoping with all her heart that was true. She tried to explain. "If and when we get married, Noah, I need to know we can make it work. I don't want to do what's conventional or reasonable or convenient. And I really don't want to get married because it's what my family expects. We'd be doomed, Noah. You get that, right?"

"I do get it," he said.

"I am going to miss you like crazy, though."

"I'm only going to be a short drive away," he told her. "Anytime you need me, all you have to do is call. And

I'll be here for all the doctor appointments." He patted his pocket. "Every one of them is already on the calendar on my cell phone."

"Of course they are," she said, smiling. "You're very efficient that way."

He gave her a stern look. "I assume they're all on yours, as well, right?"

She grabbed her phone from the coffee table. "Check for yourself."

He shook his head. "I trust you, Cait."

"I don't know why. I've certainly given you lots of reasons to question me lately."

"You wouldn't be you if you didn't need to analyze everything and reach your own conclusions. It's the same trait that's going to make you such a great doctor."

She regarded him with surprise. "Great? You think so?"

"I *know* so," he said emphatically. "You're compassionate and you're an excellent diagnostician. That's a pretty incredible combination."

Pleased, she nudged him with her elbow. "You're not half-bad yourself," she said. "I've been learning from the best."

"Okay, enough of the mutual admiration," he said, standing and pulling her to her feet. "I need to hit the road. I want to get down there and get the car unloaded before dark."

"I imagine you'll have plenty of help," she told him. "I have it on good authority there will be an O'Brien welcoming committee on hand. For all I know they've scheduled their annual physicals with your new receptionist already."

Noah looked startled by that. "Seriously?"

"Knowing Grandpa Mick, it'll be his way of sending a message to the entire community. Trust me, you're going to be very successful."

"I suppose there are worse fates for a new doctor in town than having the support of the town founder," Noah said.

"Well, none of those fates are likely to befall the father of an O'Brien great-grandchild. As long as you stick with the program Grandpa Mick has in mind for the two of us, there will be only cheers to greet you in Chesapeake Shores."

He studied her closely. "What about you, Cait? What fate awaits you next time you come for a visit?"

She shuddered at the thought. "Nothing good until we announce a wedding date," she said direly. "Which is why I'm not setting foot in town."

Noah looked taken aback by the vehemence in her voice. "You can't mean that."

"Oh, but I do. I know I'm disappointing everyone. I just can't bear to see it in their eyes."

"They love you," Noah corrected. "They're not judging you."

"I know they love me," she agreed. "I'm not so sure about the judgment part. But I do know for certain that they're disappointed that I haven't done what they view as the sensible thing yet. I hear it in Grandpa Mick's voice every time we talk. I'm actually starting to look forward to him leaving for Africa."

"And when will that be?"

"He, Grandma Megan and Carrie are going to look over a couple of the villages in September. He wants to talk to the doctors and get a sense of what they really need and what sort of help he can count on before he finalizes his designs for the medical facilities."

"You don't seem to be as upset about that as you were before," Noah said.

"I'm making peace with it," she agreed, then smiled ruefully. "About time, wouldn't you say?"

"Your turn will come, Cait," Noah said with conviction. "And when it does, you'll do amazing things."

She wished she were half as certain of that as he seemed to be. She felt their baby kick and rested her hand atop her belly. For now, she had a pretty amazing project under way right here. She needed to keep reminding herself of that.

When Noah drove up to his new home and office, thanks to Cait's warning, he wasn't surprised to find Mick, Connor, Kevin and Trace awaiting him.

"I see you've rallied the troops," he said to Mick as he exited his car. He paused to shake hands with Trace, too, hoping to win him over eventually. His silence the past few weeks had been worrisome. "Are you all here to help or is this a lynch mob?"

Mick scowled at his attempt at humor. "So far we're all on your side," he told Noah, then gave him a hard look. "That could change in a heartbeat, though."

Kevin put an arm around Mick's shoulders and grinned at Noah. "Pay no attention to my father. You won't die at his hands, at least not until after you've made an honest woman of Caitlyn."

"Something I'm all in favor of doing," Noah assured them.

"Which is why you're still in one piece," Mick said.

"Now let's get your things inside. Ma's got dinner waiting at my place."

"I wouldn't say no to one of Nell's meals," Noah said eagerly.

"None of us would," Connor chimed in. "There are very few in the family who can match her skill in the kitchen, though my brother here has come close. Kevin seems to have inherited her knack for cooking."

"I spent a lot of time cooking when I was an EMT," he said with a shrug. "Firefighters and paramedics need good hearty food and most of them were useless with everything except spaghetti or take-out pizza and Chinese food. And Gram would have taught all the rest of you to cook, too, if you hadn't behaved like big sissies about it being women's work."

"Which not a one of us would ever have dared to say to her," Connor admitted with a shudder. "I hate to think of her reaction to such an excuse. And you seem to be forgetting that Abby, Jess and Bree didn't exactly take to preparing anything edible, either."

Mick chuckled. "Yeah, Ma does think of the kitchen as an equal opportunity domain, even if she does tend to kick out anyone who doesn't measure up to her standards. She's despaired of ever getting a decent meal from my Meggie. For all her talents in other areas, Meggie is hopeless in the kitchen. Sadly all the girls seem to have taken after her."

"Amen to that," Connor said. Kevin concurred.

Noah noticed that Trace held his silence throughout the exchange, but he pitched in over the next half hour as they unloaded Noah's things from the car and from the small trailer of furniture he'd brought from Baltimore. He'd need to shop for a lot more to fill up this place and turn it into a real home, but he was counting on Cait to help him with that. In the meantime, he could make do.

When they'd finished, Mick looked around the sparsely furnished living room and shook his head. "I think you could use some help here, son. We'll put the women on the case."

Noah shook his head. "It's fine for now," he insisted.

"He wants Caitlyn to have a say," Connor guessed.

"Is that it?" Mick asked.

Noah nodded.

"He's right," Trace said, giving him an approving look for the first time. "Every woman wants to have a say in creating their own home." His expression turned nostalgic. "When I bought our house and moved Abby in with the girls, even at that age Caitlyn and Carrie had very set ideas about decorating their rooms. Carrie's was filled with frills and pink. Caitlyn's was lined with bookshelves and a good solid desk for studying."

Noah could imagine that. Her apartment now had a couple of homey touches, but it was mostly set up for function and bookshelves dominated.

"But he can't live like this in the meantime," Mick protested. "That sofa looks as if it would give a man a backache."

"It does," Noah confirmed. "But it will do for now."

Mick continued to look dismayed, but he finally shrugged. "Your call."

Connor glanced around. "Of course, it wouldn't hurt to put a big flat-screen TV on that wall over there," he suggested. "Seeing that you're the only bachelor in the family at the moment, the men could come here to watch sports."

Noah laughed. "I don't watch a lot of sports," he admitted. "Ask Cait."

Kevin and Connor exchanged a shocked look. "No sports?" Connor said.

"Not a one," Noah confirmed.

"That's just pitiful," Kevin said. "You don't follow the Ravens or the Orioles?"

"I know one is football, one is baseball, but I'm not a hundred percent certain which is which," Noah claimed, enjoying their stunned reactions.

Connor's expression brightened. "We'll teach you," he suggested. "And, in the meantime, we'll take your money by getting you to make completely absurd bets."

"I'm not much of a gambler, either. Residents tend not to put their paltry salaries at risk."

"So, no poker, either," Kevin deduced.

"Afraid not."

Both men regarded him with disappointment.

"Leave the man alone," Mick ordered. "We need to remember that there must be some reason our Caitlyn loves him."

Connor held up his hands. "Well, I for one really don't want to think about why that might be."

"Me, either," Kevin was quick to say.

"And it goes without saying that I don't want to know," Trace chimed in. "I'm still trying really hard to convince myself that this pregnancy is some sort of miracle."

Mick chuckled. "I'm pretty sure it's safe to say that there's only been one of those in history and the church has laid claim to it."

Trace merely scowled at him. "Don't take away my illusions, please. They're all that let me sleep at night.

And now with Carrie back under my roof, I have more than enough to worry about."

"You don't need to fret about her," Mick told him. "I'll be taking her under my wing when we go to Africa. That girl needs to see there's more to life than chasing men all over the globe."

Trace leveled a look at him. "And thinking about her in Africa is just the tip of my iceberg of worries where that girl is concerned."

"Don't you think I'm capable of looking after her?" Mick inquired indignantly.

"Of course he does," Connor said quickly. "Now let's go before Gram's meal gets cold." He winked at Noah. "There's no greater sin than ruining dinner."

Noah laughed. "I'll keep that in mind."

Figuring out O'Brien priorities and trying to find his place in the family was going to make life in Chesapeake Shores a lot more interesting than he'd anticipated. At least he had allies in his quest for Cait, or he did as long as he didn't manage to mess up and blow any chance of winning her forever.

12

Before Caitlyn realized it, summer had flown by. It was already mid-October, the leaves were turning and there was an occasional chill in the air. It would only be a couple of months until the baby was here. She tried to imagine it and couldn't.

Now, between her schedule at the hospital and carrying what felt like a twenty-pound weight around her middle, she was constantly exhausted. She spent what little spare time she had either sleeping or helping Dr. Davis with her foundation.

The latter at least gave her the illusion of making a contribution to a cause that meant the world to her. Dr. Davis had even included her in the talks with her grandfather about the medical facilities when he, Grandma Megan and Carrie had returned from their trip. To her surprise and relief, she'd found herself listening without envy and was able to make suggestions that Grandpa Mick had claimed were invaluable. The first clinic, in the village where she'd spent time, would be small, but it would be state-of-the-art and would, she decided, go a long way toward making up for her delayed return.

Even with everything else on her plate, Noah's visits for her prenatal checkups were the highlights of her life. For an entire twenty-four hours at a stretch, she allowed herself to focus on shopping for the baby, sharing a quiet dinner with Noah and catching up on the life he was building in Chesapeake Shores.

He seemed to have settled in not only with the town, but with her family. She was constantly getting calls singing his praises. Those calls were always accompanied by less-than-subtle hints that it was time she paid a visit home. She knew that day would come, certainly by Thanksgiving, but she was determined to postpone it as long as possible. Noah, thank goodness, wasn't one of those pressuring her. He seemed resigned to the pace she'd set for taking the next step in their relationship.

She glanced over at him now as he studied the directions for assembling the crib they'd purchased earlier. For a man who was intimately acquainted with the complex inner workings of the human body, he was surprisingly inept at this, it seemed.

"May I make one tiny suggestion?" she asked carefully, not wanting to wound his male pride.

"Sure."

"Maybe you should just leave that till Grandpa Mick comes up here."

Noah frowned at the suggestion, or perhaps it was the implication that he didn't like. "Your grandfather and I are getting along great these days. We respect each other. I don't want him to know I don't know my way around a simple project like this."

"Which is more important, your male ego or the safety of our baby, because right now it looks to me as if that crib is about sixty seconds from collapsing into a heap."

Noah surveyed the lopsided crib, then sat back with a sigh. "You win."

She hid a smile. "Not me, the baby. And before you start feeling like a failure, try to imagine Uncle Connor, son of the great Mick O'Brien, having not a single skill when it comes to construction, crib assembly or anything at all of that nature."

Noah's expression brightened considerably. "Connor's hopeless?"

"Oh, yeah. Uncle Kevin's only moderately better. He assembled a few things in Shanna's bookstore when they first met, but my grandfather went right along behind him to make sure they were solid. He said he owed it to Shanna to help her avoid a lawsuit from having the shelves collapse on her customers."

There was no mistaking Noah's relief. "Thank goodness," he said. "I envisioned all sorts of male bonding over tools I can't even identify. I was afraid that might be part of the criteria for winning acceptance into the O'Brien clan."

She frowned at the wistful note in his voice. "I thought you all were thick as thieves down there. Am I wrong about that? Is there a problem you haven't mentioned?"

"I think they may be starting to lose patience with my progress in sealing this deal with you," he lamented.

That was something she could easily relate to. "Then you can just imagine how exasperated they are with me," she countered. "And they don't hesitate to tell me that. Since they know you're on board, you probably don't get the same full-court press I get every time I answer one of their calls."

Noah regarded her with sympathy. "Now that I've

seen for myself how persistent they can be, especially when they start ganging up, I actually feel a little sorry for you."

She laughed. "Thanks, but I've pretty much learned to tune them out. That used to be difficult, but I'm getting a lot better at it with all this practice."

He put aside the screwdriver he'd been using and folded up the crib's assembly directions. "How about dinner? Where would you like to go?"

"We were shopping for hours. I thought we could stay in," she said.

"Sure. Want me to go pick something up or do you want to order takeout?"

She probably should have been offended by his assumption that dinner at home meant food from a restaurant, but he was only going by past experience.

"I cooked," she said casually. "One of Nell's recipes."

He studied her worriedly. "Really?"

"Oh, don't look like that. If you must know, Dillon brought her up here yesterday and she helped me. I called, mentioned you were coming and she took pity on me. Or maybe it was you she took pity on."

"That's good, then," Noah said, his relief unmistakable.

As Caitlyn lumbered awkwardly to her feet, she gave him a wry look. "Careful, pal. I could revert to being the princess of takeout."

"Princess?"

"Mom's the queen," she said, grinning. "Much to Trace's despair."

"He did mention something like that," Noah admitted.

"Not in front of her, I hope."

"Come on. The man is smart," Noah said. "He loves

your mom, and he values his life." He gave her a long, tender look. "As much as I love you."

"And value your life?" she teased.

"Something like that," he agreed, eyes twinkling. "So, what's on the menu? And what can I do to help you get it on the table?"

"Table's set and the meal is already warming in the oven. I can do it. Sit back and relax. Turn on the news. It should be about time for the sports report. You might learn something new about the Ravens. I gather the guys are trying to educate you on the finer points of football."

"They are trying," he confirmed. "But I'm still at the stage when all I see are the potential injuries during every tackle. I hope this baby is a girl. I'm not sure I could take sending a kid of ours onto a football field and I doubt there's any chance I could stop it."

"And what makes you think our daughter wouldn't be a tomboy?"

Noah actually shuddered at that. "You weren't, were you?"

"Not really, but Carrie and I were little daredevils. Ask Mom to fill you in on how many times we nearly gave her heart failure."

Noah held up his hands. "Oh, no. If I hear those tales, I might try to come up with some way to keep that baby in the womb until puberty."

"I'd kill you first," Caitlyn said, rubbing her huge belly.

She was on her way to the kitchen when Noah snagged her hand and pulled her down onto his lap.

"I love you, Cait." He rested his hand atop hers on her stomach. "And I love this child we've created."

She held his gaze. "I know. Me, too."

He started to say more, but she touched a finger to his lips. "Don't," she whispered.

Because if he asked her right now to marry him, she was feeling just sentimental enough to say yes. And no matter how close she might be to that moment, it still didn't feel a hundred percent right. And until she could say yes without a single reservation, it would be less than Noah deserved.

Spending the evening with Cait had been exactly the way Noah had envisioned their married life to be, filled with laughter and talk about the impending arrival of the baby. Despite his determination to wait her out, it was getting harder and harder to miss out on all the memories they should be making together right now.

He'd almost pushed once more for her to marry him, but she'd immediately silenced him before he could get the words out. Once again he'd bitten back his frustration and let her have her way.

As they sat in the kitchen over breakfast, he noted that she was watching him warily.

"What?" he asked.

"I know you started to ask me a question last night and I stopped you," she began.

"True. What's your point?"

"We never seem to talk about how you see the future shaping up," she complained.

Noah stared at her incredulously. "And that's my fault? Believe me, I'll talk about it whenever you're ready," he said reasonably. "You keep saying you need time. I've been giving it to you."

"Well, stop. It's annoying."

"Exactly the sort of rational response I'd expect from you," he commented dryly.

As soon as the words were out of his mouth, he saw the temper spark in Cait's eyes. He honestly couldn't say he regretted it, either. Maybe it *was* past time to force the issue. His current strategy certainly didn't seem to be getting them one bit closer to his goal of being married before the baby arrived.

"Are you trying to start a fight with me?" she asked. "If you mention me being hormonal, we can go from round one straight to a knockout."

"Actually, I've been trying very hard not to," he said, fighting a smile. Any hint that he was amused by her reaction really would lead to war. He needed some sort of in-between stage when rational conversation was still possible.

Cait apparently heard how ridiculous she sounded and sighed. "Sorry. What is wrong with me?"

"Not much from my perspective," he said, studying her with an appreciative look. "You look amazing. You're positively glowing. Impending motherhood suits you."

"Men always say that, especially around the time they figure anything else will set off a tantrum."

"No, they say it because it's true. A woman carrying a child is beautiful."

"I don't feel beautiful," she said, her expression wistful. "I haven't seen my feet in weeks."

"Then you can take my word for it. They're beautiful, too."

"Now I know you're lying. I need a pedicure in the worst way, but I can't reach my feet."

"Is this how it's going to go?" he inquired. "Anything nice I say, you disagree with me?"

"Pretty much. Welcome to my perverse world."

"There is one thing I'd like to talk about seriously before I head back to Chesapeake Shores," he ventured carefully.

"Oh?" Her expression promptly turned wary.

"The house is pretty bare, except for a few essentials," he began. "Your family has been all over me about that."

She shrugged. "So buy furniture."

"I thought you might want to have something to say about it," he said. "Any chance you could find a day to come down and go shopping with me?"

"Noah, it's your house. You don't need me to pick out furniture."

Her words cut right through him. "Is that how you really see it?" he asked, his tone suddenly icy.

She flinched visibly, but held her ground. "It's how it is. I'll be right here in Baltimore for the foreseeable future. You live in Chesapeake Shores."

"I know where we live *now*," he retorted in frustration. "I thought you might want some say over decorating where we might live together in the future."

"I can't think that far ahead," she claimed, though even as the words snapped out, she looked as if she might be regretting them.

Noah relied on what she said, though, not how she looked. What else could he do? "Okay, then. I'll get started on my own," he said as if it no longer mattered. "Your mom's eager to help. Carrie mentioned she'd go shopping with me, too."

For an instant, there was a flicker of alarm in her

eyes, but she refused to back down. "Good. They'll have some ideas, I'm sure. They both have great taste."

"They do," Noah agreed.

He stood up and pressed a kiss to her forehead, trying not to let his exasperation show. He had no intention of starting a fight over furniture or anything else. Maybe it was time, though, to reevaluate the odds that they were going to work this out, after all.

"I don't get it," Noah admitted to Connor on Sunday as they poured chips and salsa into bowls in preparation for a gathering of the O'Brien men for the Ravens game. "Was I completely crazy for thinking she might care about how this place is furnished? Or is the really crazy part thinking she'll ever actually want to live here? Every time I think we're moving forward, albeit by inches, she throws a curve like this at me and leaves me wondering."

"We're talking about a woman, man," Connor said. "We could take a four-year degree in the subject and still not know the first thing about how their minds work."

"Do you know she hasn't even set foot in here since that day she caught me here with you and found out I was buying it? Wouldn't you think she'd be at least a little curious?"

"On her rational days, I'm sure she would be, but she's pregnant. I don't know how many of those days there are," Connor said, regarding him with sympathy.

Noah looked around at the open, airy space with its gleaming hardwood floors, big windows and dream kitchen, every top-of-the-line detail chosen by Mick, whose expertise was undeniable.

It was a great starter house for a new family, with a

huge fenced-in backyard and close to the town green. Noah had planned to show it to Caitlyn right after the renovations had been completed. He'd hoped she'd begin to see the possibilities for the future they could build together in a place he knew she loved. Their child could grow up surrounded by family. Now he had to wonder if she'd ever set foot inside.

"You sprang it on her," Connor reminded him.

Noah nodded. "Obviously a bad idea. I should have mentioned it before we ever drove down here that day, instead of letting her catch us here like I was trying to put something over on her. Maybe that's forever tainted her view of this house."

"Too late now to rethink that," Connor said. "If it's any comfort, I was a really slow learner about this stuff myself. I finally figured out that women may love surprises, but that doesn't extend to anything that implies you've made a big decision without them." He gave Noah a sympathetic look. "Did you know that I bought a house for Heather before she'd said yes to marrying me?"

Noah shook his head.

"Big mistake," Connor told him. "She wanted to buy the house herself, so she was furious that I'd stolen her dream house out from under her. It took a very long time for her to believe Driftwood Cottage was hers with no strings attached. Thank goodness she finally accepted that my motives were pure—at least mostly pure—and married me despite my boneheaded mishandling of the situation."

"So, what am I supposed to do now?" Noah asked. "My medical practice is here. I'm living upstairs. Should I ditch it and start over?"

"That would be a crying shame," Connor said. "You

couldn't find a better place than this. It's one of Dad's original houses in the town."

"Well, what, then?" Noah asked in frustration.

"In our family we're big fans of groveling," Connor said, looking entirely too happy about the prospect of watching Noah do just that. "The men have had to do it a lot. It comes with the territory. We're stubborn and impulsive and we spend a lot of time trying to make up for our mistakes."

Noah laughed, despite the sour mood he'd been in ever since returning from his latest visit to Cait.

"You're laughing, but I'm serious," Connor said. "The big romantic gesture is another favorite. Figure out what Caitlyn wants more than anything else in the world, then prove you understand by getting it for her."

Noah absorbed Connor's advice and realized he'd just been given the best clue he was ever likely to get. From here on out, he was pretty sure he knew exactly what to do to ensure the future he wanted, one that would make both of them happy. What he couldn't figure out was why it had taken him so long to see it, when the clues had been there all along.

When Caitlyn hadn't heard from Noah in days and he continued to ignore her messages, she swallowed her pride and went in search of Jill Marshall for a heart-to-heart talk. She needed an outsider's objective perspective. She sighed. No, what she really needed was advice from the one person on staff who Noah had always considered to be a friend.

"Do you have time for coffee?" she asked Jill.

The nurse regarded her with surprise. "Something the matter? Is Noah okay?"

It was telling that Jill immediately assumed that she was only talking to her because there was a problem with Noah.

"He's fine. At least, I guess he is. I think I upset him the last time he was here, and now he's not speaking to me."

Jill regarded her with immediate sympathy. "Give me five minutes to finish up this chart and I'll meet you in the cafeteria," she said, then added, "I take my coffee with cream and a lot of sugar."

"Thank you," Caitlyn said. "I'll have it ready."

She found a table with some privacy. Though there were always people around, most of those nearby were patient family members, rather than hospital staff.

When Jill finally joined her, she sat down with a sigh. "Boy, is it good to be off my feet for a few minutes." She studied Caitlyn with concern. "You must feel that way, too. You're not pushing yourself too hard, are you?"

"I'm fine," Caitlyn assured her.

"How much longer before the baby's due?"

"Sometime between Christmas and New Year's," Caitlyn replied. "I can't wait."

"Is that because you're eager for the baby or because you're tired of being pregnant?" Jill asked.

"A little of both," Caitlyn told her.

"Well, I know Noah's on top of the world. He can't wait for the baby to get here," Jill said.

Caitlyn thought she heard a chiding note in the woman's voice, but she let it pass. She'd probably deserved it.

"Look, I know how you feel about Noah and how close he is to you," she began.

"Out of all the medical students, interns and residents who've come through here over the years, he's one of the best," Jill confirmed. "They all have a place in my heart, but Noah's something special."

"I agree," Caitlyn said softly, unable to stop her eyes from filling with tears. "And I am so afraid I'm going to blow things with him. He's tried so hard to be patient, but I know he's tired of waiting for me to come to a decision."

"Then why haven't you made one?" Jill asked bluntly. "If you don't mind my saying so, he doesn't deserve to be jerked around the way you've been doing."

Oddly, Caitlyn found the direct talk reassuring. She needed to speak to someone who wouldn't pull punches. Better yet, she needed that from someone who wasn't an O'Brien.

"I know that," she told Jill. "I just don't want to make a huge mistake. On my sane days, I know I should have figured this out months ago. I love Noah with all my heart."

Jill looked dismayed. "Then why would you believe that marrying him would be a mistake? Half the women on staff would be smart enough to jump at the chance." She leveled a look into Caitlyn's eyes. "I've told him that, too, but he wants you. That makes you incredibly lucky in my book."

"Mine, too."

"Then say yes," Jill said as if it were a simple decision.

"What if I get it wrong? I could wind up breaking his heart."

"He seems willing to take that chance," Jill reminded her. "He believes in the two of you. A word of caution, though," she added. "Even a man as patient as Noah won't remain in limbo forever. And there will always be women around who'll be eager to jump in and console him, even in a town as small as Chesapeake Shores."

Caitlyn frowned at that. "Have you heard something?" she asked, even though she doubted any rumors floating around in Chesapeake Shores would have reached Baltimore.

"Of course not," Jill said with a touch of exasperation. "He's in love with you. I'm just warning you that could change. Don't drag your heels forever, Caitlyn. You wanted my advice and that's it." She stood up. "I need to get back on the floor. You coming?"

"I'll be there in a couple of minutes," Caitlyn told her. She needed to think about what the older woman had said. It was one thing to feel pressured from all sides by her own family, but Jill was unmistakably on Noah's side. She, better than anyone else, probably knew the limits of his patience, and she'd left Caitlyn with the distinct impression that she might be testing them.

Exhausted by the end of a very long day at the hospital and fretting over what might be going on with Noah, Caitlyn fell into bed that night expecting to sleep soundly. Instead, her thoughts were whirling in a hundred different directions. She was almost grateful when her phone rang, even though it was nearly midnight. She yawned as she answered.

"You can't possibly be asleep already," Carrie said. "I called the hospital first and they said you'd just left for home a half hour ago."

"After twenty-four hours on call," Caitlyn told her. "What's up? And please make it quick, because I can't promise not to fall asleep on you."

"I thought I'd fill you in on what's going on down here," Carrie said. "Mom, Noah and I went furniture shopping today."

Caitlyn felt a quick stirring of jealousy. It was particularly unreasonable given the fact that she'd told him she had no interest in going with him.

"Really? For Noah's house?" she asked, careful to keep her tone neutral.

"Of course. He told us you weren't interested in helping." Carrie, who rarely shut up, suddenly fell silent. "Was he right about that, Caitlyn?" she asked as if she couldn't quite believe it.

"I did tell him he should get whatever he wanted," she admitted.

"And he took that to mean it would be okay, because you have no intention of ever living in that house," Carrie concluded. "No wonder he kept telling me to choose whatever we thought worked as if he couldn't care less about what went into the house." She sighed heavily. "Sweet heaven, Caitlyn, for a smart woman, you don't have a grain of sense."

Caitlyn winced at the condemnation she heard in her sister's voice. "I didn't mean it that way."

"Then what's your interpretation, because I don't know how he could have taken it another way."

Caitlyn struggled to come up with an explanation that made any sense at all. "I was only saying that I was too busy to come to Chesapeake Shores right now and look at furniture."

"Not much better," Carrie said. "Caitlyn, this is your life and I'm certainly in no position to tell you how you should be living it, but Noah's an incredible man. People in Chesapeake Shores—and I don't mean just family— have fallen in love with him. Pretty soon you're going to come off looking like the bad guy. Believe me, it's tough for any O'Brien to lose favor like that, but you just might do it."

"I'm not worried about what people there think of me," she claimed, though it did hurt just a little to imagine being viewed as the one in the wrong, while Noah came off as the local hero. "I can't let that influence me."

"Then you need to explain what will influence you," Carrie said. "It's certainly not Noah or your family."

"I'm trying to do the right thing here," Caitlyn insisted. "For Noah, the baby and me."

"Want to know what I see?" Carrie asked. "I think you keep telling yourself that you're considering all three of you, because you know that's what you should be doing. The way it looks to me, though, your needs are the only ones that actually count with you right now. I almost feel sorry for Noah."

Caitlyn thought she heard something a little too protective in her sister's voice. Noah was exactly the sort of man Carrie had always wanted. She could almost see the two of them together, and when she did, it made her blood run cold.

"Stay away from Noah," she ordered fiercely.

"What?" Carrie said, sounding shocked.

"You know exactly what I mean, Carrie. He's not available. You don't want to be in the middle here."

"And you think that's what I was suggesting, that I'm right here to pick up the pieces when you break his heart?" Carrie asked, her voice filled with indignation or maybe genuine hurt that Caitlyn would think her capable of trying to steal Noah.

"Weren't you?"

"Boy, you really are messed up if you think I would ever hurt you like that," her sister said heatedly. "I think

I'd better hang up before I say something I'll regret. I hope you're already regretting what you said to me."

The call disconnected before Caitlyn could muster a single word of apology. She knew she owed her sister that. She'd known it the instant the hateful words left her mouth. But with Jill's earlier warning echoing in her head, she'd leaped to a dark and unwarranted conclusion.

If she kept on doing that, she *would* lose Noah. And she'd lose all respect for herself in the process. It was probably past time to head to Chesapeake Shores and make her peace with everybody. Especially with Noah, she thought, before it was too late.

13

Mick had heard enough of Carrie's side of the conversation with her sister to know that it had gone exactly as he'd hoped.

When Carrie turned to him with a dark scowl, he wasn't a bit surprised. Sometimes, though, sacrifices had to be made for a greater good.

"I hope you're satisfied," his granddaughter grumbled. "My sister hates me. She thinks I'm after her man, which is absurd. I would never do that to her. Never!"

She gave Mick a defiant look as if daring him to contradict her or to suggest that she ought to make a few moves toward Noah to up the ante in this game. Even Mick, for all his certainty that they were on to something, wouldn't be quite that foolish. He was hoping to stir the pot, not open a permanent rift.

Carrie was just getting warmed up apparently because both hands went on her hips in a pose he recognized all too well.

"And, just so we're clear, I doubt Noah would ever look at another woman, at least not without Caitlyn cutting him loose once and for all," she said. "You should know that about him, which makes this whole scheme of yours crazy. Caitlyn should know that, too."

"Your sister's not thinking all that clearly these days," Mick responded. "It's up to us to give her a little shove and get this situation handled. That baby of hers needs its daddy."

Carrie sighed. "So you've mentioned about a thousand times. And I know you're right. Besides that, Caitlyn needs Noah way more than she realizes. Otherwise, I would never have let you talk me into making that call and implying that I'm interested in Noah. What if she never speaks to me again? I could hardly blame her when I'm the one who actually hinted that I wanted to steal Noah away from her."

Mick waved off the possibility. "You're twins. You've always squabbled. You get over it."

Carrie regarded him with exasperation. "It's one thing to squabble over who has the bigger room or who gets the bigger piece of cake at our birthday party. It's quite another to start fighting over the same man, especially when one of us isn't even interested. You do realize this could blow up in both our faces. If Noah ever figures out what we've been up to, he won't be too pleased, either. And forget Mom's reaction. She'll never speak to either one of us again. She hates playing games."

His granddaughter buried her face in her hands. "Why did I let you talk me into this?" she mumbled. "I should call Caitlyn back right this second and tell her everything. She'll believe me if I tell her you were behind that call. She knows the lengths you'll go to in order to get your way."

Mick refused to let himself feel even a moment of regret for making Carrie so miserable. Extraordinary circumstances required extraordinary measures. "Stop your fussing. There's no reason your mother or Noah will get wind of this," Mick said calmly. It's the one thing he was certain of. "I'm not talking. I don't need your grandmother or Ma on my case, either. And your lips are sealed, correct?"

"Locked tight," she confirmed, though she sounded a little less convincing than he might have liked. She could prove to be the weak link in this plot, after all.

Still, he nodded happily. "Then we'll just sit back and wait to see how long it takes your sister to come roaring down here to claim what's hers."

"If you don't mind my saying so, Grandpa Mick, I think you just might have gone too far this time," Carrie said direly. "Worse, you've got me out there at the tip of that rotten limb with you."

Mick laughed. "Oh, who are you trying to kid? You enjoyed every second of wiggling that knife around in your sister's back. You've got my genetic code when it comes to adventure and meddling and pushing the boundaries."

Carrie sighed heavily, but there was the faint hint of a smile tugging at her lips. Mick waited her out.

"Oh, okay," she finally admitted. "It was kind of fun trying to pull that off. Caitlyn's being too stubborn for her own good. She needs to get with the program before Noah loses patience." She leveled a look into Mick's eyes. "I'll tell you one thing, though. None of this would have been necessary if Jenny had just tossed her bridal bouquet in my direction."

Mick couldn't say what he really wanted to in response to her lament, that not catching that bouquet had been the best thing that could have happened to her. Unlike Caitlyn, Carrie needed to figure out her own value before she got attached to the first man to come along. The very last thing he wanted for her was to see her spending her life in the shadow of some man.

That trip to Africa they'd taken together had been an eye-opener for her. She'd realized there was a whole big world outside of her comfort zone and that she had what it took to make a real difference in it. He figured there were a few more lessons in store before she lived up to her full potential the way her sister had.

Noah always kept his cell phone off during office hours, though most days he found time to check it once or twice for messages. Today he hadn't even had a chance to do that. Thankfully, calls from patients came to the front desk and were handled by his receptionist or nurse unless there was an urgent need to interrupt him. Personal calls could wait.

When his last patient had left for the day, he pulled his phone out of his pocket, turned it on and found several messages from Cait. One would have been a surprise. The six he found came as a shock.

Heart pounding with fear and without listening to a single message, he hit speed dial for her number. She answered on the first ring, which only kicked his anxiety level up another notch.

"What's wrong?" he asked at once, panic threading through his voice. "Is it the baby? Are you cramping? Bleeding? You haven't gone into labor already, have you? It's too soon."

"It's none of those things," she responded. "The baby and I are fine. Why would you think otherwise?"

"Six messages, Cait. You haven't called for days and

now, all of a sudden, I get six messages. What did you imagine I'd think?"

"I thought you'd listen to the actual messages, not jump to conclusions," she told him, her tone wry. "Obviously you didn't do that. I'm really sorry if I worried you."

Noah felt his heart rate finally slow to something close to normal. "There's no crisis?"

"No crisis," she confirmed.

"Then what is going on?"

She was silent for what seemed like an eternity.

"Cait? For you to call that many times, there had to be something on your mind."

"I spoke to Carrie earlier," she revealed slowly.

Noah didn't get the significance. "Okay," he responded, then waited.

"She said you, she and Mom had gone furniture shopping."

He couldn't imagine why that was a news bulletin. She'd pushed him to do exactly that. "We went to a few stores," he confirmed.

"Did you find anything?"

"We picked out a new sofa and a matching chair," he replied, still bewildered by her odd reaction to the shopping expedition.

"Good," she said, though without much enthusiasm. "That old sofa was a nightmare."

"It was," he agreed. "Cait, does it bother you that I went shopping with your mom and Carrie? You did say you weren't interested in going with me."

"That was before," she began, then cut herself off. "Never mind."

"Before what?"

"Before I realized that my sister finds you attractive," she blurted.

Noah held the phone away from his ear and stared at it, not quite believing what he was hearing. "Carrie? Are you kidding me?"

"She told me so herself," Cait insisted. "And it would make sense that you could fall for her. After all, we are identical twins, and she's not all fat and swollen and cranky these days."

Noah closed his eyes and counted to ten. Otherwise, he was likely to burst out laughing. "Sweetheart, I am not interested in your sister. She might look like you, but the resemblance ends there. Not to mention the fact that you are carrying my child, which ties you and me together in a way that will last forever. That bond means something to me."

"I'm sure Carrie would be happy to give you a child," she said. "She's always wanted a husband and family. You'd be a perfect match."

Noah wasn't sure how much longer he could control his desire to laugh. He'd finally realized that Cait, who under normal circumstances was the most rational, stable woman he'd ever met, was actually pea-green with jealousy. The jealousy might be misdirected and ridiculous, but it was the most promising conversation they'd had in ages. He was tempted to run with it, but he knew that no good came from fanning jealousy, no matter how flattering it might be on the surface.

"I love you, Cait," he said solemnly. "Nothing's changed for me. It's not going to, either."

"But one of these days you're bound to lose patience with my indecision," she said. "I can't blame you, either. It's taking me an absurdly long time to sort through what's going on and get to a solution that makes sense for all of us. It took you about a nanosecond to get there."

"Because, as you once pointed out, this baby fit very neatly into *my* dream," he reminded her. "And you are the heart and soul of my future."

"Noah, sometimes you say the sweetest things." She sighed. "I think that's what scares me so much. You keep telling me I'm the center of your world and I believe you mean that. Shouldn't I be able to say the same thing about you?"

Noah could actually understand the depth of her struggle. "Here's how I see it," he told her. "I always knew that I wanted three things: a medical practice in a small town where I could be a real part of a community, a woman I loved with all my heart, and children. With you, our baby and Chesapeake Shores, I'm getting all of that, and more."

"More?"

"The whole O'Brien support system and the promise of huge holiday gatherings," he told her. "Even the meddling is a blessing because it shows just how much your family cares. I wish you could see it through my eyes and appreciate it even half as much as I do."

"Me, too," she admitted.

"Hear me out," he told her. "You take all of that part for granted. You've been surrounded by it your whole life. Your priority for the future has always been based on your enormous, generous heart. You found a mission you believed in and you've spent the past few years totally focused on making it happen. Marriage and a family weren't on your radar the way they were on mine. It's little wonder that our relationship caught you by surprise."

"It was a shock, all right."

He smiled at the dismay he heard in her voice. Cait obviously wasn't a big fan of surprises, not when she had her life all mapped out. He'd been a big one, but the baby had been monumental.

"You need time to adjust your thinking," he said. "Believe me, I get that. If I didn't believe you'd make that adjustment eventually, I'd have pushed for some sort of custody arrangement and let you go long before now. I'm patient, but I'm not a masochist."

"You could be a saint," she told him. "There are rumors in my family to that effect."

Noah laughed. "Not with these thoughts I have running through my head about you. Believe me, there's nothing remotely saintly about those."

Cait laughed at last. "Are you absolutely sure those images aren't of Carrie?"

"Very sure. You're the one with the ripe-melon belly and the glow."

"There you go talking about that glow again," she said with mock exasperation.

"I like knowing that maybe I'm a little bit responsible for it," he said.

"Well, you're definitely responsible for the belly."

"I love you," he said again. He hesitated for a minute, then decided maybe it was finally time to reveal something he'd been keeping to himself, something that might help to convince her just how serious he was about the choice he'd made to move to Chesapeake Shores. Maybe it would convince her of the true depths of his feelings.

"You've gone awfully quiet," Cait said, interrupting his thoughts.

"Do you remember me talking about Dennis Logan?"

"Your mentor in med school? Sure. Have you heard from him?"

"I had a call from him a few months back, around the same time you found out you were pregnant."

"Oh?"

"He'd had an inquiry from a town in West Virginia that was in desperate need of a physician. He thought the job might appeal to me. He said it was exactly the sort of situation I'd always talked about."

"Oh, Noah," she protested, sounding dismayed. "Why didn't you say anything?"

"Because I knew it would freak you out to think that I was giving up my so-called dream job."

"But that's exactly what you did, apparently. I'm so sorry."

"Don't you dare be sorry," he said fiercely. "I'm telling you now because I want you to understand that dreams, even the very best and most noble ones, can evolve and turn into something that's much better. That's how I feel about being here in Chesapeake Shores and having you and our baby in my life. It's the best trade-off ever. I think if you open your heart just a little bit, you might be able to look at the future the same way. There's a way for you to have everything you ever wanted, Cait. The only real sacrifice might be that it won't be on your timetable. Will you think about that?"

Silence greeted the question. "Cait?"

"I'll think about it," she said. "I promise."

"That's all I'm asking. Now, go get something to eat. I suspect letting your imagination run wild and all of this overthinking has left you starving."

"Not me, but the baby is a little hungry," she said. "He or she seems to be craving a pepperoni pizza."

Noah winced. "At this hour? How about some roasted veggies instead of the pepperoni?" he coaxed. "Though even with that, there's a good chance you'll never get to sleep."

"Sleep is highly overrated," she claimed. "That's the first thing they taught us in medical school."

"I doubt they were talking about interns who are nearly eight months pregnant," Noah said.

"I know you have very impressive medical credentials," Cait replied, "but your kid is demanding pepperoni pizza. Love you."

"Good night, sweetheart."

He clicked off his phone, smiling as he did so. As crazy as the entire conversation had been, he was actually starting to see the finish line ahead and was pretty sure they'd be crossing it together.

Two weeks after her conversation with Noah in which she'd revealed just how insanely jealous she'd gotten because of an offhand remark by her sister, Caitlyn was still struggling to figure out the rest of her life. Noah's revelation about that job he hadn't even looked into left her feeling ashamed that it was taking her so long to find the same sort of magical, satisfying compromise.

She'd also spent days considering the possibility that she just might owe Carrie an apology, but she hadn't made that call. She figured her sister needed to stew awhile for planting those seeds of doubt in her head. She had a hunch it had been deliberate. She also thought she detected Grandpa Mick's hand in the plot.

Alone after another twenty-four-hour shift at the hospital, she sat in her apartment staring at the walls and wondering how things had gotten so twisted around in her head, to say nothing of the actual disruptions to her well-considered plan for her life.

It was crazy that she was here, alone, her baby growing in her belly, while Noah was down in Chesapeake Shores setting up a medical practice. She'd stubbornly resisted accepting his invitations to come home for a weekend to see the renovations to the house he'd bought, the furniture he'd chosen, anything that might even hint that she was ready to accept the situation and move forward with a life with him in Chesapeake Shores.

Maybe it was irrational, but she had a feeling once she crossed the threshold of that house, the decision about the future would be ripped out of her hands.

In the meantime, though, she hadn't been able to keep herself from peeking at the house online. As soon as she'd caught Noah there with Connor and realized his intention, she'd gone on the real estate website to take the tour she'd refused to take in person. Even though the renovations remained a mys ry, she could picture every nook and cranny of the hou e.

She could envision every detail of the street it was on, just a block off Main in downtown Chesapeake Shores. The house itself was one of the traditional beach cottages Grandpa Mick had designed when he'd developed the town. There was a wide porch. Mature trees in the yard provided shade and flowerpots filled with bright red geraniums had been left behind by the previous owner. It was a home just right for a family, she thought with a troubling sense of longing. There was little doubt that she could move right in and find happiness with Noah and their child.

But at what cost? It would be the end of that dream she'd been so passionate about. No matter what anyone else believed, she knew she couldn't do it justice by half measures. Whatever she did with her future, she had to be fully, one hundred percent committed to it.

A knock on the door snapped her out of her reverie. She opened it to find her mom standing there.

"What are you doing here?" she asked, startled by the unexpected visit. "Is everyone okay?"

"Everyone's fine. May I come in?"

"Of course," she said, stepping aside. "I'm just surprised to see you. Generally you don't pop in unannounced. And you've been amazingly silent recently. Not even a phone call."

Abby smiled. "I thought you'd be grateful for that. I'm sure your grandfather hasn't been nearly so reticent."

Caitlyn laughed. "Of course not. So, what brings you by?"

"I thought you might be feeling lonely," Abby told her, studying her closely. "With your sister and Noah both gone, this place must seem pretty empty."

Caitlyn sighed and nodded. "I miss Noah." She regarded her mother curiously. "Have you seen him?"

"A few times. Dad's insisted he come to Sunday dinners with the family."

For some reason that made Caitlyn feel even worse, as if they'd taken Noah in, and left her out. Apparently her irrational thinking knew no bounds these days. She could blame it on pregnancy hormones, but she had a hunch she had her own recent insecurities to thank.

Her mother smiled. "I know what you're thinking. You're thinking we've somehow taken his side over yours."

"Haven't you?"

"I'd like to think there aren't sides. I believe there's a

solution that can work for both of you, but I get the feeling you've stopped trying to find it."

Caitlyn frowned. "Just because I haven't dropped everything and moved down to Chesapeake Shores?"

"Nobody ever expected you to do that," Abby said impatiently.

"Oh, please," Cait said. "That's exactly what Grandpa Mick wants."

Abby smiled. "One of these days, Dad has to figure out that he can't always get his way. The point is that you should have made a commitment to Noah by now." She leveled a hard look at Caitlyn. "Or let him go."

Caitlyn regarded her mother with dismay. "You think I should break up with Noah? Why? So he can move on with Carrie?"

Now it was her mother's turn to look stunned. "What would ever give you the idea that Noah and Carrie want to get together?"

"She practically told me as much," Caitlyn said. "Noah thought I was crazy, too." She shrugged. "I probably was. I suspect I jumped to exactly the conclusion I was meant to jump to."

"So that explains why Noah's been giving Carrie these odd looks," Abby said thoughtfully.

"Odd as in interested?" Caitlyn asked, her heart once again thumping unsteadily.

"Of course not," her mother said impatiently. "Odd as if something strange were going on. Since I know with absolute certainty that your sister thinks you belong with Noah, I can't imagine her doing or saying anything to give you a different impression."

They both fell silent. Abby suddenly looked as if a lightbulb had switched on in her head.

"Your grandfather is behind this," she said. "I'd put money on it."

Caitlyn was almost relieved that her mom had reached the same conclusion that she had. "You think Grandpa Mick got Carrie to plant that idea in my head?"

"Don't you?"

"As a matter of fact, once I calmed down, I thought exactly that. Carrie would never have done anything like that on her own and it is exactly the sort of thing Grandpa Mick would do. He loves to stir the pot until he gets his way."

Her mother nodded. "No question about it. Trust me, I'll have a word with him when I get home. Now, let's get back to the real issue why you haven't told Noah you'll marry him. The man is crazy in love with you. Just look at what he's done to prove it. He bought a home in the town you love. He's opened a medical practice there. He's getting to know the family he knows is important to you. How can you not realize that he's done all of this for you?"

"I know you're right, but it feels like a trap," Caitlyn said. "Ironically, he told me just the other night that he didn't even look into a dream job that came his way because of me and the baby. I know he thought there was a lesson in there for me about compromise, but it just added to my guilt."

"Guilt? What on earth are you talking about?"

"He's made this grand sacrifice and I'm holding out."

"You're not holding out exactly," her mom said in her defense. "You're exploring all your options. Sometimes it's possible to get so bogged down in that process that you can't see the answer that's right in front of you."

She picked up the notebook Caitlyn had left sitting

on the coffee table and flipped through the pages and pages of pro-con lists, her attempts to find a balance between goals and reality. "Exactly as I thought. Have these helped?"

"Not really," Caitlyn admitted. "Did you get bogged down in all the choices when Trace wanted you to get married? I might have been a kid back then, but it seems to me you panicked when he bought that house without talking it over with you."

Her mother flushed at the reminder. "That was different."

"How?"

"My life was still in New York. I hadn't agreed to marry Trace at that point."

Caitlyn just looked at her until her mom sighed.

"Okay, it was exactly the same," Abby said. "But looking at it in hindsight, I was an idiot. Don't you be one, too."

"Do as I say, not as I do," Caitlyn suggested, using words she'd had thrown in her face about a million times as a kid.

"Something like that," Abby confirmed. "What Noah has done is a gesture, sweetie. A big one. Just like the one Trace made years ago. Can't you meet him even halfway? Or are the children you want to save more important to you than this baby you're carrying and the man you claim to love?"

Caitlyn frowned. It wasn't anything she hadn't heard before and she still didn't like the accusation. "That's not fair."

"Just calling it like I see it."

"Are you speaking for yourself or can I assume the O'Briens have reached a consensus about this? Have you all come to the conclusion that I'm being selfish?" Caitlyn asked, unable to keep a hint of bitterness from her voice.

"Not selfish. None of us would ever deny that your intentions are wonderful. Your goal is definitely a noble one." She held Caitlyn's gaze. "I just think maybe you're being shortsighted. There's a way to have everything you want, but instead of trying to figure it out, you're viewing everything Noah has done with suspicion. Remember that expression I used to use with you and Carrie when you'd dig in your heels and be totally unreasonable?"

"You'd tell us not to cut off our noses to spite our faces," Caitlyn repeated, her lips twitching into a smile at the memory. "I always thought that was silly. Nobody would cut off their nose."

"Isn't that exactly what you're doing right now? You love Noah. You're having his child. But you'd rather cut him out of your life and be a martyr to this cause of yours, instead of trying to find a way to be together, especially if the solution requires you to give up anything, even for the short term."

"We're back to my being selfish."

"Shortsighted," her mother corrected yet again.

"I don't get it," Caitlyn complained in frustration. She'd been raised by this very woman to believe she could have it all. Now she was being told to give up who she was and accept a different future.

"You might not get it right this second, but you're a brilliant young woman," Abby told her. "I'll bet if you give it some thought you'll understand what I'm saying."

"Couldn't you just tell me what you think I should do?"

Abby laughed. "I could, but I suspect you'd rebel at

being told what to do, the same as always. It'll be better
if you look into your heart and get to the solution on your
own." She gave her a pointed look. "And while you're
at it, give Noah some credit. Every decision he's made
hasn't been manipulative. Nor has it been just about him.
He really wants you to be happy, too."

She stood up then and held out her arms. Caitlyn
stepped into the embrace.

"Thanks for coming, Mom."

"Whatever you decide, remember we all love you,
Noah included."

Alone again, Caitlyn acknowledged that her mom
was right about one thing: it was past time to make a
decision. She couldn't stay in this same holding pattern
forever. As if the baby could read her mind, there was
a solid kick in the belly.

"Okay, okay, I get it," Caitlyn murmured. She picked
up the notebook with all of her pro-con lists, took it into
the kitchen and ripped it into pieces before dumping it
into the trash. It was a symbolic gesture, but a critical
one. The time had come to go with what her heart had
been telling her all along.

14

Mick took one look at Abby's expression and knew his goose was cooked. His only regret was that his wife was sitting right here while he was about to get raked over the coals for his latest attempt to coax a member of his family into line. Meggie had disapproved of his interference in the lives of his children and in his mother's romance with Dillon O'Malley. In retrospect she might have been right about his attitude toward Dillon, but he stood by his efforts to see that their children were happily settled.

That said, Meggie wasn't likely to be one bit happier at the discovery that he was still at it with his grandchildren. He figured the best defense was a good offense.

"What's wrong with you?" he asked his daughter, feigning ignorance.

"Did you actually have the audacity to pit my daughters against each other?" Abby asked him furiously.

Mick grimaced when he saw his wife's eyes go wide with shock.

"Mick, you didn't!" Megan said, then sighed. "Of course you did. How could you?"

"Well, somebody had to light a candle under Caitlyn and get her on track. Otherwise, that baby of hers will be born without a daddy."

"Oh, don't be so dramatic," Megan chided. "The baby has a devoted father. Noah's never going to turn his back on his child, no matter what happens between him and Caitlyn."

"She's right," Abby said. "Which you know perfectly well. I can't believe you'd involve Carrie in one of your schemes. Jealousy is a terrible, corrosive thing. You could have destroyed the relationship between my girls. As it is, I don't think they've spoken in weeks."

"That's only because my plan was working," he said defensively. "It got Caitlyn to thinking, didn't it? She even came crying to you apparently."

"She wasn't crying," his oldest daughter told him with a hint of impatience. "She was ticked off, especially when the two of us added two and two and came up with you as the real culprit."

"Means to an end," Mick said blithely.

"What exactly was the end you envisioned?" Abby inquired, regarding him with curiosity.

"Getting her to face facts," Mick replied readily. "She loves Noah. Everybody can see that. They're having a baby. They belong together. Simple as that. And if you weren't in such a self-righteous snit, you'd admit I'm right."

"Do you see her around here?" Abby asked. "Has she rushed down to stake her claim? Have you even considered the possibility that you've given her yet another reason to stay away?"

The suggestion took Mick by surprise. "Why would she do that?" he protested. "Do you think for a single second that she'd walk away from Noah and let her sister have him? Do you not know your own daughter?"

Abby's frown deepened. "Of course I do!"

"Then you should know it's not in her nature to give up the man she loves without a fight. Just look at how tightly she's holding on to that dream of hers," Mick reminded her. "If she were wishy-washy about the things she cares about, she'd have let it go months ago. Instead, she's done everything she could think of to hold on to it. She'll do the same with Noah."

Megan smiled for the first time and gave Abby a reassuring look. "He is right about that much at least. Caitlyn will always fight for what she perceives as being hers. That's what O'Briens do."

Abby continued to scowl, but Mick saw the precise instant when her temper gave way to a smile. "Oh, I know that," she grumbled, relenting. "I just can't believe you'd resort to something like this, Dad. Do you have any idea how risky it was?"

"Only big risks net big gains," Mick said. "So, when is she coming home?"

"She didn't say," Abby admitted.

Mick regarded her with frustration. "Why not? I go to all this trouble to set things in motion and you can't even seal the deal?"

Megan laughed. "Mick, have you considered that the real problem is that Caitlyn is exactly like you? She's stubborn. She wants things on her timetable. She'll come around in her own good time, and there's not a thing in the world any of us can do to rush the process."

"I think Mom's nailed it," Abby said. "We should probably take a page out of Noah's book and sit back and relax. We've done everything we can. The rest is up to those two."

Mick was about to argue, but even he could recognize when it was best to bow out and let nature take its course. The baby wasn't due for a few weeks yet. If that due date got a little too close without any signs of progress, well, then he could take matters back into his own hands.

Caitlyn had spent her entire day off with Dr. Davis going through reports on the status of the foundation's projects in eight villages in Africa.

"There are so many more that desperately need help," Caitlyn said, her heart aching with regret that there wasn't more they could do.

"But thanks to us, there are eight that are in far better shape today than they were a few years ago," Dr. Davis reminded her. "That's how you have to look at it, Caitlyn. Never stop fighting to do more, but recognize how much you've already accomplished in the meantime. Allow yourself to feel a sense of pride in every small success. Otherwise, it'll be all too easy to wind up in a deep pit of despair."

She studied Caitlyn with a worried expression. "Now, moving on. There are a couple of things I wanted to discuss with you."

"Sure," Caitlyn said at once. "Is there some other project you'd like me to take on?"

The pediatrician smiled at her eagerness. "Actually, I was thinking it might be time for you to take a step back. That baby of yours is going to be here in a matter of weeks. You're pulling a full load at the hospital. You need to take better care of yourself right now. I don't want Noah up here yelling at me for overworking you."

"But this is a critical time of the year for fund-raising," Caitlyn protested. "People always feel especially generous between Thanksgiving and Christmas. I have three groups lined up next week to hear me talk about the foundation's work."

"And I've cleared my calendar to handle those," Dr. Davis told her.

Caitlyn felt an immediate sense of loss at having her role in this project taken from her. "You don't need my help anymore?"

"Of course I do," Dr. Davis replied firmly. "After the baby's here and your life has settled into a new routine, any time you can spare to help will be more than welcomed. Right now, though, I sense you're using this work to put off making some important decisions." She smiled, her gaze on Caitlyn's ever-expanding middle. "Seems to me there's not a lot of time left for making those decisions."

Caitlyn didn't pretend not to understand. "One thing has nothing to do with the other," she insisted. "If anything, working with you has helped me to see that I won't have to entirely abandon my goals in order for Noah and me to plan a future together. You've set a good example for me."

"If I've done that, I'm glad, and I hope you'll take a word of advice to go along with it."

"Of course," Caitlyn told her, though she was surprised that the older woman, who was usually so businesslike and professional, wanted to delve into something more personal. Such occasions were rare, so she knew to listen carefully.

"I'm a lot like you, Caitlyn," Dr. Davis revealed. "Or at least I was when I was your age. I was incredibly fo-

cused when I was younger. I thought it was up to me
to singlehandedly save the world. And I walked away
from someone important so I could do that. By the time
I finally recognized what I'd sacrificed, it was too late."

"He married someone else?" Caitlyn asked.

"No, he died serving in the military. Aside from being
a terrible tragedy, it was ironic. He would never have
joined if he hadn't wanted to prove something to me,
that he could find a goal every bit as noble as mine. I'll
always bear the weight of my responsibility for the decision he made that led to his death and the sorrow of
losing the life we should have shared."

To Caitlyn's shock, Dr. Davis blinked back tears and
looked away. When she turned back a moment later, she
was once again composed.

"Don't have those kinds of regrets in your life, Caitlyn,"
she said gently. "Not when you still have time to avoid them."

She gave Caitlyn's shoulder a squeeze, then left her
alone to think about what she'd heard.

Caitlyn took Dr. Davis's advice to heart. That night
at home, she pulled the bouquet from Jenny's wedding
from its box on the top shelf in her closet. She'd meant to
give it back to her after the reception in New York, but
she'd been in such a state of shock, she'd held on to it.

The flowers in the simple bouquet had turned brown.
The ribbon had faded. But the memory of the happiness
that had shone on Jenny's face that night was still crys-
tal clear in Caitlyn's memory.

Jenny, far more than Caitlyn, had reason to question
the decision she'd made to marry. Caleb had betrayed
her in the worst possible way. She'd been publicly hu-
miliated by a cheating scandal broadcast in the tabloids.

But Jenny had clearly believed in love and second

chances, rather than dwelling on that past. She'd taken the leap of faith that everyone has to take when walking down the aisle, that there's nothing they'll face that can't be resolved if the love is strong enough.

Noah had done everything to earn Caitlyn's trust. The love she felt for him was strong and enduring, the kind meant to last a lifetime. Surely she could hold out her hand and take that leap into the future with him, for the sake of their child and because that's what people in love did. They didn't wait for perfect timing or omens. They jumped in and prayed they could get it right, then worked every single day to ensure it.

She oh-so-gently touched a finger to the dried petals of the roses in the bouquet, then smiled as she found one of the forget-me-nots that Bree had tucked in.

"I think it's time I give you back to your rightful owner," she murmured as she nestled the bouquet back amid the tissue paper in the box.

The bouquet, which she'd once regarded with dismay, had done its job. She couldn't say for sure if it had brought Noah into her life, but it had steadied her nerves just now and made her see what she needed to do, the *only* thing she could do.

Setting the box on the bed next to her suitcase, she began to pack. It was time to go home, maybe not forever, but at least long enough to tell Noah how much he meant to her and claim the future he'd been offering all along.

It was a Friday evening the week before Thanksgiving and the last of Noah's patients had just left the office. The yard was covered in colorful leaves he needed to rake up and there was a sharp nip in the air.

Main Street had skipped right over Thanksgiving and was already decked out for Christmas. The window displays and lights made downtown Chesapeake Shores seem even more festive and special than usual. It was exactly the atmosphere he'd hoped to find, exactly the sort of community he'd wanted to call home.

When the front door to the office opened, letting in a chilly draft, he looked up and saw Caitlyn hesitating in the doorway.

"Is it okay?" she asked.

A smile broke across his face. "Of course it's okay. You know you're welcome here anytime. I wasn't expecting to see you till next weekend, though. Your mother told me you'd promised to come home for Thanksgiving."

Though he'd continued to go on all of her prenatal checkups, Noah hadn't seen her often beyond those overnight visits to Baltimore. Despite Connor's advice to grovel or make some huge grand gesture, he'd taken a step back and waited for Cait to reach her own conclusions about the future, trusting that she'd find her way back to him.

He had made a few plans, though. He'd wanted to be ready when the time came. He couldn't help wondering if this was it.

"Want to look around?" he asked.

She nodded, her expression curious, but a little wary.

Noah showed her the offices and exam rooms downstairs first.

"They're really modern and well equipped," she commented, clearly impressed.

"Did you think I'd do this without doing it right?" He gave her a rueful smile. "Your grandfather wouldn't have allowed it, for one thing. When he noticed that I'd put a few pieces of expensive equipment on the back burner, he insisted on buying them himself. He said the town deserved the best." Noah shrugged. "You know that talking him out of anything is like talking to a wall. I accepted, but I am paying him back every penny."

"Of course you are," she said, clearly aware that he wasn't the kind of man who'd accept being indebted to anyone, even family.

"The same's true with the house," he said. "Mick put upgrades everywhere, but he'll get that money back, too. He grumbles about it, but I can be just as stubborn as he can."

"Show me," she said with a level of eagerness that surprised him.

Noah led the way to the private living quarters upstairs. He showed her the fancy kitchen, the sparsely furnished living room with its huge windows and polished oak floors, the oversize master bedroom and marbled bath and the guest room. Caitlyn seemed fascinated by every detail.

He walked to the end of the upstairs hallway and opened the door to yet another room, a small one tucked away behind the staircase. He saw her eyes widen when she saw that he'd turned it into a cozy nursery, decorated with pale green walls and white trim. The white crib had sheets with yellow ducks and there were parades of yellow ducks in a framed picture, a mobile over the bed and across the back of the changing table. An old rocker—an O'Brien heirloom, according to Abby— had been brought back to life with a careful sanding and polishing of the oak.

"You made a room for the baby," Cait whispered, looking around with a sense of wonder.

"Is it okay?" Noah asked worriedly. "I know we hadn't really talked about it, but you kept mentioning ducks and since we decided to be surprised about the baby's sex, I just ran with a neutral color scheme. Connor's wife helped. Carrie and your mom picked out the furniture."

"It should have been me," she said.

Noah tried to read her expression. He couldn't tell if she was mad that he hadn't consulted her or disappointed. The tears in her eyes when she looked up at him and then away suggested the latter.

"I've been such an idiot," she murmured. "I should have been around so we could do this together. I've missed too many moments we could have been sharing."

"You were dealing with a lot," he said. Understanding that had made patience easier. He stepped closer and tucked a finger under her chin until she met his gaze. "I never wanted to hold you back, Cait. I want you to have everything you've ever dreamed of."

"And I couldn't imagine how that was possible," she said. "Not until my mom gave me a not-so-gentle shove in the right direction. Then Dr. Davis gave me another push earlier today. I realized I could still have it all, just maybe not in the order I'd planned. Lots of doctors volunteer overseas after they're established here at home. Even Gram pointed that out to me months ago, but I wasn't ready to hear it yet."

She gave him a look filled with regret. "Here's the crazy part. I was so worried about losing one dream, I almost blew the chance to fulfill another one, a dream I have to wonder if I even deserve."

"If you're referring to us, I think we both deserve to have this dream," Noah said. He put a hand on her stomach and felt the baby shift, almost as if he or she was aware that what was happening here and now was momentous, and was snuggling into the comfort of Noah's touch. "God wouldn't have given it to us otherwise."

"You've never once lost faith that this is right, have you?" she asked, a sense of wonder in her voice. "You don't have a single regret about that town in West Virginia."

"Not a single one. I recommended one of the other residents to my old mentor. He's a good fit, so it worked out for the best." His gaze held hers. "Is it really okay with you? Waiting to go back to Africa, I mean, at least for a little while?"

She nodded. "I realize that the work might be important, but none of it would matter if I lost you in the meantime. I want us to be together to raise our child. Or at least as together as we can be with you here and me in Baltimore. I want the commitment, Noah. I was raised to believe in marriage and family, as much as I was to make a difference. I just lost sight of that."

Noah finally released the breath it felt as if he'd been holding for months now. "Wait here," he said. "I have something for you."

He went to the master bedroom and took a small jeweler's box and a thick envelope from the dresser. He went back to the nursery. He found her standing beside the crib, her hand on the railing, a smile on her lips.

"Cait?"

When she turned, he caught her gaze and held it. "I've been waiting a very long time to ask you this. Officially, I mean. Will you marry me? Will you let me try to give you everything you've ever dreamed of? Once you've finished your residency, will you join me here in this town that means so much to you to make a home for our child?"

Tears spilled down her cheeks as she nodded. "I love you, Noah McIlroy. I really do. I can't imagine my life without you."

He slipped the engagement ring on her finger, then smiled. "There's one more thing." He handed her the envelope.

"What's this?"

"Open it."

Inside was the paperwork from Doctors Without Borders, forms for both of them to serve as volunteers. More than likely, it would be several years before they'd be able to submit them, but he needed her to know it was something he intended to share with her.

"Oh, Noah," she whispered. "You really do get it."

"Of course I do. It's just one of the million and one reasons I love you." Once again he rested a hand on her belly, felt their baby give a good strong kick this time and smiled. "I think our little one approves of our plans."

"Either that or he or she is kicking me for waiting so long to get with the new plan," she said, covering Noah's hand with her own.

"When do you want to get married?" he asked. "Have you given that any thought?" Even as he asked, he laughed. "Of course you have. You're not the kind of woman who leaves anything to chance."

"Christmas," she said at once, proving his point. "Maybe one day between Christmas and New Year's."

"But the baby," he protested. "It's due in December. What if it comes early?"

"It won't," she said confidently. "It was the bouquet from a Christmas wedding that set us on this path. I think it's only fitting that we celebrate that."

Noah thought they were taking a chance on having

the wedding upstaged by the birth of their child, but he nodded. How could he deny her anything that obviously meant so much to her? She was giving up part of her dream to marry him and raise a family. He could only pray that over time she'd believe that she'd gotten even more in exchange.

"If that's what you want, then that's what we'll do," he told her. "Have you got one more plan up your sleeve? Like what happens after the baby gets here?"

"That one's a little trickier," she confessed. "I'm planning on the shortest maternity leave on record. I'd like to nurse the baby, but that'll mean having it in Baltimore with me." She regarded him with bewilderment. "That's as far as I've gotten."

"A nanny during the week when you're working?" he suggested. "Me on weekends when I can join you?"

There was no mistaking the relief in her expression. "You'd do that?"

"Did you think for a single second I'd suggest you take a long leave of absence in the middle of your internship? If you think you can juggle everything, I'll do whatever I can to support you."

"Grandpa Mick's not going to be very happy that a nanny is caring for his first great-grandchild."

Noah laughed. "Grandpa Mick doesn't get a say, not unless he wants to take over the babysitting himself."

"Don't even joke about that," Cait responded with a shudder. "I suggested something similar to Mom about my little brother and she reminded me that letting my grandfather have undue influence over a child is probably a very, very bad idea."

Noah nodded. "I see her point." He gave Cait a reassuring smile. "There's no need to worry about any of this just yet. We'll work it out. The toughest hurdle is behind us."

Cait stood on her tiptoes and linked her hands behind his neck. "I'm sorry it took me so long to get here."

"The important thing is that you did." He ran his hand over the curve of her hip. "Want to take another look at that master bedroom?"

She smiled at the suggestion. "Did I notice a brand-new king-size bed in there?"

"You did."

"Then by all means, let's check it out."

"We could wait till our wedding night," Noah said.

She put both hands on her belly and grinned at him. "I think that particular ship has long since sailed. Love me, Noah. Remind me of how we got here," she said, then added softly, "And how it's going to be for the rest of our lives."

The holiday season, always chaotic in the O'Brien household, took on an added frenzy after Caitlyn and Noah announced their wedding plans at Thanksgiving dinner.

"You don't need to worry about a thing," Carrie promised the next morning after most of the family had left to take advantage of the Black Friday sales. "I'll call in every favor I'm owed to find you the perfect wedding dress." She frowned. "That is, if you don't mind me being involved."

Caitlyn hugged her twin. "Sanity has been restored," she assured her. "I know exactly who was behind that attempt to make me jealous. What I don't get is why you went along with it."

"Because as sneaky and ill-advised as the plan was,

I know you well enough to know it would work," Carrie admitted readily. "And you needed something big to shove you into realizing just how much Noah means to you."

"Maybe so, but you won't get any thanks from me, just an apology for not trusting you."

Carrie grinned. "Fair enough. Now, do I get to find that perfect wedding dress or not?"

Caitlyn uttered a sigh of regret. "Do they even make elegant dresses for women who are nine months pregnant?"

"That's what seamstresses are for," Carrie said blithely. "And I know the best ones." She gave Caitlyn a sly look. "Who's going to be your maid of honor?"

"You, of course. Who else would I want?" Caitlyn replied. "And yes, you can pick out your own dress and decide the color scheme and anything else you want to do. Just keep it simple, please. We don't have a lot of time and we don't want a lot of fuss."

Carrie rolled her eyes. "It's an O'Brien wedding at Christmas. Of course there's going to be a fuss. Do you not remember how spectacular Matthew's impromptu wedding in Ireland was with practically no notice? We can surely top that with all of the resources at our disposal here."

"All that matters to me is marrying Noah before this baby comes," Caitlyn insisted.

"You say that now, but you'll thank me someday for giving you the very best wedding memories. Aunt Jess and I will see that the Inn at Eagle Point is magical."

"No," Caitlyn said. "We want to get married at home, though I imagine we'll lose that battle. Gram's going to want the ceremony to be in the church. But the reception will be at home for sure."

Carrie frowned. "Are you certain?"

"A hundred percent certain."

"Then we'll make *that* magical," Carrie said. "It'll be a winter wonderland when we're finished."

"I'll leave all of that to you," Caitlyn told her sister. "Now let's walk into town and have a huge breakfast at Sally's. I'm starving."

"You're just hoping for a glimpse of Noah," Carrie said. "I can't believe you sent him home alone last night. It's a little late for your sense of propriety to be kicking in."

Caitlyn thought of the hours she and Noah had spent alone in that king-size bed after she'd accepted his proposal and smiled to herself.

"I know that look," Carrie said, grinning. "Don't think you're fooling me."

"It just seems as if we should make an attempt to preserve the whole wedding-night-anticipation thing," Caitlyn said.

"Not buying it," Carrie replied. "But let's take that walk. Even with all that turkey, dressing and pie I consumed yesterday, I'm ready for a good breakfast, too. And I love the Christmas decorations and the music that Grandpa Mick insists having piped into the speaker system in the town square. The only other place that's ever filled me with as much holiday spirit is New York."

Caitlyn studied her sister closely as they left the house. "So, when are you moving back to New York?"

Carrie let the question hang in the air as they walked into town. Caitlyn waited until they were seated at Sally's before prodding. "You never answered me."

Carrie sighed as she sipped her hot chocolate with a mound of whipped cream on top. "Because I don't know the answer to that. Can we not talk about this? It'll spoil my otherwise festive spirit."

Caitlyn backed off. Outside the loudspeakers crackled to life with "It's Beginning to Look a Lot Like Christmas." The song brought a smile to her lips. In Chesapeake Shores Christmas was synonymous with magic and love. In her life these days, there suddenly seemed to be a whole lot of both.

Epilogue

With almost no time for planning a fancy wedding, even with Carrie's eager help, Caitlyn went to her aunt Bree for the one thing she wanted to be sure was perfect—the bridal bouquet.

"I don't want it to be exactly like Jenny's," she told her. "I was thinking a small bouquet of lily of the valley if you can find it this time of year with maybe a few red ribbons, something that will look Christmasy without being too cheesy."

Bree looked indignant. "Have you ever known me to create anything cheesy?"

Caitlyn laughed. "Of course not. Everything you do is elegant and special."

"Thank you," she said, a twinkle in her eyes. "That was just the right touch of respect and reverence for my creativity."

"One more thing," Caitlyn requested. "If you don't think Jenny and Caleb would mind, could you put a few forget-me-nots in there, too?"

Bree smiled. "I don't think they'd mind a bit. There's nothing those two appreciate more than an old-fashioned love story. That's what inspires their music."

Caitlyn smiled. That's exactly what she and Noah were living, she thought, a love story. Of course, given how out of whack their timing was, it would probably be a stretch to describe it as old-fashioned.

They'd finally caved in to Nell's pleas and decided to have a small wedding at the church on the day after Christmas. Caitlyn had tried holding out for a simple ceremony in the huge sunroom at Abby and Trace's. It was filled with light and had a view of the bay, but Nell had prevailed. Then she'd used her considerable powers of persuasion on the priest to ensure he'd fit it in with all the holiday services and dispense with any other roadblocks. He'd given in without too much of a fuss, because that's what happened when Nell took charge of anything.

Noah was pacing the small groom's waiting area minutes before the wedding, Connor at his side trying to match him stride for stride.

"You seem awfully nervous for a man who's been anxious to get married for months now," Connor commented.

"Because Caitlyn admitted to me she's been having these twinges all day long," he said. "She swears she's not in labor, but I think she's in denial. She flatly refused to let me examine her. She told me her medical degree was just as good as mine." He shook his head at yet more evidence of the stubborn streak that was going to keep life interesting. "I'm just praying we get through the ceremony before my child shows up."

An hour later with the ceremony barely behind them and a glass of nonalcoholic champagne lifted in a toast in the sunroom, which had been chosen instead for the family reception, Caitlyn's face contorted and her eyes went wide.

"Um, Noah," she whispered. "You might have been right."

He laughed at her obviously reluctant confession. "The baby's coming?"

"Oh, yeah," she said. "Any minute, if I'm any judge of these things. I think getting to a hospital is out of the question."

Which is why their son, Jackson Noah O'Brien McIlroy, his Irish and Scottish heritage now formally noted, was born in the house where Caitlyn grew up, in her very bed, in fact. His father delivered him with a whole slew of O'Briens just outside the door, waiting noisily and impatiently for the news of his arrival.

"He's beautiful," Caitlyn said when Noah placed their son in her arms.

"Looks like his mom with that red hair," Noah said. He nodded toward the door. "Think he's ready to meet the family?"

She smiled. "Absolutely. I think he's going to feel blessed to be a part of it."

"At least until his great-granddaddy decides to try to run his life," Noah said.

Cait held his gaze. "Are you complaining? We're here today, in part at least, because of him."

Noah laughed. "You sure about that? I'm thinking it's more in spite of him." He brushed one of those wayward curls he loved from her forehead. "And because we were just meant to be together."

"Amen," she whispered. "But let's not tell him that. He likes believing this family can't stay on track without him."

Noah nodded. "It wouldn't be the same, that's for sure. Mick O'Brien is one of a kind."

"So are you," she told him.

Noah opened the door and then got out of the way as the O'Briens rushed past him to get a first glimpse of the newest member of the family. To his surprise, it was Mick who held back, his eyes misty.

"Thank you," Mick said quietly.

"For what?"

"Making my girl happy."

Noah put an arm around the older man's shoulders. "I plan to do my best to see that her happiness lasts a lifetime."

Mick nodded. "I couldn't ask for more."

They stood side by side, watching the joyous scene before them, for once in perfect harmony. Knowing the O'Brien temperament, Noah imagined there'd be plenty of dissension in the future, but, God willing, there would be many more moments just like this one. He'd certainly do his best to see to it.

* * * * *

Turn the page for an exclusive
CHESAPEAKE SHORES *novella*
BAYSIDE RETREAT
from #1 New York Times
bestselling author Sherryl Woods.

BAYSIDE RETREAT

1

"Retreat?" Jaime Alvarez groused disparagingly as he hobbled onto the front porch of the cottage that Mick O'Brien had insisted he use for his recovery. The cheerful yellow sign with its bright blue lettering that was hanging above the front steps might declare it a quaint Bayside Retreat, but for him it might as well be a prison.

Ever since he'd tumbled off a roof and broken half the bones in his right leg, he'd been completely out of sorts. Who wouldn't be with a whole lot of hardware now holding him together and a cast up to his hip that restricted his mobility to whatever he could accomplish on crutches? The doctors and nurses had repeatedly reminded him he should be very grateful just to be alive.

At first, when his boss and longtime business mentor had shown up in that little town Jaime had designed and the company was building on a scenic Puget Sound cove in the Pacific Northwest, Jaime had been grateful to see a friendly face. He'd been too groggy and in too much pain to argue when Mick had put him on a private jet and flown him back to Maryland.

Their first stop had been Johns Hopkins in Baltimore

to see a top orthopedic surgeon and assure Mick that Jaime had been treated properly. Within 24 hours of that, Jaime had been ensconced in this cottage on the bay in Chesapeake Shores, where Mick could rest easy knowing that the O'Briens would see to it that Jaime had everything he needed.

Now, however, three weeks into what promised to feel like a lifetime of tedium, he wasn't feeling the gratitude. He wanted to work. He *needed* to work. For more than twenty years now he'd been first an eager-to-learn intern, then Mick's executive assistant and then the top designer and architect on small planned communities of his own, under the umbrella of Mick's company. That was the only life Jaime knew. He'd been married to his job, which had always suited Jaime—and Mick—just fine.

Now, apparently, Mick was all caught up in some crazy notion that the world should exist in pairs. On that endless plane ride across the country, he'd lectured Jaime about getting balance into his life, finding the right woman, settling down and having a family while he was still young enough to enjoy them. Thank heaven he'd been too doped up on painkillers for most of Mick's words to set off alarm bells.

A couple of days later, when he'd been settled in at the bayside bungalow with O'Briens wandering through the house at all hours with food and offers to do whatever he needed done, it finally registered with Jaime that Mick had sentenced him to take an actual vacation. Mick refused to allow a computer in the house. Jaime's calls to the local office received a friendly enough response, and there was even a visit or two from other architects on Mick's team, but not a one would bring Jaime so much as a pencil or a sketchpad, much less his laptop with its sophisticated design apps. The secretaries on whom his charm usually worked were suddenly too busy to chat. They quickly passed him off to the less-susceptible men.

"Uncle Mick's orders," Matthew O'Brien finally admitted on his second visit. "He thinks it's long past time for you to take a break."

"And do what? Go stir-crazy? You ask your uncle just how he would have felt when he was building this company if someone had sent him on vacation in the middle of a project."

Matthew had only grinned. "Yeah, well, that's exactly what broke up his marriage to Aunt Megan all those years ago. Now that my uncle has reformed, he wants to make sure the rest of us see the error of his ways."

"But I'm not married," Jaime argued in frustration.

"And that, as he sees it, is the worst sin of all. A successful man past forty should have a wife and a houseful of kids. If it's up to Uncle Mick, there will be wedding bells before you ever get out of that cast."

Jaime had stared at him in shock. "I need a drink."

"Sorry, pal. You can't drink while you're taking pain-killers," Matthew had responded. "Anything else I can bring you?"

It was a testament to how single-focused Jaime's life had been for years now that he couldn't think of a single thing that might alleviate his boredom. A book or two might help, but he was so used to reading his favorite authors in brief snatches, he doubted he could concentrate for hours on end, no matter how good the story might be. And there wasn't a single woman who'd come running if he picked up the phone and called. Or, maybe the truth was, many might eagerly accept his invitation, but there were none he'd want to spend more than an evening with.

"Could you at least bring me the reports on progress at the Puget Sound project?" he'd pleaded. "Maybe have the guys out there send some pictures?"

"I can do that," Matthew agreed then took off, leaving Jaime to stare at the bay and wonder how he'd ended up here, not just in Chesapeake Shores, but in his early forties without a family of his own or even the kind of friends he could count on in a crisis. He had Mick—all of the O'Briens, for that matter—but that wasn't the same as having buddies to drink with or women with whom he shared a real connection. To his regret, he realized that was probably the point Mick had been trying to make.

Now, standing at the top of the two steps that led down to the sidewalk, he debated risking the maneuver just to pick up the morning paper that had been tossed on the lawn despite his repeated calls, asking that it be left on the porch. Apparently, whoever drove by and tossed the thing had a lousy arm or bad hearing.

Up until his fall off that roof in a freak accident, Jaime had been considered as nimble as a mountain goat. Surely he could make it down a couple of steps and a few feet into the yard with the assistance of a sturdy railing and his crutches.

Feeling like a baby who hadn't quite mastered his footing, he eased down to the sidewalk then across the lawn to the newspaper. He stood there staring at it, stymied. Bending with a cast to his hip and staying balanced wasn't exactly an easy maneuver. He was plotting it out in his head, when he heard a *whish* of sound that announced the sprinklers were coming on. Before he could take a single step, much less grab that paper, he was soaked to the skin.

Uttering a string of profanity, he hobbled away from the sprinkler's reach, only to look straight into the face of a woman whose chiding expression could have silenced an entire room filled with unruly children.

"Really? Is that any sort of language to use in a neighborhood where children live?" she scolded.

Jaime recognized that look and that tone, because his mother would have said much the same thing, only this woman appeared to be anything but motherly. She was in her thirties, he guessed. She was slender, with long, shapely legs displayed by her running shorts and a surprisingly curvy torso, shown off by a sports bra covered by a tank top. Thick chestnut hair had been scooped into a careless ponytail. Now if she were his angel of mercy, perhaps the next few weeks of recovery wouldn't be quite so painful.

Unfortunately, she didn't look terribly sympathetic.

"Sorry, that was three weeks of frustration spewing out," he apologized. "I didn't realize anyone could hear me." He tried out a rusty smile, the one everyone told him could charm the halo off an angel. This might be the perfect time to discover if that were true. "I'm Jaime Alvarez."

She hesitated then nodded. "Emma Hastings. I didn't realize someone had bought Bayside Retreat."

"I didn't buy it. It's just on loan to me from Mick O'Brien, while my leg heals."

For the first time since she'd confronted him, her expression warmed. "Ah, you know Mick?"

Jaime laughed. "Doesn't everyone in this town? He built it, after all."

"Fair enough. Then tell me this. How do you know him?"

"I've worked with him for years," Jaime replied. "I was lucky enough to get an internship with the company while I was still studying architecture. By the time I'd graduated, I was Mick's executive assistant and soon after was designing my own projects for the firm."

Though her expression was warmer, she didn't look entirely convinced. "I've never seen you around town."

"I've handled on-site management all over the country for Mick. I was working in the Pacific Northwest when I toppled off a roof. Mick insisted I come back here to mend. He wants me to think of it as a long-overdue vacation. I view it as more of a prison sentence."

She laughed at that, blue eyes sparkling even brighter than the morning sun on the bay. "A bit of a workaholic, are you?"

"So they tell me." He shrugged. "What can I say? I love what I do."

"We should all be so lucky," she said, her tone hinting at dissatisfaction.

"Dead-end job?" Jaime asked. "Want to come in for a cup of coffee and tell me about it?"

"Sorry, I can't. I have to finish my run and get to that *dead-end* job on time. See you around, Jaime. Can you get back inside okay?"

"I think so, but you might take a peek to see if I'm on the ground when you pass by on your way home."

"I'll do that," she promised.

"And you'll stop by soon for that cup of coffee?" he pressed, feeling a sense of urgency to get that much of a commitment from her.

"Sure. In the meantime, watch that language."

"It's a promise," he said as he watched her head back to the road and take off at an impressive clip. Clearly she was a woman who took her running seriously. Maybe one of these days, he'd be able to join her.

But first he had to get back to walking on his own two feet again.

* * *

Emma ran until she was out of breath and her legs felt wobbly. For once her workout hadn't been about pushing all thoughts of her disastrous marriage or her recent writer's block out of her head, but getting rid of those delicious images of a soaking-wet Jaime Alvarez. His T-shirt had clung to an impressive chest and biceps likely toned by hard work, rather than workouts. Damp, his coal-black hair had curled in a way he no doubt detested. And that smile… She sighed just thinking about it. It could curl the toes of an angel.

Yes, indeed, Jaime Alvarez was quite possibly the sexiest man with whom she'd ever crossed paths, so definitely not her type. If she ever had another relationship—and that was a huge and probably insurmountable *if*—it wouldn't be with a man who likely had women falling at his feet. Been there, done that, wrote the book on it. Literally.

Emma had dissected the end of her marriage to a man just like Jaime in a bestselling book. She'd laid bare all of her emotions, every insecurity, every destructive, hurtful act that had chipped away her self-esteem. It had been published as fiction, but there wasn't a paragraph in those pages that she hadn't lived.

In the book, though, the heroine triumphed. Emma really envied that.

In real life, Emma had retreated to Chesapeake Shores and taken a job at the library, working for her mother, because it was safe and the hours were flexible enough to allow her time to write another bestseller…if only she could. That wasn't the triumphant ending that had drawn readers to her first book. Rather, it was downright pitiful.

"But I'm going to fix that," she promised herself as she showered and walked to the library that had been

built eight years ago and over which her mother ruled
with an iron fist. Emma might have scolded Jaime for
his language in her best imitation of Jessica Hastings'
censure, but Jessica herself might well have gone a step
further. She would have reported him to Mick as being
a bad influence and suggested he be run out of town.

"You're late," her mother said when Emma walked
into the bright airy library.

No good morning. No asking if everything was okay.
That was her mom, a stickler for the rules, even when it
came to her only child. Rather than taking the attitude
to heart, Emma focused on her surroundings. Mick had
done himself proud with this building. The main room
was filled with sunlight filtered by a grove of surrounding trees. In the spring a garden of azaleas bloomed
right outside the windows, and benches invited readers
to sit quietly and enjoy the small, burbling fountain in
the middle of the peaceful setting.

Restored by the sight, Emma forced a bright smile.
"Sorry. I stopped to help a neighbor."

Now that was something Jessica understood. She was
all about good deeds. "You met a neighbor? How wonderful! Someone new to town?"

"In a way, I guess. He works for Mick O'Brien, but
from what he said, he mostly handles Mick's projects
in other parts of the country. He's here now because he
fell off a roof at a construction site and broke his leg."

"Oh, dear. The poor thing must be miserable if he's
used to being busy." A worrisome, calculating expression crossed her face. "You should make a casserole and
take it over. I'm sure he'd appreciate it."

Emma smiled at the predictable suggestion. "Mom,
he has Mick looking out for him, which means all of

the O'Briens are looking out for him. I doubt he needs another casserole."

"Then perhaps you can pick out a few books you think he might like and take those by. Now that's something you're more than qualified to do. I doubt anyone else has thought of it."

Emma loved to read, a passion that her mother had inspired in her at an early age. She'd always thought having a librarian as a mom, despite Jessica's sometimes starchy demeanor, made her the luckiest girl in the world. She'd grown up with unlimited access to the newest books, and no one had ever chastised her for preferring to sit on the front porch with a book to hanging out with a bunch of giggling teenage girls and hormonal boys.

Of course, maybe that was why she'd been so unprepared to deal with a man like her ex-husband. He'd been handsome. He'd possessed Southern charm to spare. And he'd been determined to win over the only girl in the entire freshman class at the University of Alabama who hadn't given him a second glance.

In retrospect she'd seen that the whole romance had been about the challenge. Derek Watkins, as she'd discovered much too late, had taken a dare that he could convince the shy little wallflower to go out with him. Emma had said *no* repeatedly, which had only fueled his determination.

Ironically, she hadn't been playing hard to get. She'd been terrified. A worldly man like Derek had seemed larger than life, a hero out of the pages of a book. Clark Gable as Rhett Butler had come to mind the first time she'd met him, in fact. She'd long since accepted her limitations. She wasn't Scarlet O'Hara. She wasn't anybody's heroine.

But a part of her had apparently wanted to be, and eventually she'd allowed herself to be convinced to go on a first date, then a second. By their sophomore year they'd been a couple. To her shock, Derek had asked her to marry him just before graduation from college. By then he'd managed to convince her that their love had been inevitable, that it was real and lasting.

Only later had she discovered that he was just fulfilling his parents' demand that he settle down. She wasn't exactly a trophy wife. She was smart, presentable and eager to please. Apparently, that was sufficient proof that the previously reckless, devil-may-care Derek was capable of making good choices and being responsible enough to manage his trust fund. His parents had adored her.

For a couple of years Derek had put on a good show of being a loving and faithful husband. He hid his affairs. After that he didn't bother, assuming Emma was so grateful to have such a prize in her life that she'd ignore the behavior. And, stupid woman that she was, she had until she'd overheard one of their friends whispering about what was going on behind her back and wondering why on earth she put up with it.

Emma considered the evidence to which she'd clearly been blind, did the math and concluded she was the most naive woman on the planet. She didn't like the label.

The very next day she'd walked out, filed for divorce and moved to Chesapeake Shores to join her mother, who was in full command of the new library and blessedly short on part-time help.

A few months later, after frenzied writing day and night, Emma had submitted her first book to a publisher. A year after that it had hit store shelves. Her story resonated with a whole lot of women, because sales had immediately skyrocketed, which Emma actually found a little sad. Were so many women living lives of quiet desperation that a book about a woman who'd gotten out of a lousy marriage actually inspired them?

"Emma!"

She blinked and saw that her mother was regarding her with a worried frown. "What?"

"I've been talking for the past couple of minutes about books I think this new friend of yours might like. Did you hear a word I said?"

"Not really," she admitted ruefully. "Sorry, Mom."

"Sometimes I don't know what goes on in that head of yours," Jessica said with real regret. "Why don't you shelve all those books that I checked in earlier? We can discuss books for your new neighbor later."

"Sure, Mom."

With a sigh, Emma went to work on the tedious task that would keep her occupied for the rest of the morning. As she shelved the books, she discovered several to put aside for herself, but none she thought might appeal to the man she'd met that morning. Why was she not surprised? All she really knew about him was that he could curse like a sailor, was sick of being cooped up in that charming little cottage and that her hardened heart had taken a couple of surprising little stutter steps when they met.

That last was more than enough reason to stay far, far away from him.

"Why's your newspaper soaking wet?" Mick inquired when he stopped by for his daily visit with Jaime. He held the soggy mess in one hand, scanning the living room for a trash can.

"Sprinkler came on," Jaime reported succinctly.

"And the paper hadn't made it onto the porch," Mick concluded. "I thought you'd called and explained the situation."

"Several times. It's okay. I can survive without the paper. That's what TV news is for, right?"

Mick gave him a sharp look. "You seem a little testier than usual this morning. Something happen?"

"When the sprinkler came on and soaked me, too, a neighbor caught me expressing my annoyance," Jaime said with regret. "She wasn't impressed."

"And this neighbor was someone you'd otherwise like to impress?" Mick asked, his eyes lighting up. "Female? Pretty?"

Jaime recognized that gleam. He'd seen it often enough. "Yes to both, but get any ideas about matchmaking out of your head, Mick. You're my boss. My social life is no concern of yours."

"When was the last time you actually had a social life?"

"I've dated plenty," Jaime said defensively.

"Name one woman you've been serious about in all the years I've known you. And remember we met when you were still a wet-behind-the-ears kid, totally focused on college and work. You're, what, forty-two now? I don't see that much has changed."

"There was Yvette," Jaime said at once, thinking fondly of the woman with big blue eyes, a pixie haircut and incredible athleticism in bed.

"Yvette was perfectly safe because she lived in Paris and had no interest in moving to the States. Name an available woman." When Jaime remained silent, Mick gave a nod of satisfaction. "I thought so."

"Mick, not every man is cut out for marriage."

"The ones who claim they aren't just haven't found the right partner," Mick countered. "Tell me more about this neighbor."

At Jaime's scowl, Mick only grinned. "Okay, at least tell me her name."

"Now, why would I tell you that? So you can go off and interrogate her?"

"I wouldn't do that," Mick protested indignantly.

Jaime laughed. "I know a whole slew of people in your family who'd say otherwise. Why don't you go pester one of them? I'm fine. Thanks for stopping by."

Mick actually looked startled. "You're kicking me out?"

"I am unless you want to sit down and fill me in on everything that's going on at work, maybe bring me my laptop so I can stay on top of things for myself."

Mick slapped him on the back. "Not happening, pal. You enjoy this break. Make the most of it. If you feel up to going to Luke's pub later, let me know and I'll come by to pick you up."

As Mick left, Jaime glanced down at his restricting cast and shook his head. To his way of thinking, a vacation would involve waterskiing, maybe some hiking, definitely some sailing and kayaking. This wasn't a vacation. It was torture.

And the only interesting prospect for breaking up the tedium had literally run away this morning without a backward glance.

2

After her half day at the library ended, Emma grabbed a tuna salad sandwich on a buttery croissant at Sally's Café and ate it sitting on one of the benches along Shore Road. She never tired of views of the bay, the ospreys and occasional eagles that swooped through the blue sky or the laughter that drifted from children playing along the shoreline. The absence of that view was her only regret about the little house she'd bought a few months ago after living with her mom when she'd first moved to town. The only cottage she'd been able to afford wasn't on the water, though if she peered between the trees in the fall, she could catch a glimpse of it across the road.

Today, feeling surprisingly content, she basked in the sunshine and view as she ate her late lunch then debated going home to stare at her computer screen in the hope that inspiration for a second novel would finally strike. Instead, she opted for some surefire fiction by heading to the bookstore. That pile of books she'd put aside at the library would only last so long.

Emma found the owner, Shanna, an O'Brien by marriage, leafing through a catalog of upcoming books.

They'd become instant friends when Emma moved to town and discovered the little shop with the outstanding collection of the latest books. Best of all, there hadn't been a single copy of her old bestseller on the shelves to taunt her. Of course, Shanna had ordered it the minute she'd realized a local resident had written a novel, but at least she didn't make a fuss about it or ask when the next book might be coming out.

"Oh, perfect timing," Emma said eagerly, pouring herself a cup of Shanna's notoriously weak coffee and joining her friend at a table in her little coffee area. "What's coming out next month? Anything good?"

Shanna chuckled. "You can't find enough books in the library?"

"Are there ever enough?" Emma asked, though she could feel color climb into her cheeks. It was true, as a bookaholic she did have an embarrassment of riches at her disposal.

"I suppose not," Shanna agreed. Her expression turned thoughtful. "I don't know why I haven't thought of this before, Emma. You probably read as much as or more than anyone else in town, including me. Why don't you join our book club?"

Emma was startled by the invitation. "I thought it wasn't a real book club. Aren't all the members O'Briens? And isn't it just an excuse to get together and gossip about your men and whatever the hottest news in town might be?"

"Mostly," Shanna agreed. "But it would be really nice for me to have at least one other person there who might actually read the book." Her expression brightened. "Or we could start another club here at the store. I do have a few customers who might be interested. They're more serious readers than anyone in my family, much to my regret."

More than ready to spend an occasional evening with company other than her own, Emma nodded at once. "Sure. Count me in for either one."

Shanna looked surprised. "Seriously? You'd be interested?"

"Why not? It would be fun to talk to other people about books they're reading. It's the best way I know to discover new authors."

"You mean aside from working in a library and hanging out with a bookstore owner?" Shanna teased.

Emma laughed. "Yes, aside from that. As to the other topic of discussion, I am woefully ignorant about town gossip, so that could be fun, too."

"Then I'll see what I can pull together, either with the family or here at the store. I'll let you know when I have something specific." She hesitated. "Changing directions, don't you live at the end of Wisteria Lane in that cute little bungalow with all the wisteria arbors in the garden?"

Emma nodded.

"Would you consider doing me a favor, then? Do you have a little time to spare?"

"Absolutely. Anything you need."

"I took a phone order earlier from someone and promised I'd have the books dropped by. He can't get around so easily. I was going to do it myself, but Davey has a soccer game, and I promised I'd be there the minute I close up tonight. My son, bless his heart, was skeptical. To my regret, he has reason to be. I've let him down too many times lately, thanks to being swamped at this place and with his two younger siblings. All that babysitting

I was counting on my oldest to handle?" She shook her head and sighed. "Henry's a great kid, but he's not really into it, at least not as often as I could use him. Now that he's getting ready for his senior year and looking at colleges, I can only play the mom card every so often."

Emma felt a little tug of anticipation even as she asked, "Is your customer Jaime Alvarez, by any chance?"

Shanna's eyes lit up. "Ah, so you know him?"

"We met this morning."

"Perfect, then I won't be asking you to stop by some total stranger's. It shouldn't take more than a minute. Jaime's not feeling very social these days."

"So I gathered."

"Uh-oh. Did you two get off on the wrong foot?"

Emma described their meeting that morning. "I came off as a snippy librarian. I sounded a lot like my mom, I'm afraid."

Shanna chuckled. "Knowing Jaime, that just fueled his interest."

"He's a big flirt?"

"Always has been," Shanna said. "Doesn't matter if a woman is short, tall, thin or fat, married or single, Jaime flirts. It's very flattering, as long as a woman's smart enough not to take him seriously. I don't think he's a settling down kind of man. Of course, I've only been around him when he joins the family for dinners at Mick's on these whirlwind visits of his. Could be my impression is all wrong."

"Unfortunately, that was my impression, too," Emma admitted.

"Just flirt back. It's good practice," Shanna advised. "I'll grab those books for you."

Emma reluctantly accepted the bag and headed toward home, her steps dragging as she got closer and closer to Bayside Retreat with its neat lawn and a flower garden that needed tending. Before turning up the walk, she finally gave in to the urge to peek inside the bag.

A new James Patterson thriller. Predictable. A Louise Penny mystery. Hmm. That was less predictable—a little intriguing, in fact. And what was this last one? A signed first edition of an old Thomas Black mystery by Earl Emerson, a Seattle author. That series had been one of Emma's secret vices. Thomas was a little sexist, but the relationship in the books was wonderfully written.

"Find anything interesting in there?" an already familiar masculine voice taunted from the shadows of the front porch.

Emma nearly dropped the books. Knowing her cheeks had flushed red, she took her time approaching the house. "Sorry. I work at the town library. I love books. I couldn't help wondering what you'd chosen."

"You could have waited and asked," he suggested, though the twinkle in his eyes hinted he wasn't all that offended by her prying.

"I suppose that would have been the polite, less-nosy way of handling it. Or I could have asked Shanna what you'd ordered when she asked me to drop them off." She noted that he looked no less delicious in his perfectly dry, well-worn jeans and a faded University of Washington T-shirt. One leg of the pants had been cut off to accommodate the cumbersome cast. "Were you expecting me?"

He nodded, a grin spreading across his face. "Shanna called and alerted me to clean up my language before you got here." He studied her with warm brown eyes. "So, the two of you were talking about me. I'm flattered."

"You wouldn't be, if you'd heard what I told her."

"Which explains why she was so clear about my minding my manners," he said. "Would you like a glass of iced tea, a cup of coffee, a glass of wine?"

"That's okay. I don't want you to go to any trouble. I was just going to give you these and head home."

"Stay," he said.

There was an oddly pleading note in his voice.

"I'd enjoy the company," he added persuasively.

Emma felt herself caught up in the intensity of his gaze. Against her better judgment, she sat down in the wicker chair next to his. "Wouldn't you be more comfortable with your leg elevated?"

"Comfort is relative these days," he said. "Truthfully, I couldn't figure out a way to get the ottoman in the living room out here."

"And being a man of action, not being able to figure things out is just one more thing that's driving you nuts," she guessed.

"You have no idea," he confirmed. "Any thoughts?"

"Actually, yes. Let me see if I can find a solution," she said, jumping up and heading for the door. She hesitated. "Do you mind?"

"Be my guest, but don't judge me on my housekeeping."

Emma laughed. She walked into the house expecting the worst, but discovered that the living room was surprisingly tidy. The ottoman he'd mentioned was definitely way too cumbersome to be dragged onto the porch. An afternoon shower blowing in the right direction would ruin it, anyway.

In the kitchen, also neat as a pin except for a glass in the sink, she found exactly what she needed, a small plastic step stool. She grabbed that, found a pillow in the living room that looked more shabby than chic, and took both outside.

"Here you go," she said triumphantly, arranging both in front of him and getting his casted leg settled just right. "Feel okay?"

"Perfect," he said. "Thank you."

Emma sat back down, her hands folded primly in her lap in an attempt to keep herself from reaching out to touch the coal-black hair that was just long enough to allow a few strands to curl against the tanned skin of his neck. With his olive complexion, the faint shadow of a beard and the occasional amused glint in his eyes, he reminded her of the sexy pirates she'd read about in some of the romance novels she'd once loved.

When she finally dared to meet his gaze, she discovered he was studying her intently. "Why the look? Do I have chocolate on my face? I ate a brownie at lunch."

"You say that with an awful lot of guilt," he teased. "Are brownies against the rules?"

"What rules?"

"I'm not sure, but you seem to have a lot of them."

She sighed. "I suppose I do. My mother's a stickler for the whole quiet-in-the-library thing, handling books with respect and so on. She was a single mom, so that carried over to the way she raised me. I grew up with a lot of rules meant to keep me on the straight and narrow."

"And did you stay there?"

"Most of the time," she conceded. "A part of me really wants to rebel, but it's a pattern that's hard to break." Uncomfortable with the whole topic of living according to the rules, she said, "Tell me about the books you ordered. The James Patterson I can see, but the other two surprised me."

"You've read Louise Penny?"

Emma nodded. "I love the Canadian setting and Inspector Gamache."

"Any reason you think I wouldn't love them, too?"

"Not violent enough?" she suggested then winced. "I'm stereotyping, aren't I?"

"Just a little. How about Earl Emerson? Have you read his books?"

"Love them," she admitted. "I'm so envious that you snagged a signed first edition."

"Pure luck. When I mentioned his name to Shanna, she said she'd just gotten this book from an estate sale. She's trying to increase her selection of signed books, especially first editions. I've spent enough time in the Pacific Northwest now that I love anything that's set there. Emerson tells a good story. I've read this one, but I like the idea of having a signed first edition. Maybe I'll start collecting the whole series." He chuckled. "You look surprised."

"I guess I am."

"Didn't think I could read?" he taunted.

"Didn't think we'd share the same taste," she countered. She stood up quickly. "I really do have to go. Enjoy your books. If you need more, I'd be happy to bring you some from the library or pick them up from Shanna if you prefer to buy them."

"Can I ask one thing before you go?"

"I suppose," she said.

"You love books, but just this morning you referred to your job at the library as a dead-end situation."

"Actually, that's how you described it. I just didn't disagree," she corrected then sighed. "Unlike my mother, who has a degree in library science and loves every nook and cranny of the Chesapeake Shores library, this wasn't my goal. It's just a way to fill some hours of the day."

"While?"

She regarded him blankly. "While what?"

"What are you waiting for? What goal is eluding you?"

Emma always hated that question. Once upon a time she'd answered eagerly. She was going to be a writer. Then she'd actually had a book published. She'd *been* a writer, one with a bestseller, no less.

It was hard now, though, to explain that she was a washed-up writer at the age of thirty-three and after only one book and countless failed attempts at a follow-up. She didn't like sharing all that with anyone these days, but for some reason she was especially reluctant to tell Jaime her sad life story.

"Long story," she said succinctly, instead. "Maybe we can get into it another time."

Thankfully, Jaime didn't push. He just nodded knowingly. "Another time, then. I'll be looking forward to it."

Emma started down the steps. Just when she thought she was safely away from that knowing scrutiny and her skittering nerves, he called out. She should have known he wasn't the type to let her off the hook that easily. Boredom evidently made him even more inclined to be persistent. Taking a deep breath, she turned back.

"How about tomorrow around one? That's when you get off, isn't it? I can have some lunch delivered."

"Mr. Alvarez—"

"Jaime, please."

"Jaime, then. I don't think that's a good idea."

"Any particular reason?"

Since she wasn't about to tell him that he made her

nervous with that glint in his eyes, their shared love of certain authors and the way her pulse scrambled in his presence, she said only, "It's for the best, okay?"

And this time when she walked hurriedly away, he didn't try to stop her.

Jaime watched Emma leave at a hurried clip, then tried to focus his attention on the opening pages of the Patterson book. But for reasons that weren't especially hard to figure out, the words weren't nearly as intriguing as his recent guest.

"She's a real mystery, that one," he murmured, staring up the block in the direction she'd taken.

And for the first time since he'd arrived in Chesapeake Shores, he had something fascinating to keep him occupied—unraveling the mystery of beautiful, uptight Emma Hastings, who was trying like crazy not to acknowledge the sparks flying between them.

3

Without his computer and with phone books a thing of the past, Jaime was forced to call the office first thing the next morning. He requested the number for Brady's, the best seafood restaurant in town. Fortunately, he had the number for Flowers on Main already programmed into his phone because he always sent flowers to Megan and Nell after he joined the O'Briens for Sunday dinners on his trips into town to meet with Mick.

"I'll get Matthew to help you," the obviously nervous receptionist said a little too quickly.

As he waited for Mick's nephew to pick up, Jaime wondered what the devil Mick had told his staff to make the women at least clam up around him. He'd asked for a little help with a phone number, not state secrets, for heaven's sake.

"Are you finally planning to leave the house?" Matthew asked when he'd been persuaded to take Jaime's call. "It's about time. You've been holed up there too long. I'm surprised it hasn't driven you over the brink."

"Who says it hasn't?" Jaime replied dryly. "But no, I'm not going out. I've been thinking about crab cakes this morning. I thought I'd ask Brady to deliver some."

"I can pick them up and bring them by," Matthew offered after he'd passed along the phone number. "I'd be happy to join you, if you're sick of your own company."

"Not necessary, but thanks," Jaime said.

"Are you by any chance expecting someone else?" Matthew asked with almost believable innocence then ruined it by adding, "Uncle Mick mentioned there might be a woman you're interested in."

"Your uncle has a big mouth. Thanks for the phone number, Matthew. Have a good day." He hung up before he could be pestered with more questions he didn't want to answer.

Brady was more than happy to send over the crab cake sandwiches, along with side orders of cole slaw and potato salad and a key lime pie for dessert. Jaime hoped he wouldn't be eating all that food alone, but just in case, he'd ordered the key lime pie because it had been a staple when he'd been growing up in Miami. Maybe it would offer decent consolation if his anticipated guest couldn't be persuaded to join him.

Next he made the call to the flower shop and, after exacting a promise of complete confidentiality, asked Mick's daughter Bree for some additional help. She was there in minutes, did as he'd requested and exited with barely a single taunt, just a smirk as she left.

The boxes of food arrived promptly at one. Jaime had the delivery boy put them in the kitchen, then he settled on the porch to wait. Emma might have said no to lunch, but he was oddly optimistic that she'd wander past any minute on her way home, and he'd be able to convince her to change her mind. Much as he hated using it, he'd noted her quick capitulation when he'd dared to play the pity card. He'd never wanted to be pitied by anyone, but at the moment he was willing to seize whatever tactic worked.

He tried to read while he waited but kept glancing up the street for some sign of his neighbor. It was closer to two when he finally spotted her coming…on the opposite side of the street. Apparently, she was giving his house and him a wide berth. That made him smile.

"Hey, Emma!" His cheerful greeting startled her so badly, she stumbled.

She gave him a wave but kept right on moving.

Jaime was undeterred. "Had lunch yet?"

She stopped and faced him, her expression visibly torn. Obviously, she was no good at little white lies, because she finally heaved a sigh and shook her head.

"I have crab cakes from Brady's," he called out. "They're the best in town."

"They are," she agreed.

"It's not too late to decide to join me." Again, he added the clincher that had worked so well the day before. "I could really use the company."

She stayed right where she was, clearly debating what to do. Judging from the hard glint in her eyes, visible even at a distance, she was more than a little suspicious that she was being played.

"Couldn't you talk whoever brought the crab cakes by into sticking around?"

"Didn't try. The delivery boy was some pimply-faced kid. It's your company I want."

"Why? Just because I'm a challenge?"

Jaime sensed the question was loaded with more importance than her light tone suggested. He sorted through various responses, all of them true, then settled for the one he thought most likely to reach her. "Because you're interesting."

"And you're bored," she concluded.

"Out of my mind," he admitted.

He watched as she weighed the invitation some more then finally relented and crossed the street. She frowned down at him. "This won't work again, just so you know. I might be a sucker for Brady's crab cakes, but I won't give in to temptation a second time."

Jaime bit back a smile. "Not to worry. I try never to repeat myself."

She looked startled by the response, just as he'd intended.

"I have everything set out in the kitchen," he said briskly. "Shall we eat in there?"

"Or I could bring the food out here," she suggested.

Another smile tugged at his lips. "Emma, Emma, Emma. Don't tell me you're scared to be alone with me inside."

"Why would I be?" she said, a touch of defiance in her tone. "You're a flirt. You're not dangerous."

"Ah, so you've heard some more about my reputation. Interesting that we've barely met and you've already found out so much about me."

She gave him a wry look. "It's Chesapeake Shores. People talk. It's the town hobby."

"So you didn't go looking for the inside scoop about me?"

"Hardly."

He laughed. "Okay, then, get the food and bring it out here if it makes you feel safer."

"More comfortable," she corrected emphatically. "And it's a lovely afternoon. We should take advantage of the weather."

"Whatever you say."

When she returned a few minutes later, there was an odd expression on her face.

"Something wrong?" Jaime asked.

"You went to a lot of trouble, given the fact that I told you no yesterday."

"I guess I was just hoping I could change your mind. And how much trouble did I go to, really? I called Brady and placed an order."

"I'll bet Brady's delivery person didn't set it out on the table with cloth napkins, decent china and a vase of flowers."

Since it was something she was likely to hear about sooner or later anyway, he admitted the truth. "Fine. You caught me. I made a call to Bree at Flowers on Main. She brought the flowers by and set the table." He gave her a lingering look with a hint of defiance in it. "Most women like flowers on the table."

"Like I said, you went to a lot of trouble."

"My mother taught me to treat women with respect, to pay attention to the things that made them happy. It's a habit that's served me well."

"I knew a man like that once. Good Southern manners and all that. It couldn't quite make up for the fact that he was a liar and a cheat."

Jaime heard the unmistakably bitter note in her voice. It was hard to miss and spoke volumes about her hard shell. "Old boyfriend?"

"Ex-husband."

"Ah, so that explains it."

"Explains what?"

"The wariness."

"No doubt about it," she agreed.

"Well, for whatever it's worth, I am not a liar, and I've never cheated on anyone. I could give you references."

He saw the twinkle in her eyes even as she tried to fight a smile of her own. "Not good enough?" he asked.

"Sorry. Words and promises are too easy."

"Then I suppose I'll have to make my actions count."

She gave him a disconcertingly long, hard look. "Seriously, Jaime, why would you bother? Are you that bored?"

"Sure, boredom motivated me to seek out your company," he acknowledged candidly, "but I find you fascinating, Emma Hastings. I'd like to spend some time getting to know you. We do have the same taste in books, after all. Isn't that a good starting point?"

"That depends on where you're heading," she said. "It's a great starting point for some lively conversation, but anything more?" She shook her head. "I don't think so."

"Not even the story of your life? You did promise to tell me that."

She frowned at him. "And you intend to hold me to that, even though it must be obvious that I don't want to talk about my past?"

"That just convinces me it's even more critical that I get you to open up about it, if I'm going to really get to know you."

"Maybe we're just destined to share crab cake sandwiches and nothing more," she said, pointedly taking a bite of hers then sighing with pleasure.

Jaime followed suit, and, for a few minutes, they focused on Brady's food. He was the first to finish his sandwich then sat back to watch Emma. She could have been savoring every bite, but he had a hunch she was deliberately delaying the moment when the questions might start to flow again.

"Ready for dessert?" he asked. "It's key lime pie, something my mother used to make on special occasions. Brady's isn't the same, but it comes close."

"I don't think I could eat another bite," she protested.

"You have to at least try it," Jaime said, offering her a forkful of the tart pie.

She accepted the offering with undisguised reluctance then moaned with equally obvious delight. "That is so good. Your mom made pies like this?"

"Even better," Jaime confirmed. "You'll have to come to Miami with me sometime and try hers."

She gave him an odd look, but didn't bother debating the out-of-the-blue suggestion.

Jaime regarded her with amusement. "You know, Emma, just because I've stopped asking questions, doesn't mean I've forgotten them. One of these days you will tell me the story of your life so I'll understand what put that wariness in your eyes."

"Not today," she said with a touch of defiance. "Probably not any other day, either. Sometimes the past is best forgotten."

"Is it ever truly forgotten?" Jaime asked. "I think we're all shaped by the lives we've lived. One of these days I'll put some serious effort into changing your mind and getting you to open up." He winked at her. "Bet I can."

She shuddered a little at that, but she didn't look away. That was enough for Jaime. She might be scared, but now that he'd called her on it, she wasn't going to run. He'd have to be sure he didn't give her any reason to regret that.

Emma had barely walked into the house after her disconcerting and surprisingly pleasant lunch with Jaime, when Shanna called to see if she was available for an impromptu book club meeting that night at the store.

"We'll make it a quick getting acquainted meeting tonight," Shanna said. "We can decide how often we want to meet and pick our first book."

"That was fast."

"A couple of my regulars happened to stop by today and immediately said yes. I made a few more calls, and it turned out everyone was eager to get started and available tonight at seven. So the store now has its first official book club. These are real readers, who are actually eager to talk about books. Are you in?"

"I'll be there," Emma promised, looking forward to the distraction from her very wayward thoughts about Jaime. The possibility of making some new friends appealed, too. "Do you need any refreshments? I can run by the Inn at Eagle Point and see if they have any cookies or pastries they can spare."

"That's okay. I spoke to Nell earlier. She baked today. She's sending cookies with Bree."

"So Bree's coming?" Emma said.

"Why did you say it like that?"

"Just that her hand took a little dip into the matchmaking pond earlier today. No big deal."

Shanna laughed. "Matchmaking is what we do around here. I learned a long time ago when people were pushing me together with Kevin to accept it in the loving spirit in which it was intended."

"I'll try to remember that."

In fact, she hung on to Shanna's words with a determined grip that night as she watched a car pull up outside the bookstore and saw Jaime emerge with a little assistance from Mick O'Brien. She turned to Shanna.

"You, too?"

Shanna shrugged. "Family curse. O'Briens can't help themselves."

Emma just shook her head, poured herself a cup of coffee and dragged a chair into a cluster of people who were already chatting excitedly about possible books to read. The fact that her mother happened to be one of those people made her cringe a little, but Jessica Hastings did know her books.

And judging from the way her sharp-eyed gaze was darting between Emma and Jaime and back again, she knew her daughter, too.

Jaime knew it had been a mistake to ask Mick for a ride when he saw him grab a cup of coffee and take a seat right in the thick of things. Since he doubted Mick had read a book for the sheer pleasure of it in years, he was hanging out on a reconnaissance mission. Apparently, he hadn't bought Jaime's explanation that Shanna had simply sweet-talked him into coming tonight.

Given his boss's avid interest, Jaime made it a point to steer clear of Emma. He sat on the opposite side of the room and introduced himself to the others who'd come. When Bree arrived, she set a tray of desserts on a table then glanced around. She gave a little nod of satisfaction when she spotted Emma then frowned when she caught sight of Jaime nowhere near her. She made a beeline in his direction.

"Don't start on me," Jaime warned.

"But how are you supposed to woo Emma if you're sitting clear across the room?"

He gave her a dark look. "Who said anything about me wooing Emma?"

"Oh, give it a rest. I know she's the one you were hoping would come to lunch, and Shanna told me the two of you would be here tonight."

"As is your father," he said, nodding at Mick, who was regarding the two of them suspiciously.

Bree blinked, clearly startled by his presence at a gathering to discuss books. "What's he doing here?"

"I stupidly asked him for a lift," Jaime said. "Now he's spying on me."

She tried in vain to swallow a laugh. "I'll take care of it," she told him. "Two minutes."

Jaime watched as she took her cell phone out of her pocket and made a call, although he couldn't hear what she was saying. She quickly tucked it away, looking extremely pleased with herself. Mick's phone rang within seconds. He frowned as he listened, glanced suspiciously at Bree and crossed the room.

"It seems my wife has some sort of problem at her art gallery that requires my immediate attention," he informed Jaime. "How long do you figure this thing will last? I'll come back for you."

"Not necessary, Dad. I'll see that Jaime gets home," Bree offered cheerfully. "You run along and help Mom. I'm sure she wouldn't have bothered you if it wasn't urgent."

Mick simply shook his head. "You're not fooling me, young lady. This is your doing. What I can't quite figure out is what you're up to. Jaime, you okay with Bree getting you home?"

"Absolutely," Jaime said, thoroughly amused by Mick's obvious frustration.

When Mick had gone, Jaime turned to Bree. "Nicely done."

"Years of practice. Now, if I can just get Emma over here, my mission will be complete."

Jaime was about to tell her to back off, but he was too late. She was already on her way to Emma's side. He caught Emma casting a quick glance in his direction, a frown on her lips. Then she sighed and nodded. And Bree, after casting a smirking look in his direction, walked out of the bookstore.

As Emma approached, he studied her wary expression. He definitely had his work cut out for him. He doubted that Bree's slick maneuver just now had helped the cause. He decided to make light of it.

"Two sneaky O'Briens gone," he remarked. "If only there were a way to get Shanna out of her own bookstore, there'd be no more prying eyes to worry about."

"You're wrong about that," she said wearily, turning to the woman who'd just slipped up to join them. "Mom, have you met Jaime Alvarez? Jaime, my mother, Jessica Hastings."

Jaime almost choked on his sip of coffee. "Mrs. Hastings. I'd get up, but as you can see, I'm in a bit of a bind when it comes to mobility right now."

"Don't you worry about that," the older woman said, regarding him with sympathy. "Emma mentioned you fell off a roof."

"A foolish misstep," he acknowledged. "Given the number of roofs I've been on over the years, I'm lucky it hasn't happened before."

"Well, if you need anything, anything at all, don't hesitate to call. Emma lives right up the street. You have her number, don't you?"

"Actually, I don't," he said, shooting a pointed look at Emma.

"Emma, dear, what were you thinking? You're probably closer than Mick or any of Mr. Alvarez's other friends. He should know how to reach you in an emergency." She reached into the depths of an enormous tote bag and pulled out a fancy clothbound notepad with its own gold pen. She quickly jotted down a few words then handed him the slip of paper. "There you go. I put my name and number on there, too. I'm a few blocks away, but I could still get to you quickly. I've taken several CPR and first aid certification classes, too."

"Good to know," Jaime said, suddenly envisioning Emma's lips—not her mother's, please, God—on his for some mouth-to-mouth resuscitation.

Thankfully, before that disturbing thought could have a predictable effect, Shanna called the book club meeting to order.

"Has everyone had a chance to get acquainted?" she inquired cheerfully.

Jaime's gaze caught Emma's, saw the color rise in her cheeks. She might not be entirely happy about it, but they were getting acquainted. Heck, he'd even met her mother now. He couldn't recall the last time he'd ever met a woman's parents. He usually ducked and ran long before they ever made that suggestion.

Maybe Mick had been right. Perhaps he had deliberately avoided relationships over the years. Was he honestly willing to consider one now? It was evident that Emma was a woman who needed serious intentions. By her own all-too-brief account, she'd been burned by a jerk. She didn't need another man treating her badly and adding to her conviction that men weren't to be trusted. That would be a crying shame.

Jaime tried to focus on the conversation swirling around him about books, but all he could think about was whether he was making the worst mistake of his life by pursuing Emma…or finally doing something exactly right.

4

"You were surprisingly quiet during the meeting," Emma commented as she drove away from the bookstore with Jaime settled awkwardly in the passenger seat. The seat had been pushed back as far as it would go to accommodate the cast, because he'd stubbornly refused to sit in back where he could prop his leg across the seat. "Are you in pain?"

"Nope."

She glanced over at him and caught a dark expression in his eyes. "In a mood?"

His frown deepened. "I don't have moods," he growled.

She laughed at that. "Really? Evidence would suggest otherwise."

He sighed heavily. "Sorry."

"You don't have to be sorry. Anything you want to talk about?"

He gave her a lingering glance that heated her blood and made her heart race.

"Not unless you'd care to discuss my sudden obsession with the idea of kissing you," he responded.

Emma was so taken aback, she came way too close

to missing the light that was changing to red. She hit the brakes so hard, Jaime nearly slid off the seat. Only the seat belt saved him. "Excuse me?"

He shrugged as he straightened in the seat. "You asked what was on my mind. I'm thinking about kissing you. I can't seem to get the image out of my head."

Thoroughly flustered, she simply stared. When she could finally speak again, she only managed to ask, "But when? Why?"

"Something your mother said."

Her mouth gaped. She didn't even notice the now-green light until an impatient driver honked behind her. Still rattled, she pulled into a parking space on the far side of the town green. Thankfully, it was well away from the tourists walking around downtown and any lingering O'Briens.

With dusk falling and a few lingering pink and purple streaks reflecting on the calm bay waters, it was a lovely night, but Emma barely spared a glance for the view right in front of them. Instead, she seemed to be laser-focused on the man seated next to her and *his* mouth. His mouth on *hers*. A kiss that was tender, yet intensely passionate. And complicated, she reminded herself sternly. It wouldn't do to forget complicated. Oh, sweet heaven, now she was obsessing about a kiss? It was her turn to sigh heavily and try to get a grasp on her straying thoughts.

How her mother had gotten involved in this particular scenario was beyond her, but thinking about that was definitely enough to clear her head of wicked images.

"My mother said something about kissing me?" she said in a voice that sounded only a tiny bit breathless. "How'd I miss that?"

"Not exactly," he said, his mood seeming to lift just a little. "She mentioned CPR and first aid, and my mind took a leap." At Emma's still incredulous look, he fought a grin. "I'm a man. It happens." He looked into her gaze, a hopeful glint in his eyes. "Maybe if we just did it, that would put the whole thing to rest."

"You want me to kiss you so you can stop obsessing about kissing me?" she asked, trying to make sense of his ridiculous and thoroughly self-serving suggestion. "Are you thinking it will be really, really terrible?"

He sighed. "It's not going to be terrible, Emma."

Emma thought she heard a touch of regret in his voice, possibly because he knew as well as she did that once the deed was done, chemistry would kick in, and common sense would fly right out the window. Nope, it definitely wasn't going to be terrible. She was as sure of that as he was.

"Then what purpose would this experiment serve?" she asked, trying to cling to reason and steer away from temptation. "What if it gets us all stirred up?"

He seemed a little too intrigued by the possibility. "Would that be so horrible?" he asked, his tone deadly serious.

She actually found herself considering that then mentally kicked herself. "You're leaving, Jaime. Maybe not right away, but eventually. It would be crazy to start something that's not going anywhere, especially with a whole town of interested parties watching our every move. I don't want to be left behind to deal with the fallout."

"Fair enough," he agreed. He glanced over and held her gaze. "So, that's a no on just one little experimental kiss?"

Emma chuckled at his attempt to suggest she'd left room for doubt. "Definitely a no."

"Too bad. I'm thinking it would be spectacular."

Unfortunately, so was she.

"Last night was very interesting," Jessica said when Emma risked being in close proximity to her mother for the first time since she'd arrived at the library. "Didn't you think so?"

"You know how I love to talk about books," Emma agreed cheerfully. "So do you. I'm surprised you haven't started a book club here at the library."

"I tried a few times, but it never seemed to work out."

"Nobody wanted to read the classics that you wanted them to read?" Emma guessed.

Her mother frowned. "I'm more open-minded than that, but what's wrong with the classics?"

"Not a thing, but isn't the important thing that people read and get excited about books? Then, every once in a while, you can sneak in a bit of great literature."

For a moment her mom looked taken aback. "You're absolutely right," she said. "It's ironic, really, because I've said precisely that to parents who won't let their children read some of the popular series, because they consider them junk. I've reminded them that any book that holds a child's interest and gives them a break from all their electronics is a good thing."

She gave Emma a sharp look. "I know what you're trying to do, you know."

"What's that?" Emma asked innocently.

"Distract me so I won't ask too many questions about Mr. Alvarez. He's an attractive man," she said slyly. "Don't you think so?"

"Hard to deny," Emma agreed, suddenly thinking of his sensuous, tempting mouth again. She quickly shook off the image, though there was no way to hide the heat it put on her cheeks.

"Interesting, too," her mother continued, all innocence.

"He is that."

"Have you made plans to get together again?"

"Mom, Jaime is just here until his leg heals and he's back on his feet. Then he'll be heading back to Seattle or wherever his next project takes him."

"I hear the Pacific Northwest is beautiful. Wouldn't you love to visit?" her mom persisted.

"Sure. I'd love to see Seattle, the San Juan Islands, take a ferry up to Victoria, maybe even go to Vancouver or Alaska one of these days." She couldn't seem to keep the wistful note out of her voice. She quickly added, "That has absolutely nothing to do with Jaime. It's always been on my travel bucket list."

"Well, now you know someone who could make that happen," her mother said. "That's all I'm saying. It's always more fun to explore a new area with someone who knows all the best spots to see. Remember how much fun I had when I flew to Hawaii to see my old college friend? We saw the sights, for sure, but I had the chance to feel like a local."

Emma knew her mother wasn't suggesting Jaime be her travel guide. What she was really suggesting was something much more complicated and long-term. Boy, she'd have to give Jaime credit. He'd charmed her mom in just a couple of hours without even trying. Derek the weasel had never won her over. Maybe that was something Emma ought to think about one of these days. Her mom did have exceptionally good judgment.

"I need to shelve some more books," Emma said, eager to escape. She turned and walked away, well aware that no matter how much more her mother might want to say on the subject, she wouldn't interfere when there was work to be done.

Though Jaime spent the afternoon on his front porch, Emma never strolled by. Nor did she drive past. Clearly, she'd found a new route home or intended to wait until she could pass by under the cover of darkness. Since he could hardly go chasing all over town after her, the odds of her avoiding him were in her favor. He was going to have to get creative, if he truly wanted to pursue her.

Unfortunately, under the circumstances, even his sneakiest approach would have to rely on some of the very people he most wanted to stay out of the situation: the O'Briens. He sighed. It was just a question of deciding which one might be the least of all the evils. Bree had proven herself to be a good coconspirator yesterday, but overdependence on any one person would probably be a mistake, too. Emma would guess what he was up to a little too easily. She was a smart woman, and very wary.

Immediately, he thought of Nell, Mick's mother, and probably the most trusted person in all of Chesapeake Shores. She'd always treated Jaime like one of the family and chided him all the time for not finding the right woman and having a whole slew of babies she could fuss over. As if the O'Briens hadn't kept her well supplied on that front, he thought.

Nell had been fretting and fussing over Jaime ever since the first time Mick had brought him home when he'd just joined the firm. Now that he was laid up, she was even more attentive. Luckily, yesterday had been her baking day, so she was bound to be by today with Tupperware containers filled with treats and a few meals for his freezer. Perfect, he thought, suddenly looking forward to her visit for his own devious reasons, reasons that had nothing to do with melt-in-his-mouth cookies and triple berry pie or comforting Irish stew.

Sure enough, just after five, Nell's familiar car turned into the driveway. She emerged right along with Dillon, her husband of just a few years, an old flame she'd met again on a family vacation in Ireland.

"What on earth have you brought?" Jaime called out at the sight of two armloads of containers. "I'm not starving."

"I worry about you just the same, living here by yourself and not able to get around so well," Nell said. "I wish you'd agreed to stay over at Mick's. I could keep a closer eye on you."

"Believe me, you—the whole family, in fact—do more than enough as it is," Jaime said with genuine gratitude.

"That's as it should be, given the responsibilities you've taken on so Mick could spend more time with his family," Nell said.

Jaime grinned. "Are you so sure they'd thank me for that, now that they've had a few years of his meddling? They might welcome him being back on the road again."

"More than likely," she agreed with a chuckle. "Dillon, love, can you put these things in the refrigerator while I chat with Jaime and make sure there's nothing more he needs?"

"Done," Dillon said.

He gave his wife a quick kiss on the cheek and the kind of doting look that always made Jaime envious. The renewed love between those two, who were in their early eighties now, was an inspiration. That, far more than Mick's lectures, made Jaime wonder about the solitary life he'd fallen into over the years he'd been devoting himself to work.

"Everything okay?" Nell asked, her gaze sharp. "You seem to be in an odd mood."

"Just bored, which seems to be the norm these days."

"Nothing to catch your interest?" she asked in a way that told him she'd been hearing stories.

"What have you heard?"

"Just that there seem to be a few sparks flying with that lovely Emma Hastings," she said. "Must be hard to chase her from your front porch."

Jaime sighed, seeing little point in denying it, especially if he wanted Nell's help. "Exactly," he said. "Any ideas?"

Nell's expression turned thoughtful. "I know her mother quite well from the library and our church group. I could see that they're included at dinner this Sunday."

As badly as he wanted to see Emma again, there would be far too many prying eyes. "I don't think so."

"Too much, too soon," she said with a nod. "You're probably right. We don't want to overwhelm the woman and scare her off."

Jaime held back a grin at the way she'd taken ownership of the problem.

She fell silent as she gave the matter some more thought. Jaime sat and waited.

"From what I hear," she said eventually, "Emma's been at loose ends. She's having a bit of writer's block and it's frustrating her."

Startled, Jaime held up a hand. "Hold on. Emma didn't mention being a writer." He thought a second. She had mentioned that her library job was some sort of stop-gap measure, but had quickly clammed up after that.

"A bestselling novelist," Nell informed him with as much pride as if Emma were one of her own.

Filled with curiosity, Jaime asked, "Has she written a lot of books? Does she write under her own name?"

"Just the one, I think," Nell said. "And yes, it was her name on the cover."

"How long ago?"

Nell's expression turned thoughtful. "Several years now. Her mother says she's been working on her next book, but seems to be struggling with it. Now, I don't know much about writers, but it seems to me that sometimes the best way to solve any problem is to stop picking at it."

"In other words, you think she needs a distraction," Jaime said, focusing on formulating a plan. He could think about the implications of Emma's not mentioning her writing another time. "I'm all for providing as much of a distraction as she needs."

"Too obvious," Nell said, dismissing his eager offer. "I think I'll ask her to help me with planning the fall festival at the church."

"Sounds perfect, but that won't help me win her over."

"It will if you're the other person on the committee," Nell said, clearly pleased with herself. "It'll be good to have a fresh perspective. You two will provide that."

"I might not even be here by the time this fall festival rolls around," Jaime protested. "I'll be out of the cast by the end of summer, God willing. And—"

Nell cut him off before he could say he'd be on his way back to Seattle.

"And then you'll need physical therapy," she reminded him. "Which you'll take right here, if you have a brain in that head of yours, and if you're serious about Emma. You won't go running straight back to Seattle."

Jaime considered that option. He did have that sort of flexibility. If he could fly by then, he could certainly make a couple of quick visits and come right back here until after the fall festival was over and his duties were done.

"What exactly is this committee assignment of yours going to involve? I can't build booths and run all over the place on errands."

"But you can direct others to do that. Isn't that something you excel at doing?" She frowned at him. "What's with these excuses, Jaime? Do you want to spend time with Emma or not?"

"I'm in," he said quickly.

"Then I'll send Dillon by to get you tomorrow at two. We'll meet at my house because there aren't any steps to trip you up. Play your cards right and you'll both be staying for dinner, and Emma will be bringing you home."

Dillon had emerged from the house just in time to overhear enough to figure out what the two of them were up to. "And here the whole family thinks Mick is the mastermind of all the matchmaking," he said, shaking his head. "He has nothing on my Nell."

"I've had a lot more years of practice," Nell said. "And I'm subtle. Mick's like a bull in a china shop. That's why no one trusts him. They're always alert to an ulterior motive."

"And you're practically a saint," Dillon said, amusement written all over his face.

Nell's blue eyes flashed. "Are you suggesting otherwise?"

Dillon laughed. "I wouldn't dare. Watch out for this

one, Jaime. Once she gets a bit in her mouth, she's relentless."

"I'm counting on that," Jaime said. He'd take all the help he could get until nature kicked in and did the rest.

Nell's cottage overlooking the bay was like something from a fairy tale. Her gardens, in full bloom now, were a riot of color and fragrance. Rather than going inside, Emma was tempted to wander out there and sit, absorbing the sound of the birds and the beauty and tranquility of the setting.

Unfortunately, the front door opened and there was Nell, a beaming smile of welcome on her face. "There you are," she called out cheerfully. "Just in time."

"How are you?" Emma asked, kissing the older woman's cheek. "You look incredible."

"Hardly that, but I'll thank you just the same," Nell said, leading her toward the kitchen. "I thought we'd meet in here. It's cozier, and I've made tea and scones."

In the doorway, Emma came to a sudden stop. There, already munching on a blueberry scone, was Jaime, his casted leg propped up on another chair, a chintz cup of tea steaming in front of him. That cup looked ridiculously dainty next to his large, work-roughened hands. The fact that he hadn't asked Nell for a more masculine mug made Emma's heart swell for some reason. A man who did that would be strong, yet gentle in other ways, too.

"You know Jaime, of course," Nell said briskly. "I've asked him to help us, as well. I'm hoping for lots of new ideas from the two of you so this year's festival won't be more of the same old thing. It needs a fresh perspective."

Emma suspected what Nell was really hoping for was a firsthand look at the sparks her family had been describing between Jaime and Emma, but she wasn't about to toss that accusation in Nell's face. She merely gave Jaime a wry look.

"Do you have a lot of experience with planning a fall festival?" Emma asked him, her skepticism plain.

"Not a bit," he admitted readily. "I attended my share of huge Calle Ocho events in Miami and enough art festivals to last a lifetime, but something tells me this is entirely different." He studied her. "How about you? Are you experienced at planning festivals?"

"Hardly. I've been to a few since I've been back in town, but I've never planned one. Nell, are you sure we're the best choices? I know the community counts on this for added fall tourism, and the church relies on it as one of their big fund-raisers."

Nell gave her a serious look. "Then you'll work really hard not to let me down, won't you? Now, shall we get started?"

Emma sighed and took a big bite of her blueberry scone to keep from saying something impolite.

"I have a list of the vendors who've already paid their fees," Nell began. "We'll have the usual apple cider booth. That's always a big favorite."

"They do sell the most amazing apple cider doughnuts," Emma added, barely containing a sigh at the memory. "And candied apples and caramel apples."

Jaime chuckled. "So, you're all about the food. I was hoping for a kissing booth. Is there one of those?"

"No," Emma said very firmly, frowning at him.

"But an interesting idea," Nell said.

She seized on it in a way that made Emma wonder just how deeply she was involved in the whole O'Brien

conspiracy to throw Emma and Jaime together as frequently as possible.

Her expression thoughtful, Nell added, "I imagine the
single men in town would spend quite a lot for a chance
to kiss some of our most eligible young women."

"I know I would," Jaime said, his gaze never leaving
Emma's face. "Depending on the woman, of course, and
only because it's a good cause."

"Yeah, right," Emma muttered. "Why not put a few
sexy hunks in the booth and let women pay for the privi-
lege of kissing them? I'm sure you'd volunteer for that,
wouldn't you, Jaime?"

Jaime merely held her gaze in a way that had color
flooding her cheeks.

Nell chuckled. "An equal opportunity kissing booth.
I like it. I'll put it on the list as a possibility."

"What other vendors are on the list?" Jaime asked.

"Several local crafters, a few artists, some of the
local shops, a variety of food vendors and a few civic
clubs that sell various things for their own fund-raising efforts," Nell said, scanning over her list. "It hasn't
changed much in years. We have a small carnival set
up for the kids to enjoy, and the church has booths with
games and small prizes."

"So it's a real, old-fashioned small-town event," Jaime
concluded. "I can't believe I've never been here for it.
What are the dates again?"

"Last weekend in October."

"Have you considered a Halloween costume parade?"
he suggested.

Emma regarded him with surprise. "What a great
idea!" she conceded. "The kids would love that, especially since a lot of parents seem to be discouraging trick-

or-treating these days. People along the route could be encouraged to hand out candy, and we could give a small prize for the best costume in two or three age groups."

Nell clapped her hands with delight. "A wonderful thought!" she concurred. "I knew I did the right thing by inviting the two of you to be on the committee. Any other ideas?"

"Do you have any music?" Jaime asked. "It might be nice to have a band perform so some of the adults and teens could dance." His gaze settled on Emma. "Perhaps by then I could even manage to take you on a spin around the dance floor."

Emma wanted to comment that she hadn't expected him to be around town that long, but she remained silent, even as her pulse skipped a beat or two at the look in his eyes.

"It would encourage people to stay into the evening," Nell said thoughtfully. "And I imagine Luke could suggest some musicians. He has bands at the pub quite a lot. Perhaps he'd even consider underwriting the performances in return for a banner advertising the pub."

A half hour later they had a list of intriguing new ideas. Nell assigned each of them several possibilities to investigate.

"Next week at the same time?" she suggested. "Jaime, would you like us to come to you? Would that be easier?"

"If I can catch a ride with Emma, coming here works for me," he said. "I enjoy getting out of the house."

Nell's expression brightened. "If you're eager to get out, then how about this, instead? Luke has a lively Irish band performing at O'Brien's on Friday night. Why don't we go there to check it out?"

"Works for me," Jaime said at once. "Emma, if you're available on Friday, would you mind picking me up?"

Though she knew perfectly well that she was falling into a neatly set trap, Emma also knew there was no reasonable way to decline. If she claimed to have other plans, sooner or later she'd be caught in the lie. "No problem. Do you need a way home now?"

"Sure, if you have the time. Dillon picked me up, but there's no reason to put him to any trouble if you're going right by my house."

"No reason at all," she said dryly.

In the car, she glanced over at her passenger. "Did you put Nell up to this?"

"Up to what?"

"Putting me onto this committee with you?"

"Do you honestly think anyone tells Nell what to do?"

Emma considered that. Nell was notoriously independent. "But it works out rather nicely for you, doesn't it?"

"Does it? It means I'll be in Chesapeake Shores longer than I'd initially planned, so if you think about it, it's actually inconvenient."

"And yet you don't seem to be the least bit upset by that."

He grinned. "After today, I'm definitely seeing the upside, especially if I can convince Nell to move forward with that kissing booth and the whole dance thing."

"If she goes along with you, I'll be sure to point out some of the available women in town," she offered, even though her stomach knotted at the thought.

"No suggestions necessary. There's only one woman I'm interested in," he said, his gaze steady.

Emma held his gaze then finally shook her head in exasperation. "What am I going to do with you? You don't give up," she murmured.

"Definitely something you should keep in mind," he said as they pulled up in front of his house. He got out of the car without assistance then stuck his head back in. "Pleasant dreams, Emma. See you Friday night."

Coming from anyone else the comment would have meant nothing more than a casual reminder, but somehow coming from Jaime, it was filled with innuendo. Emma wasn't sure which was more disturbing, the likelihood that he'd be sneaking into her dreams tonight or that Friday night was going to feel an awful lot like a date, even if they would have a couple of chaperones and a whole slew of curious onlookers.

5

There was already a large, noisy crowd at O'Brien's by the time Emma and Jaime arrived on Friday night at seven. Jaime noticed that Nell had managed to snag a great table by the window for the four of them. It was far enough away from the bandstand that they'd be able to hear each other and, thanks to some shifting around of chairs, there was room for Jaime to prop up his leg without it being in the way of the waitstaff. He noticed Emma glancing around with a surprised expression.

"What's that look about?" he asked as they settled in to await Nell and Dillon's return. Dillon was getting ales and soft drinks at the bar, and Nell was apparently in the kitchen telling the chef what to do. Jaime had heard all the stories about Nell taking a proprietary interest in the pub's Irish menu.

"I've never seen it this crowded in here before," Emma confessed.

"You haven't come to hear the music?" Jaime asked. "I know Luke has bands playing pretty regularly. I've even managed to come a couple of times. It's always packed."

Emma shook her head. "This is a first for me."

Jaime considered the implications of that. "Surely there are men who've asked you out since you arrived in town. It's been at least a couple of years, right?"

"Three years, actually. And I have been asked out."

"But you've turned them all down," he concluded.

"I don't really have time for a social life. I do my best writing at night."

Ah, there was the opening he'd been waiting for, a chance to explore the career she hadn't even mentioned to date.

"Writing?" he inquired carefully. Clearly, it was a touchy subject, so best to satisfy his curiosity slowly.

She looked away, obviously regretting the slip of the tongue.

He refused to let it pass. "What do you write, Emma?"

"I wrote a book. I've been working on another for a while now." Her gaze narrowed. "But you knew that, didn't you? And you've heard about the writer's block?"

"It's been mentioned. What I don't understand is why you didn't tell me yourself. That seems to be where your heart lies. You've said yourself that working at the library is just a job."

"It's hard to explain to someone that I wrote this book that had a moderate amount of success, but have nothing to show for all the hours I've spent in front of the computer since then," she said, noticeably embarrassed. "I haven't written anything worth reading for a couple of years now, not even a discarded manuscript I can point to and claim I'm still a writer."

"But if I were to pin you down and ask what you care most about in terms of a career, writing would be it for you, no question about it?"

She nodded. "Unfortunately, what I am at the moment

is a part-time library employee, living off my savings from my one big bestseller."

Jaime understood what it was like to be filled with frustration and uncertainty when the ideas wouldn't flow. He, however, was more patient with himself than she was with herself.

"Why do you sound so mad at yourself? It's a creative endeavor."

"It's my job, or at least that's what I intended it to be. I diligently sit down in front of my computer every day and wait for the words to pour out of me," she said with a touch of defiance.

"Admittedly, I don't know a thing about the writing process, but does the command-performance thing work?"

Her expression turned rueful. "Not that I've noticed."

"Then maybe you need to change things up, get some new experiences under your belt, meet some new people."

She seemed startled by the suggestion. "You could be right," she conceded. "My first book was heavily based on my experiences in my marriage. That well has definitely run dry. I'm sick of even thinking about it."

"But not sick of letting it dictate your future," he observed, deciding he needed to get a copy of that bestselling book of hers to see exactly what it might reveal.

She frowned at his words, but he let them hang in the air. Finally, she met his gaze.

"You're really annoying, you know that? We've barely even met, and you seem to know me better than I know myself."

"Outsider's perspective, that's all," he said. "And a sincere interest in the subject."

Before she could respond to that, Dillon and Nell had joined them and it put an end to any sort of personal conversation. It was just as well, Jaime thought. Let his words and his insights sink in. Emma might be exasperated by them, but that didn't make them any less accurate. Perhaps his view of her would prove inspiring, not in terms of her writing, but in terms of opening her heart and convincing her to start living again.

More and more, he was hoping that if she did that, he'd be around to be the man she let into her life.

Though Jaime's insights had thrown her more than a little, Emma found herself relaxing as the evening wore on. Nell and Dillon were great company, and the music was even better than Nell had promised. While the band relied heavily on the expected Irish songs, they played a few familiar pop tunes, as well. She found herself tapping her foot, regretting that she couldn't join those who'd moved to the small dance floor that had been cleared right in front of the bandstand.

Jaime leaned in close. "You should dance. I know you're dying to. Your foot's been tapping to the music for the past hour."

"No partner," she said. "And I don't know the Irish dance moves the way those couple on the floor seem to."

Dillon apparently overheard them. "I might have a solution for that, if you don't mind having an old man teach you a thing or two. Nell, love, would you mind?"

"Absolutely not," Nell said at once then gave Emma a sharp look. "Just don't go getting any ideas, young lady. He's only on loan to you."

Emma laughed. "Everybody in town knows Dillon's heart belongs to you, but if you don't mind, I would love to learn a few steps."

"Then come with me," Dillon said happily.

Emma followed him onto the dance floor, where he showed her a series of steps so intricate and so fast, it was a wonder she didn't get her feet completely tangled and land in a heap.

"How do you do that?" she asked breathlessly when the song ended.

"Years and years of practice. It's second nature to me now. You'll catch on. I imagine when Jaime's back on his feet, he'll be eager to give you a few lessons. He's surprisingly good. Must be all the years he's hung out around Mick. The Irish traditions have rubbed off on him."

"Mick dances an Irish jig?"

Dillon chuckled. "With Nell as his mother, do you imagine her letting him or his brothers off the hook? They might have grumbled mightily, but when they came to Ireland, you couldn't tell them from the locals on the dance floor."

Back at the table, Emma regarded Jaime curiously. "Is Dillon right? Can you do all those dances?"

"All those and a mean tango and salsa, too," he said with a wink. "I'm very diversified. Just wait till the fall festival. If we hire a couple of bands, I'll show you all my moves."

"What do the two of you think of this band?" Nell asked. "Would they be a good choice for the festival?"

"Absolutely," Emma said. "Their music really does make you want to get up and dance."

"I agree," Jaime said. "I think their mix of selections would be perfect for a community event."

Nell nodded. "Then I'll go and speak to Luke. Dillon, you coming?"

"Yes, love," he said, and dutifully followed her to

the bar, where Luke was pouring ales and chatting with customers.

"You look like you're having fun," Jaime said.

"I am," Emma said, a little surprised by the admission. It had been a long time since she'd done anything just for the sheer pleasure of it. And here in one week she'd joined a book club and gone to the pub for an evening of music and dancing. Perhaps her horizons were finally expanding a bit. Was that due to Jaime, or had it simply been time? She couldn't be sure, but it did seem he was at the center of the changes she could feel taking place in her life.

What she didn't know was how she felt about that.

After she'd dropped off Jaime, Emma felt so exhilarated, her flagging energy of late restored, she went home and sat down in front of her computer. For the first time in months, the words seemed to flow easily. As they flooded out, page after page of a new story inspired by an image of a sexy Latino, she was almost scared to stop. What if she did and the words were gone by tomorrow? What if her imagination failed her yet again?

Even as her doubts crowded in, the flow of words seemed to slow to a trickle then stopped altogether. She stared at the computer screen, dismayed. Had just thinking about her writer's block brought it back?

She stood up and began to pace, but her small office wasn't big enough to contain her level of frustration. Despite the lateness of the hour—well after midnight—she grabbed her keys and left the house.

Carefully avoiding the route past Bayside Retreat, she went around the block in the opposite direction, walking for perhaps a mile before her steps slowed and brought her back to Wisteria Lane. In front of Jaime's she noticed the lights were still on in the living room.

She stopped and stared, indecisive. She knew if she crossed the street and knocked on his door, things between them would change. That kiss she'd banned would happen. Maybe even more than a kiss.

In her present mood, though, filled with a conflicting mix of heady exhilaration and frustrating defeat, she was ready to risk anything…maybe even her heart.

She crossed the street, stepped onto the porch and knocked. Through windows left open to the cool night breeze, she heard a loud thump, a mild curse and then the slow but steady rhythm of crutches tapping on the wood floors.

There was time to turn and run. Jaime might even chalk up the knock to kids playing a prank, but Emma told herself that for once she shouldn't be a coward. Jaime had brought something unexpected into her life, and she needed to know where it might lead. Even nowhere would be okay, as long as the experience broke up the tedium she'd come to accept as the norm for her future.

The door swung open, and then it was too late to run.

Jaime's expression registered only mild surprise. "Emma! Is everything okay?"

She swallowed hard. She looked away for a heartbeat to gather her composure then looked into his eyes. "I'd like to try that kiss, if you haven't changed your mind," she said boldly.

Heat turned his eyes dark, and his hand reached out to caress her cheek. "You sure about that?"

"No," she admitted. "But yes."

He chuckled. "Now, there's a decisive answer if ever

I've heard one. A wise man would exercise caution before moving forward. Want to come in and talk about it?"

"I want to come in," she said. "But not to talk. I mean not about the kiss or whether or not it's a good idea. I just want to do that then talk about other things." She took a deep breath. "Or not."

He stepped aside. "Come in, then. Can I get you something to drink? A midnight snack?"

She shook her head.

"Then have a seat."

She noted that the Patterson book he'd apparently been reading had fallen on the floor. That must have been the thump she'd heard right after she knocked. A glass of water was on the table beside his chair, along with the remains of what must have been his own late snack—some cheese and crackers, a few grapes, a perfectly respectable snack for a health-conscious man.

Then Emma spotted a few graham cracker crumbs in an aluminum pan and knew he'd thrown caution to the wind and finished that key lime pie from their recent lunch together. That made her smile, at least till she thought about why she'd come by.

Scared out of her wits by the implications of her impulsive decision, Emma sat on the sofa and waited to see what Jaime would do. He sat next to her and put his crutches aside.

"Look at me," he said softly.

She glanced into his eyes, noted the concern, then looked away.

"Emma?"

She sighed and held his gaze.

"What's going on?"

"A willing woman shows up on your doorstep in the middle of the night and you really want to dissect it?"

"I think we probably should. I don't want to take advantage when you're feeling vulnerable."

"Maybe I'm just coming to my senses," she replied. "You did say I needed to open myself up to new experiences."

"Ah, so I planted this notion in your head. Good to know you were listening and taking my advice seriously."

"It sort of worked," she told him. "I went home tonight and wrote for a couple of hours. I won't know till I look at it tomorrow if it's good or if it's garbage, but the words did flow."

"Then why aren't you happier about that?"

"They stopped almost as fast as they'd started."

"So you're here for more inspiration?"

She winced at the lightly made accusation, because it was probably true. "More than likely. Then again, that whole kiss thing has been on my mind ever since you brought it up."

He smiled at that. "The power of suggestion."

"Have you changed your mind?"

His expression turned serious. "Not a chance. You were the one with doubts. Do you still have any?"

"About a million," she told him candidly. "But I want to know, Jaime. I want to feel something again."

He beckoned her closer, leaving it to her to come to him. When they were sitting thigh to thigh, he caressed her cheek again, his eyes locked with hers. His thumb brushed across her lower lip, stirring sensations she hadn't felt in years, hadn't expected to ever feel again.

And then his mouth was on hers, his breath a whisper against her skin. Her heart, empty for way too long, filled with a heady mix of anticipation and joy that sent her pulse scrambling. Her brain tried to argue against this, but it was too late. She wanted the sweet touch of Jaime's lips, the lingering caresses that left fire in their wake, the whispered endearments that seemed to reach into her soul and replace the cold with unexpected heat.

Jaime was the one who broke off the kiss before it swept away the last of their control. He didn't let her go, though. He managed to stretch out on the sofa and pulled her snugly into his embrace. The cast was a definite hindrance, but they made it work.

Emma sighed as her head rested against his chest, the sound of his steady heartbeat soothing and reassuring.

"Did you get what you came for, Emma?" he asked softly.

She could hear the smile in his voice. "I did, and then some."

"It's just the beginning, you know."

She did know, and while that terrified her, she was suddenly eager to see where it might lead...even if it ended in heartbreak.

6

Early Saturday morning Emma awoke to the sound of birds chirping like crazy and to the smell of real coffee brewing and bacon frying. Since she kept her windows shut tight much of the time and rarely cooked, it took her a minute to realize it wasn't a dream. She was still on Jaime's sofa, snuggling up with a soft throw that had apparently appeared sometime during the night.

She wandered through the house till she found the bathroom, washed her face, used a finger and some toothpaste to freshen her mouth, then padded into the kitchen, coming to a halt in the doorway and simply staring.

Jaime stood precariously balanced on one crutch in front of the stove cooking breakfast. Wearing only his customized jeans, a pair that had clearly been well-worn even before he'd taken scissors to the one pants leg, and a snug white T-shirt that emphasized his muscular build and his tan, he looked totally male. She had to pause to catch her breath at the glorious sight then forced herself to focus on the riskiness of his awkward balance.

"You shouldn't be doing that," she scolded. "You could fall and break something else."

He turned, and a smile broke across his face. "You're worried about me," he gloated.

She frowned at his interpretation. "I just don't want any broken bones on my watch."

"Maybe another broken bone or two wouldn't be such a bad thing. It would give me an excuse to hang around Chesapeake Shores even longer. And if you felt guilty, you might volunteer to be my personal angel of mercy."

Emma gave him a disbelieving look. "Pretty extreme measures just to have me wait on you. And I guarantee you wouldn't be getting a breakfast like this one if the cooking's left to me."

"Your cooking skills aren't what interest me," Jaime informed her with a wink before turning back to the bacon.

Emma used the time to catch her breath for a second time and to try to find safer conversational ground. "Isn't Mick's company headquartered here? Shouldn't that be all the excuse you need to stay in Chesapeake Shores?" she asked as she poured herself a cup of coffee then breathed in the scent of the strong brew. A man who could make coffee like this might be worth considering. When she was writing well, she drank gallons of the stuff.

"True, but my responsibilities for the company are on the other side of the country," he reminded her.

He gave her a quick glance as he spoke, and she thought she detected real regret in his eyes. Was that because his work was elsewhere and he wished otherwise, or because he was stuck here even temporarily? She couldn't be sure. "Do you miss it? The work, I mean. Or the Pacific Northwest, for that matter."

He glanced at her. "Do you miss writing?"

"Of course, but it's not exactly the same, is it? The minute you're able to move around freely, you can jump right back into your work. You can go back to Seattle and pick up where you left off."

"Some of it, sure. The actual construction just requires me to oversee the work, make sure it's on schedule, that nobody's skimping on the workmanship, but that's just a necessary part of the process. Like yours, my real work is creative."

"How so?" she asked, genuinely interested. She'd watched houses go up, even housing developments, but she'd never thought about the forethought that went into the process. Or how that might compare to what she did, building a story from a tiny nugget of an idea.

"I have to find parcels of undeveloped land that inspire me then design the sort of homes that might work there without spoiling the environment. Neither Mick, Matthew nor I design little cookie-cutter developments. We take pride in creating communities that fit in with their surroundings, the way Chesapeake Shores is exactly right for this bayside setting. That's not coincidence. It takes vision and commitment."

Emma smiled at the passion in his voice. "You do love it."

"From the first rough sketch to the last nail that's hammered in," he agreed. "And I love going back when the homes are sold and the businesses thriving to see how it's all come together, to see the events on the town greens and the kids laughing and running on the playgrounds in the parks."

"You're clearly as devoted to it as Mick notoriously is," she guessed.

"Was," he corrected. "Mick's retired, or *reformed*.

At least that's what he likes to tell everyone. He's come to understand that his family is his greatest achievement, not this town or any of the others he's designed and built."

"But you haven't made that leap," she suggested.

Jaime smiled as he piled crisp bacon onto a plate and handed it to her to set on the table. Then he turned his attention to scrambling eggs. He seemed to be happy to have an excuse not to respond to her right away.

Eventually, when she simply waited for an answer, he said, "You have to have a family to put them first."

"And you don't?"

"My mother's still in Florida. I get home to see her once a year at least. No wife, if that even needs to be said, given what's going on between you and me. No ex-wives, either. No kids. Mick had Megan, five kids, two brothers and their families, to say nothing of Nell, waiting for him right here, no matter where we were working. At least he did until Megan tired of it and walked out. Those were dark days, apparently. I joined the company after the divorce. Once they reconciled, I took on more responsibilities to free up Mick's time."

"Which left you with none of your own," Emma concluded.

"Pretty much. This enforced inactivity, which Mick likes to refer to as a vacation, is the longest break I've taken in more than a decade. I snatch a three-day weekend from time to time, but that's about it."

"And that's the way you want it?"

"It's always been enough," he said simply then gave her a lingering look. "I might be rethinking that, though."

Emma trembled a little at the intimacy in that look. Did she want to be responsible for anyone even considering shaking up their lives, especially when her own was such a mess? "Not on my account, I hope," she said lightly.

"Why is that?" he asked, setting the eggs on the table then adding a plate of scones he'd obviously gotten from Nell. "You have something—or someone—in your life I don't know about?"

"No, but that doesn't mean I want a relationship."

"You did last night."

"A gentleman wouldn't remind me of that," she chided. "Maybe all I wanted was inspiration."

His expression darkened slightly. "Did you find what you came for, Emma? I was teasing last night, but now you have me wondering."

"I won't know till I sit in front of the computer again," she said blithely, though the truth was she'd gotten a whole lot more than she'd bargained for. The kisses they'd shared, the warmth of sleeping in his arms on that cramped sofa, those things had set off a yearning for something she'd never expected to want again.

Yearning wasn't the same as reaching for, she told herself sternly. And sparks in the night weren't the same as reality in broad daylight. She was wise enough to know the difference, strong enough to resist the temptation.

At least she hoped so. And given Jaime's disappointed expression, she had to wonder if he'd ever give her another night like the one they'd just shared.

Jaime didn't know whether to be exasperated or relieved by Emma's mixed signals. One thing he did know was that the key to understanding her might be in that book she'd written. He didn't want to stir up talk by asking Shanna if she had the book and without his computer, he couldn't order it online. Instead, he called the main office and had one of the assistants, who luckily was in on a Saturday morning, if she'd look up the closest chain bookstore. He jotted down the number and made a call to order a copy.

"How quickly do you think you can get it to me?"

"We have it in stock," the clerk said. "I can put it aside and you could pick it up today."

"I can't get there," he said with real regret. "I'll pay for a courier to bring it to me, if you can arrange that. I'd really like it today, rather than waiting for it to get here by mail next week."

"That's awfully expensive," she said.

"It's important," he told her. "Can you arrange it?"

She put him on hold then came back and promised it would be there by early afternoon. "One of our part-time employees lives not too far from there. He said he'll bring it. You can work out the payment with him, if that's okay."

"Perfect," Jaime told her. "Thanks so much."

Even though it might be hours before the book turned up, he showered and dressed quickly then poured himself another cup of coffee. After that he settled on the porch to enjoy the late-morning breeze and wait for something that might tell him everything he needed to know about the woman who'd gotten under his skin so darn quickly.

Emma wrote as if the house were on fire, and she had to get finished before the walls collapsed around her. She couldn't recall ever feeling such a sense of urgency, such passion for the words that were flowing onto the screen. She was almost breathless by the time she reached the end of the chapter and knew in her heart that readers would be the same.

She sat back, drew in a deep breath and smiled for the first time in ages at the work she'd accomplished. Jaime had apparently been right about one thing. She had needed some new people and new experiences in her life to recharge her creative batteries. Not Jaime, specifically, she assured herself, but what he represented: a fresh outlook, new inspiration.

There was, of course, a huge danger in buying in to that notion. Jaime would be gone in a few weeks, a couple of months at the most. Then what? Would her well dry up again? She shuddered at the thought, not only of losing focus, but of Jaime out of her life as quickly as he'd entered it.

At least he'd brought her out of her shell enough to see the world around her again, to start appreciating what she had, rather than focusing on what she'd lost. She'd have to be sure to thank him for that before he left for good.

Her thoughts were interrupted by an impatient knocking on her front door and the sound of her mother's frantic voice calling out to her. Emma hurried to open the door.

"Mom, what on earth? Is everything okay?"

"That's what I want to know," Jessica said, sucking in a deep breath as she visibly tried to calm herself. "Why weren't you answering your phone? I've been calling for hours. I was sure you'd fallen in the shower and broken something or who knows what. I've been worried sick."

But not worried enough to leave the library early to come to check, Emma thought, noting that it was now just past the library's early afternoon Saturday closing time.

"I was writing," she told her mother. "My phone was charging in the other room. I never heard it ring."

Her mom put a hand to her chest. "Please don't do that to me again, Emma. You really scared me."

"I'm sorry," Emma said sincerely, giving her mom a hug. "Come in and I'll fix you a cup of tea, or would you like something stronger? I have a bottle of wine I could open."

"Tea would be nice."

She followed Emma into the kitchen. "I called until late last night, too. Were you writing all night?"

Emma flushed. "No." She described the evening she'd spent at the pub with Nell and Dillon, avoiding any mention of Jaime. "Then I stopped by to visit a friend."

"Mr. Alvarez?" Jessica asked hopefully.

"As a matter of fact, yes."

"I'm glad," her mother said, a note of satisfaction in her voice. "I think he's good for you. You've seemed happier since you met him."

So her mother had noticed it, too. She couldn't be sure if that was good or terribly worrisome.

"Is there any potential for something more?" her mom pressed. "Will he be staying in town?"

"Only until his bones heal and he's done some therapy," Emma said. "He's helping out with the planning for this year's fall festival, so I imagine he'll stick around for that. Sooner or later, though, he'll go back to his real life."

"And where will that leave you?"

"Right here in Chesapeake Shores, Mom. You don't have to worry that I'm going to take off and leave you."

"Actually, I was hoping you would," Jessica said. "Not that I don't want you around," she added quickly. "But I would like to see you sharing your life with someone again. Writing is isolating enough without distancing yourself from everyone just to protect your heart."

"Someone else said something similar to me recently," she admitted.

Her mom chuckled. "Mr. Alvarez, perhaps? I imagine he had his own motives for mentioning it."

"He probably did," Emma agreed.

She studied her mother thoughtfully. In her late fifties, she was still a lovely woman with not a single strand of gray in her short, dark brown hair. Her porcelain skin was flawless, and she had a slightly curvaceous figure despite the rigorous walks she took every evening. Men should be flocking around her. Emma wondered if they were.

"Mom, did you ever think about marrying again after Dad died? You were so young. I'm sure you had your chances." She thought back, trying to remember if there had been any suitors. If so, her mother had been discreet about them. Emma only recalled one. "There was our old neighbor. Steve Tate thought you were something pretty special."

"Steve Tate thought my cooking was better than his," Jessica corrected. "I told him to hire himself a chef if a good dinner every night at six was what he was looking for."

After a startled instant, Emma laughed. "What about after you moved here to run the library?"

"I was too busy."

"So the advice you were just handing out to me wasn't valid for you?"

Surprising mirth sparkled in her mother's eyes. "A mother never likes to have her own words turned on her," Jessica scolded.

"Doesn't mean they aren't true," Emma said. "Maybe I should get the matchmakers to turn their attention to you."

"Don't you dare!" Jessica's expression turned sly. "I'll

tell you what. You get married again and settle down, give me a couple of grandbabies to cuddle and I'll consider going on a date again."

"You might be in a retirement home by the time that happens," Emma cautioned.

"I'll take my chances. If you have any real consideration for my social life, you won't wait that long now, will you?"

Emma shook her head at the sneaky trap. "You're hanging out too much with Nell."

"Can you think of a better role model? When it comes to getting things done for her family, no one in town is any better."

Feeling closer to her mother than she had in some time, Emma impulsively asked, "Mom, would you like to go somewhere for a bite to eat?"

Her mother looked startled by the invitation. "You don't have plans with Mr. Alvarez?"

"Don't look so disappointed. No, I don't have plans with Jaime, and I would enjoy spending the evening with my mother. We don't do that nearly enough."

"Then that's what we'll do," her mother said decisively. "Where shall we go?"

"Brady's is the place for special occasions," Emma suggested.

"And this is a special occasion? I know perfectly well it's not your birthday or mine."

"No, but it is the day you and I officially got off to a fresh start, not as mother and daughter, but as friends."

Surprising tears promptly filled her mother's eyes. "Do you mean that?"

"I do," Emma assured her. "Just don't think that entitles you to give me unsolicited advice and paw around in my closet to borrow my clothes."

"As your friend, I wouldn't dream of it," Jessica promised. "But as your mom, I wouldn't count on my not speaking my mind, if I have something to say. That will never change."

For once, though, Emma thought she might not mind it so much. Today was turning out to be full of miracles and new beginnings. Thinking back to her exchange with Jaime earlier, the one that had left him looking as if she'd actually hurt him, made her wonder, though, if there had been an ending today, too.

She pushed aside the concern and linked her arm with her mother's. "Let's show this town that the Hastings women are a force to be reckoned with."

Her mom laughed. "I'm not sure what's gotten into you today, but I like it."

"Me, too, Mom. Me, too."

7

Jaime spent most of Sunday immersed in Emma's book, pausing only to fix a sandwich for lunch and another for dinner. He was totally absorbed all the way through, in part because the story was so well written, but mostly because he could picture Emma in the heroine's journey from psychologically abused victim to a strong independent woman.

There were sections that infuriated him as he imagined Emma living with a man like the character's ex-husband. In some ways, though, the chapters at the end, when she put her life back together bit by bit and found the love she was meant to have, were worse. The heroine—Quinn Anderson—had completed a transition to a rich, full life that continued to elude Emma. Only the fact that he could see Emma starting to reach for such a life gave him some small measure of satisfaction and conviction that she was on her own road to recovery.

On Monday morning he was on his porch at dawn with his mug of coffee. He'd brought out a thermal pot and extra cup, as well. With any luck he was early enough to catch Emma before or after her run.

It was just past seven when he saw her coming down the street, her skin glowing from the exercise, her hair damp from the humidity and her exertion. He thought she looked beautiful.

"Good morning," he called out as she neared his gate.

Her step faltered as she glanced his way, her expression oddly wary. "Good morning."

"I have coffee," he said then added, relieved that he'd thought of it, "or bottled water, if you'd prefer."

She hesitated. "I could use some water," she admitted finally.

"Then join me."

As she stepped onto the porch and accepted the cool bottle of water, her gaze landed everywhere but on him. "I don't have a lot of time."

He smiled. "It's not even seven-thirty. You're not due at work until at least nine."

She frowned slightly. "You checked on my schedule?"

"Didn't have to. You walk past here predictably at eight forty-five most weekdays. You come back just after one. It wasn't that hard to figure out. And before you suggest that I'm stalking you, remember that I'm stuck here. Observing what goes on in the neighborhood keeps me from going stir-crazy. I even know which day Mrs. Kelly goes to her art class and which day Mr. Davis cuts his grass."

She sighed. "Sorry. I seem to be in a prickly mood."

"Turnabout's fair enough. You've seen me at my worst a time or two. Is this mood about me or has something happened?"

"I have no idea," she admitted. "More than likely I just woke up on the wrong side of the bed." She finished the water then looked longingly at the thermal pot. "Any of that coffee left? That might help."

He nodded. "That's why I brought out an extra cup." He poured the coffee and handed it to her. "How was your weekend?"

"Productive," she said, sitting on the very edge of the chair beside his as if she was ready to bolt at any second. At last, though, there was a faint spark of life in her eyes.

"You're back in your writing groove?" he asked, pleased for her. "That's great."

"I had dinner with my mother on Saturday, too."

"Something you don't do often?" he asked, hearing an odd note in her voice.

"Something I almost never do willingly. Saturday night it was my idea. We had a good time."

She sounded surprised.

"Your mother seems like a very nice woman," he said, treading lightly to see what she might reveal about that relationship.

"She is. I don't think I noticed that before the other night. She was always my mom, if you know what I mean. She was always picking at me to do things her way."

"That's what moms do," Jaime said. "You should meet mine sometime. She can reduce me to being a twelve-year-old faster than you can say *media noche*."

"What does that mean?"

"A *media noche* is one of the Cuban sandwiches that's so popular in Miami," he explained.

"I think I'd like to watch your mom take you down a peg or two," she said, smiling.

"Then I'll have to arrange it."

She looked flustered by his promise. "So, how was

your weekend? I probably should have come by to check on you."

"Despite what I said the other day about you being my angel of mercy, you're not my caregiver, Emma. I was fine. I was totally absorbed in a new book."

"The Louise Penny mystery or the Earl Emerson?" she asked eagerly, sitting back at last and starting to look more at ease.

"No, this one was different. It was by a writer who was able to move me with the depth of the emotions in her story."

"Really? That doesn't sound like your taste."

"It's not my usual taste, no," he conceded. "But I have a particular fondness for this writer."

"Anyone I might have heard of?"

He held her gaze then lifted the book from the table beside him.

Emma stared at it in shock. "My book? You read my book? Why?"

"I thought it might be revealing. It was."

Emma looked dismayed. "I know I shouldn't feel like this, but it feels like an invasion of privacy."

Jaime was totally taken aback by her reaction. "The book was a bestseller. You shared your innermost thoughts with a lot of people. Did that bother you?"

"No, but now it's you who's reading it. You know I was writing about my own experiences in a lot of ways, deeply personal experiences I don't talk about. Most readers had no idea about that." She gave him a defiant look. "Just so you know, though, I'm not that heroine. I'm nothing like Quinn Anderson."

"I know it's fiction, Emma, but you said yourself that you'd poured a lot of your story into the book. I thought it might help me to get to know you, to figure out why you're still keeping this barrier between us."

"I keep a barrier between us because you're leaving, Jaime," she said with exaggerated patience. "I've told you that already. It's one thing to be caught off guard and get your heart broken. It's another altogether to walk right into it with your eyes wide open."

"Emma, I'm not going to break your heart," he said solemnly with a level of certainty that even surprised him.

"How can you say that? I already feel more than I should. The other night when I was here..." Her voice trailed off before she finally admitted, "I felt too much, Jaime."

"So did I," he said quietly. "But I'm not going to run from it."

That silenced her. He saw what might have been a tiny spark of hope in her eyes, but she didn't acknowledge it.

"I mean that, Emma. I was so antsy to get back to work when we met that I would have crawled back to Seattle if I'd been able to. Now I'm already dreading the day I'll have to leave. I'm thinking of ways to stick around. When Nell asked me to work on the fall festival, I seized that like a lifeline. She reminded me I could do my therapy here and, instead of balking at a longer stay, I've already asked the doctor for the names of physical therapists in the area."

"Why didn't you mention this before?"

"I didn't want you to feel pressured. I thought maybe the longer we had together, the more you might start to trust me."

"I do trust you."

He gave her a skeptical look.

"I do," she repeated. "As a person."

"Ah, I see. But not necessarily as significant-other material?"

She sighed. "That will take time."

"Time we might not have if I hadn't shaken up the original plan," he explained.

"What does Mick have to say about all this?"

"I haven't discussed it with him. These are my decisions, Emma. Make no mistake about that. However long I stay or when I go will be up to me." He held her gaze. "And to you."

Her expression faltered a little at that.

"Don't look so scared. There really is no pressure here. I'm just being clear about what I want. Now you need to figure out what you want."

"You say that as if it's easy."

"It's only difficult if you can't hear what your heart is telling you."

She looked momentarily startled. "That's a line from my book."

He grinned. "I know. It seemed to work out pretty well for your hero. I thought I'd try it. Is it working?"

She set aside her coffee, stood up and came closer. Then she leaned down and kissed him, a slow, lingering kiss that got them both all stirred up.

Then she released him and winked. "Pretty well, I'd say. How about you?"

Jaime laughed. "Not bad. I think I'll reread that final chapter before I see you again tonight."

"Tonight?"

"We're having dinner."

"Where?"

"Right here."

"You're cooking? That's too much trouble."

"I'll manage. See you at seven."

She nodded slowly. "I'll be here. I'll bring wine."

"I'm still not drinking," he reminded her.

"Who said it was for you?"

Jaime laughed as she trotted down the steps and headed toward home. Definitely a promising turn of events, and it wasn't even eight a.m.

Emma didn't mention her dinner plans to anyone. In fact, she kept Jaime's invitation to herself so she could savor it without a lot of commentary from her mother or her friends. She did take a drive the minute she left the library to shop for a new dress, something summery and feminine.

There weren't a lot of clothes like that in her wardrobe these days. They'd been the expected attire when she'd been striving to be a suitable Southern belle. The minute she'd left Derek, she'd donated every single designer dress to a local charity. She'd hoped his snobbish friends would recognize them being worn around town by the very people they often treated with scorn.

Today, her mood extraordinarily upbeat, she wanted to wear something special to knock Jaime's socks off. It was interesting to note, though, that he'd seemed pretty blown away this morning when she'd been wearing workout clothes that had faded over time. He didn't strike her as the sort of man to be impressed by designer labels. That worked very much in his favor.

She even spent the afternoon primping, taking out her seldom-used curling iron and fixing her hair in a loose, casual fall of waves that were a far cry from her usual pulled back ponytail that she liked because it was easy and, maybe just a little, because Derek had hated her hair that way.

Even as that rebellious thought crossed her mind, she recognized that it was one more indication of how deeply her ex-husband was still embedded in her head. It was time to free herself from the last of those taunting memories and move on.

When she arrived at Jaime's in her cotton dress with its spaghetti straps and flowing skirt and a pair of kick-ass high-heeled sandals, she smiled in satisfaction at his thunderstruck expression.

"New look?"

"New outlook," she corrected.

A smile tugged at his lips. "Are you hoping to seduce me, Emma Hastings?"

"The thought has crossed my mind."

He grinned. "You don't have to work that hard, but I'm glad you went to the trouble. You look fabulous. I love your hair like that." His voice took on a low, sexy tone, and his eyes darkened with a smoldering heat. "It makes me want to tangle my fingers in those curls and kiss you senseless."

He sounded so serious, so hungry for her, that her pulse scrambled. "Before dinner?" she said, barely able to squeak out the words. The whole slow, sweet seduction game was a new one for her.

"Or after," he said, his gaze steady. "What's your preference?"

She blinked at the question. She could barely form a thought, much less answer him.

"Now, please," she finally managed, a hint of desperation in her voice. She wanted to move past the anticipation, past the insecurities and the million and one doubts crowding out her tiny shred of self-confidence.

As if he sensed just how skittish and uncertain she was, he nodded at once. "Let me turn off the heat on the stove."

She trailed him to the kitchen. "Will dinner be ruined?"

He turned, a spark of amusement in his eyes. "Do you really care?"

She hesitated then shook her head. "Not that much," she confessed.

When burners on the stove were off and pots set aside, Jaime stepped closer. "You still have time to change your mind, Emma. I don't want to rush you into something you're not really ready for."

He trailed a finger along her cheek in a gesture that had her trembling. She was ready for this. More than ready, in fact.

It was the possible consequences—falling even more deeply in love with a man who was destined to leave—that she wasn't entirely sure she'd be able to handle.

And yet, with his eyes locked with hers and his hand so gentle on her face, she moved forward and straight into his waiting arms.

"Were there fireworks? I definitely think I saw fireworks just now," Emma said as she lay cradled in Jaime's powerful embrace.

He chuckled. "I saw them, too, if that means anything. It's possible the town was celebrating something, but I think it was just us, Emma. I think you and I together made something incredible."

She thought so, too, and was annoyed with herself for

allowing that bliss to fade away under wave after wave of panic. *Live in the moment*, she cautioned herself. *Don't ruin things by looking too far ahead.* She sensed Jaime studying her with concern.

"What?" she asked.

"Your mind is racing ahead, isn't it?"

She sighed and nodded.

"You do know that we have some control over what happens tomorrow or the next day or the day after that?" he reminded her.

"I wish I could believe that as strongly as you do."

"How can you not? You took control of your life and got out of a bad situation. You wrote a bestselling novel. You've built a new life for yourself in Chesapeake Shores. You're a strong woman, Emma. Every bit as strong as Quinn Anderson in your book. She's not the woman you want to be. I think she *is* you."

Despite his reassuring assessment, she wasn't convinced. "Okay, for a whole year, maybe a little longer, I felt like I really was moving forward, that I had it all together," she acknowledged.

"And then you were hit with writer's block," he guessed.

"Exactly, and I felt as if my flimsy hold on my life was slipping away."

"Okay, I don't know if this applies, but someone once told me that holding on to anything too tightly is a surefire way to lose it. I suppose that's a take on the idea that if you truly love someone, you set them free, and, if the love is real, they'll come back to you."

Emma smiled a little at his words. "Listen to you, going all philosophical on me. I actually believe everything you just said. But I also know that panic does funny things. It's not so easy to release your hold on something or someone when you're scared."

Jaime tilted her chin and looked deeply into her eyes. "You don't need to be scared, Emma. I will always come back."

She wasn't sure how they'd come back to this same topic, but he was right. She was terrified that he'd go, get caught up in his own life again, and she'd just become a distant memory of a lovely summer fling.

"How can you sound so sure of that?" she asked him.

"Because I know what's in my heart. I know the kind of man I am. And I would never take a commitment like that lightly."

"I want so badly to believe you, to believe in us and what's happening right here and now." Here, safe in his arms, she could almost make the leap.

"Then do it," he encouraged, seeming to sense that she was so close to trusting in what they had. "Believe in us, Emma. I do."

She drew in a deep breath and tried to absorb just a little of the faith he seemed to have, but in the end she couldn't quite quiet the doubts that echoed in her head. Jaime wasn't the one she didn't trust. It was herself, her judgment.

And then, of course, there was her marriage, entered into with such blinding joy and hope. That had taught her well that sometimes the very best intentions in the world weren't enough.

8

Jaime knew he had his work cut out for him convincing Emma that he was in her life to stay. He wasn't entirely sure why he was so certain that she was the woman for him or why he was so determined to reach for the sort of commitment he'd never made before, but it felt right. Maybe it was just time. Maybe it was all that O'Brien influence, their philosophy that life was meant to be lived in loving pairs.

Or maybe it was simply that Emma had been irresistible from the very first moment he'd set eyes on her. She was intelligent, beautiful, complicated and sensitive. It was that last trait that could trip them up. She was too quick to react to the slightest shift in mood. Her feelings were raw and tender. And, to his deep regret, the hit her self-confidence had taken during her marriage was still very much with her.

He might wish he could magically change that, but he had to deal with what existed—and all that pain, suffering and cynicism was still a force to be reckoned with. It was a pall that hung over even their happiest moments together.

And it was thick in the atmosphere as she drove him

home from an appointment with the orthopedic surgeon, who'd pronounced his progress to be exceptional, removed his heavy cast and replaced it with a lighter cast that went only to his knee.

"A couple more weeks in this cast should do it," the surgeon had said. "Then you'll be ready for physical therapy. I know you're chomping at the bit to get started with that, but you're not to overdo it. You let the therapist set the pace. Is that understood?"

"Absolutely," Jaime said, though he knew he'd want to push himself. He'd been idle for far too long. He'd never been one for going to a gym, but his daily life had been jammed with nonstop exercise of one sort or another, and he'd always managed to squeeze in a run at the end of even his busiest days.

When Jaime had reported the conversation to Emma as they headed back to Chesapeake Shores, he'd expected her to be as thrilled as he was. She'd managed all the right words, but the light in her eyes had dimmed just a little, and he'd known the doubts about their long-term future were flooding back.

He'd also known words weren't enough, but he'd tried just the same, focusing on all the things they could now do together. "Pretty soon we'll be able to take walks together, maybe even take that spin around the dance floor that I promised you," he enthused.

"That sounds great," she said, giving him a quick glance and an unconvincing smile before returning her gaze to the road ahead.

"If I didn't know better, I'd think you weren't happy about this news," he said quietly, watching her closely.

Color flooded her cheeks. Again, she glanced his way. "I am happy for you. I know the inactivity has made you miserable, and I know how much you're looking forward to getting back to work."

"All true," he said. "But I'm not looking forward to leaving you behind, Emma. We're going to work that out."

She regarded him apologetically. "I'm sorry. You must be sick of having to reassure me."

"I get it, Emma. I really do. And I'll do it until you believe me," he said.

But two days later, when Mick O'Brien stood in his living room early on Sunday morning and announced that he needed Jaime to fly out to Seattle to resolve a problem with his pet project, Jaime realized just how difficult it was going to be to keep that promise he'd made to Emma.

"I'm an idiot," Emma announced to Shanna as they drank coffee before a meeting of the now-thriving book club, which had surprisingly eclectic taste. They'd read everything from autobiographies to horror in recent weeks. For the past couple of days, though, Emma hadn't been able to focus on anything other than Jaime's abrupt departure and what it said about how easily he could walk away from her.

"Why would you say such a thing?" her friend demanded. "Jaime cares about you. You know he does."

"He says he does," Emma conceded. "But he could hardly wait to get on that private jet of Mick's and take off for Seattle."

"Sweetie, he poured his heart and soul into that community that's being built out there. The way I understand it, he needed to deal with some big permit snafu that was about to derail the whole project."

Emma stubbornly refused to listen to reason. "Mick could have handled it, I'm sure."

Shanna smiled. "I'm sure he could have, but Jaime was the one with the contacts. It's his baby. Would you want someone to pull your book away from you before you've written the final chapter and tell you not to worry, they'll finish it up for you?"

Emma frowned. "Okay, I see your point. I'm just not quite ready to be logical."

"Have you talked to Jaime since he left?"

"A couple of times," she said. "Maybe three."

Shanna smiled. "A couple of times, maybe three, and he's barely been gone 24 hours? Is that all? That scumbag!"

"Okay, I'm being insecure and silly."

"Just a little." Shanna gave her hand a reassuring squeeze. "Let's take a step back from this unexpected business trip he had to take. Have you two talked about the future? About what happens when his leg is fully mended, his therapy is behind him and he's ready to go back to work full-time? Sooner or later you were going to have to deal with the long-distance thing."

Emma shuddered just thinking about it. The closer that day came, the more she fretted about how impossible their situation would be to resolve. This trip to manage a crisis had reminded her of just how quickly reality would be setting in.

"Only to the extent that he insists he wants a relationship and that we'll work it out," she told Shanna. "I have no idea what he means by that."

"And you're frustrated because you wanted it all spelled out," Shanna concluded. "Relationships rarely come in tidy little packages on a precise timetable, sweetie. This one has moved along pretty quickly. You've barely been together a couple of months now."

"And I'd known Derek for years and still didn't real-ize what a jerk he was or how he was using me," Emma said. "I should have my head examined for even think-ing Jaime and I might be involved in something more than a casual fling. We all know the definition of insan-ity—repeating the same old mistakes and expecting a different outcome."

"Is Jaime anything at all like your ex-husband?"

"Honestly, no," Emma said then added ruefully, "but I can be pretty blind to someone's flaws when I choose to be."

Shanna had the audacity to laugh at that. "I'd say, if anything, you're more determined than ever to find the slightest little flaw in people. That's why you're so worked up about Jaime right now. You think he's not going to live up to his promises, but has he given you even the tiniest indication that he won't? Be honest."

"Not really," Emma said. "But we haven't really been tested till now. Isn't that what flings are all about, just having fun and not taking anything too seriously?"

"Stop calling what the two of you have a fling," Shanna commanded, sounding surprisingly impatient.

Emma winced but didn't back away from the charac-terization. "Weren't you the very person who first told me about Jaime's reputation for flirting, and that you couldn't see him settling down?"

Shanna frowned at her, unable to deny it. "Oh, what do I know? Obviously, things changed when he met you. Anyone who sees you together knows there's a whole lot more going on. More important, you have Nell's blessing, something she doesn't give lightly. She has a lot of expe-rience recognizing the real thing when it comes along."

Shanna's expression brightened, and a twinkle appeared in her eyes. "You should have heard her at dinner yesterday when she found out Mick had sent Jaime back to Seattle."

Emma allowed herself a chuckle. "I'll bet that was fun."

"Not for Mick. Nell asked him if he was determined to ruin Jaime's life." Shanna gave her best Nell impression, complete with a hint of an Irish lilt. "'Isn't it enough that you've turned the man into a workaholic in your image. Now that he has a chance at having someone special in his life, something you yourself claimed you wanted for him, you go and ship him out of town at a critical moment, just when there's progress being made. I can't imagine what you were thinking, Mick O'Brien.'"

Emma could picture Nell taking on her beloved son in front of the entire family, with most of them taking sides and landing on hers. "How did Mick take it?"

"He promptly pulled out his cell phone and called Jaime. Right there in front of God and everyone, he demanded that Jaime get back to Chesapeake Shores."

"But Jaime hadn't even gotten to Seattle at that point," Emma said, startled. "He was probably somewhere over Colorado."

"True. Mick told Jaime he was going to call the pilot and order him to turn the plane around."

"But Jaime's meeting with the planning officials was scheduled for first thing this morning," Emma protested, shocked that Mick would go that far to try to fix things. "That was the whole point of the trip."

"Which Jaime told Mick, who'd put the call on speakerphone. He actually asked if Mick had lost his flipping mind."

Despite the mood she'd been in, Emma couldn't help smiling. "I imagine that went over well."

"Everyone in the room started laughing, and when Jaime figured out he was on speakerphone, he hung up on Mick. Mick looked around at the rest of us, shrugged and told us he'd tried to make things right. And then Nell smacked him on the shoulder and told him he hadn't tried hard enough."

Emma frowned as a thought crossed her mind. "Jaime never mentioned that Mick had called and told him to come home."

"Would you? Especially since he had no intention of turning right around and flying straight back." Shanna studied her. "Oh, no! Please tell me you are not twisting this all around and deciding that it means Jaime doesn't care about you, after all, that he chose work over you, because that is absolutely not the point of the story."

"The point might have gotten a little lost," Emma conceded.

"It's that Nell, and even Mick, are on your side in this. They want to see you and Jaime together. Mick would never have made that call otherwise, not even with Nell's very public disapproval making him squirm. You have powerful allies. We all want this to work out."

Emma gave her a weary smile. "But none of you are the ones who count. I'm not sure I have it in me to fight for this relationship."

Shanna regarded her with real concern. "But you do love him, don't you?"

Emma nodded. "I can't deny that, much as I'd like to."

"And he loves you," Shanna reminded her emphatically. "I'm pretty sure he has enough determination to get both of you across the finish line."

"The finish line?"

"Down the aisle, whatever," Shanna said. "You're the one who's good with words. You write the perfect ending."

Emma suddenly had an image, not of her in a fancy white gown and veil, but in something simple yet elegant; not in a church crowded with strangers and business associates, but in a small chapel surrounded by family and close friends. There was Jaime, gorgeous and sexy in his black suit, waiting for her by the altar. Was that the ending she'd write for their story?

Or was it sitting hand in hand on the lawn with the Chesapeake Bay shimmering before them and a couple of olive-complexioned kids running around the yard?

Or years and years from now, in rockers, still hand in hand, fighting over whether the surprisingly twisted ending to a book had been pure genius or a creative cop-out.

Were any—or even all—of those endings in the future for her and Jaime?

Or would their relationship die long before they ever reached the point of saying I do? And was any of that within her control…or even his?

"How was book club?" Jaime asked when he reached Emma late on Monday night.

"Lively. Half the people hated the book we'd read. A third loved it. And the rest hadn't read beyond chapter one."

"Where did you come down?"

"I hadn't finished it," she admitted, sounding sheepish. "I felt awful. Shanna looked at me as if it was a personal betrayal. Then she publicly excused me by saying she knew I'd had a lot on my mind."

"Am I at fault, Emma? Am I the one who's making you lose focus?" he asked, thinking of Mick's call the day before.

"Maybe a little," she said. "I miss you even more than I expected to."

"I miss you, too."

"Any idea when you'll be back?"

"I'm supposed to get this cast off next week, and my first therapy session is a few days later, so I'll have to be back before then."

"Okay," she said, her voice suddenly flat.

"If I can wrap things up sooner, I will."

"I know how important this project is to you," she said. "Of course you have to untangle whatever this latest holdup is."

"I do, you know, but I'm getting the feeling you don't entirely buy it."

She fell silent, and Jaime knew he'd struck a nerve. He decided to wait her out. When she was nervous or upset, she couldn't seem to stand silence for very long.

"Shanna mentioned that Mick ordered you back here," she said eventually. "And that you refused to come."

Jaime sighed. That explained why she sounded a little off. "Just because Mick had a change of heart, which frankly I don't understand, doesn't mean he wasn't right to send me out here in the first place. I've dealt with the local officials from the beginning. They trust me. If Mick had come charging in here to save the day, I'm not sure he wouldn't have made things worse. This isn't something that can be resolved by caving in to absurd demands or throwing money around to pacify them."

"You're probably right," she agreed. "Mick may be a genius on a lot of levels when it comes to his profession, but he certainly doesn't have the same finesse you have."

"To put it mildly," Jaime said. "That's one reason we make a good team. So, you're okay? You understand why I had to come?"

"The suddenness of the trip threw me, but I really do get it," she said.

Jaime sensed she still had more than her share of uncertainty. "You could fly out here," he suggested. "I can arrange a ticket for a flight first thing tomorrow." He warmed to the idea. "I'd love to show you this community. It's really starting to take shape, Emma. You could see what it is I do."

She hesitated. "Are you just trying to pacify me, or do you really want me there?"

"I want you here," he said at once, suddenly needing to get her wholeheartedly on his side and involved in his life, his *whole* life, not just the fantasy world they'd created for themselves in Chesapeake Shores for a brief moment in time. "This is important to me. I want to share it with you."

Another of those long silences fell, and once again he waited while she sorted through her feelings.

"How about this?" she said at last. "This is a quick trip and you're dealing with a crisis. Why don't we plan it so I can go with you next time, when you're under less stress and you can maybe even spend a couple of extra days showing me around Seattle?"

"I would love to do that," he said eagerly. If she fell in love with the area, all the better. Now that the words were flowing again, he felt certain she could write anywhere. Of course, who knew where his next project might take him, but most likely it would be somewhere else in the Pacific Northwest. He'd come to love the beauty of this part of the country, the shimmering blue waters wherever you looked, the sunny days when Mount Ranier's snowy peaks were on full display.

"So, we have a plan?" he persisted.

"We have a plan," she confirmed, sounding happier.

"I told you we could figure this out, Emma. Will you try to have a little more faith?"

"I'll work on it," she promised. "Now, tell me about this crisis. Have you charmed those officials into your way of thinking?"

Jaime filled her in on the contentious meeting he'd had that morning and the amount of paperwork he had to supply by tomorrow morning. "It's nothing they haven't seen before, but they claim it's not in their files. They're suddenly demanding excessive proffers that weren't in the original agreement, more roads, a bigger school—the list goes on and on. I think they figured out Mick's company has deep pockets, and they're trying to backtrack to dip into them."

"Can they do that?"

"Not if I can help it."

"Then I should let you get to it," she said.

"And you should get back to your writing," he suggested. "When are you going to let me read what you've written so far?"

"We'll see," she said evasively. "It's not quite there yet."

"But you're happy with the direction it's going? You feel as if you're in control again?"

"I'm hopeful," she said carefully.

"Need any more inspiration?" he teased.

She laughed at that. "It definitely couldn't hurt. Sweet-talk me for a minute," she suggested, "and I'll write a love scene that will set the pages of the book on fire."

So that's exactly what he did, which made it a whole

lot harder to concentrate on all those dull pages the planning officials wanted to see first thing in the morning. Suddenly, he was highly motived to wrap up these endless meetings. All he could think about was getting back to Chesapeake Shores as quickly as possible and getting Emma back into his bed. He still had a whole lot of moves she'd never experienced, and once this cast was off for good, he intended to share every one of them with her.

Come to think of it, a lifetime might not be long enough for all the plans he had for the two of them.

9

Jaime's anticipated return to Chesapeake Shores had been delayed yet again. His original surgeon in Seattle had removed the cast, and he'd been to physical therapy twice out there. Emma's resolve to keep the faith in their relationship was being sorely tested despite Jaime's repeated requests that she fly out to join him.

"Why won't you go?" Shanna asked, regarding her with exasperation.

"Because if this crisis is dragging on and on, he needs to focus on resolving it. He doesn't need me around as a distraction."

"If you two were together permanently, you wouldn't be a distraction. You'd be his support system," Shanna suggested lightly. "That's how a real marriage works, Emma. You're there for each other in the tough times, not just when everything's perfect."

Emma took her friend's words to heart, but she still didn't make a reservation to fly to Seattle. She wasn't sure whether she was deliberately trying to let the relationship die, testing Jaime's commitment to her, or her own to him.

Whichever it was, she wasn't going to take a chance on flying out there and being in the way.

She was just finishing up her shift at the library, when Mick walked in.

"Do you have a minute?" he asked.

"Sure. Can I help you find a book?"

He shook his head. "This is personal."

Startled, she simply stared at him. "Then we should probably go somewhere else to talk. My shift's over. Let me get my purse."

As she grabbed her purse in the office, her mother cornered her. "What's Mick doing here?"

"He wants to talk to me."

"About?"

"I have no idea, Mom."

"Well, he might be chairman of the board of this library, but he doesn't have the authority to fire you," her mother said, her expression grim.

"Please don't jump immediately to some worst-case scenario. I'm sure it has something to do with Jaime and whatever it is that's keeping him in Seattle for so long."

Her mother looked relieved by the suggestion. "You're probably right. Call me later and fill me in. Okay?"

"I will," Emma promised.

A few minutes later she and Mick had cups of coffee from Panini Bistro and were sharing a bench overlooking the bay on Shore Road. The air was still, too still. Emma thought they were likely to have a storm before the day was over.

She studied the man beside her. She didn't know Mick well, but he looked worried. A frown marred his handsome, weathered face. "Is something wrong?" she asked eventually.

"I was going to ask you that. I know it's not my place to meddle…"

She gave him an amused look that had him shrugging.

"Okay, meddling is exactly what I do," he conceded. "But it's different with Jaime. He's been with me a long time and I count on him. But I also think of him as a son, and I want him to find the happiness he deserves."

Emma had some idea of where he was heading, but she said only, "I know he appreciates the faith you have in him. He'll do anything not to let you down."

Mick nodded. "But I might have put him in an untenable position sending him back to Seattle too soon. He seems distracted, and that's not like him."

"And you think that's my fault?" she asked, shaken.

"I do," he sai, then quickly added, "but it's not something I'm blaming you for, or him, for that matter. I think it's wonderful, just inconvenient, given the situation we have out there."

"He says it's complicated."

"Complicated enough that my lawyers are now involved," Mick said. The revelation surprised Emma. Jaime hadn't mentioned that things had progressed to an even more serious level. "I had no idea it had gotten that bad. I just knew it was taking longer than Jaime had anticipated to resolve. Could the whole development be scuttled?"

"I doubt it, since we're already pretty far along in the building process, but it's going to require a lot more time and energy to resolve than any of us were counting on. The greedy sons of—" He censored himself. "Well, they're trying to change the rules in the middle of the game."

"Jaime had mentioned something about that."

"Then you understand why he needs to focus."

"Of course."

"The problem is that he's clearly worried that the delay is going to foul things up with you. Ma's been all over me about the mess I'm making of things for the two of you. I offered to go out there and take over, but Jaime wouldn't hear of it. I'm out of ideas on how to fix this."

She could hear the frustration in his voice, but even more she heard genuine concern. "This is Jaime's work. It matters to him. You have nothing to feel guilty about."

"I do if it causes problems for you and him. That matters more than anything that's going on out there. Jaime knows that. I just want you both to understand that I get it, too."

Emma took a slow sip of her coffee and let Mick's words sink in. He'd somehow succeeded in accomplishing what Jaime hadn't been able to with all of his reassurances, or Shanna with her prodding. Mick had convinced her of the depth of Jaime's feelings by letting her know that he was allowing those feelings to interfere in doing what he needed to do for his job, a job that up until recently had meant everything to him.

"I can resolve this," she said, her voice filled with quiet resolve.

Now it was Mick who looked startled. "How are you going to do that?"

"I'm going to Seattle. Until just this minute I thought I'd only be in the way, but I'm beginning to think that I can do more if I'm there to support Jaime, if he knows I'm with him no matter what."

Relief spread across Mick's face. "You're ready to do that? I don't want to push you, but I do think you're right. He needs you by his side, so he's not worrying that he's going to lose you over this untimely absence."

"I'll make sure he knows that we're solid," she promised. "Don't tell him I'm coming, okay? I'll fly out tomorrow. I'd like to surprise him."

"My jet's at the airport now," Mick said, his expression hopeful.

Emma shook her head. Mick O'Brien had never lacked confidence in his powers of persuasion, that's for sure. "You knew all along what I'd do, didn't you?"

"I'd hoped," he corrected. "I know what I would have given years ago if my Megan had shared my work with me. It was my own fault that she didn't. I was comfortable leaving her here with total responsibility for our children, but I shut her out of something that was a huge part of my life. That was a mistake. Maybe you and Jaime can get that part right. You'll have a stronger life together, if you can."

She nodded. "Thank you for making me see that."

"Shall I tell the pilot you'll be ready to leave in an hour?"

She stood up, eager to get started, but realistic about what she needed to accomplish, including explaining to her mother that she was quitting her library job with no notice. "Make it two. I have some arrangements to make and some packing to do."

"Whatever you want. I'll have a car pick you up to get you to the airport here, and another car waiting at the airport out there. Thank you, Emma."

Impulsively, she reached out and hugged him. "As meddlers go, you're not a bad one to have on our side."

He laughed at that. "I have a whole lot of people in my family who'd argue that point with you."

"They're all happy now, aren't they?"

"Come to think of it, not a one of them could deny that."

Emma was pretty sure Jaime wouldn't, either, when he figured out that her arrival in Seattle was as much Mick's handiwork as it was an epiphany on her part.

At the end of another totally frustrating day, Jaime returned to the house he'd built on a piece of land overlooking Puget Sound. It wasn't far from the community he was building. Eventually, in fact, when the planned houses were all in place, it would be within the city limits of the newly built Puget Village. He'd hoped to keep it for himself, just as Mick had his home in the heart of Chesapeake Shores.

Tonight, though, the house felt empty. Now that the painkillers were a thing of the past, he poured himself a glass of wine and went onto the deck with its amazing view of the sound. Towering trees reflected in the water, along with streaks of color from the setting sun. Sailboats glided across the water on the evening breeze. Not even the sound of a powerboat or a Jet Ski could entirely disrupt the serenity of the setting. Usually the view alone was enough to calm him, but tonight he felt particularly restless.

He was sick of the back and forth with the local officials and the sudden demands for more infrastructure than had been in the original deal. He knew the whole country was hurting when it came to roads and bridges, but he didn't think the solution to that should be to rip off a developer who was already being more than generous when it came to fulfilling those needs. Moreover, contracts had been signed at the beginning, spelling out exactly what Mick's company would provide for the new community and the surrounding area.

Just about the time he usually called Emma to check

in, his doorbell rang. Eager to make that call, he hoped he could put off whoever was at the door.

When he opened the door and found the very woman who'd been in his thoughts standing there with a pile of suitcases beside her, his jaw dropped. Her hair fell in waves, just the way he liked it, and she was wearing one of those revealing camisole things under a white linen blouse and matching linen pants. He thought she looked like an angel, but that red silk-and-lace camisole that dipped low was pure wicked sin.

"Surprise!" she said, her expression charmingly hesitant.

Jaime couldn't get a single word past the huge lump in his throat. He just reached for her and pulled her into a tight embrace. Immediately, his restlessness seemed to ease.

When he finally released her, she gave him a tremulous smile. "I guess you're glad to see me."

"You have no idea," he said. "Come in. How did you find me?"

"Mick had a driver waiting for me."

Jaime laughed. "Of course he did. Did he fly you out, too?"

She nodded. "I could probably get used to the whole private jet thing."

"It is a perk, that's for sure."

He brought her suitcases in, but left them sitting in the foyer to be dealt with later.

"Which do you want first, a tour or a glass of wine? Or something to eat? I have some salmon in the freezer. It's fresh. Or rather it was, when I caught it. And there's stuff for a salad." He was babbling nervously, like a boy on his first date. Or maybe he sounded like exactly what he was, a man stunned to have his nightly fantasy turned into an unexpected reality.

"Take the salmon out of the freezer," she suggested. "And pour me a glass of wine. By the time we take the tour and catch up, maybe the salmon will be thawed enough to put on the grill." She regarded him with amusement. "I imagine you have a grill."

"Of course I do. I'm genetically wired to barbecue."

He led the way into the kitchen then listened with pleasure as she gasped.

"This may be the most beautiful kitchen I've ever seen outside of a magazine. Is it wasted on you?"

"Are you asking if I can do more than fix a simple meal once in a while?"

She nodded, even as she reverently touched the granite counters and ran her fingers over the six burners of a professional-grade gas stove. She lingered in front of the oversize refrigerator.

"You could cook for a really big family in this kitchen," she said.

"That was the idea."

"There's even a huge eat-in area, plus a great room with a fireplace. You've taken the open concept to a whole new level." She turned to him. "You designed and built this, didn't you?"

Jaime nodded.

"It's nothing like Chesapeake Shores and the homes Mick built there."

"I told you that every community is designed to fit in with its surroundings. Chesapeake Shores is all about cozy cottages, built with families in mind. Puget Village is about soaring windows and spectacular views. Not that we lack for creature comforts," he added.

"Amazing," she said, awe in her voice. "Will the other homes be like this?"

"In one variation or another. Some will be similar in size, others smaller. All will take advantage of the views. They'll all come with top-of-the-line appliances and fixtures."

"I can't wait to see the rest of the house, the whole community, in fact." She paused and tilted her head, studying him. "The crutches are gone. No cane, either?"

"Depends on what I'm doing. Around the house, no. I manage."

"Then let's take that tour, unless you need to get off your feet."

"I'm fine, but one thing at a time. Let's take our wine onto the deck and relax first." If he showed her the master bedroom right now, he was afraid they might not leave it. He owed her time to unwind before he put some of those wicked thoughts he'd been having into practice.

He poured her glass of wine then brushed her fingers as he handed it to her. Sparks flew.

"I've missed you, Emma," he said, holding her gaze. "More than you can possibly imagine. Even more than I'd expected to."

"I've missed you, too. And I'm sorry I was so stubborn about not coming for a visit. I don't know if I thought you wouldn't really want me here, or if I was hoping you'd hurry up and come home faster if I stayed away, or what. I wasn't exactly thinking clearly."

"It's okay. You're here now. I'm still a little stunned by that."

"But in a good way, right?" she asked, searching his face as if she needed proof even now that she hadn't intruded.

He took away the glass he'd just handed her and set

it aside. Then he stepped closer, brushed a wayward curl off her cheek then lowered his head until his lips were on hers. It was like coming home. Suddenly, his world, which had been upside down for a few weeks now, righted itself. His life made sense again.

"I swore I wasn't going to rush this, that I was going to give you time to settle in here, but I want you, Emma. I've missed being with you even more than I'd expected to."

Her eyes filled with light. She tucked her hand into his. "Then I guess you'd better lead the way to the bedroom, because I absolutely refuse to make love with you on one of these shiny countertops."

"You sure about that?" he teased.

"I don't even want to know why you're so eager to give it a try," she said. "But I want to see your bedroom, Jaime. I want to see for myself if you designed it for two."

He laughed at that. "There's an empty walk-in closet just waiting for you and a spare sink that I promise is all yours. No sharing with the messy man in your life."

"King-size bed?"

"Of course."

Her expression faltered slightly. "Right this second, I'm actually thinking a single bed holds a lot of appeal. I don't want to be that far away from you."

He put his arm around her as he led the way to the master suite. "Believe me, the bed could be the size of the ocean and I'd still keep you close to me."

There were more sweeping views from the wall of glass in the bedroom, but Emma barely seemed to notice now. Her gaze never left his face as she began to unbutton her blouse then slipped the straps of her camisole off her shoulders and let it fall. Jaime's heart began to thud in anticipation. The silk caught on the tips of her breasts.

"You're taking too long," he said, finishing the job with a sharp tug that had delicate silk and lace tearing.

At Emma's gasp, he murmured, "I'll buy you another one tomorrow. I'll buy a dozen, in every color they come in, though I'm suddenly awfully partial to red."

Against the backdrop of a splashy orange sunset, she looked spectacular. Her skin glowed, and her eyes flashed with heat. She was everything he'd remembered, everything he'd ever need.

"I don't want to be separated again, Emma."

"Me, either."

"Then we'll always work it out. We can split our time between here and Chesapeake Shores or wherever I'm working. I'll make sure you have an office in every house."

She grinned at him. "And inspiration like this 24/7?"

"That will be my pleasure."

"Good, because I sent my book off to my editor three days ago. It's good, Jaime. At least I think it is. I won't know anything right away, but it's never too soon to start coming up with a fresh idea, maybe something set in the Pacific Northwest this time."

His eyes darkened. "Then you wouldn't mind living here?"

"Wherever we can be together is home, though I do hope we won't ever leave Chesapeake Shores behind completely."

"That will never happen," he promised. "I've already spoken to Mick about buying Bayside Retreat. I know I wasn't happy about being stuck there, but I have some pretty fond memories of it now."

"Me, too," she whispered.

"What about your place? Would you rather keep that as home base?"

"I'm not attached to it. For one thing, it doesn't have a view. More important, it's not where all this started." She snuggled closer. "I love you, Jaime. I don't know how it happened, how you managed to slip past my defenses, but you did. The most amazing part to me is that you didn't give up."

"On you? How could I? You're my heart." A simple declaration, but oh, so true.

And then he set out to show her not only how much he'd missed her, but also how happy he intended to make her for the rest of their lives.

Epilogue

The Chesapeake Shores Annual Fall Festival at the end of October drew hundreds of neighbors from around the region to town. Businesses were swamped, and the booths set up on the town green were doing a brisk business. An Irish band was tuning up on the bandstand when Nell joined Jaime and Emma on a bench under an old oak tree that was shedding leaves of orange, gold and brown.

"It's the best festival ever," Nell said, clearly pleased. "I have the two of you to thank for that."

"How can you say that?" Emma protested. "We've both been clear across the country for most of the past month. It was the worst possible time for us to abandon you. You've done all the heavy lifting to make sure this came together."

"And haven't we talked at least once a day?" Nell countered. "Haven't you both made phone calls and used your powers of persuasion to make things happen? I believe in giving credit where credit's due. You came up with the fresh ideas that put us on a new track." She gestured toward a nearby booth. "The kissing booth is doing a very brisk business."

Jaime grinned proudly. "I told you it would. Emma, when's your shift?"

She frowned at him. "You actually want me to take a turn kissing a bunch of strangers?"

"I'm thinking a very brief shift that earns the church a very big donation," he corrected.

Nell chuckled. "You could just hand the money to me right here and I'll wander off and leave the two of you alone."

Jaime shook his head. "If we start kissing over here, it would probably violate some rule about public displays of affection. Come on, Emma. Let's go show these amateurs with their little pecks on the cheek how it's done."

"If you do it right, maybe Dillon and I will take a turn, too," Nell said.

Jaime led the way to the kissing booth, whispered something to the girl who was currently working it, and Emma took her place. He handed over a hundred-dollar bill that had the girl's eyes widening. Then he beckoned Emma closer.

"Come here, love."

"That was a lot of money. What if I can't deliver the kind of kiss you're looking for?" she teased.

He laughed. "You haven't failed me yet."

He leaned into the booth and put his hands on her shoulders, drawing her closer. When their lips met, fireworks went off. It was getting to be pretty darn predictable every time he touched her. When he finally let her go, they were greeted by applause.

Jaime looked around, clearly pleased with himself. "And that, my friends, is how you kiss a woman to let her know you love her."

Emma felt heat climbing into her cheeks when she saw her mother watching the two of them. She had on her stern librarian's face as she marched in their direction.

"Uh-oh," Emma said, nodding in her direction.

Jaime was quick to take the hint. "Mrs. Hastings," he said happily. "How are you?"

"I'll be a lot happier when I understand the meaning of that display just now," Jessica told him, though to Emma's surprise there was a twinkle in her eyes that belied her tone.

"Just staking my claim," Jaime said.

"Branding my Emma as yours?" she questioned.

He smiled. "I suppose you could put it that way, yes."

"There are more appropriate ways of doing that, young man."

"Mom!" Emma protested.

Jaime stepped in. "No, sweetheart, she's absolutely right. There is a better way. I'd intended to wait until tonight when there's a full moon shining and music in the background, but now seems as good a time as any."

Emma wasn't sure who was more startled, her or her mother, when Jaime dropped to one knee, uttering a faint groan as he did so. That recently repaired leg of his wasn't always as cooperative as he wanted it to be.

"Emma Hastings, I know we've been talking about the future we want, and that there are still a lot of things to work out, but there is one indisputable fact we're agreed on. Whatever that future is, we're in it together. I love you, Emma. I need you in my life, by my side, wherever we are. I need you—not Mick—to remind me when it's time to take a vacation. You've proved yourself to be pretty good at making time off even more appealing than work." He reached for her hand and looked into her eyes. "So, what's it to be, Emma? Will you marry me and take on the task of reforming me full-time?"

Jessica gasped then clamped a hand over her mouth as her eyes filled with tears. "Emma?" she prodded, when Emma couldn't seem to get a word out.

"Married?" Emma whispered. "You really want to get married?"

Jaime smiled. "Did you think I intended to keep you living in sin for the rest of our lives?" He glanced at her mother. "No offense, Mrs. Hastings."

"None taken," she said, clearly enjoying being in on the big moment.

"Emma, could you maybe give me an answer before my knee cramps up and I land on my butt? This is supposed to be a romance, not a comedy."

She knelt down, facing him. "Do you mind if I laugh just a little, not at you, but because I'm happier than I've ever imagined being again? Yes, I'll marry you."

Then she was in his arms, and the crowd around them seemed to drift away to give them at least a tiny bit of privacy.

"I love you, Jaime Alvarez."

"Right back at you," he declared.

He pulled her to her feet. "Now, if we're going to dance at our wedding, we'd better get out on that dance floor and start practicing. The band's just starting. I want you to be able to keep up with me."

"Is that a challenge?"

"It is," he said solemnly. "You up for it?"

"As long as we're together, I can handle anything," Emma declared.

And for the first time since she'd walked out on her disaster of a marriage to Derek, she believed it was true. She was ready for anything that came her way! In fact, she could hardly wait to see what might come next.

* * * * *

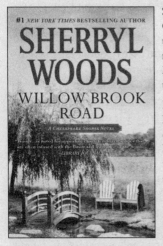

New York Times bestselling author

BRENDA NOVAK

welcomes you back to Whiskey Creek, where one Christmas can change your life...

Kyle Houseman believes he'll never find anyone he could love as much as Olivia Arnold, who's now married to his stepbrother. Not only did he lose her, he's been through one divorce and has no desire to go through another—which is why he fights his attraction to the beautiful stranger who rents his farmhouse for the Christmas holiday.

Lourdes Bennett is a country music artist. She's only planning to stay in Whiskey Creek long enough to write the songs for her next album. Her dreams don't include settling in a town even smaller than the one she escaped. But as she comes to know Kyle, she begins to wonder if she'd be making a terrible mistake leaving him behind...

Available now, wherever books are sold!

Be sure to connect with us at:

Harlequin.com/Newsletters

Facebook.com/HarlequinBooks

Twitter.com/HarlequinBooks

www.MIRABooks.com

MBN1844R

LIFE IN ICICLE FALLS

SHEILA ROBERTS

Icicle Falls is *the* place to be at Christmas...

Everyone's getting ready for Christmas in Icicle Falls, especially on Candy Cane Lane, where holiday decorating is taken *very* seriously. Tilda Morrison, town cop, is looking forward to celebrating Christmas in her first house...until she discovers that she's expected to "keep up" with the neighbors, including Maddy Donaldson, the inspiration behind the whole extravaganza. But this year, someone's destroying Maddy's precious candy canes! Thank goodness for the cop in their neighborhood.

Then there's Tilda's neighbor Ivy Bohn. As a newly single mom, Ivy can sum up the holiday in two words: *Bah, humbug*. But she's determined to give her kids a perfect Christmas.

Despite family disasters, irritating ex-husbands and kitchen catastrophes, these three women are going to find out that Christmas really *is* the most wonderful time of the year!

Available now, wherever books are sold!

REQUEST YOUR FREE BOOKS!

2 FREE NOVELS
FROM THE ROMANCE COLLECTION
PLUS 2 FREE GIFTS!

YES! Please send me 2 FREE novels from the Romance Collection and my 2 FREE gifts (gifts are worth about $10). After receiving them, if I don't wish to receive any more books, I can return the shipping statement marked "cancel." If I don't cancel, I will receive 4 brand-new novels every month and be billed just $6.49 per book in the U.S. or $6.99 per book in Canada. That's a savings of at least 19% off the cover price. It's quite a bargain! Shipping and handling is just 50¢ per book in the U.S. and 75¢ per book in Canada.* I understand that accepting the 2 free books and gifts places me under no obligation to buy anything. I can always return a shipment and cancel at any time. Even if I never buy another book, the two free books and gifts are mine to keep forever.

194/394 MDN GH4D

Name	(PLEASE PRINT)	
Address		Apt. #
City	State/Prov.	Zip/Postal Code

Signature (if under 18, a parent or guardian must sign)

Mail to the **Reader Service**:
IN U.S.A.: P.O. Box 1867, Buffalo, NY 14240-1867
IN CANADA: P.O. Box 609, Fort Erie, Ontario L2A 5X3

Want to try two free books from another line?
Call 1-800-873-8635 or visit www.ReaderService.com.

* Terms and prices subject to change without notice. Prices do not include applicable taxes. Sales tax applicable in N.Y. Canadian residents will be charged applicable taxes. Offer not valid in Quebec. This offer is limited to one order per household. Not valid for current subscribers to the Romance Collection or the Romance/Suspense Collection. All orders subject to credit approval. Credit or debit balances in a customer's account(s) may be offset by any other outstanding balance owed by or to the customer. Please allow 4 to 6 weeks for delivery. Offer available while quantities last.

Your Privacy—The Reader Service is committed to protecting your privacy. Our Privacy Policy is available online at www.ReaderService.com or upon request from the Reader Service.

We make a portion of our mailing list available to reputable third parties that offer products we believe may interest you. If you prefer that we not exchange your name with third parties, or if you wish to clarify or modify your communication preferences, please visit us at www.ReaderService.com/consumerschoice or write to us at Reader Service Preference Service, P.O. Box 9062, Buffalo, NY 14240-9062. Include your complete name and address.

SHERRYL WOODS